# GHOULSMEN

## Book One

## A. C. Hughes

*Cahill Davis Publishing*

CAHILL DAVIS PUBLISHING LIMITED

Copyright © 2025 A. C. Hughes

The moral right of A. C. Hughes to be identified as the Author of the Work has been asserted by him in accordance with the Copyright, Designs and Patents Act 1988.

First published in Great Britain in 2025 by Cahill Davis Publishing Limited.

First published in paperback in Great Britain in 2025 by Cahill Davis Publishing Limited.

Apart from any use permitted under UK copyright law, this publication may only be reproduced, stored, or transmitted, in any form, or by any means, with prior permission in writing of the publishers or, in case of reprographic production, in accordance with the terms of licences issued by the Copyright Licencing Agency.

All characters in this publication are fictitious and any resemblance to real persons, living or dead, is purely coincidental.

ISBN 978-1-915307-24-8 (eBook)

ISBN 978-1-915307-23-1 (Paperback)

Cahill Davis Publishing Limited

www.cahilldavispublishing.co.uk

# The Ghoulsmen Series

1. Ghoulsmen

2. Bloodmarsh

3. City of Champions

4. The World

# Chapter One

Rav stood panting, heart rattling, legs on the cusp of giving out and dropping him to join the corpse at his feet. *Close.* If he'd been an instant slower, he'd be the one lying limp in the mud. Just another one of the dozen dead soldiers strewn down the hillside below him.

He tore off his animal skin mask, took a breath, and looked at the man he'd just killed. Gone were his twisted snarl and crazed eyes, both replaced with the hollow, glazed expression of the dead. Only the fetid, now bloodstained froth dribbling from his lips remained as proof of his prior frenzy.

The man was maybe twenty-five, only a few years older than Rav, with greasy brown hair a shade darker and a finger-length longer than Rav's. He even had matching hazel eyes. Did he have a family? A home? A sense of honour and duty? Rav spat on the corpse. Whatever he'd once had, he'd thrown it all away for greed. The Sink did that to people, the allure of its riches too compelling for fools to realise all they'd find in that place was death. At least this man had been killed before he arrived there; at least he'd died quickly on the end of Rav's spear and not been mauled by some twisted monster.

Rav drew back his spear and thrust it once more through the soldier's blue and white gambeson armour to confirm his end, then looked below to the other gambeson-clad bodies. Six were clustered towards the top of the rocky hill he was standing on, while the last five were strung out towards the bottom after being cut down as they'd fled from the Ghoulsmen ambush. His comrades were still in pursuit of the last surviving soldiers and had chased them into the surrounding hills.

The dense pack of clouds overhead darkened further to block out more afternoon light and herald the coming rain. Rav got to work surveying the battlefield before the torrent started and the grass became even more slippery.

Dressed in thick black goat furs for armour and protection from the cold, Rav looked more beast than man as he moved down the hill from corpse to corpse, making sure every invading soldier was dead. Some were more mature than his last opponent, their beards greying and their skin wrinkled, but none were old. Most had square faces and lighter skin than Rav, while a few others had darker complexions, indicating that they hadn't all come from one region. Armies preparing for the Sink recruited from every settlement they passed through on their journey to their demise, accepting anyone able into their ranks. Rav glanced at a dead woman before stabbing her throat.

Had all these people been fighting of their own free will, or had they been forced into combat after having their families taken hostage, like they'd threatened to do to him? Rav shook his head to scatter the question. There was no point asking that; he already knew the answer—none of these soldiers were innocent. When armies like this one had first started marching past his home on their way to the Sink, he'd been ignorant enough to believe they'd been acting under coercion. Hadn't it been easier to think there were only a few vile people ruining their family legacies by catching slaves and sending them to war? But these seemingly ordinary people were always the most vicious in their attempts to capture his family. They'd *chosen* to do this... they all had. He spat at another corpse.

As he approached the body of an older man, slight movement caught his eye. One of the supposedly dead man's fingers twitched.

"Are you trying to trick me?" Rav growled. "You're the one who came here to attack us; at least face your death with courage. You bring shame to your ancestors."

The injured man opened his eyes and stared up at Rav. "Please let me live," he whispered. "Please. Have mercy."

"Would you have shown us mercy?" Rav readied his spear for a killing strike.

The man's eyes widened before a sneer consumed him. "We already did," he hissed. "We weren't going to kill you. Not all of you, anyway. Even after you rejected Baron Kiln's conscription, he was still gracious enough to ask for most of you alive. After executing the murderer, Rav Carvell, we were just going to take his conspirators as captives."

Rav tightened his fist as his lip wobbled. It was his stupid mistake that had given cause for these soldiers to invade Stone's Way. What if they'd made it through the hills to Pitt? What if they'd attacked his home and harmed his family? The Ghoulsmen's families?

"See? We were going to take you to the Sink and let you share in our glory," the man continued. "You'd have been rewarded for your treachery."

Rav snapped out of his daze as a frown cracked his forehead. "Entering the Sink is no reward. Why do fools like you keep saying that? If you and your Baron wish to march off and die like all the others, leave Pitt out of it. And don't insult me by calling them captives; those you shackle are no different to slaves."

"We'd *never* dishonour ourselves by using slaves," the man shouted. "Catching murderers and those who protect them is a noble duty; we respect our Names and the ancestors who gave them to us."

Rav's expression hardened. "No, I've seen dozens of people like you before. Nothing is more important to you than your greed, not even your legacies. Even without an excuse, you would have come here seeking captives. You'll destroy your reputations, your lineages, your Names, and for what? When our original Baron called to conscript from Pitt, we answered. Half the town set off in pursuit of riches and not one person returned."

The man's eyes gleamed as a fervour possessed him. "Some will fail, that's true. That's why we need a bigger army; that's why we need your people and your supplies. With all that, surviving the Sink and claiming its spoils becomes a certainty."

"That's just not true. Baron Kiln has about three hundred soldiers, right? And they're all outfitted like you—in cheap gambeson armour and wielding uneven spears."

The man's jaw tensed as he drew in a sharp breath. "*What?* Do you have a spy among our ranks?"

"We don't need one; we've seen dozens of armies like yours pass through Greenfield on their way to the Sink. Better armies than yours. Those soldiers didn't return with riches." He stared the man hard in the eyes. "Those soldiers didn't return at all."

The soldier shook his head as though convulsing. "No, no, no, you don't understand what the Sink holds. How can you be so ignorant of the opportunity you're squandering? The Sink's formation is the greatest event of our generation... the greatest event of *any* generation. Can't you see that? You could earn more wealth there in a day than you could in a lifetime lived in this insignificant place. Isn't that what you want?" He paused, as though to give Rav time for his words to sink in. "Think about your family; one venture into the Sink and your children and their children and their children's children would never want for anything ever again. And that's not even the best of what the Sink has to offer. You can achieve the impossible." The man looked at the sky and smiled as his imagination seemingly took hold. "Run faster than a horse, become stronger than a bull, or you could even obtain something more special, like the power to turn your skin into iron. Think about it. If you join Baron Kiln and serve in his army, you can come with us to claim the Sink's spoils. You can wield power only heard about in stories."

Seeing the deluded frenzy that had consumed the man, Rav knew his hope of persuading him would be in vain. Still, he tried. "The mutants in the Sink are worse than the monsters from stories and yours is not the only army looking for power. Either you'll kill each other, or the mutants will butcher you. *Maybe* one of you will survive. Do you think you're that one out of three hundred?"

The man's frenzy grew. "This is why you deserve to be captured. How could you let the mere threat of danger stop you from obtaining everything you could ever want? To be so spineless is *inhuman*. It's better for you and your family to labour for us and our goals than to waste away in a tiny place like this. All of mankind is working to conquer the Sink. Not giving everything you have to further that goal is shameful. Is that the legacy you want to leave behind? Is 'coward' the association you want with your Name? And just because my predecessors haven't returned doesn't mean they're dead. They're alive, I believe it, still fighting for their families."

Rav snorted at him. "Those are passionate words for someone about to die in this 'insignificant place', having never even seen the Sink. Where's your wealth? Where are your powers? How can you still look down on my home when your unit was defeated by just six of us?"

"Defeated?" he wheezed, laughing. "The only reason we lost is because of that brute leading you, but he *will* fall. Not even the great Cyrn Carvell can hold off our army for long. Baron Kiln only sent fifteen of us to capture your town this time, but once news of our failure reaches him, he'll send thirty soldiers or fifty or all of them. We'll never stop. And if it isn't us, then it'll be the next Baron to march past Stone's Way that will catch you, or the next, or the next. Can't you see how futile your fighting is? Pitt's the only settlement we know of that isn't giving everything it has for the Sink. It won't be long until you have to join a Baron; make a choice to serve while you still can."

Rav sighed. The man remained just as crazed as before. He'd expected this result and yet tears welled in his eyes. Why couldn't they just leave Pitt alone? Why were they all so greedy?

He locked his gaze onto the soldier. "Cyrn won't fall, not with the Ghoulsmen supporting him. Not with me at his back. I'll give my life to ensure that. My brother's greater than you could imagine."

"Brother?" His eyes widened. "You're the murderer Pitt's fighting to protect? *You* dared speak to *me* about Names and legacies?" the man screeched, hysteria consuming him. "Every day Cyrn fights, he tarnishes the Carvell Name. How can you bear that shame? How can you stomach watching your brother and his warriors risk their lives for you? You should've been exiled. You don't deserve your Name."

Rav began to tremble but remained silent.

"It's such a waste," the soldier seethed. "All this time you've lost ruining your legacies could've been spent conquering the Sink. You've been blessed to live this close to it; I travelled for years to get here, crossing oceans and deserts to reach a place you could walk to within a month. How could you not snatch at an opportunity like that? How could..."

Rav's vision blurred with tears, his trembling turning violent until the roil of pain within him could no longer be suppressed. He loomed over the soldier, who kept blabbering on about how great the Sink was.

"We intercepted a messenger a few days before we ambushed you," he spat, voice cold enough to silence the soldier. "Three days ago, Baron Kiln called you back to Greenfield so you could help defend the city. The death I warned you of has already arrived. Baron Kiln is currently at war with another Baron and will be for months to come, so you see, there won't be anyone else coming after you. Your efforts were meaningless. All you unfilial brutes have tarnished your Names for nothing. Your corpses will be left to rot as animals pick them apart, never to be returned to your home. All anyone will remember about you is your pathetic failure. I hope the shame of that crushes your Bloodlines so that none of your families will ever be respected again."

The man gasped, snatching at Rav with filthy nails. "No, that can't—"

Rav pierced his throat, then wiped the blood off his spear on the man's torso. He gagged, stomach churning, acidic bile clawing up his throat as he turned away from the corpse. *What have I done?* That wasn't an honourable killing. That wasn't how a Carvell behaved. Looking around, he took a relieved and shaky breath upon seeing that none of the Ghoulsmen had returned in time to see his cruelty. Cheeks burning, he wiped his face, the grit on his hands scratching his skin. It took a few deep breaths for him to cool down and settle his stomach. This wasn't him; he wasn't supposed to be someone who tormented *anyone* even if they were his enemies. He wasn't supposed to be vicious or cruel or callous or...

Rav blinked away his tears and tensed his jaw to stop its tremble. The others were still out fighting, doing their duty in guarding their home. He had his duties to do, too. Carvells *always* performed their duties. To keep their families safe, to make up for his stupid mistake that had put them all in danger, to spare them from having to leave their homes, he'd do his part.

After adjusting the grip on his spear, Rav hardened his gut and headed to the next body, thrusting clean through it to confirm it to be another corpse, not a pretender. Then he stabbed another. And another.

As the sun waned further during its descent, Rav took a moment to rest and gazed north, where the other Ghoulsmen had given chase, a flutter of worry in his chest. How long had it been since they'd left? They were alright, weren't they? He shook his head and turned back to his hillside. Aye, of course they were. Cyrn was with them. Cyrn had formed the Ghoulsmen, and he was the one who led them into battle. His older brother was twice the man he was, a true Carvell. All Rav could do was his duty. He readied his spear and stabbed another body.

As Rav ran through the last soldier's chest with his spear, he spotted movement from the direction the Ghoulsmen had left in and instinctively whipped his spear up into a combat stance. A giant fur-clad figure strode across the hills towards him, its face hidden behind a grotesque animal skin mask. Rav lowered his weapon and waved. Cyrn leaned his spear into his shield arm to free his hand and waved back. Rav exhaled in relief. They'd been successful. He found himself pulling a stretched and shaking smile as he watched the figure approach, his joy strained by his knowledge of what his brother would've had to do to win this skirmish. Even from a distance, it was obvious that Cyrn's armour had been darkened by dried blood.

Rav looked back to the body beside him and kneeled to hide his face, picking through the soldier's pockets in search of valuables, hoping Cyrn had been far enough away to only notice his smile and not the torment beneath it. With some effort, Rav regained control of his face to flatten his lips, and by the time Cyrn arrived at the hill, Rav wore a blank, almost bored expression.

Cyrn stood next to Rav and patted his shoulder, his seven-foot frame of muscle brimming with violent power towering over him. "Sorry we left you to handle the last soldier here alone. I wouldn't have given the order to chase them down if I wasn't certain you could handle him yourself. I needed to ensure none of Baron Kiln's soldiers returned to Greenfield with information about us. Did it go well?"

Rav managed to force a non-strained, fake smile as he stood, only reaching Cyrn's shoulders at his full height. "Aye, it did. There were no problems."

Cyrn pulled off his mask, revealing his thick black beard and thinning head of hair, which combined with his weatherworn skin to make him seem much older than he was. Nine years of bloodshed had forced him to mature early. Rav scratched his own smooth chin, finding it hard to believe his brother was only two years older than him.

Cyrn smiled softly. "You're getting stronger."

Rav further forced a chuckle. "I'd have to be with all the training I've done."

Cyrn frowned in concern. Rav's smile faltered as he chided himself for making such an obvious mistake. He had to show confidence rather than nonchalance to stop his brother worrying about him.

"I wasn't as good as I thought I'd be." Rav looked up the hill at the body of his last opponent. "There was a moment when he charged at me, consumed by this... wild desperation. I knew that if I didn't manage to kill him before he reached me, he was going to hurt me. Maybe even kill me." Rav took a breath. "But I did kill him. I thrust forward like you taught me and buried my spear in his gut. You were right; I handled it, and I can handle it again."

Cyrn's face softened as he pulled his brother into a hug. "I hope this never happens again."

Rav almost winced, having heard that same sentence after every battle for nine years now. "Aye." He hugged his brother back, clutching the thick furs that formed Cyrn's armour while trying not to think about how sticky they were. "But if it does, know that I can do whatever you need me to."

"You don't have to if you don't want to," Cyrn whispered. "You don't have to be out here with me."

Rav pulled out of his hug to look Cyrn in the eye. "I *want* to be here helping. Trust me to be fine and focus on the things that matter. Stone's Way will always be more important than me, just like the Carvell Name is."

Cyrn shook his head. "Everything we're doing is for the people of Pitt. It's for you, Ma, Pa, and everyone else who *makes* Stone's Way our home. There's no point in me doing this if it harms you. There's no point in fighting if what we're fighting for gets ruined anyway. You don't have to be fine."

"Aye, I know all that, but I *am* fine, Cyrn." Holding his brother's gaze a moment longer, Rav relaxed upon seeing Cyrn finally nod in acknowledgement. "What happened with you? Where are the other Ghoulsmen?"

"Wakeman is scavenging the dead for equipment and will be here soon. I sent the other three back to camp so they could rest early. It was a long chase."

"And did we get them all? Is Stone's Way free of soldiers once more? I know we captured Baron Kiln's messenger, but what if the message was wrong? What if Baron Kiln sends more soldiers to kill us anyway?"

Rav must've let some of his fears show because Cyrn held him by the shoulders when he answered. "That's not going to happen. One of my contacts near Greenfield confirmed that Baron Kiln is under siege and won't be able to deploy any more units here for at least two months. His opponent is a rival Baron called Baron Hewett, and supposedly, he's come to Greenfield *from* the Sink, so he should give Baron Kiln a tough fight."

Rav gritted his teeth. "I hope they kill each other to the last man. I hope none of them are left alive to come here when their battle's over. Do you think we could stay in Stone's Way another year if that happens?"

Cyrn sighed as he hung his head. "That's not going to happen, Rav. We've tried waiting it out, but more and more Barons keep marching this way to the Sink. We can't fight them off forever. They won't give up trying to conscript us or our families. We've got a few months of peace now; it's best we use them to gather as much food as we can carry. After that, we need to escape from Stone's Way while Baron Kiln is still at war and can't spare any soldiers to pursue us."

*No.* The word sat on the tip of Rav's tongue, on the verge of being uttered. Of course he wanted to refuse to leave his home. The place where the Carvells had lived for generations. How could he leave Pitt and Stone's Way when they held so much of his lineage's history? How could they leave when he knew what would happen if the Ghoulsmen weren't here to protect it? Everything would be torn down by greedy soldiers to be used in their endless wars, soldiers who wouldn't care about the sense of love and community that had gone into every creation. No, they'd use Pitt's stone in fortresses soon to be stained in blood or fling it from war machines at terrible monsters. Just the thought of abandoning everything his Bloodline had built sat like a knife in his soul.

Rav grimaced. Maybe his desire to stay was more selfish than that. Maybe he just didn't want to leave so he could avoid the humiliation of finally undergoing the punishment he deserved. His recklessness was a stain on the Carvell Name, but as long as he kept fighting for his family, couldn't he clean it? If he managed to protect Pitt and everything he loved, couldn't he undo the blight hanging over him? Right now, everyone in Pitt ignored his crime, but if they had to leave, wouldn't they curse him under their breaths? Wouldn't they hate him for causing this mess and despise him for failing to fix it?

Everyone in Pitt would suffer for his actions, including his brother. Cyrn certainly didn't deserve that and yet he'd been the one to suggest it. Rav bit his tongue. Seeing the tortured expression on Cyrn's face, Rav knew he'd also struggled with this decision. Of course he had; he was the one who'd taught Rav about the greatness of the Carvell Name and was the living embodiment of everything it represented. More than that, Cyrn was smart enough to have already considered Rav's every worry and had decided to do it anyway. Rav dug his nails into his palms. If Cyrn thought leaving was necessary, then it had to be done. He'd rather have Pitt's citizens hate him than be dead.

"Alright. We'll leave."

As soon as he said the words, Rav's heart burned. *I want to stay, I want to stay, I want to stay,* flooded his mind as the tears he'd suppressed earlier wet his eyes.

Cyrn gazed at him with pride, as though he understood Rav's every thought. "Good. Let's get this done, then." His voice became sombre as he indicated to the body next to them. "It's not good to be around the dead."

"Aye," Rav said, his voice shaking as his lip wobbled.

Bodies of soldiers stiffened around them, filling the once-beautiful hillside with pools of coagulating blood. As Cyrn went to scavenge equipment off the ones at the hilltop, Rav stood watching him. Cyrn looked menacing in his thick goat hides, looming above the land like a conqueror as he strode across the battlefield. Cyrn would tear his enemies in two barehanded to stop them reaching Pitt. Rav flinched at a sharp pang of guilt, its familiarity doing nothing to dull its edge. *What have I turned my brother into?*

# Chapter Two

*Clank.* Rav threw a broken spear point onto a growing pile of looted equipment being built on the hilltop. While the shafts of the soldiers' spears were too wonky to be of use, the metal heads could be reforged into new points. Aside from them, there were three intact kettle helms, two sets of decent gambeson padding, and four pairs of quality boots. Neither he nor Cyrn had found any jewellery yet, all of it likely having been sold off during the soldiers' journey here. Rav sucked his teeth as he looked at the heap. Nine years ago, this would've been a fantastic haul for the Ghoulsmen, but now it was little more than junk compared to the other equipment they'd scavenged over the years. Wasn't it ironic that they'd gotten rich from those chasing their fortunes?

*Ting, ting, ting.*

As Rav headed back down the hill to search the last soldier, icy shards of rain began pelting everything, bouncing off his armour. He tightened his collar and hurried. This soldier was one of Cyrn's victims, made evident by the gaping holes in the man's chest. Rav tried not to look at the wounds, nausea swirling in his stomach whenever he glimpsed the bone and organs inside. He was reasonably skilled with a spear and had a precise strike that was good for finding gaps in enemies' armour, but Cyrn was strong enough to not bother with that, instead using brute force to punch his spear through anything in his way. It was Cyrn's reputation alone that made invading soldiers wary of facing the Ghoulsmen.

Rav turned out the soldier's pockets and found nothing, but just as he was leaving, a glint of silver caught his eye. Through a hole by the man's sternum, he spotted a small necklace. Rav braced himself before reaching inside to pull it free, then wiped the plain, silver disk on the grass and examined it. This wasn't an ordinary necklace; it was a symbol to be earned by outstanding soldiers who'd gained their Baron's recognition. It was a universal signifier that this man had been a Contender, a high-ranking member of a Baron's army second only to the Champions, who led all of their Baron's forces. This man had been this unit's leader.

"Have you got everything?" Cyrn called from the hilltop.

"Aye."

"Wakeman's nearly here. Help load up this equipment, then let's head back."

Rav looked back out across the hills, spotting another giant fur-armoured figure lurching towards him with a large bag. Also near seven feet tall and clad in goat hides, Wakeman was the only person Rav knew who had a physique as staggering as Cyrn's. His hair was long and wild, matching his scruffy black beard, and although his cheeks were still a little thin from his time fleeing slavers before he'd arrived in Stone's Way and joined the Ghoulsmen, he was undoubtedly the second strongest member of their crew.

Rav headed back up the hill and added the necklace to the pile before helping Cyrn organise their spoils while Wakeman arrived. He heard a grunt from below as Wakeman stopped at the bottom of the hill. He went down to help him.

"Tired?" Rav asked.

"Tired," Wakeman grumbled. "I need to rest for a moment, then I'll be good to continue." He released the bag and flexed his hand.

"I'm not surprised. You fought side by side with Cyrn today. I've never seen anyone keep up with him like that." He patted Wakeman's shoulder. "It won't be long before you're just as strong. You already look the part, and after watching you dispatch those soldiers, I'm certain you'll be as good as him one day soon."

Wakeman sighed as he shook his head. "We didn't fight side by side; Cyrn led, and I barely followed. I've still got a long way to go if I want to even get close to matching your brother."

"I promise you, you're not that far off. The two of you together will be unstoppable."

Wakeman ruffled Rav's hair. "I'm a good fighter and I'll get better, but your brother's not just strong, he's wicked smart too. We're lucky to have one of him; asking for two is being greedy." He looked up at Cyrn, and Rav followed his gaze, love and pride swelling in his chest.

"Stop staring and get moving," Cyrn shouted. "I'm getting soaked."

Wakeman laughed.

Rav made to help Wakeman with the bag, but Wakeman shooed him away and lifted it on his own. After joining Cyrn at the hilltop, they loaded the bag and set off.

A freezing wind blew over them, the rain caught in it slapping Rav in the face. "I thought winter was ending," he said with a scowl whilst shivering.

"The seasons have been changing year by year since the Sink appeared," Cyrn grumbled. "Even things like that have become unreliable. We just have to hope it gets warmer by the time we set off."

"We're definitely leaving, then?" Wakeman asked.

"Aye," Cyrn said. "We'll take two or three months to rest and prepare for the journey, then we'll head out. Hopefully, it should be spring by then."

"Do you know where we're going yet?"

"No, but we've got no time to find out. We need to leave before Baron Kiln or Baron Hewett recover from their battle, or worse, before another Baron arrives to cause more trouble." Cyrn grimaced. "Staying here means certain death. Wherever we end up going, it's better to risk our lives on the road."

Wakeman nodded. "If you're sure we need to go, then let's go."

Rav fought to suppress his roiling emotions once more. It wasn't fair. Why had the Sink appeared near their home? Why couldn't it have formed on the other side of the world?

He looked out across the rocky hills that formed Stone's Way. Littered with boulders and twisted formations, traversing the landscape was treacherous for enemy soldiers and merchant caravans, but he knew its shortcuts and its dead ends. He knew there was a ridge to the east that had the best view of the sunrise and a valley to the west that had the best view of the sunset. Grass grew thin but green around the rocks, with patches of rustic-orange moss blooming over great stretches of bog, and the air smelled fresh with a hint of soil. This was the place he'd grown up, and he loved every part of it.

Stone's Way was supporting him the same way it had supported his parents and their parents before them. The Ghoulsmen were a small group, but with the aid of this terrain, they could defend against many times their number, as though Stone's Way had been designed to help guard their home. Rav dropped his head. Even with all its help, he still wasn't strong enough to protect his town. He wasn't good enough at fighting or strategizing or negotiating. If only he could be more like Cyrn, then they might have had a chance to keep their home.

Wakeman grunted, lurching forward with weary steps as he lugged the sack filled with equipment.

"Here." Cyrn reached out and grabbed the side to help lift it.

"It's not heavy; it's my armour. It keeps sliding." Wakeman lifted the top layer of his furs to show two flapping sections of hide hanging loose at his waist, the thread supposed to be binding them broken.

Looking closer, Rav spotted a cut in the hide where a blade had slashed them, the ends of the thread severed, not snapped. Only the last layer of chainmail Wakeman was wearing had saved him from having a gaping hole in his gut. Rav rubbed his hands together to get some feeling back in his fingers, then pulled a needle and thread out of a pouch on his belt. Wakeman set the bag down, then lifted his furs higher, Rav kneeling before licking the string of wool and tying it around the needle's hook.

"Someone almost got you. If not for your chainmail, you'd be bleeding out right now." He pushed the needle through the left hide section, then the right, starting to bind the two pieces together again.

"Ha, but I got him first. And I did have my chainmail. It's always protected me." Wakeman patted his chest, observing Rav's work. "You're as good as your Ma," he commented.

"He's better," Cyrn corrected.

"I'm not." Rav's cheeks went warm, his skin tingling as hot blood clashed with the bitter cold that had seeped into them.

"Aye, you are," Cyrn affirmed. "It's cold and wet and you're just as fast as she is."

"I'd have pricked myself a dozen times already," Wakeman added.

Rav looped the thread across itself, the top half of each section secure, then started on the bottom. "Doing repairs like this is easy. It's nothing compared to what you two can do."

Cyrn flicked Rav's head. "If all of us only focused on fighting, then we'd have no equipment to fight with. We all have our gifts, Rav, and don't forget that you're also pretty good with a spear."

"And a knife," Wakeman added.

Rav pulled a small smile as he tied the last bit of thread and snapped off the end. "How does it feel?" he asked Wakeman.

Wakeman twisted from side to side. "Good."

Cyrn still grabbed the other side of the sack to help carry it despite Wakeman assuring Cyrn that he was fine. Wakeman and Cyrn continued talking about what supplies they'd need to take with them when they left. Cyrn asked most of the questions and Wakeman answered them as best as he could from his experience travelling outside of Stone's Way. Rav mulled over the idea of leaving for what felt like the thousandth time. The decision to leave had been made, but was there really no way they could stay?

Leaving would give them a peaceful life free from Barons and the Sink and these constant battles. The answer seemed obvious when he thought about it like that, but then why was he struggling so much with the decision?

Rav pinched himself between his eyes. Stone's Way had made him; its rock was in his bones. When he felt that searing pain in his chest at the thought of leaving, it was almost like the pieces of his home inside him were getting wrenched out, and if that happened, who would he be? How could he be a Carvell when he couldn't save anything the Carvells had left their descendants?

Rav glanced at Wakeman, who noticed and smiled softly. There were only two people Rav knew who'd left their homes, and they were both like brothers to him. Although he hadn't known Wakeman before he'd stumbled upon Stone's Way, Rav knew him now and he was sure Wakeman wasn't a desiccated phantom of himself like Rav feared he'd become if he left Stone's Way. Wakeman's circumstances were different to Rav's, though, but how different could escape and exile be? The result was the same. They'd both been—

"*Get down!*" Cyrn hissed as he pulled Rav to the ground and covered Rav's mouth with his hand.

Rav scanned the hillside below him, breathing fast and shallow, the wet grass tickling his face. Wakeman was lying beside them, also staring at the beast at the bottom of the hill. Rav gulped. This was the other problem with living so close to the Sink.

"It's a Spine," Cyrn whispered.

Its mutants had begun roaming here. The beast below them had once been a goat, but after its body had been corrupted by whatever strange power had formed the Sink, it had taken on a far more vicious appearance. The Spine was much larger than a normal goat, reaching Rav's height when standing on all fours, with wicked black horns covered in spikes. If it was like the others of its kind, then Rav knew its hide had also become tough enough to withstand projectiles like arrows and bolts, leaving close-range spear thrusts as the only means to wound it. The change wasn't just to its appearance; this mutant was no longer grazing prey. Rav stared as the Spine gnawed on the bones of a hare.

Cyrn signalled for them to crawl away from the beast. Rav moved as quietly as he could, but all he could hear was his beating heart.

*Meeh*, it bleated. It must have noticed something. Rav wished it wouldn't come searching for them. *Tak, tak, tak*. He could hear it walking across the rock below them. He looked to Cyrn again, who signalled for them to get ready to fight. Rav accepted a shield that Wakeman slid over to him from the bag as Cyrn drew his own spear and shield. Rav and Wakeman copied him. Even with Cyrn and Wakeman at his side, Rav's hand trembled as he gripped his spear. *Tak, tak, tak*. The sound was getting closer.

"*Attack*," Cyrn bellowed, bolting up with Wakeman right behind him.

Rav shot to his feet, moving into position behind them as they rushed towards the lip of the hill to ensure they had the high ground for the coming fight.

"*Waaaaah*," Cyrn roared whilst brandishing his spear at the Spine.

*MEEEH.*

The mutant bounded up the hillside straight at Cyrn. Rav flinched at the horned boulder hurtling towards them.

"*Waah*," Cyrn shouted again while he darted to the left.

The mutant followed Cyrn, and Rav snapped to. Cyrn was doing the hard part. Wakeman acted first, thrusting his spear into its hind leg while it was distracted. The monster didn't budge under the blow. Wakeman shuddered after the impact, his spear unable to drive any deeper into its flesh. Rav stabbed his spear into the shallow wound Wakeman had opened with all his strength.

*MEEH.*

The Spine halted its charge. It turned to face Rav, who hurriedly retracted his spear and braced behind his shield. In a single bound, the beast closed the distance between them, ramming straight into Rav's spear, but its skull was too thick to be pierced and Rav's arm was smacked to the side. The beast was right in front of him. His shield wouldn't save him.

*MEH.*

The Spine went sliding down the hillside. Cyrn and Wakeman had struck it in its other leg, sending it tumbling to the bottom of the hill. They drew back into defensive positions, never taking their eyes off the monster.

Rav found his breath again. He rushed to Cyrn's side and braced himself there, sweat cold. The Spine broke its fall and stood on shaking legs before limping back up the hill towards them, still locked onto Rav. The Ghoulsmen waited for it, letting it tire itself out, and once it reached them again, Cyrn bellowed as he drove his spear at its head. The mutant ducked to block the blow with its thick skull, but Wakeman had predicted the action and stabbed at its eye while Rav aimed for its snout.

Wakeman missed his target, his spear tip slicing across the side of its head, while Rav struck true, his spear biting deep into the soft flesh of its nose. The beast reeled back, giving Cyrn an opening to bury his spear tip into its eye socket. With a guttural bleat, the mutant collapsed and went still. Cyrn stabbed it twice more while Wakeman scanned their surroundings for any other threats. No signs of movement anywhere else; they were safe for now.

Rav jittered in place, that moment before the Spine had almost trampled him replaying in his mind.

"Why's one of those things over here? Aren't they supposed to stay in their territory on the other side of the river?" Wakeman asked Cyrn.

"Aye, that's what they're *supposed* to do. Which means this might be a new one that's come all the way from the Sink."

"Another one?" Wakeman huffed. "Why can't those things just stay in the Sink where they belong? Why do they keep wandering here?"

"I think they're like us—these weaker mutants can't survive in the Sink, so they have to leave."

Wakeman spat on the grass with a grimace. "If monsters like this can't live there, no one can."

"We need to count the goat herds near here to confirm if this is a new Spine or one that's just crossed over the river," Cyrn said. "If this is a new Spine that's come here with others from the Sink, we might need to leave Stone's Way sooner than we think to avoid fighting them. One Spine is dangerous enough; if we face a group of them, some of us are going to get killed."

"These things are like an infestation," Wakeman growled. "We already have to avoid half of Stone's Way to stay out of their territories. If any more come, they'll take over this place."

Cyrn nodded. "Rav?"

*I'm alive, I'm alive, I'm alive, I'm—*

"Rav?" Cyrn barked. "Do you know which herd this Spine could have come from?"

Rav scrambled to get his notebook from his satchel and flicked through his pencil-drawn maps. *Where, where, where*. His hands kept shaking. *There*. "The closest herd is east of here." Rav pointed. "Behind that hill."

"We'll need to count it tomorrow to check if that's where this Spine came from," Cyrn said.

"I'll do it." Rav forced a confident grin as he puffed out his chest. "I'll head out in the morning."

Wakeman gave Rav a knowing wink. "Don't worry; I'll come with you."

Rav flushed red at having been seen through before smiling at him in thanks.

"Come on, let's get back." Cyrn beckoned for them to follow him. "I want to check on the others."

As they continued back to their campsite, Rav's jitters faded as a wave of exhaustion set in. Legs failing him, he used his spear as a walking stick to keep himself moving at a quick pace. His arm ached from his clash with the Spine and the heat seemed to have left his body, leaving him shivering despite his furs. Cyrn and Wakeman marched on the same as they had before the fight. Rav gritted his teeth and pushed on. Why was he so weak? Why had he needed Cyrn and Wakeman to save him? The thoughts sat like splinters under his skin. If he'd encountered the Spine alone, he'd have been killed and left Stone's Way unguarded. He could only rely on others to risk *their* lives for his home and family. He couldn't keep doing that; the guilt had already eaten through him.

He stepped in a divot and ended up stumbling forward. Rav spun around, intent on stamping the earth into place to vent some of his frustration when he froze, his eyes widening. There, in the dirt, was an enormous cloven hoofprint.

"Cyrn," he called.

Cyrn and Wakeman looked back.

Rav stepped next to the print. His foot wasn't even half as big as the print was. If the shape of the cloven hoof weren't so clear, he'd have thought that a small boulder had once been sitting there. Was it real? The Spine they'd just fought had hooves the size of his hand and that had been as tall as him. Whatever had left this track would be more than twice its size.

"You need to see this."

"What am I looking at?" Cyrn asked as he came over.

"I think." Rav gulped. "I think it's a hoofprint."

Cyrn went silent as he stared at the groove.

Wakeman studied it and frowned. "It can't be. There's no way there could be a Spine this big."

"I think Rav's right," Cyrn muttered. "The shape is identical to Spine tracks."

"It'd have to be massive, Cyrn." Wakeman raised his eyebrow as he pointed at the surrounding hills. "We would've spotted something that big long ago."

"Or it's only entered Stone's Way recently," Rav whispered. "Maybe it walked through while we were fighting Baron Kiln's soldiers."

"We need to get back to camp now and make sure the others are alright," Cyrn ordered.

They set off running as a coiling sense of dread set in Rav's gut. There was a monster unlike anything they'd ever seen roaming Stone's Way. He pushed himself to move as fast as he could. What if the mutant had already encountered the other members of the Ghoulsmen? They could be injured right now, desperately hoping to be saved as they took their last stand.

None of the Ghoulsmen would have to fight without him by their side if he could help it. No one would die before him. He'd make sure of it.

Rav rushed over a hill and down into a valley, seeing the boulder that marked the Alley Camp entrance. No Spines or screams. Cyrn tilted his head to signal for him to continue to the camp. Rav readied his spear just in case, but having seen no signs of danger, he relaxed his shoulders a little. Cyrn reached the boulder first, Rav just behind him, and Wakeman at the rear, the trio peering inside the cave beside it.

The Alley Camp was the closest Ghoulsmen camp to Pitt and had been dug deep into the hillside like a mine shaft, a fire burning a dozen paces away at the back to light the narrow tunnel. A large rock was sitting next to the entrance that was used to block them in at night to prevent anything from getting at them while they slept. Rav heard laughter and spotted the three other members of the Ghoulsmen moving around the fire. He chuckled with relief, nudging Wakeman with his elbow, who then nudged him back.

"They're alright." Cyrn's shoulders relaxed.

"Phew." Wakeman wiped his sweaty forehead with the back of his sleeve. "Worrying really tires me out."

"I know it's still light outside, but can we block the entrance early today?" Rav asked.

"Aye."

Cyrn and Wakeman worked together to shift the boulder across the entrance, sealing out the waning sunlight so only flickering orange firelight filled the cave.

One of the other members walked over to them from the fireside. He was Rav's height, thin, ginger-haired, and always brimming with energy, but beneath the childish gleam in his eye was someone who had seen all the horrors of the world. He was the only other person Rav knew, aside from Wakeman, who had lived outside of Stone's Way.

"You're finally back." Thorley laughed. "We were wondering when you were going to join the celebra..." He frowned. "Why are you all so pale? Did something happen?"

"I need to speak to everyone. Let's sit." Cyrn strode down the narrow cave to the fire, reaching it in a few steps.

Already sitting beside the fire on cushioned wooden stumps were Tido and Tobias. They gazed up at him with weary grins as he arrived, Tido with her shoulder-length brunette hair, full cheeks, and freckles; Tobias with his short blond hair that matched well with his pale eyes and soft features, only the burned skin around his mouth marring his good looks. Seeing Cyrn's serious demeanour, they went quiet.

Once everyone was seated on the stumps around the fire, Cyrn spoke. "It was an honour fighting beside you this afternoon. Not one of you faltered in the thick of battle. Thanks to your immense efforts and unwavering bravery, Stone's Way is free from enemy soldiers once more."

"Aye," the Ghoulsmen cheered, Tido and Tobias the loudest, while Rav, Wakeman, and Thorley held back in anticipation of what else Cyrn had to say.

"I've been awed watching you all develop into the warriors you are today," Cyrn continued, "and I'm sure you'll only get better in the future. The Sink's brought nothing but hardship since it appeared, yet you've all held strong against its dangers. For nine years, we've been under attack. For nine years, we've fought off those seeking to destroy our home. Here we are, free. Neither Barons nor mutants have broken us."

They cheered again. Rav tensed.

Cyrn's smile faded. "Right now, Baron Kiln is at war with a new Baron, Baron Hewett. While this war should last for a few months and give us time to rest, neither one of those Barons is going to defeat the other without losses to their forces, which means that no matter who the victor is, they're going to end up looking for new labourers to replace those who died. In just a few months, more soldiers will enter Stone's Way looking for slaves. No doubt they'll claim they're hunting for criminals, looking to trade with us, or whatever other lie they'll have prepared as a 'pretence' for them to enter our home.

"But we know the truth. We know what they're truly after. I never want to see any of Pitt's citizens in shackles. I never want to see another one of Pitt's citizens get dragged off to die in the Sink."

Cyrn paused. "I've been thinking of a way to solve this, of a way to keep us and our families safe, and I'll continue to do so, but there's only one solution I can see right now. There's only one way we can all survive." He gazed around the cave. "We use these few months to gather as much food as we can and then leave Stone's Way."

Thorley, Tido, and Tobias's eyes went wide, their complexions paling, Cyrn's words seeming to weigh their heads down. Rav did his best to keep his expression as stern as Wakeman and Cyrn's.

"We've been sacrificing ourselves to save our town and now we need to sacrifice our town to save ourselves." Cyrn cleared his throat. "We need to get everyone in Pitt ready for the journey as soon as we can. That's what we're going to focus on now. It'll take us about a month to gather enough food and equipment, but I'd like us to work as fast as we can to hopefully be ready earlier than that in case anything unexpected happens. We've fought here for as long as we can; now it's time to escape."

"But won't it be all right if this new Baron kills Baron Kiln?" Tobias asked.

Behind Tobias' eyes, Rav could see the same pain he had at the thought of leaving.

"Baron Kiln's the only one who knows about... about *that* event," Tobias continued, "and him wanting to arrest Rav is the only valid reason anyone could have for catching us. If he dies, then Baron Hewett will have a hard time finding a good enough pretence for attacking us. He might give up on it, deciding Stone's Way's too small to bother with."

Rav flinched. *Murderer.* Which was worse—that he'd done it or that he couldn't face it, to the point that the people he trusted most had to avoid talking about it? Carvells weren't cowards and yet that's what he was. Maybe he'd stopped being a Carvell the moment he'd stabbed that guard and everyone was just too scared to tell him.

"This has nothing to do with that," Cyrn said, breaking Rav's mire. "If the Barons don't have an excuse to attack us, then they just won't use one. There are no laws anymore, not among those heading to the Sink. They'll lie and cheat and steal with not even their Names to hold them accountable. And besides that, there's another reason for us to leave."

"Is this about whatever happened after we left the battlefield?" Thorley asked. "Were you attacked?"

"Aye, that's the other part of it." Cyrn stared into the fire for a moment as he gathered his breath. "We encountered a wandering Spine on our way back here. Rav also found a hoofprint larger than any we've seen before, which means there's a new giant Spine wandering Stone's Way. I think another group of mutants have migrated here from the Sink."

The air turned heavy at his words.

"How big do you think this new Spine is?" Tido asked.

"Judging by its tracks, it's at least twice the size of the usual ones."

Tido sucked in a breath through her teeth.

"Aye, it's that bad. I don't ever want to fight this thing, so let's get away from it as soon as possible."

Thorley stared at the floor, tugging at his sleeve, expression heavy with foreboding. "If it's really as big as you say," he muttered, "then it might be a mutant called a 'Zet Ar."

Everyone looked at him.

"Have you learned something about mutants like this before?" Cyrn asked.

Thorley looked up at him, pale. "I was taught about them in my old home. 'Zet Ar is the name for a mutant that comes from the Ar'za, the Sink's outer ring. The usual mutants we've fought are from the fringes of the Sink, but the further in you go, the stronger the mutants become. None of those things should've come to Stone's Way, though; I don't know what one would want here."

Cyrn smiled softly, as though to comfort Thorley. "Isn't it after the normal things animals want, like food and territory?"

Thorley shrugged with a hopeless shake of his head. "I can't imagine Stone's Way has more of those to offer than the Sink does. It might be after something else."

Rav adjusted his collar, which suddenly felt too tight around his neck. "Well, let's hope this 'Zet Ar just got lost and isn't intelligent enough to want things beyond its animal instincts."

"If we avoid it, its intelligence won't matter," Thorley said. "But, Cyrn, do you know where we're going?"

"No. We'll just have to hope there's some safe land for us to settle on out there."

"Cyrn, I've been 'out there', and Stone's Way was the only safe place I found. All the other territories have sworn allegiances to Barons... they're all training their sons and daughters for war in the Sink. Their fanaticism runs far too deep for them to ignore us. If we don't join them, they'll attack us." Thorley dropped his shoulders and lowered his voice. "And there are thousands of Barons leading their armies to the Sink from every direction. How are we going to hide from them? We're trapped in a net here."

Cyrn took a breath before breaking into a grin, a gleam in his eye, dispelling the worry that had seized the camp. "Well," he said, "there are two ways to escape from a net. We can either wriggle free through a gap, or we'll cut our way out. There's only one place where things are hopeless and that's here. If we stay, we'll die, it's as simple as that. Whether it's Barons or mutants, our enemies will keep coming until they overwhelm us, but out there, we have a chance to escape that fate. Thorley, you managed to find us, and I don't believe we're unique. There *will* be another place for us to live. Will you find it with me? Will you work with me to escape our fate so that one day we might have the peaceful life we want?"

"Aye." Everyone nodded.

Rav hardened his resolve. Stone's Way wasn't special because of its stones or its sunsets, it was special because of its spirit, and that could never be taken away.

It was quiet in the Alley Camp that night. Cyrn's words had killed any hope that they could stay here, and now it felt as though Stone's Way were a grandparent on their deathbed. Everyone milled around the cave saying their silent goodbyes. Rav sighed. Maybe Stone's Way had been dying from the moment the Sink appeared and it was just that they could only now see the signs of it wasting away. His eyelids grew heavy as his exhaustion overwhelmed him. He sat listening to the *tss* that sounded whenever a raindrop fell through the small hole in the cave ceiling that acted as the chimney and sizzled on the fire.

"Rav..."

He snapped upright from his slumped position and looked at Wakeman tending to his shaggy Spine-hide armour next to him. "Did you want something?"

Wakeman glanced up from cutting the clumped mud from his furs and raised an eyebrow at him. "What?"

Rav raised an eyebrow back. "I heard you call my name."

"I didn't."

Rav looked around the cave to see if it had been someone else. No one was looking at him. "Did you hear it?" he asked Wakeman.

"I didn't hear anything. It must've been your imagination."

"Oh." Rav rubbed his eyes as he settled back down in his seat, deciding that it was just his tired mind playing tricks on him.

"Rav…" the voice called again.

Rav peeked around the room, but no one was trying to get his attention. *Oh*. He smirked but remained still, as though he hadn't noticed it this time. The others were clearly messing with him, calling his name, then pretending that they hadn't to confuse him. Smoothing his grin, he played along, ready to catch whoever called to him next.

"Rav…"

Rav snapped his head up, only to see everyone else tiredly minding their own business around the fire. There were no grins, no signs of suppressed laughter, or even anyone facing his direction. He frowned deeply. Hallucinating hearing his name once was strange, but having heard it three times, he was certain the voice was real.

Just as he was about to tell Wakeman, something in the fire caught his eye.

Rav leaned closer to see the shadow of a Spine rampaging around in the flames as a group of tiny people tried to kill it. He blinked and tried to focus on what he was seeing but struggled to make out any details in the figments. There were six people fighting the Spine, two of them a head taller than the others, all wielding spears and shields. Rav rubbed his eyes before looking back at the fire, yet nothing changed. The figures continued battling in the flames while none of the other Ghoulsmen noticed.

It became hard for Rav to tell whether he was awake or dreaming. His body wasn't responding to his commands, and all he could do was watch the battle playing out before him. The

Spine trampled one of the smaller fighters, the boyish figment vanishing as it died, and from there, it picked off the next three, leaving only the two tallest people remaining. They fought well, but soon, they too were killed. The Spine bleated in victory, the noise rumbling through his mind as if the Spine were right in front of him.

Rav regained control of himself and stood up panting.

"Woah there, Rav." Wakeman grabbed Rav's shoulder and steadied him. "It's alright. Did you have a nightmare?"

Rav slumped back down with a shudder, muscles twitching as his heart pounded. "Aye. It was... odd."

"I see things too, sometimes," Wakeman said as he stared into the distance. "Old battlefields, old opponents, even the occasional ghoul from Pitt's stories. And while it's terrifying, they're just dreams. Why don't you settle down for the night and get some proper sleep?"

Rav found his sleeping place—a pile of furs on a straw-stuffed mattress—and tucked himself under the first layer while thinking about what he'd seen. Dreams were supposed to fade out of your memory when you woke up, but this one was stuck with him in perfect clarity. Rav shivered as realisation struck him. One of the tallest fighters had moved exactly the way Cyrn did. The other fighters also matched up with each member of the Ghoulsmen. If the figures were supposed to be them, then they weren't small, the Spine was massive. The cloven hoofprint. He had just seen the giant Spine kill them all.

# Chapter Three

Rav took a deep breath before exhaling slowly, his panic threatening to spike out of control. What he'd seen must've just been a dream, a figment of his imagination born out of his fear of the giant mutant. It wasn't real. The Ghoulsmen were alive, and he hadn't even seen the new Spine, so how could he know what it looked like? He shivered. The dread didn't leave him. It was that voice. Someone had called him. Someone had wanted him to see the figures in the flames. Why? What did the vision mean? Who...

Rav pinched himself. He was being childish, no better than when he had been a boy believing gruesome stories about Pitt's dead rising again as ghouls to protect the town. Only the Ghoulsmen existed. Only they could protect their home. He'd had a bad nightmare, but he'd had worse ones before; dreaming about failing to guard Pitt and seeing everyone he loved die was almost common by now. His heart rate slowed. He needed to sleep. It had been a long day of difficult decisions, and there were many more problems that needed his attention; he couldn't be distracted by his wild imaginings. Besides, why would he suddenly start getting visions anyway?

As Rav lay in his bed, a tempting thought crept back to the front of his mind. He hadn't actually seen the giant Spine. No one had. There was a single hoofprint, sure, but what other evidence was there proving its existence? What if they were just making a big deal out of nothing? He was being hopeful to the point of delusion, he knew that, but wasn't there a chance this thought was right?

If he could find proof that there was no giant Spine and no new mutants in Stone's Way, then the pressing danger they posed would disappear. That would ease some of the pressure on them to leave. Then if Baron Kiln and Baron Hewett caused grievous damage to each other during their war, every threat forcing them to flee Stone's Way right now would be resolved. He could do his duty and protect his home for a few more months. For a little longer, his friends and family could avoid enduring unknown hardships travelling to a place that might not even exist. He could delay suffering the exile he deserved.

Cyrn had said none of that would ever happen, and he'd never been wrong before, but wouldn't this be the best thing to be wrong about? The delusion grew, Rav's mind concocting a perfect future scenario. Maybe after the current threats facing them were resolved, more things would go in their favour. Maybe the mutants would decide to return to the Sink; after all, if they'd wandered out, they could wander back in. Or all the Barons coming this way could decide that this wasn't a good path to the Sink and stop marching through here. Maybe he'd be even luckier and the entire Sink would disappear just as quickly as it had appeared, taking all its supposed riches with it.

*But what are the chances of that happening?*

He firmed his mind. Ten years ago, no one would've believed that half the continent was about to be terraformed by a cataclysmic event that would fill the land with monsters, and yet a year later, the Sink came into existence. So many unthinkably bad things had happened already; why couldn't something good occur?

Rav sat up and faced Wakeman, who was still cleaning his armour by the fire. "Wakeman," he called.

"What?"

"Will you still come with me to count the goat herd tomorrow?"

"What's the point, Rav? We already know there are new mutants from the Sink."

"I just want to be sure."

---

Rav and Wakeman sat on a hillside overlooking the large riverbank where the eastern herd usually gathered to drink in the morning. They'd set off before first light so they could sneak into position undetected for the scouting mission, and the sun was now sitting above the horizon, casting golden rays of light across the landscape. Sky clear, air crisp, everything peaceful, birds flitting overhead before dropping to the ground, tweeting as they hunted for worms. It was moments like this when everything bad that had happened and everything bad that was happening felt far away, as though it were taking place in a different world. Rav pulled out his notebook and started sketching. The river gradually came to life on the page, with a few birds swooping over it.

"That's good," Wakeman commented as he watched Rav.

Rav finished up a bird's reflection in the water. "Thanks."

"You could become an artist if you wanted to; I'd decorate my house with your drawings."

Rav laughed. "I don't think I'll ever get the chance to do that, and besides, this is just for memory." He focused as he shaded the shadow of a rock. "I don't want these moments to be forgotten; I don't want the beauty of Stone's Way to be lost. Do you still remember your home?"

"I do." Wakeman pulled a sombre smile. "You don't have to worry; your home's not a place you can forget. Stone's Way is inside you. It's inside all of you. I'm sure..." his eyes glistened.

"I'm sure that just as I can see Stone's Way in you, you can see my home in me."

"I'm sorry," Rav whispered, lifting his pencil from the page before his now-shaking hands ruined the memory. "I shouldn't have brought up your home. I know your life wasn't pleasant there."

"Don't be." Wakeman looked out across the hills. "Sometimes it's nice to remember. There was far more good there than there was bad. I won't let that man spoil it all. I only regret that I ever honoured him with the title Pa."

"Being made Nameless should only be a punishment for those who've done something so evil it brings shame to their entire Bloodline." Rav dug his hand into the soil beside him, squeezing it into a fist. "How could your pa exile you for *refusing* to commit a crime? It's cruel, especially because... because of what I did." Lifting the ball of dirt, he released his grip and let it crumble in his palm. "My Ma and Pa protected me even when I didn't deserve it, while yours cast you out for doing the right thing."

"My pa had just as much a right to take away his lineage Name from me as your parents do to take away the lineage Name Carvell from you and Cyrn. No one could have stopped him, and no one should have. Being made Nameless is not just a punishment for committing crimes, it's for anyone who *dishonours* their lineage, no matter what their lineage regards honour as. My parents cut me off from my heritage and tried to shame me by having me wander the world without a Name, but honestly, I'd be more ashamed to still be part of that family.

"Being exiled from my home hurt, but having to obey such terrible orders under the threat of being made Nameless hurt far more. Imagine your own Pa telling you to go beat up some poor soul just because they refused to pay him for protection. To my pa's mind, I dishonoured my lineage by refusing to hurt others. I'm glad to be rid of him. And besides"—he smiled at Rav—"if I wasn't Nameless, then I wouldn't be here with you. I wouldn't have met Cyrn or your family or joined the Ghoulsmen. I wouldn't be the man I am today."

Rav smiled back. "I'm glad you are who you are. Do you think Thorley feels the same about being Nameless as you do?"

"Thor's different." Wakeman chuckled. "I think he deliberately made himself Nameless. From the few times he's mentioned his past, I've gathered that his family might be Sink fanatics. When he mentioned families training their sons and daughters to head out and join their Barons, he seemed to be speaking from experience. Perhaps the only way for him to escape that life was through exile."

Rav bit the inside of his cheek. "I completely missed that."

Wakeman watched Rav for a moment, looking to catch his eye and give him a sympathetic look but unable to. "Aye, I understand why. Do you ever talk to Cyrn about *that* event? He was one of the only people there at that time, right? Him and your Ma."

"Not really. If I even think about it too much, I start to get dizzy, or..." *Vicious*. "...Or confused."

"Well, from what I've heard, I think you did the right thing. And you still have the Name Carvell, so you can't have dishonoured your lineage."

Rav nodded, pretending that the words had comforted him in order to end the conversation before everything started spinning around him.

---

"That's one." Wakeman pointed at a Spine drinking from the stream amidst a herd of ordinary goats.

Rav added a mark in his notebook.

"And there." Wakeman indicated another. "And there. That's three out of...?"

"There should be four Spines amongst this goat herd."

They scoured the herd for the last one but failed to spot it. Rav's hopes grew.

"I don't see it," Wakeman said. "Does this mean the Spine we ran into yesterday came from here?"

"Aye," Rav replied. "Maybe a new group of them hasn't migrated here from the Sink after all."

Was this the good news he'd been wishing for?

"Ah, there it is." Wakeman pointed out the fourth Spine as it raised its head from drinking at the river. "Are you satisfied? We have to leave; there's no getting around it."

Rav lifted his head to face the deep blue sky, a self-deriding chuckle at his foolishness building in his chest. "You knew why I wanted to count the herd?"

"It wasn't hard to figure out your intentions. We've been living together for over four years now and I know you'll do everything you can to protect your home, but sometimes everything's not enough. We must accept the reality before us."

"I know." Rav huffed. "I know I'm not strong enough to fight off our enemies and I know that I've been putting you all in danger for my stupid wants, but how can I just accept that? I want to change it."

Wakeman flicked the side of Rav's head, Rav flinching, then facing him. "Firstly, *everyone* wants to stay here, not just you. We've all chosen to remain in Stone's Way up until now; you haven't forced us into anything. Secondly, it's the Sink that's put us in danger. You're not responsible for that. And lastly, how are you going to change anything if you're dead? If you really want to change our circumstances, isn't it better for you to retreat for now so that you can grow strong enough to do that in the future?" Wakeman gleamed with infectious hope. "Leaving Stone's Way isn't the end of us, Rav, it's an opportunity to potentially find solutions to our problems. Who knows what the future will be like? There isn't an endless number of people who can march into the Sink. A decade or two from now, we might be able to walk back into Stone's Way stronger and better experienced to reclaim your home."

Rav's lip twitched, almost rising into a matching grin. "I suppose that sounds like a pretty good plan. I'm not abandoning everything; I'm readying myself so I can fight to get it all back to the way it was."

"Right." Wakeman nodded to encourage him.

"Thank you. Do you think Cyrn knows how I'm feeling?"

Wakeman snickered. "Cyrn's twice as smart as I am. Aye, he knows, and he's probably also guessed that I'd be able to help you; otherwise, he wouldn't have let us waste our time. He can read situations to a degree I can't even comprehend. He's clever enough to know everything that's going on and wise enough to let us solve our own problems."

Rav rubbed the back of his neck. "Hearing you say that makes me feel so silly for keeping things from him to stop him worrying about me."

"I reckon if you stopped, Cyrn would become more concerned, and besides, he's too busy to spend all his time managing you. Him knowing that you have the confidence to solve your problems on your own must be reassuring."

"Well"—Rav nudged Wakeman with his elbow—"I'm not quite solving my problems on my own, am I? Thank you for helping. With you and Cyrn being so similar, it's almost like I have two brothers looking out for me."


Returning back to the Alley Camp, Rav found Cyrn leaning on a boulder half embedded into the hillside beside the camp entrance, gazing vigilantly in their direction before breaking into a relieved smile as he spotted them. "Any good news?" he asked.

Rav shook his head as he dropped into the valley. "I didn't find what I was looking for, but"—he looked to Wakeman at his side—"I'll be alright anyway. We all will."

Wakeman stepped ahead and leaned across the entrance to peer inside the cave. Rav followed him to see Thorley, Tido, and Tobias picking through the spoils they'd recovered from the battle yesterday, discarding some pieces while wiping others clean.

"What's going on?"

Cyrn stood and looked in with them, his smile falling. "We're checking our supplies before we head back to town and inform everyone that we're leaving."

Wakeman glanced at him with understanding. "We've got a tough day ahead of us, then."

"Aye, we do," Cyrn muttered. "I've got people doing menial tasks first, so they've got time to prepare what they're going to say while they keep busy. Even I'm not quite sure how to tell my wife."

Wakeman touched Cyrn's arm. "I'm sure whatever you say, Enna will understand. Come on, Rav; we'd better help." He pulled Rav inside towards the loot pile at the back and lowered his voice. "What about your girl? Any idea what you're going to say to Kayla?"

Rav gave a firm nod. "Aye, the truth."

He headed over to the pile of scavenged equipment and began sifting through it, thinking about his parents. They'd be hard to convince, just like he was, but Cyrn would manage it; their trust in him surpassed their love for Stone's Way too. As for his future fiancée... Rav found himself smiling as he thought of her. She'd—

*Clop. What is that noise?*

*Clop.* The sound was faint, like an echo from far away.

*Clop.* Rav realised what he was hearing and hurriedly glanced at the others, hoping he was hallucinating again. His eyes met Thorley's, who looked as panicked as Rav felt.

*Clop.* This time, everyone was startled by the sound.

"Is that...?" Wakeman whispered.

*Clop.*

"Aye." Cyrn dashed inside the cave to grab his spear and shield. "That's the sound of horses on the through road. Someone's entered Stone's Way. Get ready for battle."

Everyone dropped what they were doing and rushed to equip their armour.

"Rav," Cyrn barked, "I'm going to scout ahead. Come with me. Wakeman, lead Tobias, Thorley, and Tido to the choke point and ready an ambush there, understood?"

Cyrn set off running out the cave without waiting for a reply, Rav scrambling to grab his own equipment before chasing after him. Arriving outside, Rav spotted Cyrn already climbing out the valley towards the clopping and sprinted to catch up, breath ragged by the time he reached Cyrn's side, the pair continuing at a quick jog.

"Has... Baron Kiln... sent more soldiers after us?" Rav panted.

"I don't know. I was sure he wouldn't be able to," Cyrn growled, seeming to bristle as he flexed his shoulders.

Seeing his brother so angry increased Rav's sense of panic. Who was coming? More soldiers? *Wait.* That didn't make sense. If Baron Kiln were attacking Stone's Way, wouldn't he have his soldiers travel the hills, not the road, so they couldn't be detected easily? Rav gritted his teeth. He wasn't good at guessing things like this. But Cyrn always knew what was going on. If he didn't know what was happening, then Rav had no chance of figuring it out.

Running directly over the hills was a far faster method of traversing Stone's Way than the through road, which was twisted and winding. They soon closed in on the noise. Cyrn guided Rav behind a rocky outcrop where they couldn't be seen from the road but maintained a good view of it for themselves. As they waited—*clip clop, clip clop*—the echoes got louder.

It was definitely the sound of metal-capped hooves hitting rock, making Rav certain horses were coming. He could now hear wheels squeaking, which meant there were also carriages. Rav got his notebook out and skimmed over his sketches of all the Baron insignias he knew. He paused at Baron Kiln's emblem, a blue and white shield, wishing that the coming carriage wouldn't belong to him.

A grand white stallion rounded the corner, carrying someone tall, blond, and handsome. The man was wearing a breastplate lined with gold that served to highlight the dark red handprint in the centre of the chestpiece. It was a Blood Palm, identifying this man as a Champion—a Baron's greatest fighter and representative. Rav flicked through his notebook. Baron Kiln's Champion was called Mars Epo, but Champion Epo was supposed to have black hair.

Following the Champion were four horse-drawn carriages, each guarded by two saddled soldiers. A blue banner with a mountain insignia was mounted atop the second carriage. Rav checked his sketches. The insignia wasn't there.

He looked at Cyrn, who was staring at the leader. "We've never encountered them before. What should we do?" he hissed, eyes wide.

"We'll defend our home, like we always have."

Cyrn had given the call to fight a hundred times and a hundred times it had set Rav's blood boiling, but this time, he trembled. Rav stared at his brother's face, seeing the slight tension in his cheeks, the way he pursed his lips. It was an expression he knew too well from having to hide it from his own face. Cyrn was scared.

# Chapter Four

Rav's stomach jittered, nerves eating him alive as he and Cyrn raced towards the choke point to meet with the other Ghoulsmen. Not only were Champions expert fighters, they were also second-in-command to Barons' armies and could mobilise them themselves. With one order from this man, Stone's Way would be filled with soldiers. Still, the brother Rav knew would have usually been fearless even in the face of a threat like that. Cyrn and scared were two ideas that had never coincided in Rav's head. Until now.

"That Champion probably represents Baron Hewett," Cyrn growled.

"Are there any other Barons nearby?"

"I don't think so. I could be wrong, but the most obvious answer is the likeliest, which leaves Baron Hewett as our attacker."

"But he's at war," Rav pointed out, as if Cyrn could have possibly forgotten. "This Baron Hewett shouldn't be able to send his Champion, his second-in-command and greatest fighter, here while he's in the midst of a siege against Baron Kiln at Greenfield. Doesn't he know Stone's Way is treacherous? Doesn't he know that this is the Ghoulsmen's land?"

"No, Rav, the message we intercepted said that he *was* at war. If Baron Hewett has sent his Champion here, then that war has likely already ended with his victory. I know I said Baron Hewett and Baron Kiln would be fighting for months, but that fight is probably already over. I think Baron Hewett has already sent out his Champion to conscript new soldiers from the local area to replenish his losses. It also means that Baron Hewett defeated Baron Kiln in a very short time."

Rav gasped, stumbling in his run as his thoughts swirled, the true meaning behind Cyrn's words sinking in. Baron Kiln wasn't the strongest Baron, but he wasn't weak either, and while Greenfield was only a market city, it still had tall walls and a great view of the surrounding plains. Baron Kiln would've seen Baron Hewett coming from far away, giving him plenty of time to prepare for the siege.

Mouth dry, Rav wet his lips and managed to choke out his words. "To defeat him so quickly, Baron Hewett would need a much stronger army."

"Aye," Cyrn spat, "which is why things are now extremely dangerous."

Rav slowed, watching Cyrn break ahead of him, the jitters in his stomach spreading until his whole body was trembling. The Ghoulsmen had just been fighting. They were tired. *He* was tired. How were they going to defend Stone's Way this time?

Wakeman, Thorley, Tido, and Tobias were waiting outside the Alley—a choke point in the road before Rav's hometown that was set between two long rock faces as tall as two men to mimic a canyon. It was narrow enough for carriages to have to scrape through even when they travelled in single file. The Ghoulsmen had brought their crossbows and all had their grotesque masks made from animal skins stretched over their faces.

"Here." Wakeman handed Rav and Cyrn their masks and crossbows. "Who's coming?"

As Cyrn explained what was happening, Rav donned his mask and inspected his crossbow to ensure it was working properly. One of the reasons the Alley was a perfect place to set up ambushes was because once enemies entered it, the Ghoulsmen could shower them with crossbow bolts from the top. With limited space, enemies couldn't dodge the bolts and could only use shields to defend themselves, which kept them pinned down. From there, other members of the Ghoulsmen could safely drop boulders into the Alley to crush them or simply trap them inside.

"Are the boulders ready?" Cyrn asked after he'd caught everyone up on what was going on.

"Aye," Wakeman answered. "If they try and force their way through, we'll stop them."

"Good. We'll try using the 'pretences' first to see if these people still respect the law. We don't know anything about Baron Hewett, so we need time to investigate him, and pretending to acknowledge him as our new Baron will get us that time, understood?"

Everyone nodded.

The pretences were the guises under which everyone's behaviours were hidden. Barons couldn't legally enslave people, but they *could* conscript soldiers from the citizens in their territory. The most important difference between the two was that citizens could negotiate the terms of their conscription. Conscripts had to be treated well, with good pay, a solid status within the army ranks, and they would only have to fight for a single war. It was a fair deal between Barons, who defended their territory from invaders, and the citizens, who benefitted from the peaceful life Barons provided.

Under these pretences, the Ghoulsmen weren't a group rebelling against their Baron, they were people guarding a road, and the Barons weren't forcing people to go to war for them, they were looking to hire people for their army.

Cyrn faced Rav. "I'll need you to lead the negotiations. I need to watch this Champion as he speaks to you to see what he's like. I also need to see if he genuinely still obeys the law, or if upon confronting you, he'll attack, thinking that we're weak. I'm using you as bait, which is dangerous but necessary. Are you willing to do it?"

"Aye." Rav's response was immediate. He understood that because of Cyrn's stature, the Champion might feign adhering to the law to avoid fighting him. Cyrn needed someone smaller, like Rav, to represent the Ghoulsmen to ensure the Champion's honesty.

"Thank you." Cyrn patted Rav's shoulder before facing the others. "Wakeman is in charge of the ambush. Don't attack them unless they attack us first."

"Aye."

"This is our land," Cyrn roared. "Our home. Our duty. Let's show them what it means to enter Stone's Way."


Rav stood outside the Alley entrance, listening as the *clops* got closer. The sun was shining bright across Stone's Way, but the Alley was dark and dank, giving him an intimidating backdrop. Cyrn was hiding within the Alley's shadows, close enough to help Rav if he was attacked, but still out of sight. *Be confident. Be brave.* Rav took a deep breath and double-checked that his crossbow was ready and loaded. *Be smart.*

"They're here," he heard Cyrn murmur.

Rav looked up to see the sun glinting off the Champion's breastplate in the distance. *Clip clop, clip clop, clip clop.* As the Champion approached, Rav marched out to meet him with his crossbow raised. He deepened his voice and shouted, "*Halt.*"

The Champion gazed at him with a toying sneer before flattening his expression as though showing Rav respect, pulling his reins to stop his steed, then raising his hand to signal the caravan to follow his lead.

"Who are you?" Rav continued, heart rattling enough to shake his voice even as he reminded himself that this Champion had no reason to attack him and that Cyrn was close by to save him just in case.

The Champion stared down at Rav from his stallion, his gaze shifting over his neck, shoulders, and wrists—everywhere there was a gap in his armour. Rav's weaknesses were laid bare before the Champion, as if he were about to be dissected. All the confidence he'd had in Cyrn being able to save him in time crumbled to nothing.

"Tibald Sar, Slayer of Mars Epo and Champion to Baron Hewett," Tibald finally responded, his voice echoing down the Alley. "And you are?"

Cyrn was right; Baron Hewett had defeated Baron Kiln. Rav puffed out his chest in a show of bravado and answered with as much gravitas as he could muster. "The Ghoulsmen."

"The Ghoulsmen?" Tibald snorted. "I heard the leader of the Ghoulsmen was seven feet tall and strong enough to crush a man's head between his hands, not some boy who can't hold a crossbow without shaking."

Rav grimaced at having been seen through and squeezed the crossbow with a white-knuckle grip to stop his hands trembling. "Aye, some of us can crush heads barehanded," he growled, "and some of us can shoot bolts into peoples' throats. We all have our talents. Do you have the toll?"

"What toll?"

"The toll for passing through Stone's Way," Rav answered using the pretences of who the Ghoulsmen were. "There are mutants and bandits that roam these hills. We get paid to keep the road safe for travel."

"Under the command of which Baron?" Tibald asked, also abiding by the pretences. Rav regained some confidence.

"Baron Kiln currently sits in the capital, Greenfield," Rav said, acting ignorant of the outside situation to maintain their cover. "Doesn't this land belong to him?"

"Baron Hewett has killed Baron Kiln, taking control of Greenfield and its surrounding territories," Tibald announced.

"And does Baron Hewett intend to stay at Greenfield?"

"For a time, yes."

"Then we'll serve our new Baron." Rav lowered his crossbow. "But we still need to get paid for our work."

Tibald raised an eyebrow, a hint of derision rising with it. "You expect Baron Hewett's Champion to pay for travelling his land?"

"How else will we buy our food?"

Tibald watched him a moment before speaking. "Since this is the first time you're learning about your new Baron, I can make an exception for this journey and pay you." He emptied all the coins from a pouch on his belt into his hand and offered them to Rav.

Rav set his crossbow down and collected the money, finding it to be twice the amount usually paid for a toll. "This is too much," he said, trying to hand back half of the coins.

"I'm paying for two caravans to come through here. Ours is the first; the second will come through in two weeks."

"Two caravans?" Rav frowned.

"I intend to conduct some trade between Greenfield and the town of Pitt. That's your hometown, is it not?"

"Aye." Rav nodded slowly, watching Tibald's every move through squinted eyes.

"Then you should be celebrating." Tibald smiled. "Pitt's about to become rich."

*Ah*. Tibald wanted to "buy" conscripts from Pitt. It was a strategy other Barons had tried before, and Rav was familiar with how to use that pretence to delay the call to conscription by constantly renegotiating the price and other aspects of their employment. His fear of Tibald marching through to capture his home using violence faded.

"That's good," Rav said. "I'll let you head on, then."

"Thank you." Tibald suddenly glared at him like a snake looking at prey. "Ah, yes. Some of my men spotted a few bodies scattered around a hillside north of here. You wouldn't know anything about that, would you?"

That was where they'd killed off Baron Kiln's unit yesterday. Rav's mouth went dry. "There are mutants that roam these hills. Perhaps a few travellers who didn't pay the toll were attacked by them?"

"I see." Tibald faced the road ahead. "I only ask because I don't want anything like *that* to happen to my men. Is that understood?"

"Aye." Rav hurried to nod, immediately understanding what Tibald was implying. It was oddly polite, the Champion somehow following the law whilst also acknowledging that it was just a front. Rav squinted from behind his mask as he stepped to the side, Tibald signalling for his caravan to keep moving. Did he actually respect the law?

Cyrn stepped out of the Alley's shadows as Tibald passed by, and the two locked eyes.

Tibald grinned. "You must be the one who can break skulls."

Cyrn grinned back, stretching his mask. "Actually, there are two of us who can do that."

"Two of you?" Tibald looked genuinely surprised. "Would either of you want to spar with me sometime? I have great respect for the strong. Perhaps you do too."

"My apologies, but we don't fight for fun. If either of us face you in combat, then someone *will* die."

Tibald winked at him. "Let's hope I don't have to kill you, then."

Stood at the roadside as the caravan trundled after Tibald, Rav gazed up at Tibald's soldiers while they gazed down at him. The two riding closest behind Tibald acted the haughtiest, looking at Rav as though he were some pesky nuisance to be swept away. Rav thrummed his fingers against his crossbow as he glowered back, still keeping it lowered, but a rearguard soldier snatched for the spear strapped to his back. A sharp hiss from his partner had him release it, the man snapping his head forward to ignore Rav as he entered the Alley. Once the caravan had passed into the gloom, Rav darted to Cyrn, who also climbed up the steepening hillside, and handed him the toll payment before scampering up the remaining slope to reach the Alley top.

Wakeman stood looming over the caravan, a boulder held in place by smaller rocks but ready to be pushed down the canyon and block this entrance beside him. Four hundred winding feet away at the Alley's exit were Thorley, Tido, and Tobias beside another boulder, watching Wakeman for a signal to drop this one down too. Cyrn shook his head at Wakeman, who then stepped back from the boulder and raised his arms in an X to Thorley, Tido, and Tobias. They also stepped back and came running over. Cyrn waved his hand forward for Rav and Wakeman to accompany him across the stone ground as he strolled alongside the slow-moving caravan below, staring down at it.

Rav tugged his furs, peeling them off his sweaty skin while flexing his muscles to try and relieve the ache that had set in them.

"Here," Cyrn said, voice low, handing him his waterskin.

Rav grabbed it and took a sip to wet his mouth. "I must be tired from not sleeping well."

"No, you're feeling like this because of Tibald Sar. The first thing he did was make you feel exposed by highlighting the gaps in your armour, then he belittled you for being afraid. It took a lot of courage for you to respond the way you did." Cyrn smiled as he ruffled Rav's hair. "But you don't need to worry about Tibald Sar; I'll be taking care of him."

"What should *we* do?" Wakeman whispered.

"Tibald's abiding by the pretences, so we shouldn't be in any immediate danger, and while Tibald's being tricky about it, we can still use those pretences to get us some time to investigate Baron Hewett," Cyrn answered. "From there, we'll have to find out how Baron Hewett's positioned his army around Stone's Way to see if there's a gap for us to escape through. We might have to stay here a while longer than we thought."

"Does that mean we might have to fight Baron Hewett?" Rav asked.

"Maybe." Cyrn shrugged, then nodded to Thorley, Tido, and Tobias as they joined them in stalking the caravan. "We'll have to see what happens. There's too much we don't know right now."

"So why don't we just attack?" Wakeman murmured. "There aren't many soldiers guarding the Champion. If we'll fight each other later, why not ambush Tibald now when he's vulnerable? We might not get another opportunity like this."

Cyrn's mask crinkled as he grimaced, his gaze never leaving Tibald, his usually steady steps disharmonious as he fidgeted with his shield. "It's not a bad idea, but I think this might be Tibald giving us the same test we gave him. He's seeing if we'll attack him while he's vulnerable, which means he probably has some means of escape. I think striking now will go wrong in ways we can't predict because we don't know enough about him. Right now, Tibald's trusting us a lot. Can you see how he's riding?"

While the other soldiers occasionally glanced up at the Ghoulsmen from under their kettle helms, squinting as they faced the bright sky from the alley's shadows, Tibald kept his eyes firmly on the road ahead.

"We could attack him at any time, but rather than behaving skittishly, like we'll betray the deal we've just made, he's calm. He's showing us respect by believing that we'll honour our word."

Trust? Respect? Rav took another swig of water before staring back at Tibald, trying to see what his brother could.

"He's also setting an example for us," Cyrn continued. "We're at our weakest in Pitt, where our families live. I think that by trusting us here, Tibald's asking us to trust him in Pitt, when he's capable of attacking our loved ones."

It almost seemed as if Tibald was well-intentioned. Perhaps that's what he wanted them to see. Perhaps he'd been manipulating Rav's impression of him from the start to use fear and friendliness to guide Rav into thinking he was an honourable person. Then Tibald could stab him in the back and enslave them all. Rav refused to fall for it. Tibald had said he was heading to Pitt to conduct trade, but Rav didn't believe a word of it. Tibald was after conscripts for Baron Hewett's army, and he was targeting the citizens of Stone's Way.

Rav glared at the back of Tibald's head. "Well, I *don't* trust him."

"And we shouldn't. Tibald's too precise with his actions, making it obvious they're for display. He's come to Stone's Way with a plan and everything he's doing is to execute it. We need to figure out what it is and stop it, but"—Cyrn pulled out the coins Tibald had used to pay the toll—"this really concerns me."

"How much is that?" Wakeman asked.

"Exactly enough for two caravans."

That was it—everything Tibald had done was measured. He knew how much the toll was, he knew who the Ghoulsmen leader was supposed to be, and he knew to hide his desire to conscript from Pitt. Tibald Sar knew about them, but they knew nothing about him.

# Chapter Five

Once Tibald had passed through the Alley, Cyrn gathered the Ghoulsmen around him.

"I'm going to return to Pitt with Rav so we can deal with Tibald," he announced, "but we can't leave Stone's Way unguarded. Wakeman, will you keep watch out here with Thor, Tido, and Tobs? Although I doubt Tibald will attack us right now, there's still a chance he might be acting as a distraction while more of Baron Hewett's soldiers sneak into Stone's Way. We also need to look out for any other Barons and mutants."

"Aye, I'll do that."

Tido stared south with longing as though she could see Pitt beyond the slew of rolling hills hiding it from sight, wisps of brunette hair blowing in the breeze from under her helmet. "C-can you tell my Ma that I'm alright when you get to Pitt?" she asked, voice shaking at first but growing stronger as she spoke. "I know she worries about me."

Tobias looked towards Pitt too, expression stern as he squeezed his spear tight. "I've got a similar request. Let my Pa know I'm doing well, will you? Let him know I'm doing my duty. Let him know Pitt will be safe."

"Aye, I'll visit them both," Rav promised.

Thorley glanced between them, settling on Wakeman. "These hills are more of a home to me than any other place I've lived." He chuckled.

Rav and Cyrn hugged the others goodbye, gathered their weapons, then marched towards Pitt. Travelling across the hills, they quickly caught up with the caravan, where Cyrn had them watch Tibald from a distance to see if he did anything suspicious.

"What's my job in Pitt?" Rav whispered as they stalked the caravan.

"It's going to be complicated," Cyrn said. "You need to collect supplies without Tibald finding out while I focus on figuring out what he's up to. When Barons first take over a territory, their soldiers are zealous and will take their guard duties seriously, but over time, they'll become lax. If an opportunity for us to escape past Baron Hewett presents itself, then I need us to be able to take it immediately."

"Would it be worth us trying to escape west of Pitt through Ghoul Wood or loop around the east and south through the Stone Steps if Baron Hewett's army is too well-organised to sneak past?" Rav asked. "If we escape through the Stone Steps, we can even restock at Crevice Camp."

Cyrn shook his head. "The Stone Steps are too dangerous for a group to travel through. This won't be us treading in a line with small sacks of cheese, salt, and waterskins along the known route to scout from Crevice Camp once a year. We'll need carriages to carry Pitt's food and most of the ground there is too brittle to support us even when we're careful, never mind inexperienced townsfolk. The risk of people falling through the hollow top layer of stone and into the rapids below is too high. To be honest, I think the only reason bigger mutants haven't arrived in Stone's Way before now is because the Stone Steps sit between us and the Sink." He suddenly shuddered as though icy rain had rolled down his back.

"As for Ghoul Wood, in all of Pitt's history, no one has managed to traverse it. Most who've attempted to never returned and those that did were driven half-mad by the nightmares. We don't know how big it is or what lurks in its depths. Everything that protects Stone's Way and Pitt also acts as a barrier keeping us trapped here. The only safe way out is the only safe way in—we have to head north towards Greenfield."

"Aye, then. I can get supplies without Tibald noticing. I'm just worried that if Baron Hewett's army is as strong as we think it is, we won't get a chance to escape."

"Baron Hewett and his soldiers have just fought a war, so they'll have to be tired," Cyrn assured him. "Right now, their morale will be high, keeping them driven, but that will fade as they settle down in Greenfield. It's a risk, but leaving always was." Cyrn crawled across the lip of the hill they were hiding behind, mud coating his furs, as Tibald's caravan drew further away, glancing at Rav out the corner of his eye. "Also, you might have to do more than just collect supplies for us to be able to leave. That's going to be the difficult part."

"I know," Rav muttered as he crawled after him, hands numb with cold as he dug them into more wet mud for purchase. "I'll also have to convince people to leave in the first place. That's why you picked me to come with you. If I tell people they need to go, they'll know those orders come from you."

"It's a hard task, but I know you can do it."

"I *will* do it. I'll..." The wind changed direction, carrying a metallic scent. Rav wrinkled his nose. "Can you smell that?"

"Aye." Cyrn sniffed the air. "It smells like blood."

Rav sat up, facing east where the smell was coming from. "Are we investigating it? I know we should, but Tibald's about to arrive in Pitt."

Cyrn took another big sniff before spitting in the grass beside him. "The smell is too strong to ignore. Hurry. If we move fast enough, we can find out what it is and get to Pitt before Tibald."

They set off running. The further east they moved, the denser the reek of blood became until Rav felt as if he were breathing iron. They were heading towards a massacre. Thoughts of the giant Spine rushed to the front of Rav's mind.

"Move quietly," Cyrn ordered, slowing his speed and lowering his posture.

Rav copied him, his senses heightened by the adrenaline coursing through him. He twitched at every new noise, terrified of catching the *tak* of hooves on rock. Upon seeing a flock of birds circling over a valley just ahead of them, Cyrn had them slow to a crawl as they creeped forward, finally stopping at the top of a hill where they could see what the birds were frenzied over. It was a bloodbath, just as Rav had anticipated.

It was hard to tell how many bodies there were or even what *kind* of bodies they were; from this distance, everything just looked red and brown as blood mixed with mud. Rav squinted and made out what looked like gambeson armour.

"I can't see anything dangerous nearby, can you?" Cyrn asked.

Rav looked further east, seeing the boundary where the hills of Stone's Way ended and the flat stone platforms of the Stone Steps began, but he didn't spot any mutants. He faced Cyrn and the massacre once more, but as he tried to speak, he found his tongue stuck in place. Rav shook his head towards Cyrn, no words coming out. He wasn't a stranger to dead bodies, but this battlefield had him speechless.

"I'm moving closer to get a better look. Stay here." Cyrn sneaked towards the valley.

Rav blinked and began watching Cyrn's surroundings to keep an eye out for him.

After a while, Cyrn called back to him, "It's clear."

Rav reached the valley and confirmed that he had seen gambeson. There were five or six soldiers' bodies that had been horribly trampled into the ground, some of which had gaping holes in their torsos where they'd been gored. The giant cloven hoofprints all around the area left no mystery as to what their killer was. Rav tensed his stomach to stop himself from being sick and waded into the mess to inspect a soldier's spear. Though there was mud spattered over the flat of the spearhead, Rav couldn't see any blood on the weapon's edge. He found another soldier's spear and noticed that it was also the same. His horror grew as he discovered that none of the weapons were bloodied.

"Cyrn," he whispered, "I don't think they even managed to injure it."

"Hmm?" Cyrn looked up from staring at one of the bodies. "Oh, right, yeah."

Rav walked over to him. "What have you found?"

"We know what killed them." Cyrn pursed his lips. "But who were they?"

"Are they with Tibald?"

"They're wearing the same blue and white armour as Baron Kiln's men, so I think they might be deserters who fled after Baron Kiln was killed by Baron Hewett," Cyrn deduced. "We need to tell Wakeman about this; there could be more soldiers roaming Stone's Way."

"What about the giant Spine?"

"I don't know what we can do about that other than continue hoping to avoid it. Judging by the congealed blood, these killings must have happened during the night, so it might be nocturnal. That would also explain why we haven't seen it yet."

Rav and Cyrn returned to the Alley Camp, heading inside to find the rest of the Ghoulsmen sitting around the remaining hot coals of last night's fire, sorting through parcels of dried meat and cheeses for their stay. Facing the cave entrance, Tido was the first to spot them, jumping to her feet, then pointing for Thorley, Tobias, and Wakeman to do the same.

Wakeman furrowed his brow upon seeing the pair. "I thought you were heading back to Pitt?"

Cyrn strode towards them, Rav at his side, his demeanour dour. "We were, but we discovered tracks made by the 'Zet Ar. It's on the move around Stone's Way and it's trampled six soldiers east of here." Past the fire, he bent down to pick up a kettle helm and broken spear point from the loot pile, inspecting them before throwing them back. "I think the soldiers used to serve Baron Kiln and fled here after his defeat, which means there might be more of them in the area. I came to warn you."

"Why are there always more?" Tido hissed, kicking into the rock floor.

"Because they hate us," Tobias growled. "They hate that we're not unfilial brutes like they are."

"No," Thorley tutted. "It's because of the Sink. They're drawn to it like moths to a flame, except they can't tell when it gets too hot."

Wakeman glowered as he squeezed his fist, looking ready to punch something. "What do we do?"

Cyrn tilted his head as he mulled over the problem before spitting out a sharp breath. "If the 'Zet Ar is wandering around here, then I think it's too dangerous for you to stay in the Alley Camp. It might be better for you all to head north to Bear Camp and stay at the top end of Stone's Way."

"And because Bear Camp is right by the entrance to Stone's Way, we'll be able to spot any more soldiers moving into Stone's Way." Wakeman went quiet as his energy sputtered. "It's just that Bear Camp is a full day's travel from Pitt instead of just the half-day it takes to reach here; we can't have people constantly running between the two, leaving both Pitt and Bear Camp undermanned. We won't be able to talk as much."

"I'm more concerned about how secure it is," Tobias spoke up. "Right at the end of Stone's Way, it's exposed from the north towards Greenfield. The boulder field it's hidden in is also close to the hilltop caravans travelling to Pitt from Greenfield like to stay the night on. Soldiers camping there might find us."

Cyrn looked between them, gaze heavy. "You either risk the soldiers or the mutant. It's up to you."

Wakeman took a deep breath as he massaged his temples. "…How terrifying is the Spine?"

"The six soldiers weren't even able to wound it before they were butchered."

Wakeman gave a derisive snort as he shook his head. "Then I guess we're going to Bear Camp."

Rav and Cyrn jogged back to Pitt as they chased after Tibald's caravan, not managing to catch up before they reached the last hill hiding their home. Rising over it, Rav gazed down to see Pitt on a wide section of flat land below them, its stone wall standing a little taller than Cyrn, bright-coloured rooftops peeking over the simple battlements. East of the town was a small mine and to the west lay Ghoul Wood—the enormous forest stretching into the horizon. The late afternoon breeze carried smells of baked bread and dust.

"Do you think Ma and Pa will be worried by Tibald arriving in Pitt before we do? They might think he's killed us," Rav wheezed as he hurried after Cyrn down the hillside towards an open wooden gate, fresh wheel grooves and hoofprints pocketing the ground in front of it.

Cyrn waved ahead to the single gate guard as they approached it—an old man in frayed grey gambeson armour wielding a book. "They'll be concerned, but I don't think they'll presume we're dead. Let's hurry home and let them know we're alright, just in case."

The guard waved back with a cheery smile, Cyrn taking off his mask as he led Rav through the front gates. Rav also pulled off his mask, feeling the strange change that overcame him whenever he crossed Pitt's threshold—his home was a civilised place where the Ghoulsmen's violence wasn't welcome. Out on the hills, it was common to see blood and bodies as well as other signs of the Sink's malignant existence, but in Pitt, things remained unblemished. Even after Tibald's arrival, everything looked peaceful. Rav walked with relief in his step as he saw that all the effort the Ghoulsmen had put into protecting Pitt had succeeded. If only it could stay this way forever.

In the centre of Pitt was its most important building, the Council Chambers, which was four storeys and had two large statues of goats either side of its entrance. To the left of it was the Carvell House, which was two storeys with white walls and a green roof. A statue of an axe striking a tree sat in the front garden. To the right of the Council Chambers was the Seabrook House, built the same as the Carvell home but with a mine cart statue at the front. Rav knew that Tibald would be staying in the Council Chambers and couldn't help staring at it as he followed Cyrn into their home.

Cyrn opened the door, then hung his furs on a hook by the entrance and stretched. "It's good to be back."

Rav sensed that something was out of place in his house, but it was only when he sniffed the air that he figured out what it was. Having been away for so long, his home smelt different, as if it was lacking his and Cyrn's scent.

"The lord and lady have been waiting for you," an older voice called out to them.

"*Benji.*" Rav broke into a childish grin and rushed to embrace the middle-aged man who came down the stairs at the end of the hallway. The mirth in his green eyes was the same as it had been before Rav left to patrol Stone's Way last month, his brown hair and stubble tinged with grey.

Benji squeezed him back. "Welcome home, young master."

"Are they alright?" Cyrn asked.

"You'd better head upstairs and find out," Benji replied, but by his manner, Rav knew his parents were fine.

Once they reached the second floor, the brothers entered a large room bathed by warm light from a fire softly crackling within a hearth nestled in the wall to their left. Their parents were seated in high-back leather chairs facing the fireplace, cheeks glowing. Cyrn Carvell Senior, an older, balder, more furrowed version of Cyrn, was flicking through some papers while Healanor Carvell, with her softer features and Rav's brown hair, stitched pelts. While they held to decorum and waited to be greeted, Rav caught his Pa's tense shoulders relax a little and his Ma's pinched grip on her needle softening, the hints of worry flecking their eyes fading as they gleamed with joy and relief.

Cyrn and Rav walked around to face their parents, then bowed before them, paying their respects to those who had given them their Name and could take their Name away.

"We give thanks for the Name Carvell," they said. "May we bring honour to our lineage."

"You have done, my dear boys." Senior Carvell set his papers on the floor beside him, then beckoned them to stand with a strong wave of his hand. "We have important matters to discuss with the arrival of this Champion Sar."

"Have you met him?" Cyrn asked.

Senior Carvell shared a terse look with his wife, who laid her pelts on her lap.

"We held a small parade for him when he arrived," she said, eyeing Cyrn as though she could read his mind. "It was quite a shock for everyone to see someone new in Pitt. It's been months since we've had contact with the outside world."

"I hope you didn't worry about us," Rav said.

"Ha." Senior Carvell slapped his thigh as he laughed. "Tibald was too clean when he got here; if he'd have fought with my boys, then he'd be bleeding. Tell me what happened."

Cyrn explained the situation with Baron Kiln and Baron Hewett.

"And you've made the decision to leave?"

"I have."

Healanor took a sharp breath and nodded as she tapped her fingers on the arm of her chair. "Are you certain we need to go?"

"I am."

Her eyes seemed to sink into her skull, the creases across her brow and around her forehead deepening, as though the culmination of her worries from the last decade were sitting on her. Still, she stayed sitting tall, locked onto Cyrn as her eyes glistened. "Then we'll trust you." She looked away to Senior Carvell and blinked. "But while your Pa and I understand that you know far more about what's happening outside Stone's Way than anyone else in Pitt, other people here don't. It might be difficult for you to convince them to go; ours is not the only family with a deep legacy in this land."

"That's why Rav's here." Cyrn put his arm around Rav's shoulders. "While I keep Tibald occupied, he's going to get the town ready to go."

"And what about those who can't travel?" Senior Carvell spoke. "Have you got a list of those we're leaving behind?"

"Ah..." Cyrn removed his arm from Rav's shoulders and looked at him. Rav returned the look with a sour expression. "That bit's going to be hard."

Rav sighed. "I'll speak to them."

"It may be easier than you think," Senior Carvell said. "The old generation might be content to die in Pitt, or maybe once we all leave, the Barons will ignore those who can't fight."

"I can also help you talk to those who have to stay here," Healanor spoke. "My fighting days are behind me, but I can still handle matters like this. You boys have been working hard to keep our lives peaceful, so you also need to take some time to rest. You should be able to at least enjoy this evening. It's been too long since you've seen your wife, Cyrn."

Cyrn stepped forward with a wide grin, heavy thoughts shed for a single moment. "How is Enna?"

"She's been keeping to herself recently. I think she really misses you. She keeps saying that the two of you need to talk."

Cyrn paused in his jubilation, the weight returning. "I'll speak to her later; I need to make a plan for this evening first," he muttered. "I won't be able to get much out of Tibald if I go to him. I need to bring him to me. I need to see how Tibald acts by having him do things on his own accord so I can figure out why he's doing them."

Rav stepped to face him with broad shoulders, as though to take some of the weight himself. "Is there anything I can do to help with that?"

Cyrn chuckled before ruffling Rav's hair. "It's better if I do this alone. Tibald behaves differently around me than he does around you, and I can't get confused between the two ways he responds to us." He faced his parents. "Can you organise a celebration like you normally do? I think something like that will draw Tibald out of the Council Chambers."

"It spoils the surprise," Senior Carvell started, "but we already have. Everyone in Pitt has been invited to Franz's Tavern."

*Everyone?* Rav broke into a goofy grin as he thought of one particular person. "Will Kayla be there?"

Senior Carvell nodded. "Aye, she's also been waiting for your return." He looked at Healanor. "I don't think it'll be too long before both our sons are married."

She pulled a knowing half-smile and reached out to hold her husband's hand with tenderness. "Neither do I."

Rav went red, his stomach fluttering.

"We can definitely organise something in time," Cyrn added, cooling Rav's rising enthusiasm.

How could he have a wedding while they were preparing to leave? The atmosphere would be all wrong with the journey ahead hanging over their heads. They'd also need to bring as much food as they could carry, leaving little left for a feast. If he was going to get married, he wanted to do it the same way Cyrn had been wed, with festive celebrations that brought the town together, not a rushed procession under the looming threat of Tibald Sar. Kayla deserved to have a true Carvell ceremony.

"I'll think on it," Rav said.

"Good. A wedding would really bring Pitt together, but remember that Kayla hasn't agreed yet." Senior Carvell laughed as he stood up. "Now, I've got a celebration to prepare. Will you help me, dear?"

"I will." Healanor rose with him. "What will you be doing, Cyrn?"

"I need to think through a few things regarding Tibald, so I'll stay here."

"And you, Rav?"

"I'll also get to work and begin telling people we're leaving."

# Chapter Six

Rav stepped out into the late afternoon light, shadows starting to stretch across the open Pitt streets. Most people were still working at the mine or logging in Ghoul Wood. He turned right and started the familiar walk towards the eastern side of the town, pace changing from a march to a shuffle, then back again as he mulled over what was to come, unable to plan the right words. A small green-roofed cottage with smoke billowing from its chimney came into sight as he reached the town's edge, standing out from those around it due to its overgrown garden. Rav stopped, wincing upon seeing the weed-infested wildland that had once been tamed and tidy with a myriad of beautiful flowers brought from all around Stone's Way. After mustering his courage again, he waded through the garden to head around the house and tapped on a window lit by warm firelight looking into a bedroom, an old woman sitting up in the bed beside it.

"Who's there?" Aunt Judy called out as she pushed open the window, her wizened face lighting up as her eyes found focus. "Ah, Rav." She reached up to pinch his cheek, and Rav leaned closer to let her. "It's good to see you."

Seeing how thin she'd gotten since last month, Rav had to stifle his wince to pull a smile, the grip on his cheek barely a squeeze. "I arrived back in Pitt today, so I thought I'd come see you."

"Come in, come in. There's no need to knock next time; you can just enter."

Rav walked around to the entrance and stepped inside. Incense had been burned, filling the house with a strong herbal scent, but beneath the aroma, Rav could still smell the sharp scent of pure alcohol used in medicines. The hall between the door and the bedroom was cluttered with dying flowers. Rav tiptoed through it, careful not to knock over any pots. It got warmer and warmer until he reached Aunt Judy's room, the fire burning beside her bed blazing. Aunt Judy was sat up in bed by the window, wrapped in thick furs, her silver hair and bony features making her seem like a pixie.

"Have you grown since I last saw you?" Aunt Judy asked. "You look taller." She squinted. "And broader."

"It's only been a month since I've been away; I can't have changed that much." Rav laughed as he sat on the end of her bed.

"Maybe it's the way you're carrying yourself, then. You look like you've got a purpose. It suits you." She leaned forward and held his cheek, fixing him a loving gaze.

"That's part of why I'm here." Rav took a breath. "There's... We've..."

Aunt Judy tutted. "I'll not have you stutter in my company. You're not a child, Rav Carvell; speak clearly and honestly."

"We're leaving Stone's Way. Not soon, but as soon as possible."

"Good, it's about time." She looked unfazed by the news.

Tears wet Rav's eyes. "Aunt Judy..."

"Don't you dare shed a tear for me, silly boy." She flicked his head. "I've not got long left in this world and I won't spend it being pitied. I've been listening to your stories about fighting in Stone's Way for years, Rav; I know staying in Pitt is becoming too dangerous. The others here are too stuck in the past, too attached to their ideas of 'proper and improper behaviour' to let you even speak of the horrors you must commit every day to keep us all safe, but *I* understand, Rav. All I want is to last the winter so I can die in the sunshine. That's it. You don't need to lug my old bones around wherever you go."

Rav wiped his eyes and managed to stop his tears, but the words he wanted to say were like viscous syrup and kept getting stuck in his throat.

"It's that simple." She shrugged.

"No, it's not. It's—"

"Yes, it is, because I'm making it simple, Rav. I'll not be another reason for you to delay leaving. You'll find no more excuses here. Get it done and keep our Bloodline alive."

Was that really what he was doing? Was he using Aunt Judy's life as an excuse to prolong leaving? He pursed his lips. No. No, he wasn't. It was true that if she said she wanted to go with them, he'd want to wait for her to get better. But it wasn't through any excuse.

"Aunt Judy, you're family. More than that, you've done so much for me," he pressed. "What kind of person would I be if I didn't bring you with us?"

"A smart one." She reached out and gripped Rav's hand, her skin cold and sweaty against his. "We're all bound to suffer in life. This is a hard choice you're making, and in the future, you'll make more of them. Get used to it. When the Sink appeared, my husband decided to march into it under the command of Stone's Way's original Baron, hoping to bring back a fortune. Had they succeeded, my husband would be alive and we'd be rich, but I'd *still* have gotten sick." She let go of his hand and wrapped the furs tighter around herself. "I told you when you were ten that bad things are unavoidable, and it's our duty to persevere despite them."

Rav shook his head. "I wouldn't have coped after *that* event without you. What if I need you in the future like I needed you then?" His voice turned to barely a whisper. "Or like I need you now?"

"Aye, I did a lot of work after you killed that man, getting you to start eating again and helping you accept what you'd done. I did it all so that you could become a person who could help yourself. Are you going to let my effort go to waste?"

"Never."

"Then push ahead. Pitt's too traditional," Aunt Judy grumbled. "It's become too attached to ideas of laws and legacies and Names. You murdered a man, Rav—that's what all the laws told us—but what you did wasn't wrong. If you hadn't killed that man, he'd have taken your Ma away, sent her to die alongside my husband and all the other brave fools of Pitt who thought they'd claim their fortunes in the Sink when it first appeared. You shouldn't have beaten yourself up about it then and you shouldn't beat yourself up about leaving Stone's Way now. When you get stuck in traditions, you lose the flexibility needed to adapt to a changing world, and the world *is* changing, Rav, far faster than any of us realised. The old rules don't apply anymore."

She held his gaze with a soft smile. "Us old and feeble will stay behind, but our Bloodlines will travel the world, just like our ancestors did. Do you think the Carvells always lived here? No, Rav, they found Stone's Way after wandering the world in search of a safe place to settle, and now you're doing that too. They left behind their elderly, and so will you."

A teardrop slid down Rav's cheek, soon followed by more. He recognised the look in Aunt Judy's eyes, the empathy and intelligence. She'd made the decision for him with no way to wriggle out of it. "I'm going to miss you, Aunt Judy."

"I hope you live long enough to still miss me many years from now, silly boy." She pulled Rav in for a hug as he sobbed.

Rav felt her body tremble, as though something holding firm within her was about to break.

"That's enough of that." She pushed Rav off her and hardened her expression, whatever emotion that was about to leak out hidden once more. "How are you doing these days? Do you still get dizzy when you think about *that* event?"

Rav nodded. "I try and use the breathing techniques you taught me, but I don't always remember to do them in time. I killed a man yesterday who mentioned it... I was going to kill him anyway, but it was the way I did it that felt uncomfortable. It was cruel of me." He dropped his head, face twisted as though he'd eaten something rotten. "Even now, I can feel this sense of rejection of the memories, like my body is trying to flush them out. I want to silence any mention of them."

"Just keep working at it," Aunt Judy said. "With age comes wisdom. You need to remember you didn't bring shame to yourself and your lineage, Rav, you *saved* yourself and your lineage. If you'd truly dishonoured your family, you would have been made Nameless."

"But the Barons keep using what I did as cause to invade Pitt and arrest everyone, saying they're harbouring a murderer. It's my fault that Barons can easily find a reason to attack us."

She snorted. "Those Barons would attack Pitt without cause if they couldn't find any. We both know that arresting us for that supposed crime is just a pretence."

"I know that. Everyone tells me it, even Cyrn. So, why does it still *feel* like it's my fault?"

"Because you can't let go of the old traditions Pitt has instilled in you. Accept the life you're living. Once you do that, you'll realise there's no need for you to feel guilty over the awful things that would have happened with or without you."

"Can I not work to change the life I'm living?"

Aunt Judy laughed. "The thing that's changed your life is the Sink. Are you going to fight against that? You can't defeat a force of nature; focus on what you *can* do and leave the rest to others."

It was dark by the time Rav left Aunt Judy's house. Part of him had known all along how she'd respond to him telling her they were leaving, but he'd still needed to hear her words to accept them. Her words were meant to light a fire in him, and they'd succeeded, as they always did. He visited Tido's Ma and Tobias' Pa to let them know their children were alright before returning to the Carvell House to meet up with Cyrn, who had finished preparing for the evening.

"Are you ready?" Rav asked.

Cyrn rubbed his chin. "I think I know what I'm looking for."

"Then, let's go."

Rav dragged his brother out by his arm, the warm orange light spilling from Franz' Tavern glowing across Pitt while singing and laughter filled the town. Strolling down the street ahead under the star-speckled night sky, Rav laughed upon seeing many of the dozen townsfolk outside already ruddy from alcohol as they swigged ale from their mugs, ready to dash forward and join them. Cyrn kept his pace steady, posture straight, demeanour befitting a Carvell. Rav forced himself to slow until he was just behind him, taking his own expected position. Peering through the open window, he spotted more people crammed inside the tavern, shuffling around wooden tables and the great central bonfire blazing within a large firepit, but he was unable to find Kayla among them.

"Elder Carvell."

"Master Carvell."

Rav greeted the outside crowd, recognising the members of the Carvell logging business as well as employees from the pelt shops. He was handed a cup of ale and downed it while the crowd cheered. Soon, his face went warm. Cyrn also drank a cup, though he sipped his drink to uphold his decorum as an Elder.

"Rav, how've you been?"

"Where did you go?"

"Have you heard about the new Baron?"

"I've been well," Rav answered the group forming around him, planning his words with care to avoid mentioning the taboo of the Ghoulsmen and the unfilial things they did in Stone's Way. "We ventured out into Stone's Way to fight Spines and guard the through road."

Looking around the drunken faces of those before him, he caught most people pulling wry smiles or glancing between themselves as though aware he'd only told a half truth. How many knew by now? How could anyone not know what the Ghoulsmen did? Rav tensed, waiting for them to snarl at him, to denounce his behaviour, to call him a murderer for the unlawful killing of Barons' soldiers; instead, they all leaned in, knowledge of what he'd done seeming to be forgotten as they ignored it, eager to hear a good story.

"Did you find any treasure?"

"Did you see the ghouls?"

"Have you met the new Healer?"

The crowd's excitement grew.

Rav relaxed his shoulders and joined back in with the jubilation, grateful. No one said anything, the problem hidden, so it didn't need addressing. The Carvell Name could remain clean.

"Come on." Cyrn pushed Rav towards the door as he was handed another cup of ale. "There are people waiting for us."

"I've got to greet my parents, but afterwards, I'll return and tell you about our adventures," Rav yelled back as he began concocting a tale in his head, swapping Baron Kiln's soldiers for rotting ghouls.

The tavern erupted in cheers as Rav and Cyrn entered.

*"I guard my home with all I am,"* Cyrn sang.

*"To honour those who gave me life,"* everyone followed.

*"We march far to conquer our foes,*

*"A Bloodline to keep out all strife,*

*"Go forth and fight 'til your last light,*

*"Gifting land and lineage to our flesh made young,*

*"We'll love and marry for our blood to carry,*

*"Into the future bright."*

Rav gazed at his parents, who stood at the front of a crowd near fifty strong, all here to welcome him home. It was a sight he'd never get used to.

Rav hugged his uncle, who was standing next to his Ma. "Uncle Font, it's good to see you."

"Easy there, Rav." Uncle Font patted Rav's back. "I'm old and you're strong."

Rav laughed as he gave him a squeeze before pulling away, while Cyrn maintained his decorum as he bowed. Uncle Font did look old, now riddled with wrinkles and liver spots.

"Have you always been this tall?" Uncle Font asked Cyrn.

"I think you're shrinking," Cyrn countered.

"Be careful with what you say. You'll end up like me before you know it." Uncle Font chuckled as the crowd laughed.

Rav looked around the tavern from face to face, names and occupations flooding his mind, until he spotted her standing behind his Ma in a black silk dress that matched her dark hair and deep eyes. Rav saw every perfect blemish in her lightly weatherworn skin, the gorgeous wave that made her hair shimmer in the firelight, and her slight smile as she knew she'd caught his attention.

What would she do now that she had him hooked?

Rav stood enthralled by the question before anticipation drew him closer. Through the stink of ale, he found her scent, vibrant and warm, compelling him to reach out for her cheek. She leaned into him, and once he finally touched her skin, tingles ran from his fingertips to his head, igniting his senses. He drew her in and kissed her. *Euphoria*. Kayla bit his lip, shocking him back to reality.

"Oooo," the crowd called.

Rav broke away, glancing at his parents with reddening cheeks. This behaviour was improper. His Ma's expression was a mix of joy and anxiety, while his Pa maintained his jovial mood, as though he hadn't seen anything. Turning back to Kayla, he saw that while her face was slightly flushed, she was standing taller and remained close to his side. Rav smiled.

The attention was soon taken away from them as Cyrn made his way to Enna. Enna had a rosy face and was wearing a loose-fitting green dress. Her brown hair hung down to her shoulders, and her features were homely.

As Cyrn greeted his wife, Kayla whispered to Rav, "You didn't forget about me while you were out on the hills, did you?"

"Never. I missed you," he whispered back.

"I've missed you too." Her breath was warm on his cheek. "Pitt's not Pitt when you're not here."

"Then it's a good thing I'm back."

"It certainly is." She held his arm. "Do you have any wounds that need tending to? Perhaps I can help dress them."

"Do you think I'm some storybook hero that needs a maiden to soothe them?" Rav chuckled. "Things aren't so glamorous out there."

"You're definitely my hero."

"Shall we eat?" Cyrn called out before Rav could respond.

Rav and Kayla followed the rest of the Carvell family to take their seats at the main tavern table and waited as a dozen steaming dishes were laid before them, the smell making Rav salivate. Once everything was set up, everyone began eating. Hunger overwhelmed Rav, and he scoffed down plate after plate as though his stomach were an endless pit, glad to not be eating the dried meat and cheese he choked down while staying out in Stone's Way. While he was eating, the tavern's uproar softened, soon replaced by quiet conversation and nervous shuffling. Rav looked up to see someone whisper in Cyrn's ear, causing Cyrn to sit upright. It seemed the time to work had come.

Rav gazed to the tavern door and waited. A few moments later, the door swung open and Tibald Sar entered. Rav met Tibald's eyes, shivering as the Champion dissected him with his gaze once more. A tavern maid hurried forward to guide Tibald and his three companions to a table. Alongside Tibald were two men—one with brown eyes and a nose warped from a break, while the other was handsome with green eyes. They both had black hair, cut to the scalp. The other person was Elder Reuben Seabrook, a man in his thirties with smart-cut hair and crisp robes. Rav surmised that Reuben had the task of chaperoning Tibald around Pitt. Tibald took his seat, with his comrades either side of him.

"Franz's Tavern has the best food in Pitt," Reuben said as he sat opposite Tibald.

"I'm looking forward to it." Tibald raised his voice, catching everyone's attention. "It's been a long time since I've eaten somewhere like this."

"Oh?" Reuben raised his eyebrows. "Do you mean in a tavern, or in a town like Pitt?"

"Both." Tibald laughed, his companions joining him. "For the last year, I've been eating fire-roasted meat in campsites while we explored the Sink, then we ate in Greenfield's barracks after defeating Baron Kiln, and lastly, we had yet more campsite food as we travelled to Pitt. I hope kitchen-cooked food is still as good as I remember."

"I'm sure it will be."

Rav stifled his derisive scoff, certain that Tibald had only spoken loudly to show off his accomplishments.

Tibald glanced around the tavern and faked a look of surprise when he saw the Carvells sitting before a feast. "Is there a celebration going on?"

"Just a small one to welcome back one of our Elders. Let me introduce you to the Carvell family." Reuben beckoned Cyrn over to him.

Cyrn led his family as they gathered before Tibald's table.

Tibald grinned at Cyrn. "I believe we've met."

"Aye." Cyrn reached out his hand, and Tibald clasped it. "I'm Elder Cyrn Carvell Junior and this is my family."

"Yes, your parents provided a wonderful parade for me when I arrived," Tibald said as he faced them. "Thank you for your hospitality."

"We are honoured to have a Champion as our guest," Healanor replied.

Tibald locked onto Rav. "And you must be the brave young man who approached my caravan with nothing but a crossbow. You must have had a lot of faith in your brother's ability to save you to have done that."

Rav's stomach churned as he watched Tibald ingratiate himself with his family, knowing it was all just an act. "I have a lot of faith in myself," he retorted.

"Oh?" Tibald leaned in. "Do you also possess some special skills I should know about?"

"I have some skills, aye, and should the need arise, I'll use them."

Senior Carvell flicked Rav's ear. "Champion Sar is our guest, and you will treat him with respect. My apologies." He bowed towards Tibald as Rav sucked in a sharp breath and glanced around the tavern, seeing folk avoiding looking at or listening to the conversation, like his Pa had done during his greeting with Kayla.

"It's alright." Tibald waved the matter away. "It's good that Pitt has spirited young men. It's people like Rav, here, who are working day and night to protect you all from the mutants and bandits prowling Stone's Way." He faced Rav. "Isn't that right?"

Rav recovered his calm demeanour. "Aye, forgive my words; I've spent too much time away from civilised life."

"This is my wife, Enna Carvell, and this is Kayla Blaine," Cyrn jumped in, continuing the introductions.

"It's a pleasure to meet you both." Tibald pointed to his companions. "This ugly fellow is Jingo Hook, and this handsome one is Ronin Luke."

Cyrn grasped Jingo's forearm, then Ronin's in greeting. Rav motioned to do the same; however, Jingo and Ronin had already sat back down, ignoring him and the rest of his family.

"Would you like to join our celebration?" Cyrn asked Tibald. "We could bring our tables together."

"That sounds excellent." Tibald smiled. "Jingo, Ronin, help move this table."

"Rav, get the chairs," Cyrn followed.

Rav obeyed him as Cyrn and Tibald spoke between themselves. Jingo and Ronin didn't pay any attention to Rav as he helped, souring his mood. It was the same type of derision Baron Kiln's soldiers had displayed towards the Ghoulsmen when they'd invaded Stone's Way, confirming Rav's thoughts regarding Tibald's true motives. Those like them didn't regard Pitt's citizens as people and only sought to take advantage of them. Every one of Tibald's pleasant words was empty.

"I've been informed that your family are loggers," Tibald spoke as he took his seat beside Cyrn at the newly joined table.

"Aye, for nearly eight generations now," Cyrn replied. "We work in Ghoul Wood."

"Reuben told me that Ghoul Wood is rather dangerous. Is that true?"

"There are a few mutants, but they tend to live deep within the forest, far away from our logging sites. The only other danger comes from the strange nightmares that you get if you sleep underneath the trees."

Rav joined everyone else as they listened to the conversation.

"Fascinating," Tibald said. "How long have these nightmares been occurring?"

"There have always been stories about strange dreams and ghouls lurking beneath the trees, but the nightmares got much worse about nine years ago," Cyrn answered. "It was soon after the Sink appeared, around... uh..."

Rav avoided looking at anyone. Around *that* event.

"Around when Baron Gethnil, our original Baron, ventured into the Sink," Reuben spoke up.

"Did many citizens of Pitt join Baron Gethnil?" Tibald asked as though he hadn't noticed the delay.

"Half of everyone capable of fighting. That's why there are now many single-parent households. My uncle from my Pa's Bloodline was one of them," Cyrn said.

Rav thought of Tido and Tobias' Ma and Pa, as well as Aunt Judy.

"It must have taken tremendous courage for your citizens to make the journey." Tibald sounded sincere. "When the Sink first appeared, no one knew anything about it. It's only thanks to pioneers like your families that we've managed to establish a foothold within it. I'm extremely grateful for my predecessors' sacrifice. I wouldn't be alive if I hadn't had their paths to follow. Their Names deserve to be honoured."

"Thank you for your kind words."

"How old were you at the time, Cyrn?"

"I was sixteen." Cyrn tapped on the table with his nail, staring at a knot in the wood as he tilted his head in reminiscence. "I had fever, requiring both my parents and Rav to tend to me; otherwise, I would have joined them." His tapping stopped, his finger pressed down hard. "Maybe I could have helped them. Maybe I'd just be dead too."

Tibald nodded slowly. "And you, Rav? What was it like being so young in a changing world?"

Rav frowned, confused at why Tibald was speaking to him. "I didn't know the world was changing. It was only much later that I saw the signs."

"I see, I see..." Tibald touched his chin. "Forgive my questions, it's just that I find anything and everything about the Sink captivating, from the physical changes, like your Ghoul Wood, to how people are reacting to it."

"I think the whole world is fascinated by the Sink." Cyrn laughed.

"That's true." Tibald chuckled. "Do you know much about it?"

"I know it's filled with mutants."

"Yes, the mutants are a nuisance." Tibald leaned forward in his chair, eyes alight with a thousand wondrous tales. "But there's so much more to it than those creatures."

Rav knew what was coming next—Tibald was about to 'sell' venturing into the Sink to them, like so many others had done in the last few years. He glanced around the table to see if anyone else realised what was going on and found himself feeling irritated as he saw that everyone appeared to be enraptured by Tibald's words. He couldn't tell if his family were genuinely interested or not, but he knew that at least Cyrn's actions would be part of his plan to uncover what Tibald was after.

"Stone's Way *is* beautiful," Tibald continued. "I can see why you live here, but the Sink has landscapes you can only dream of. There's a mountain that rises above the clouds, a river so wide you could fit Pitt into it, and many, many other wonders." His voice softened, a teasing sliver of delight on the edge of his lips at his captivated audience. "Even before you reach the Sink, there's a field of purple-tipped long grass that makes it feel as though you're entering another world."

"I've heard of these things before," Cyrn commented.

"Then perhaps I can tell you something new." Tibald pursed his lips. "You may be wondering how Baron Hewett defeated Baron Kiln so quickly."

Rav sat forward.

"Baron Kiln was fortified within Greenfield, and though Baron Hewett does have more soldiers, it's only by a few hundred, hardly enough to scale the walls in a large assault to conquer the city. How many men do you think we lost?" Tibald sat taller in his chair, his chin slightly lifted as he brimmed with arrogance. "Two dozen. Just two dozen soldiers lost for us to capture a city. We *are* better trained and have more experience, but the true reason we were able to succeed was because of Baron Hewett.

"I'm sure you've heard stories about people entering the Sink to claim powers beyond our comprehension. These people are called Ah' ke, and Baron Hewett is one of them. Greenfield's walls crumbled before him, allowing his army to march through in a single day."

Cyrn sat back with an obviously feigned awed expression, which Tibald noticed.

"Difficult to believe, right?" Tibald laughed. "But it's true. I saw Baron Hewett charge through Greenfield's wall with his body alone, bringing down the section so that we could march in and flank Baron Kiln's soldiers. Baron Hewett didn't stop there, though." Tibald paused to ensure everyone was listening to him closely. "He charged from the wall straight into the keep, trampling over Baron Kiln's guards before capturing Baron Kiln in one move."

Cyrn whistled.

"All I could do was chase after my Baron, finishing off those he'd maimed," Tibald finished.

Rav looked at Jingo and Ronin to see if they were showing any shame upon hearing their Champion tell such an outrageous story about their Baron, but Jingo and Ronin were sitting up straight with prideful grins, as though every word Tibald had spoken was true. Rav hesitated. Surely that couldn't be real, could it?

"The easiest way to prove my words would be for you to see Baron Hewett yourselves," Tibald said. "You could all come visit Greenfield."

Rav snapped out of his stupor. Visiting Greenfield meant leaving Stone's Way and the protection its terrain provided, leaving them vulnerable to attack. Had everything he'd just said been meant to entice their curiosity so that they'd make a mistake like that? Rav raised his guard further.

"Should we arrange something for spring?" Cyrn suggested. "We've crops to plant and cattle to tend to before then, but once it's warmer, we can definitely arrange a journey to Greenfield."

Rav smiled at his brother. Cyrn couldn't outright reject an offer to meet Baron Hewett, as it would expose his distrust of Tibald as well as show that he'd also seen through Tibald's ploy, so he was accepting the proposal but using pretences to delay having to go through with it. No doubt once spring arrived, Cyrn would find another reason for them to stay in Stone's Way.

"Yes, let's do that. I have business in Pitt that will take at least a month, so we can all head back to Greenfield together."

"Excellent." Cyrn smiled as though a great deal had been struck. "Does your business involve the trade caravan on its way here?"

"That's part of it," Tibald replied. "I've also received word that a Contender is travelling to Pitt to Challenge me for my position as Baron Hewett's Champion."

Everyone gasped. Even Cyrn looked genuinely surprised.

Tibald laughed, sharing a grin with Ronin and Jingo. "There's no need for you to worry about my life; I'll win and maintain my position as Baron Hewett's second-in-command. It's my duty as his Champion to prove myself his greatest fighter and an honour to duel to the death to do so. You might have been told that Contenders are just below Champions in terms of status, but the difference between soldiers like that and soldiers like me is too big for me to be concerned."

"Do you really not fear for your life?" Cyrn asked. "Pitt doesn't have an arena for you to duel in; we haven't had a Challenge since I've been alive. We'd have to build a makeshift one, and one slip in the mud could result in your death."

"The arena doesn't matter." Tibald sipped his ale. "I doubt it will be much of a fight."

Rav scoured Tibald's face but found no sign of fear, eyes squinted in disbelief at how anyone could be so relaxed knowing a skilled combatant was coming to kill them. Surely this was just more bravado, right?

"I'll start working on it tomorrow," Reuben spoke. "There's a flat area of land between Pitt and the mine where we could build it."

Tibald shrugged. "I've had dozens of Challenges already, so I'm not bothered about details like that. As long as we have a place to fight and witnesses to oversee the event, it's enough. Being Baron Hewett's Champion is a highly coveted position, and it's my duty to continually prove to Baron Hewett that I'm worthy of being his second-in-command. Duelling is just a part of my life now."

Rav wanted to further question Tibald about the Challenge but stayed quiet after remembering that Cyrn wanted to deal with Tibald alone.

"Are all these Challenges because Baron Hewett is this... Ah' ke person?" Cyrn asked.

"Yes, who wouldn't want to serve someone so powerful?" Tibald grinned. "With Baron Hewett's Ah' ke power, he can travel deep into the Sink without worrying too much about the mutants living there, and we"—Tibald gestured to Jingo and Ronin—"can go with him, collecting the spoils along the way. If we're really lucky, people like us might also get the opportunity to become Ah' ke."

"Is Baron Hewett so generous that he'd share these Ah' ke powers with his soldiers?"

Tibald paused for a moment. "Perhaps we should discuss matters like this another time; after all, I've only just met you." He laughed, and Cyrn laughed with him, easing the tension. "In short, though"—Tibald stared straight at Cyrn—"yes, Baron Hewett would absolutely share these Ah' ke powers with his friends."

Cyrn stared back. "Does Baron Hewett have many *friends*?"

Tibald finished his cup of ale. "It's been a long time since I've spoken to someone like you; I've forgotten what it's like to plan my words like this."

Rav squinted at Tibald in confusion, unsure what he meant. Had he missed a subtle exchange between the two?

"Perhaps this *friend* crisis is why you're out here instead of in there," Cyrn spoke cryptically.

"Perhaps it is, and perhaps Baron Hewett has more friends joining him now. Not bad, right? Experience *and* an Ah' ke, along with a few capable people."

Cyrn sat back and smiled. "You're better than I thought you were."

"And I'm pleased to say the same to you. It's a relief to know I haven't come all this way for nothing."

Rav shivered at the glint in Tibald's eye.

# Chapter Seven

Rav picked at his food. Conversation about the Sink had ended after Tibald's remark, and now the topics covered simple things like Pitt's mine or the weather, leaving him free to mull over what he'd heard. It sounded as if Tibald had achieved something or at least confirmed it. Rav wriggled in his chair, his skin itchy. He kept trying to catch Cyrn's eye, to get an idea of how his brother was feeling, but Cyrn was avoiding him, and Rav didn't know why. Was Cyrn acting for Tibald, or was he really unbothered by what Tibald had said?

"I think this brooding look suits you." Kayla traced a finger down Rav's face.

Rav brushed her away but straightened his posture, realising that he was revealing his emotions too openly.

"Better," Kayla whispered. "I heard you have a story to tell tonight. That ought to distract you for a while."

Rav looked at her. She was right; Cyrn said he'd handle Tibald, so he had to leave his brother to it. Even if any problems arose, Cyrn was far more capable of dealing with them than he was. "Aye," he said, calming down as he lost himself in Kayla's eyes. "I love you."

Kayla leaned in. "I know." She brushed her lips past his, to his ear, her breath tickling his skin. "It's a good thing I love you too. Now, come on; your audience awaits."

Kayla dragged Rav outside, where he spun a wondrous tale about hunting down a pack of ghouls that had escaped from Ghoul Wood and entered Stone's Way. His audience gasped and cheered at all the right moments, Rav's story growing more outlandish as the truth that had formed the basis of his story fell away and the fantasy life he envisioned took over. After delivering the finale, Rav headed back into the tavern under cries of, "*Encore.*"

Cyrn and Tibald were still talking. Rav yawned. He'd have to wait until tomorrow to ask Cyrn what he thought about Tibald. He excused himself and walked Kayla home in the moonlight.

"Did you see Enna at the table?" Kayla asked as they ambled down the torch-lit streets.

"No, why? Should I have noticed something?"

"I know this might be mean of me, but did you see how much weight she's gained?"

"That is a little mean, but aye, I could tell. Is there more to it?"

"More to it? Did you see how much food she was eating?" Kayla covered her mouth to hide her teasing smile. "It's like she was eating for two."

"Now, that is mean." Rav laughed. "It's her first time seeing Cyrn in a month; she can celebrate however she likes."

"But she didn't drink anything. Her ale cup was full when she sat down and full when she got up. What kind of celebration is that?"

Rav went quiet, not wanting to speak ill of Cyrn's wife.

Kayla looked at him. "We can talk about something else if you want. What's on your mind? Is it to do with Tibald?"

"Aye, but I don't want to talk about him," Rav replied. "I don't want what happens outside of Pitt to bleed into it. We're here to enjoy each other's company, not brood about the Sink or Tibald or the 'Zet Ar."

"What's a 'Zet Ar?"

"A giant Spine roaming Stone's Way... Let's not get into it; you shouldn't have to worry about things like that."

"I want to help you, Rav." Kayla stopped and turned to face Rav, tenderly stroking his cheek with her thumb. "Sometimes I feel like you're irritated by what I say, like you think it's unimportant."

"Kayla." Rav held her waist. "You have no idea how happy I am that you can focus on what Enna eats for supper. Please never stop voicing your thoughts. I know I might not seem responsive now, but for you to be able to focus on things like that is everything I want because it means I've successfully protected you from all the dangers surrounding us. What happens in Stone's Way is nothing like the heroic tales I tell, but I'd far rather you believe my stories to be true than for you to know what I actually do."

"I still want to help, Rav. I don't mind the burden of knowing; in fact, don't I deserve to know what's out there too?"

"It's not good, Kayla." He shook his head. "The corpses, the fighting, the... *derision* invading soldiers have for us. Everything outside of Pitt has changed for the worse. I hate that the Ghoulsmen have to face it. I can't imagine what it would be like for you or anyone else we're sworn to protect to face it too."

"Rav, think about what you just said. Imagine what it's like for me to see you endure those things and do nothing to support you. If you were in my position, I know you'd want to help too. Please, just let me do something."

Rav stared at her, guts twisting as he tried to stomach the truth. She was right, but what would happen if she got involved? Wouldn't the safe life she had here be ruined? There'd be no hope that one day, he'd find a solution to it all and let Pitt live as though the Sink had never appeared. He sucked his teeth, clenching his stomach to steady it. Kayla's eyes bored deeper into his, her concern growing in the silence.

Rav clicked his tongue with a sigh. "There is a safe task you can help me with. I need to gather supplies so we can escape Stone's Way as soon as possible."

"We're leaving?" Kayla gasped, grabbing Rav's sleeve. "Are things really that bad? I thought that with Tibald being so polite, there might be an improvement in our situation."

Rav scoffed. "Don't trust anything Tibald says; he wants to enslave us like all the others, he's just better at hiding it. I... Cyrn's handling it."

Kayla's face scrunched and reddened as she took a deep breath. "I'll keep that in mind." She dropped to a whisper. "I can't believe I thought everything was going well. I hoped..." She gazed at him with love, her hands shaking. "I appreciate what you're trying to do, Rav, I really do, but we have to fight for ourselves sometime, or we'll only end up burdening you."

Rav held her cheeks as soft as he could manage with calloused hands. "If only it was that easy. Once you bloody your hands, you can't go back. If you saw the things I've done, you wouldn't treat me the same as you do now."

"I already know what you've done, and I love you anyway."

"But you haven't *seen* it." He shook his head and turned away as he released her, staring at the stars.

They lapsed into silence, the dull sound of fading singing from Franz' Tavern hanging like a murmur in the air, giggles and clunky footsteps echoing off the stone as other revellers waddled home.

"Rav..."

"Hmm?" He faced Kayla. "What?"

"What?" She looked up at him, her forehead wrinkling.

"You said my name. Did you want to say something?"

"I didn't say anything."

"Rav..."

This time, Rav had been looking right at Kayla, confirming that she hadn't spoken. It was that voice he'd heard in the Alley Camp again.

A wave of drowsiness washed over him, his shoulders drooping as his eyelids started to weigh themselves shut. He sucked in a sharp breath to wake himself up, forcing a strained smile as he rubbed his eyes.

"Ah, I must be tired." He yawned, his body suddenly aching. "We'll talk more tomorrow." Looking ahead, he spotted the turning towards Kayla's house and trudged towards it.

Kayla walked to his side and pulled his arm around her waist. "Aye, tomorrow." She stroked the back of his head. "I do love you, Rav."

"Rav…"

Rav forced his smile wider, hoping Kayla didn't notice the sweat starting to bead on his brow as he fought to stay conscious. Around the corner stood a small two-room house with a red-dyed roof and the Name "Blaine" carved above the wooden door.

Kayla hugged Rav tighter, then stepped out from his arm, cracking open the door to reveal the faint glow of a weak candle illuminating the dark inside. She stood there watching him, then made a coy show of looking at the empty street around them. No one was watching. She shifted to the side as though to invite him forward.

"Rav…"

Rav flinched out his stupor and wiped the sweat from his forehead with a gulp. "Goodnight, Kayla."

"Goodnight, Rav." Kayla gave him a last smile before entering her home and shutting the door.

"Rav…"

Rav started running back to the Carvell House as the voice kept calling to him. The shadows of Pitt's buildings twisted around him in the moonlight, forming wicked, spined horns.

*Tak, tak, tak.*

Rav jolted in his step. It sounded just like them. The drowsiness seeped deeper into his bones, sapping away his control over his body, like it had in the Alley Camp. Chased by braying figments of Spines that breathed down his neck no matter how fast he ran, Rav finally reached his home and stumbled inside before running up the stairs and sealing himself in his room, glad none of his family was around to see him like this. Was he safe? Safe from what? There weren't any Spines in Pitt. He collapsed onto his bed. It was all just a hallucination.

His eyelids grew heavier and heavier until they forced themselves shut, trapping him in a state of half-slumber with only the sound of his rapid heartbeat keeping him conscious. Until his exhaustion faded and control over his body returned. Rav snorted back awake, eyes wild as he scanned the dark room around him. Had it stopped?

*Tok, tok, tok.*

Clopping hooves much heavier than an ordinary Spine's approached him from a distance, slow and domineering. Rav flinched, snapping his head from side to side to see where the noise had come from. There was nothing but blackness.

"Rav..."

*Tok, tok, tok.*

No, he was still trapped in the dream. He covered his ears, but the sounds remained clear. They were in his head, inescapable.

*Tok, tok, tok.*

"Rav..."

The Spine sounded as if it were right at the end of his bed, towering over him. No, no Spine was this big. The 'Zet Ar. Rav kept still.

*It's just a dream, it's just a dream, it's just a dream...*

"Rav..."

*Tok, tok, tok.*

Rav trembled in the dark. *Wait*. The dark. It was all just shadows. If he had light, he could chase it away.

He fumbled around the bedside table until he found a candle and lit it, protecting the flame as it bloomed while warming his shaking hands. His room was clear, empty except for his bed, bedside table, and wardrobe. Rav took a deep breath as he fought to calm down.

He set the candle down, thinking about what he should do. Tell Cyrn. That was what he normally would have done. But Cyrn was busy working hard to handle Tibald Sar. His brother couldn't be distracted right now, not when he hadn't even tried to solve this problem by himself. Besides, what would he say? "Cyrn, I'm having strange nightmares about the 'Zet Ar." Then what? What would Cyrn be able to do about it?

Rav rubbed his face. A shadow on the wall caught his attention. Was that... a hoof?

Looming over his bed was the enormous shadow of a Spine. Rav froze, so sure it was about to stamp down and crush him. But nothing happened. The shadow wasn't moving. It wasn't real. Rav smacked his head and rubbed his eyes, trying to shake the image out of his mind. When he looked back, it was still there, glaring at him. He shifted away from it and noticed other shadows on the walls—the Ghoulsmen, all armed and ready for combat. Each stood blurry and indistinct with their shadow forms, yet by the ways they breathed or shifted their weight from foot to foot or held themselves tall, Rav recognised who each figment represented, the actions identical to the ones he'd seen before every battle they'd fought in Stone's Way. The figures from the fire he'd seen in the Alley Camp were all here. Was he about to see them fight all over again? Was he about to see them *die* all over again?

*Defend yourselves*, Rav screamed in his mind.

The Ghoulsmen figures all took defensive positions, then the 'Zet Ar started to charge at them before everything froze again. It felt as if... the shadows were responding to his thoughts.

*Raise your spears towards the 'Zet Ar,* Rav commanded.

They obeyed, and as they moved, so did the 'Zet Ar, which continued to run straight into them. Their spears didn't harm the 'Zet Ar, and it trampled its way into the centre of the group, the figure belonging to Cyrn crushed beneath it.

*Surround the beast.*

The Ghoulsmen did so, but it soon trampled more of them until only Wakeman remained. It wasn't long before the 'Zet Ar bleated in victory once again and the shadows turned back into ordinary darkness.

Rav collapsed onto his bed and wiped away some of the sweat streaming down his forehead. He'd lost. Last time, he'd been forced to watch their defeat, but this time, it was as if he'd been directly responsible for their deaths. *His* actions had gotten everyone killed. He lay there trembling as the realisation that what he'd experienced couldn't have been a dream dawned on him. Hallucinating was one thing, but controlling a vision was something else. It wasn't his mind playing tricks on him, it was as though he was... practising fighting the 'Zet Ar.

# Chapter Eight

Rav moved through the morning in a frenzy, the thought of fighting the 'Zet Ar consuming his every thought. There was no way the Ghoulsmen could defeat that thing; they had to escape before it came to Pitt for real. He visited Aunt Judy briefly before rushing off to start preparing provisions for everyone to leave. Kayla was already inside a large wooden storage house at the southern end of Pitt, looking over the giant pile of grain stacked from floor to ceiling with a frown. Rav glanced around Pitt with eyes weary from no sleep to confirm no one else was around before darting inside and shutting the door behind him. By the dim light shining through shuttered windows, Rav glanced over the messy pile and sneezed at the musty smell.

"How much have you done?" he grunted, tone harsher than he'd wanted.

"I-I've just started c-counting," Kayla stammered, flinching back as she turned to face his wild eyes and sweat-matted hair.

"Hurry. I'll head to the next storage house so we can get both done today." He spun around and tried to rush away, but Kayla caught him by the arm and held him in place.

"Easy, Rav. I thought we were supposed to do this in secret. What's wrong?"

"We are, but..." He huffed as he looked back and forth between the grain and the exit. *What should I do?*

"Is this because of what I said yesterday? After you left so quickly, I—"

"That wasn't because of you. I remembered something important that I needed to do." Did he need to involve Cyrn in this after all? Did he need to burden his brother further? To distract him from dealing with Tibald? No. Tibald was in Pitt already, not some strange vision. The Champion took priority. Besides, couldn't he at least get Pitt ready to leave by himself? Or was he really so useless he couldn't even manage that?

"Is it something I can help you with, or is this another thing it's better for me not to know about?"

Rav glanced at Kayla but held back his quick retort upon seeing her expression. She had the same sense of uselessness he often caught in his own reflection. She wanted to help, just like he did. "It's not *better* for you not to know these things, it's... What do you want?"

"What do you mean?"

"I mean, what kind of life do you want? What do you want to do?"

"I... well..." She blushed. "You know I want to marry you, right?"

Rav's expression softened. "I do, and I want to marry you too. What else?"

Kayla smiled. "I want to have children, as many as I can, and I want to raise them to bring honour to their lineage. I want people to see their Names and know they have all the right values, like loving their home and caring for those in their community. I want everything that anyone born in Pitt wants, that anyone with a Name wants—I want to live my life in a way that would make my ancestors proud."

Rav nodded, stroking her cheek. "I want those things too, but I fear that I can't have them all. I... I know I can't have them all.

My life is not a peaceful one, and I don't know if my ancestors would be proud of what I've done. I know I'm not." Before his head could drop, he puffed out his chest and kept himself tall, always holding her gaze. "I don't want you to feel like I do. If you truly want the life that you say you do, I don't think I can involve you in what I'm doing. You'll either have to join us in the killing, or you'll torture yourself for not being able to change anything."

Kayla's smile flattened as she hardened her expression, as though trying to mimic his stoicism, trying to prove she was just as capable of being as serious as he was. "...Does that mean the thing you have to do is kill someone?"

Rav bit his lip. He had to tell her something. "We need to escape from Stone's Way, but we can't because Baron Hewett controls the surrounding territory and will capture us if we try. Originally, we were going to wait for a gap to appear; however, I think we might need to escape now, which means fighting our way out."

"Why, though? What's made you so scared?"

Rav gave a dry chuckle. "I know this will sound silly, but I had a bad dream."

"How bad?"

Rav's eyes glistened. "Everyone is going to die, bad."

"And there's nothing you can do about it?"

Rav shook his head. "I tried to stop it, and I failed."

"Failed? How have you failed? We're all still alive, Rav. Whatever you're scared of hasn't happened. And even if you think you've failed once, why can't you try again? Giving up isn't something you'd do, ever. Where's my storybook hero?" She kissed him tenderly, then pulled back and held his face. "If it really is hopeless, then we'll have to escape now, but if there's a way for us to stay, I know you'll find it."

Rav gazed into her eyes. How could they stay longer? To do that, they'd have to defeat the 'Zet Ar, which he knew they couldn't do... yet. His eyes shone as an idea formed. Hadn't the Ghoulsmen figments lasted longer against that monster in the Alley Camp fire?

*When I go to sleep tonight, will I have another nightmare and practice battling the 'Zet Ar again? Can't I practice until I find a way to win?*

Rav caught up with Cyrn over lunch, where Cyrn assured him that Tibald was behaving himself. He asked Cyrn what he and Tibald had been talking about regarding Tibald having found something of interest, and Cyrn explained that it meant Tibald had found people he wanted to conscript. There was no longer any doubt as to why Tibald had come to Pitt. The area of concern that Cyrn raised was to do with the discussion about Baron Hewett's *friends* joining him at Greenfield. If Baron Hewett's army grew larger as more of his allies arrived, it would be harder to escape past him. Rav was once again tempted to tell Cyrn about his visions but decided not to after hearing about how much Cyrn was currently dealing with.

Rav went to bed early that night but lay awake with a candle flickering beside him, waiting.

*Tok, tok, tok.*

The shadows in his room came to life again, starting with the 'Zet Ar taking its position above him. Rav took command of the Ghoulsmen and led them as best he could. Taking a passive defensive stance hadn't worked before, so Rav chose offence this time. He had the Ghoulsmen split up and surround the beast while using his own figment to draw the 'Zet Ar's attention. His figure was trampled in an instant, but Cyrn managed to deliver a strike to the beast's snout that had it reel back in pain. Then it turned on him and there was nothing Rav could do to stop it. He watched, powerless, as the 'Zet Ar slaughtered the Ghoulsmen's figures once more.

Rav slumped down on his bed, sweat running down his face and dripping off his chin. Then he smiled. It wasn't as hopeless as he'd first thought; hadn't he done better this time?

# Chapter Nine

The next day was the same. Rav spent the day with Kayla preparing supplies and the night watching another massacre conducted by the 'Zet Ar. He managed to keep Cyrn and Wakeman's shadows alive slightly longer this time by being better at distracting the monster with the other Ghoulsmen. The beast was too fast and too powerful, so he could only buy time against it by sacrificing people, always starting with himself. He needed to find a way to keep those drawing its attention alive. Or at least alive long enough for the others to inflict some damage on the beast.

Cyrn warned him not to visit the storage houses the next day because Tibald was snooping around the area. His Ma also reminded him to rest after being away for so long. Rav spent the day working in the Carvell pelt shops with Kayla, then prepared a picnic for the two of them with wine and stew, which they shared atop Pitt's south-eastern wall during sunset.

"It's beautiful, isn't it?" Kayla said as she rested her head on Rav's shoulder.

Rav stared into the distance at the rolling hills that stretched towards the horizon before they flattened out and the Stone Steps began. "It's the last good view in Stone's Way. North faces Greenfield, west and south face Ghoul Wood, and further east faces the Sink. This is the only place to look where things aren't trying to kill us. And it's a dead end."

"Do you remember the story about the Stone Steps' giants from when we were children?" Kayla asked.

"Didn't that story keep changing depending on who told it?" Rav chuckled.

"The details don't matter, only the lesson does. Great giants built a city so big and magnificent that its mere steps were as tall as a man."

"Stop," Rav muttered. "I know how it ends."

"No, you don't. But the land the giants built on was broken. Unknown to the giants, as they were building upwards, fierce underground rivers were hollowing out the earth beneath them—"

"Until their city collapsed through the top layer of stone and into the water below," Rav finished. "Almost everything they'd created was washed away, never to be seen again, leaving only their steps behind. Even they're crumbling, soon to follow the rest of the city." He gritted his teeth as he smacked the stone beneath them with his fist. "The Sink will erode Pitt until it too disappears."

"The story doesn't end there," Kayla whispered. "Though the city was lost, the giants lived on. They shrank and weakened, eventually becoming no different from ordinary men, some of whom continued to live beside their fallen city in the hopes that they could build it again. They became the founding Carvells that built Pitt."

"The Carvells having giants' blood is just something Aunt Judy made up to explain why Cyrn was twice the size of everyone else his age. It's not true, and why would it matter if it was? The city was lost."

"The point"—Kayla sat up—"is exactly what you said. A story's ending depends on the storyteller. Judy kept those giants alive, just like you can keep Pitt alive. Who's going to tell our story, Rav? Us or Tibald Sar?"

Another night of losing to the 'Zet Ar passed followed by another day of counting grain. Four days after arriving back in Pitt, Rav received a summons to his Pa's office. Walking into the room, Rav saw his Pa pacing behind his large wooden desk. The room smelled of hide and varnish along with woodsmoke from the small fireplace behind him.

Senior Carvell looked up as Rav entered, then leaned over his desk to face him, splintered hands pressing hard on the surface, expression grim. "There's been a mutant attack at the logging site. I'm sending you and Cyrn to hunt it down."

Rav stormed forward. "Who was attacked?"

"Robert's son."

Rav blinked in surprise, fervour broken for a moment. "Finn? Is he alive?"

"Barely." Senior Carvell pinched between his eyes. "I never should have let him help scout for new trees even if we were shorthanded; I knew he was too young to protect himself. There hadn't been an attack in months, and with that new Healer living in the woods, I thought he'd be safe." Senior Carvell spat a sharp breath of air out as he faced Rav once more. "The boy's in her care now."

"There's someone new here?" Rav flinched back. "Who? Where did she come from? How did she sneak past the Ghoulsmen?"

"Aye, Lyra," his Pa muttered with a wave of his hand. "She came alone from the east about a month ago and started living in the old hunters' hut in Ghoul Wood. She traded a few salves in exchange for food when she arrived and helps treat wounds but doesn't involve herself with the town. We think she's another

Nameless wanderer like Wakeman and Thorley. I've already told Cyrn, and he seemed content to let her be."

Rav gathered his breath to ask more before simply snorting. "I'll see her when we speak to Finn." Reaching over the desk, he held his Pa's forearm. "We'll kill this mutant, I promise."

"Aye." Senior Carvell nodded. "I know you will."

Once Rav and Cyrn had changed into thick furs and were fully equipped, they set off for Lyra's hut, located within Ghoul Wood. South-west of Pitt's defensive wall was a small clearing filled with felled timber and wagons, and further ahead of that was the edge of the forest. Past the ordered logging roads, the trees grew thick, gnarled, and sickly green, each distorted by the rolling waves of mist that lingered beneath the canopy to seem as though they were breathing. Hungering.

Rav shivered as he entered the forest's depths, a cold breeze prickling his skin like a final breath. The sounds of Pitt faded, replaced by the cracking of twisting trees. The deeper into the woods he walked, the stronger the stench of rot grew, clawing down his throat until his stomach churned. It was a smell he could never forget—the stench of the phantom ghouls that plagued the dreams of Pitt's hunters.

"I hate this place," Cyrn murmured.

"Let's hope we can catch this mutant today so we don't have to spend a night in here suffering from nightmares," Rav followed, a splinter of fear piercing his mind at the thought of what would happen if the Ghoul Wood nightmares combined with his visions.

"I also need to get back soon so I can continue monitoring Tibald," Cyrn said. "Although I don't think Tibald will do anything to harm Pitt while I'm away, he might start carrying out more of his plan when I can't see him."

"Have you made any progress on that front?"

Cyrn sighed. "It's tricky. I'm learning more about Baron Hewett and the outside situation, but it's still not enough.

Tibald tells me snippets to keep me interested but never anything complete, so I have to keep going back to weasel out more information from him. He's clever like that. Also, because he's acting so well-mannered, people's guards are starting to lower."

Rav strode over a tree root that had breached the ground, then ducked under a jagged branch hanging over the path with Cyrn. "Is that part of his plan? Is he going to lull us into trusting him before betraying us?"

"I don't know yet." Cyrn slapped another hanging branch out their way with a wide palm, snapping it from its tree. "The worst part is that all the work he's putting into endearing himself with us seems genuine. He actually treats people respectfully at all times, like he cares about their wellbeing. It feels like his offer to recruit us is honest and fair."

"Well, I'm not falling for it. I've nearly finished cataloguing all the grain in Pitt and I'll soon finish counting our salted meats. I'll have a supply list ready for collection in two weeks."

"You've been working hard." Cyrn ruffled his hair. "Don't forget to sleep, though; your eyes are bloodshot."

The path they travelled down became overgrown as they entered the depths of Ghoul Wood, and before long, they spotted the great willow tree that marked the hut Lyra had moved into, its leaves drooping over the small building like matted hair. The hut's walls were dark, all gaps sealed so tight that no light could escape outside and no damp could get in. Even like that, Rav had no idea how anyone could stand living in this place.

Cyrn knocked on the gnarled door. Quick footsteps approached from inside before it cracked open a sliver, a shaft of orange firelight cutting through the woodland gloom. A brown-haired man in his forties peered through the gap at them, then hurried to open the door wider and invite the brothers inside, where he directed them to stand at the side of the small room while he shut the door tight again.

A bonfire burned in the centre of the room, lighting a bedroom on the far side and a wooden medicine table beside the door, an adolescent boy with the same dark hair as his Pa lying shivering upon it. A young woman with hypnotising blue eyes and tar-black hair tended to him, her features sharp, almost sculptured, looking beautiful in a way only glass trinkets could. She appeared fragile and untouchable, eerie and inhuman. Rav lost his breath.

Cyrn moved closer to the young man on the table but kept out of Lyra's way.

"Elder Carvell, Master Carvell." Robert bowed to the brothers.

"How's Finn?" Rav asked him.

Robert sighed, gazing at his son. "Not good. He's been unconscious for a while. I don't know when he'll wake up."

Rav observed Lyra as she worked. She kept her focus solely on Finn, her movements precise as she tended to him.

"Can you tell me what happened? What attacked him?" Cyrn spoke.

"My Finn's a brave lad," Robert said, his voice wobbling. "He went to tread a new logging path to reach a high-quality tree when the mutant bit him. Those who chased the mutant away said it was a badger the size of a hound."

"That is accurate." Lyra's voice was like the high string on a lyre. "The bite marks resemble a badger's, only bigger."

She beckoned them to look, and Rav tensed as he approached the table. Finn was sweating into his robe, his eyelids flickering as he drifted in and out of consciousness. Lyra had cut away his sleeve and the bottom of his robe to reveal three bite marks—one on his arm, two on his leg—and several oozing scratches around the bites. Lyra wiped away the drying blood so they had a clearer look at the puncture marks. Rav winced at the sight of bone.

"Are there any signs of venom?" Cyrn asked.

Lyra shook her head.

"Do you know how deep the teeth marks go?" said Rav.

"A fingertip."

Rav checked his furs to see if they were thick enough to protect him. They were, but only just.

Lyra pointed to the wounds. "The mutant's teeth are designed to puncture, not cut. If it manages to bite through your armour, you need to tie a piece of cloth over the wound to stop the bleeding. I can heal some damage with a needle and thread, but if the damage is too severe, you will have to cauterise the wound as soon as you can and hope the pain does not kill you."

"Thank you for your help," Cyrn said before turning to face Robert. "Finn was injured working at our logging site, so we'll take responsibility. Healer Lyra will care for your son, paid for by the Carvells, and while I can't promise his good health, I *can* promise to kill the creature that did this. I'll bring you its head."

"Thank you, Elder Carvell." Robert bowed.

"You will also have time off until your son is healed," Rav added. "With payment."

Cyrn and Rav left Lyra's hut and headed to where Finn had been attacked. After speaking to a few other woodcutters, they were able to find the path Finn had been treading and picked up the mutant badger's tracks.

"Will just the two of us be enough?" Rav asked.

"Aye," Cyrn said. "We'll set a trap for it once we find the badger's burrow and—"

"*Halt,*" someone bellowed from behind them.

The brothers spun around to see three figures jogging towards them, the central one shining in full-plate armour.

Tibald Sar, Jingo Hook, and Ronin Luke hurried over to them, all armed. Rav scowled.

"Champion Sar," Cyrn called. "Do you need something from me?"

"I received news that a mutant has attacked one of Pitt's citizens. It's Baron Hewett's duty to keep those living in his territory safe, so it falls upon me as his Champion to track it down and kill it. Have you found its tracks?"

"I have indeed, but this mutant doesn't require the skill of a Champion to be slain; I believe us Carvells to be enough."

"I'm sure you are." Tibald's grin was cut short as he wrinkled his nose, a waft of rot blowing over them in the breeze. After gathering his breath again, he continued, "However, I would like to take this opportunity to prove that my dedication to my duties can be trusted by taking action to back them up. If nothing else, by hunting down this mutant, I will prove what I'm willing to do for my *friends*."

Rav held back his laugh, using a hand to cover his smirk. Did Tibald really believe that by doing something like this, he would trust him?

"That's a generous offer. We accept." Cyrn glanced at Rav in warning, then pointed at the boot and claw marks imprinted in the mud ahead. "This mutant is said to be similar to a badger, but it's the size of a hound and has large teeth for puncturing. This is where Finn was attacked."

Tibald perused them with feigned interest. "The mutant's no problem. I will require a guide, though. I'm unfamiliar with Ghoul Wood and its 'nightmares', so having someone who knows how to deal with them would be most appreciated."

Rav felt Tibald's horrible gaze settle on him.

"You, perhaps?"

Rav flinched. "I... uh..."

Cyrn nodded his agreement before Rav could find his words in time to object.

"Thank you for putting your trust in me. I won't let you down," Tibald spoke.

"Oh, I don't trust you," Cyrn said, chuckling, "I trust Rav. Either you'll all make it out of Ghoul Wood alive or only he will."

Tibald remained stern, facing Rav with sincerity as he made a point of taking this hunt seriously. "Then I'll be grateful to have such a dangerous companion when we face the mutant."

What was Cyrn doing? Rav couldn't make sense of it. He looked between Tibald, Jingo, and Ronin. While Tibald at least had his usual feigned politeness, Jingo and Ronin clearly looked down on him.

Cyrn hugged Rav. "Do you trust me?" he whispered.

"Aye."

"Then believe me when I say that Tibald won't harm you. I know what he wants now and hurting you will ruin everything he's done so far."

Rav pulled out the hug and nodded.

"We'll be back in two days at most," Tibald said. "Now, come on; the creature's getting away." He marched into the foliage with Jingo and Ronin.

Rav gave his brother one last look before following them.

# Chapter Ten

Jingo moved ahead of the group, leading everyone forward. Rav stayed towards the back, giving himself enough space to escape if he needed to. He trusted Cyrn, but without knowing why Cyrn believed he'd be safe with Tibald, he couldn't relax. As they moved deeper into Ghoul Wood, the tree canopy became denser, the sunlight so faint it was as though storm clouds were clustered overhead.

"Ready the torches," Tibald ordered Ronin.

"We can't use fire here," Rav hurried to say. "Can you see how the air is shifting over there?" He pointed to the faintly visible distortions in the distance. "That's a sign that there are pockets of dense fumes around here, fumes capable of igniting into great balls of flame. The explosions only last an instant, but they're hot enough to burn skin. If you bring an open flame into places like that, you'll lose your face." A memory emerged in Rav's mind of when a young Tobias had been foolish enough to ignore the warnings. He was lucky to only have burned his mouth.

Tibald signalled for Ronin to put back the torches. "Very well, no fire." He gazed at the distorted air with a slight tilt to his head. "How interesting. Do you know where these fumes come from?"

"They seep up through the ground, then hang below the canopy."

"And have they always been here, or did they appear when the Sink did?"

"The fumes have always been here. It's only the nightmares that worsened after the Sink appeared."

Tibald glanced at Rav as they walked. "Are you sure the two aren't connected? I've heard stories about gases causing hallucinations before. Perhaps these fumes are the cause of the nightmares people experience in here. Since the Sink changed not just the ground surface but everything below it as well, maybe it caused a change to the land under Pitt, which altered the fumes too."

Rav shrugged. "Maybe."

Tibald laughed. "You don't seem convinced by my suggestion. Why?"

"When you experience the nightmares, you'll understand that they're nothing like ordinary ones. Cyrn once dreamed he was fighting off a horde of ghouls, and when he woke, he was covered in black blood, yet not one body was around. No one's ever seen a ghoul while awake, but everyone sees them when they sleep."

"How odd," Tibald mused. "Forgive my curiosity, it's just that so many places have stories like this, and most turn out to be... mistaken." He waved his hand in front of his face to push away a hanging line of dead foliage. "I've only experienced such things in the Sink, and even in there, they're rare. You said the nightmares worsened after the Sink appeared. If it wasn't due to the Sink changing the ground, then can you think of anything else that happened around that time that could've caused the nightmares to change?"

"I don't know."

Rav squinted at Tibald. What was he trying to find out? Was he really curious about anything related to the Sink, or was that just a guise he was using to collect some other information? Information about Pitt's history, perhaps? But why? Was he...?

Rav went cold. Was Tibald secretly digging into *that event*? The first time Tibald had mentioned Ghoul Wood's nightmares, Reuben told him about Pitt's original Baron; now, he was trying to get Rav to talk about other events that had occurred around that time. Was Tibald seeking to unravel the pretences preventing him from conscripting people from Pitt?

But Cyrn had said he'd be safe. That thought stopped Rav from turning around and fleeing back to Pitt. Had Cyrn made a mistake? Or did his brother know something else that nullified the threat that Tibald knowing about his crime posed? Rav stared at Tibald's back, watching for the slightest indication of hostility from him.

Tibald looked over his shoulder at Rav. "Why do you look frightened? Didn't Cyrn tell you that you'd be safe? You trust your brother, don't you?"

Rav flattened his expression. "Aye."

"Then you've got nothing to be worried about." Tibald chuckled before snapping into a grin. "Or did Cyrn tell you something else during your hug?"

Rav stopped walking.

Tibald turned to face him, bringing their hunt to a halt. "No, that's not it. Did I let something slip?" He ran his fingers through his hair while mumbling. "What was it? *Ah*. Of course you'd be fixated with that time period. How foolish of me. Well, while you're not as clever as your brother, it seems you do have some insight after all."

"Speak clearly," Rav demanded, preparing to run.

"Don't be so skittish; you wouldn't be able to outrun me anyway. It was my mistake, so it's my duty to... *deescalate* this situation. You've noticed my prying into Pitt's history; however, there's no need to be alarmed. I already know what you did. Baron Kiln had a beautifully written arrest warrant for you and the town of Pitt sitting in his office in Greenfield, which is now in Baron Hewett's possession. The spoils of war and all that."

Rav's head spun as his heart pounded.

"Easy there, Rav. Use your brain." Tibald tapped his head. "As I said, I already knew about the murder, but I haven't come to Pitt with an army to arrest you all, have I? And I don't plan to. Though, considering your distrust of me and my intentions led you to this breakthrough, I suppose you won't believe that.

"I think the best way to resolve this situation is to tell you that Cyrn already knows all of this. I mean, come on, you know your brother better than anyone—he figured all this out days ago. As to what I'm truly after..." Tibald shrugged. "I'll leave that for you to think about." He turned his back to Rav and signalled for Jingo to continue tracking down the mutant badger.

Rav paused, eyes flitting between Tibald and the way home, muscles twitching like they were about to snap into action. Should he run? *No.* Despite his instincts screaming for him to escape, he kept his feet firmly set into the mud beneath him. He had to stay for the hunt and uncover Tibald's true motives. He had to remain in danger. Was this what Cyrn had meant by *Tibald only letting you know enough to have you keep coming back to ask him more?* After wiping his sweaty brow with his sleeve, Rav followed after Tibald from a distance, trying to tread a middle ground.

"As I understand it," Tibald spoke loudly for Rav to hear, "you murdered a man. Is that correct?"

"I-I don't want to talk about it."

"That's alright, I'll do the talking." Tibald sounded cheerful. "Ten years ago, Baron Gethnil gathered an army to venture into the Sink and claim its spoils, just like every other Baron, except his territory was right next to it, so he was one of the first to arrive."

"What's the point of this?" Rav spat.

"It's a game. If you're clever, you'll learn something important."

"And what do you get out of it?"

"Isn't discovering that part of the fun?"

Rav frowned, and Tibald looked over his shoulder, catching sight of it.

"Fine, then." He sighed. "At the very least, I'll get to keep you trailing behind me for a little longer in the hopes that you might decide to complete the hunt. Seem fair?"

Rav opened his mouth to protest but didn't get time to even get the first letter out.

"I'll take your silence as agreement." Tibald stared into the mist-laden trees ahead of them. "Where was I?"

Rav huffed, fetid air sending his stomach swirling, fists clenched, ready to—his foot snagged on a protruding tree root, sending him stumbling for a moment.

Tibald muffled his snort. "Ah, yes, Baron Gethnil arriving at the Sink after recruiting citizens from Pitt. Being one of the first Barons to reach the Sink obviously wasn't the advantage it appeared to be. When there are hundreds of other competing Barons with their armies at your back and thousands of mutants at your front, defeat is inevitable."

"Defeat?" Rav hissed. "They *died*. A third of the people I grew up with disappeared, never to be seen again."

"You don't know that they're dead for sure," Tibald pointed out. "There's no memorial for them in Pitt or even any graves, which tells me many of you must still have hope for their return."

Rav shook his head. "There is no hope. If those still wishing for the return of their loved ones saw what was out there, they would reach the same conclusion I have. Besides, if they were alive, why haven't they come back yet?"

"Good question." Tibald beamed. "Maybe whatever they found in the Sink means more to them than seeing their families."

Rav stopped and slammed his spear into the mud, teeth bared as he snarled, his whole body juddering as he fought to control his rage. "Don't you dare disrespect the people of Pitt like that. They were good, honourable people who loved their home and their families."

Tibald also stopped, watching Rav's outburst with an amused raised eyebrow, as though he were a naughty child. "My apologies, I only meant to speak of the Sink's wonders."

"You've already done enough of that."

"Very well." Tibald gave an apologetic half-bow, seeming to completely concede. He tutted to himself. "It seems I've made many mistakes today. You're quite the tricky character, aren't you, Rav?" He turned and continued walking, beckoning Rav to do the same.

Rav took a deep breath, but his chest only tightened as he tasted the inescapable stench of rot. Peeling his furs from his skin did nothing to cool him, the humidity too high. Tibald was getting too far ahead. Rav took a swig of water and wiped his eyes before chasing after him.

Tibald cocked his head as Rav drew near. "Anyway, with your Baron away from Greenfield, he'd left a small garrison to govern his land in his absence, but after receiving no word from their Baron for a year, the garrison became... shall we say greedy?"

Rav spat on the ground. "Tyrants."

Tibald nodded. "Yes, that's probably better. They began demanding all the greedy things that tyrants demand from their people, threatening to send them off to the Sink if they didn't comply, which to you was the equivalent of execution. But you refused to accept that, didn't you, Rav? The Carvells are a proud lineage with deep roots—pardon the pun—and your family refused to comply with the garrison soldiers, so they sent a few soldiers marching into Pitt to force you into the Sink. However, things didn't go to plan for them, did they?"

Rav went woozy, his pulse slamming in his skull.

Tibald chuckled at Rav's discomfort, leering at him like he was unspooling his mind. "When they came for your Ma, despite your good upbringing, despite knowing that what you were about to do was evil and would bring great shame to your ancestors as well as the Carvell Name going forward, you murdered one of them. Quite the grievous crime, wasn't it? I can't imagine the amount of shame you felt."

Tibald needed to stop speaking. Rav slowly staggered forward on shaking legs. He needed to *make* Tibald stop speaking.

"I've had to piece together what happened next using a few assumptions, so feel free to correct me if I get anything wrong," Tibald continued. "Cyrn must have been nearby, perhaps he was even by your side when you committed the murder, and upon seeing what you'd done, he decided to protect you instead of joining with the garrison soldiers to arrest you. I presume several others joined in at that point—I know Cyrn is a phenomenal fighter, but at seventeen, he couldn't have fought off several armed soldiers on his own. It was a rebellion. Could you believe it? The respectable Carvell Bloodline committing treason. Truly dishonourable conduct."

Rav took another shaking step closer, his spear trembling in his hand.

Tibald watched him with a smile. "All of Pitt should have banded together to chase you out, but the Carvells have an excellent Name—or should it be had?—giving them an excellent reputation, so Pitt's other citizens were willing to rebel with them. You won, but your victory can't have been complete considering I've been able to discover all this. Did a soldier manage to escape?" He tapped his chin in an exaggerated thinking pose. "I suppose it doesn't matter, only the consequences do. Pitt no longer had a Baron, leaving the duty of protecting Stone's Way to Pitt's citizens, which required more unlawful killing. As for you, Rav, what punishment were you sentenced to for disgracing your Name and dragging your entire town into the shame-filled filth with you? Were you made Nameless? Or beaten? Or rebuked? Surely all of Pitt couldn't have forgiven you? But when I see the life you're living, I can't help but assume that there was no punishment." Tibald shook his head in disbelief. "Why, if I was in your position, the guilt would have eaten me—"

Rav managed another step forward, then the roar of his pulse became a screech and everything went black.

Rav gasped awake, finding himself lying on his back, Tibald looming over him in the mists. He scrambled back with a wince, pain flaring in his elbow. He snatched out for his spear but was unable to find it, hand cold as he pawed in the mud.

"Looking for this?" Tibald waved the spear in front of Rav before throwing it down to him, the gloom and dark canopy sharpening his features until he appeared almost as fiendish as the shadow Ghoulsmen. "Here, sit up," Tibald said, crouching to help lift Rav.

Rav grabbed his spear and held it between them.

Tibald stepped back with his hands raised. "Calm yourself, Rav," he cooed. "You collapsed. I can't have you getting injured after assuring your brother that you'd be fine."

"Stay away from me," Rav shouted. Whipping his head from side to side, all the trees seemed to lock together into a wooden cage, damp air weighing on his skin like a heavy hand. Finally, he spotted a tree twice as thick as the others with a large knot on its side, recollecting where he was upon seeing the faint crossed-out skull carved into its surface.

"That was quite the reaction," Tibald said, laughing. "That event must have had a strong impact on you for you to still be suffering now."

"*Shut up.*"

"I'm not here to torment you, Rav, quite the opposite actually—I'm offering you salvation. The guilt you're feeling isn't going to go away. Not without you taking action to make up for what you did."

Rav pushed himself upright with shaky arms and steadied himself using his spear as a crutch. "I *am* making up for it; everything I do is to make up for it."

"But what you're doing isn't working, is it? I'm here to show you the true path to redemption. You've committed a grave crime and you *need* to be punished for it. If you don't atone, the guilt will never leave.

"It's time for you to face the consequences of your actions," Tibald continued. "Cyrn can't keep protecting you. You know what must be done... you know what *should* have been done back then, so do it. No more excuses. Go into exile."

Tibald's words sounded like thunderclaps in Rav's ears. Tibald was right; he didn't deserve the Carvell Name. He couldn't discard his own Name, but he *could* leave his family and never come back so that he didn't bring further dishonour to them. It was the thing he'd thought about many times, the thing he was *terrified* of doing. He couldn't put it off this time.

Tibald took on a smug grin as he stretched his neck, turning away from Rav as though he were no longer important. "But that's a problem for another time," he said, voice oozing with pompous delight. "We've got a hunt to complete. Come on."

The faint light filtering through the canopy dimmed, cooling the air.

"We're not going to catch this mutant today; we need to find a place to camp," Tibald announced. "Is there any way to prevent the nightmares, Rav?"

"Hm?" Rav looked up. "Ah, right, no," he replied, his voice barely a whisper. "You just have to suffer through them. We should climb trees rather than sleep on the forest floor to avoid the insects, and we can't eat until morning. You have to try and stay asleep, or the nightmares can become hallucinations. Being bitten by insects will wake you up, so anything that attracts them needs to be sealed away."

"How strong are the hallucinations?"

"They're..." Rav thought of his visions. Would Tibald notice there was something wrong with him? Would—

"*Rav*," Tibald barked. "Focus."

"D-don't believe what you s-see or hear," Rav stuttered. "You'll see ghouls and you'll feel under threat, as though you're being stalked by a predator."

Tibald grumbled in displeasure.

Jingo and Ronin searched the area for suitable trees to sleep in, finding four. Rav walked up to one of them and began preparing for the night by collecting his gear into a tight pack to carry up with him. Tibald, Jingo, and Ronin copied.

Once he was ready, Rav climbed up high, wedged himself between several branches and the trunk, then tied a length of cloth over his eyes. He lay in the dark with his swirling cacophony of thoughts. He had to take responsibility, *true* responsibility. He had to end the blight on his Name.

"Rav..."

The leaves rustled over his head. It was there, the 'Zet Ar, waiting for him. Somewhere in the dark, the Ghoulsmen figments would be waiting too. At his command, the battle would begin anew.

*Crunch, crunch, crunch, creak.*

In his mind's eye, he saw a dozen decaying skeletons with ragged scraps of flesh flapping in the breeze. Their jaws clicked as strands of sinew snapped over bone, their eyes nothing but empty sockets dripping with sludge. The ghouls were here too.

They shuffled closer. Rav pulled his blindfold tighter over his eyes, confirming that it was all in his mind. Everything he was experiencing was just in his imagination. Rav listened as walking corpses lumbered out of the woods and gathered beneath his tree.

"Rav..."

An itch started under his skin as his body warned him of the coming danger, screaming at him to tear off his blindfold to face the coming threat. But he knew he couldn't look. If he did, he really would *see* them. He'd bring the ghouls to life.

*Tap, tap, tap.*

How did he know that was a rotting claw hitting the tree bark? It was impatient—

*Snap.*

Rav flinched. A branch below him had broken. That sounded real. Were the ghouls trying to climb up to him?

*Snap.*

Another branch broke, this time coming from somewhere to his left. Was it another ghoul or something worse? *Don't look*. If he gave in and peeked out... The stench of the fetid black blood that had covered Cyrn filled Rav's nostrils.

The noises continued, everything lingering just out of his reach.

*Crash*. Something heavy fell. Where? Rav didn't know. It wasn't too close to him, though.

The voice kept calling his name, kept enticing him to fight the 'Zet Ar. Hot air blew across his face, as though the beast breathed over him. Rav held on until the nightmares stopped and he felt himself waking up. When had he managed to fall asleep? He peeked out from under his blindfold to see that it was morning. It was time to get moving again. A memory of Aunt Judy surfaced in his mind, replaying over and over again. *"Silly boy,"* she kept chiding him.

*Thud*. Tibald landed at the bottom of his tree, looking like a hazy shadow in the dim light. "Is it safe now?" he asked with a rough voice.

"Aye," Rav answered, climbing down from his tree and unpacking his equipment.

Tibald rubbed his bleary eyes and stretched his neck, a deep haggard expression etched on his face. Jingo and Ronin joined them, also looking as though they hadn't slept.

"It's safe to eat now," Rav informed them.

Tibald nodded but stayed silent as he unwrapped dry cheese for the four of them. Rav spotted a splotch of black blood on the Champion's boot. Had he fought the ghouls like Cyrn had? Shouldn't he be covered in more blood if he had?

"Did you see them too?" Jingo whispered to Ronin.

"It was just a dream," Ronin hissed back. "Those ghouls weren't real. Don't fall for the ignorant superstitions of a place like this; you're better than that."

Jingo stared at him for a moment, then went back to nibbling on his cheese. Ronin bit a large chunk off his provision and munched on it in an obvious display of nonchalance.

"Thank you for warning us about the nightmares, Rav," Tibald said, patting him on the back. "Without your help, I doubt I would've gotten any sleep at all. Pitt's a fascinating place."

Rav didn't miss the sharp glare Tibald threw at Ronin. He continued staring at Tibald while he chewed, trying to think on what the Champion had said about him achieving salvation through exile, but that memory of Aunt Judy kept interrupting him. Rav grumbled. Sleep had helped dull the ache of his despair, but he was still weighed down. If he was going to leave, when would he go? He still had to help prepare everyone in Pitt for escape, then he'd have to travel with them to help protect them, and after that, he'd have to help people settle in a new land. Even then, his work wasn't done. As Wakeman had said, in a decade or two, he could try to return to Stone's Way. He was needed. Was going into exile just running away from his responsibilities? But then how else could he be punished? How else could he achieve salvation and stop this horrid feeling?

*"Silly boy."* Rav scratched his head.

Once everyone had eaten, they continued tracking the mutant badger. Jingo led them into a deep section of Ghoul Wood with steady steps, as though he were the one who'd lived here all his life. Rav looked around but failed to recognise where he was. Wherever Jingo had led them was somewhere he'd never been.

Jingo came to stop by a tree and leaned close to sniff it before recoiling and wrinkling his nose. "We're in the mutant badger's territory now," he announced.

"Get ready for combat," Tibald ordered while tightening his buckler and drawing his spear.

Rav shook away his errant thoughts and focused on the upcoming fight; he needed to be alive to do whatever he was going to do. He readied his spear and shield, while Jingo and Ronin equipped short swords with their shields.

"Look for burrow holes," Tibald barked.

The area ahead had fewer trees and more open space, allowing a little more light to filter down. They spread out between the trees, cautious as they marked out a wide area consisting of a dozen holes surrounding a thick central tree.

"Get the flares," Tibald said.

Jingo and Ronin went searching in their packs.

Rav frowned. "Aren't we going to lay bait and set traps?"

"I suppose you haven't come across flares before," Tibald answered while he scanned the area. "They're cylinders of powder that can be burned to produce thick smoke good for driving people and animals out of an enclosed space, like a burrow."

Rav hurried to examine the air above them, seeing that the distortions were faint and fleeting.

"Flares only smoulder, like coals," Tibald explained. "And we'll be lighting them in the burrow holes, so no flames will rise high enough to reach any fumes overhead. We'll also be a distance away before they catch, so there won't be any danger."

Rav stepped back from the area. "Are you sure the flares are even big enough to smoke out the entire burrow network?" he asked upon seeing the forearm-sized tubes retrieved by Jingo and Ronin.

"Just watch," Tibald snapped. "Set them off, Jingo. We'll make a stand there." He pointed to a tree at the edge of the area. "Backs to the tree. I'm taking centre position, Rav and Ronin will flank me, then after Jingo returns, Rav will drop to the backline while Jingo takes his place. Understood?"

"Aye." Rav was glad to be at the back, furthest from the flares and where he could better protect himself.

"Yes," Jingo and Ronin called.

Rav took his place, and as he waited, his muscles grew taut. He hadn't fought beside Tibald before. Tibald was a Champion who had travelled to the Sink and boasted about his combat abilities; however, Champions were used to fighting men in duels or on the battlefield. How would one fair against a mutant? Rav brought his shield closer and focused on guarding himself.

Jingo sparked some flint to ignite the first flare and dropped it down a burrow hole. Smoke trickled out for a few moments until Rav heard a *fwush* and it started billowing out in earnest as a red glow shone through the haze. The hole disappeared under a white cloud while Jingo moved on to the next burrow entrance to do the same. Soon, the ground was steaming.

"There's too much," Rav shouted, watching as the ground disappeared underneath a shifting grey cloud.

There was no wind to clear the smoke, leaving it to settle and obscure Rav's vision. He lowered his posture, guarding his legs as best as he could against anything hiding out of view. Jingo came back to switch positions with him, which Rav was only too happy to do.

Tibald had also crouched low, scanning the smoke for any movement. "Which hole did it come out of?"

"I didn't see it," Jingo replied.

"Movement right," Ronin called.

Everyone looked to a swirl drifting towards them. Tibald swept out his spear, clearing away a section of smoke to reveal clear ground that was soon engulfed again.

"We should climb the tree," Rav suggested.

"Leaving our position will make us too vulnerable. It can't get through my armour. We hold," Tibald ordered.

"Your plan is to wait for it to attack you, then counterattack?" Rav asked. Wasn't that something Cyrn would do?

"Yes. Now, quiet."

The smoke settled on the ground, only rising in occasional phantom tendrils. Rav let out a long breath. His hand started to shake as he gripped his spear, the strain of keeping his guard up for so long beginning to sap his strength.

"*Right,*" Ronin yelled.

Smoke shifted, roiling out from a burrow. They saw flashes of black and white dart in all directions—there was more than one badger here. Tibald cleared the area before them once more, startling two badgers heading towards them. Rav thrust out between Ronin and Tibald, skewering one of the badgers as Tibald stabbed the other. Ronin also lunged forward but was too slow to hit anything in time.

"None were the mutant. *Reform,*" Tibald roared.

"*Ah,*" Jingo cried as he slammed into the ground.

Rav watched a blur of claws swipe Jingo before diving back beneath the smoke. Now that Jingo was injured, the left flank was left open. Rav realised that he was now in the most vulnerable position. He needed a plan, a plan to survive. Or could he do more than that? What would Cyrn do? He leaned his spear against the tree, choosing to palm a knife into his hand. Tibald and Ronin hurried back to their positions, guarding Jingo as he struggled to get up.

"Injuries?" Tibald barked, never taking his eyes off the smoke.

"I think my shield hand is broken," Jingo hissed through gritted teeth. "*Ah.*" He kneeled back down. "My leg's been bitten."

"It pierced your armour?" Ronin snapped his head from side to side as he scoured the mists for the mutant, stepping back towards the tree with suppressed trembling.

Jingo traced the wound with his fingers. "It bit into the gap behind my knee."

"It's intelligent." Tibald scowled.

Instead of guarding the left side, Rav turned his exposed thigh towards the gap and watched the top of the smoke. The mutant could stalk them beneath the cloud, but it would have to come up for air sometime.

*There.* Behind one of the rising tendrils, a snout emerged to take a breath. It would come for him now. Rav stood taller, inviting the attack.

A wave of smoke wafted against the tree, and as it receded, Rav saw white fur barrelling towards him. Teeth bared, claws slashing, it charged straight at his thigh. Rav threw his knife at the beast while heaving his shield back across him to protect his leg. The blade struck the mutant's nose, stuttering its momentum, but its claws still reached him, cutting into his arm. Rav screamed as he slammed his shield down onto the mutant's shoulder to knock it back.

Tibald's reaction was rapid, jabbing the mutant with his spear just as Rav blocked it. The mutant whimpered from the blow, turning to try to vanish beneath the smoke once more, but Ronin threw his shield into the smoke in front of it, clearing the area. It was exposed again. Tibald was ready, spear righted, stabbing at the creature's back leg, where he drew blood and a snarl. Rav and Jingo grabbed the edges of their shields and fanned them to further clear the area, following Ronin's lead. The space cleared, the hound-sized badger laid bare.

It was one on one—Tibald against the mutant.

The beast turned to face him, growling in warning. Tibald took a defensive stance, with his spear resting on his buckler arm, aimed at the beast. It lunged with speed faster than a hound, but Tibald kept his spear point aimed at it, keeping it back while he used gliding footwork to move to the right, circling the creature again. Rav blinked. Tibald's skill was extraordinary.

The mutant glared at Tibald with beady eyes. Tibald flourished his spear around him, clearing away more of the encroaching smoke. Rav drew another blade from his side, waiting for his moment, only for Ronin to grab his arm.

"Don't. Just watch Champion Sar fight."

The beast charged again, meeting the same sequence as before. Tibald predicted its attacks and put it on the back foot. It hesitated. Tibald moved in. It should have been harder for Tibald to keep pace with it as he got closer, but Rav watched his gliding footwork pull him from danger again and again, as if he were toying with the mutant. It wasn't a battle; it was a domination. Champion Sar wouldn't take a single blow.

The mutant's stamina faltered, giving Tibald more opportunities to strike. He opened more wounds across its body to bleed out more of its energy. The mutant made to charge, feigning the attack, then fled back towards the smoke, but Tibald lunged forward, stabbing it through the back of its head before retrieving his spear and flicking it to scatter the brain matter off.

"Get the carcass," he ordered, not even out of breath.

Rav stood in place, the final blow replaying in his mind. Ronin helped Jingo to stand, then got a hook from his pack, stabbed it into the mutant's corpse, and lugged it over his shoulder.

"Let's go. I don't want to spend another night in here." Tibald stowed his spear on his back and started the walk back to Pitt. "Come," he called to Rav. "We've only got the afternoon to get back."

Rav trailed behind the three, staring at Tibald. "How did you move like that?"

"It's a technique I learned in the Sink."

He could hear the gloating in Tibald's voice. Rav looked at Jingo and Ronin. They weren't special, both using ordinary combat manoeuvres. Was Tibald the only one who could perform those feats? No. Baron Hewett probably could too. Were there others? What kind of army did Baron Hewett lead? What kind of place was the Sink to produce such strong fighters? Could there be an entire army of people like Tibald? Or... an army of people more powerful than Tibald? Was the Sink a world where you survived one disaster just to see another? A tomb for all but the very few who lasted until they reached the pinnacle? If there even was a top. It *was* a sink—an endless, relentless fall until you were buried.

The adrenaline wore off. Rav winced as he shifted his grip on his shield, the cuts on his arm starting to sting.

"We'll rest where we slept," Tibald commanded. "You and Jingo need treatment."

Rav turned his arm over to see the damage. His furs had been cut through, leaving four shallow slashes from his wrist to his elbow. He gingerly touched the area to feel the extent of the damage, finding three gashes to be painful and one to be excruciating. Pulling up his sleeve, he inspected the worst one, blood oozing out to coat his forearm dark red. With nimble fingers, he pried open a pouch at his waist with his free hand and pulled out some cloth to tie over the wound, grimacing.

"Tend to Jingo," Tibald ordered Ronin once they'd reached the campsite. "Come here, Rav. Show me your wound."

Rav undid the cloth, seeing that his arm was now turning purplish black from bruising. Fortunately, the wound had clotted, the blood like jelly.

"You made a stupid decision," Tibald remarked as he looked at the extent of the damage. "I thought you were turning away because you were scared or inexperienced, but you were inviting it to attack, weren't you?" He pulled out some gauze and medicinal paste from a pack to dress Rav's arm.

"It worked," Rav mumbled.

"You shouldn't have done it. I was the one wearing plate armour; I should've been the one to draw the mutant out." Tibald pulled the gauze tight, and Rav squirmed. "You could have died."

Rav glared at him. "You tried drawing it out with your stupid flares and look how that turned out. If you'd have thought about how the fumes here clog the air and how there wasn't a breeze, you'd have realised how foolish your plan was."

Tibald glared back. "You put the formation at risk."

"Jingo had already broken it."

"Then you should've helped reorganise things."

Rav frowned. Was it just that Tibald's pride was wounded, or had something else annoyed him?

Rav thought over the fight and stepped back from Tibald. "That's why Ronin stopped my throw. You wanted me to watch as you killed the mutant alone so that I would tell people what an amazing fighter you are. You're angry that your perfect plan didn't go so perfectly, aren't you?"

Tibald bristled. "We've fought side by side, so I'm going to forgive your accusations. I killed the mutant; the matter is over."

"We," Rav spat. "*We* killed the mutant."

Tibald huffed. "Are you afraid you won't get recognition? It was a good throw. You're skilled with a knife."

Rav turned away from him. It was obvious that Tibald had only said that to distract him from the main point of how he intended to use Rav to further his own reputation. Rav hadn't only been brought out here to divulge information about the murder. What other plans were being enacted?

*"Silly boy,"* Aunt Judy's memory chided. Rav kicked the ground. Why did she keep interrupting him? He looked back at Tibald, who was now tending to Jingo.

Tibald's duel against the mutant had intended to be a performance for him, but what had Cyrn said before about observing Tibald's actions to determine what he wanted? What had Tibald said about uncovering important information if Rav was clever enough? Aside from the flares, what other mistakes had Tibald made? He hadn't just defeated the mutant badger physically, he'd defeated it mentally too by giving it a clear path for escape that only made it expose its back to him.

When Tibald had first seen Rav, he'd focused on all the gaps in Rav's armour, but what if he had also noticed the vulnerabilities in his psyche? Was all Tibald's talk about salvation, while perhaps true, designed to get Rav to isolate himself and leave Pitt weakened?

"You're despicable," Rav spat at Tibald. "All you do is lie."

"I've only ever spoken the truth," Tibald responded with an even voice. "I hope that in time you'll be able to see that, and if that's not enough, you may judge me by what I do. At the end of the day, the mutant that attacked Pitt is dead."

"How can you be so callous? What would your ancestors think of your beha—"

"*How dare you speak to Champion Sar like this*," Ronin roared, dropping Jingo to stomp forward while brandishing his short sword. "You don't deserve to march beside us. Without Cyrn, you and your backwater town would be nothing better than s—"

Tibald punched Ronin, knocking him to the ground.

"Finish what you were saying," Rav demanded.

Ronin looked up at Tibald, who stood over him, and swallowed the rage that had warped his expression. "My apologies, Rav. I spoke out of turn. I have not slept well due to the nightmares, and I fear my exhaustion has gotten the better of me."

"Get up. We're leaving." Tibald wrapped Jingo's arm around his shoulder to help him walk and headed back to Pitt.

Rav clenched his fists. "Without Cyrn." Was that the missing piece that tied everything Tibald was doing together? Tibald had mentioned friends before, which Cyrn had translated to allies. Did Tibald want Cyrn as his ally? So, Pitt didn't matter, only Cyrn did. That was why he hadn't used the arrest warrant. Tibald didn't need a band of conscripts to labour for him, just Cyrn to be a willing participant in Baron Hewett's army. His offer to recruit Cyrn *was* genuine, and he was working hard to get Cyrn to accept.

Rav racked his brain for more details about what Tibald had said. He knew Tibald had been targeting his mental vulnerabilities, but doing that to hurt him would anger Cyrn, worsening their relationship, which was the opposite of what the Champion wanted. If Tibald was trying to manipulate him, wouldn't he also try the same with Cyrn? What was Cyrn's weakness? No, that was wrong. What would Tibald *think* Cyrn's weakness was? Why did Tibald talk to him about the murder? Rav's eyes went wide as realisation struck. It was him. Tibald would think *he* was Cyrn's weakness. Cyrn had risked everything to save him after he'd murdered that garrison soldier, exposing that his love for his family triumphed over anything else.

Perhaps all this was only the start of Tibald's scheming. Rav thought about the questions Tibald had gotten him to ask himself. Where would he go if he entered self-exile? Was Tibald planning to offer him a place with Baron Hewett's army, hoping that if Rav accepted, Cyrn would go with him to protect him? Tibald was preying on Cyrn's love.

A rage Rav had never experienced before burned within him, coursing through his veins like lava. The desire to stab Tibald in the back nearly overwhelmed him, and it was only the thought of Cyrn that held him back.

Cyrn wanted to maintain an amiable relationship with Tibald so that they could take him by surprise when they escaped. Rav took a deep breath. Cyrn had also accepted Rav going on this hunt, giving Tibald direct access to his "weakness". Did he have faith that Rav would weather Tibald's scheming and report back to him so he could analyse Tibald further? Tibald thought he was gaining an advantage, when in fact Cyrn was only creating an illusion of vulnerability. It was hard for Rav to believe, but if it was his brother, then it could very well be true.

Returning to Pitt was quicker than heading out, even with Jingo's limp, as they no longer had to find tracks, soon cutting across Ghoul Wood from where they'd started their hunt to reach the hunters' hut Lyra was staying in. Rav slowed as they approached the door, ready to knock and wait, when Tibald simply threw the door open and barged inside.

Robert jumped from his chair, fists raised as he guarded his son, who'd been moved into a chair beside him in the far corner of the hut. Finn also jolted back in his chair with what little strength he had, only Lyra remaining calm, not even glancing in their direction as she continued focusing on concocting medicines on her table. Recognising Tibald, Robert lowered his fists before turning to stroke Finn's head, settling the boy.

Tibald shrugged Jingo onto Ronin, grabbed the mutant off his back, and beheaded it on the edge of the medicine table before carrying the bleeding head over to Finn and placing it on his lap. "This beast will never attack anyone again."

Rav shut the door behind them, glancing at Lyra. She tutted as the pool of thick blood trickled towards her, some dripping onto the floor, but maintained her plain expression.

"My most sincere and deepest thanks, Champion Sar." Robert bowed. "For Champion Sar to seek revenge on my son's behalf is an honour."

"I was aided by my companions," Tibald said, "Jingo Hook and Ronin Luke as well as Master Rav Carvell."

"I will remember your service."

"Tell me..." Finn wheezed, "Cham... pion... Sar."

Ronin stepped forward. "Champion Sar fought the beast in single combat out in the deepest depths of Ghoul Wood, slaying it with a single thrust."

"It's true," Jingo followed. "The mutant struck a lucky blow and managed to take me down; however, Champion Sar defended me from further attacks before stepping forward to challenge the beast alone."

"I was helped by Master Carvell, who threw a knife to force the beast into the open." Tibald looked to Rav.

Rav relented, too tired to enter another verbal spar. "Aye. Though I drew the beast out, I took a strike to my arm. Champion Sar killed the beast without suffering a single blow. I've never seen a technique like it; Champion Sar fights like three men."

Finn attempted to raise his good arm to bow, but he started to shake halfway, sweat dotting his brow.

"Do not move," Lyra warned. "If you weaken any further, you will lose a limb. Do either of you require my healing?" She looked at Rav and Jingo.

"I'm fine." Jingo waved her away.

"Aye, give me a look over." Rav wasn't happy with Tibald's dressing.

Jingo and Ronin snorted at him before looking to Tibald, who spoke, "We'll be taking our leave."

Ronin collected the mutant's carcass, and the three exited the hut.

# Chapter Eleven

When Rav looked to Finn and saw the awe in his eyes, he understood why Tibald had come here. It was all to do with his reputation. If anyone asked them what had happened, this was the story they'd tell, and who was most likely to check on them? Robert and Finn's co-workers from the Carvell logging site, which meant any favourable opinion of Tibald would inevitably reach Cyrn and his parents.

"If you'd like, I can have the head stuffed and mounted," Rav spoke to Robert.

He wanted to do something *genuinely* good for them, but Finn glared at the head and waved his hand.

"We don't want it," Robert said. "You've been generous enough, Master Carvell; the spoils of the hunt are yours." Robert returned his attention to Finn.

Rav nodded, then went to stand next to the medicine table, where he eased his sleeve up and peeled off the bandages. "Its claws cut through my furs. I've got three shallow wounds and one that's deeper." He presented his black-clotted arm to Lyra.

Lyra inspected the wounds, then leaned in and sniffed them before going to her medicinal vials. "I will clean them and redress you."

She retrieved a vial of clear liquid and returned to collect Rav's old bandages. Instead of throwing them away, she scraped the medicinal paste that Tibald had applied to them into a pot.

"You are lucky," Lyra murmured, avoiding his gaze. "This medicine is very strong. It will stop any infection."

Rav frowned. "How can you tell?"

"I can smell the herbs used." Lyra washed Rav's wounds with the clear liquid, causing him to squeeze his fist, the tendons in his arm writhing. She examined the wounds again after Rav's arm was clean. "These cuts should heal quickly; they are narrow and the deepest has only broken through your skin." Lyra opened a jar and pulled out fresh cloth.

"Aren't you going to sew it closed?" Rav spoke through gritted teeth.

"Bandages will be enough." She took her time to unspool the cloth, gazing between it and the pot, then she flicked her eyes towards Finn, catching Rav's attention.

"How good is this medicinal paste?" he asked.

"It is excellent. Pitt does not have anything like it." Lyra's voice lulled him. "With enough of it, you could leave a wound open and still not get sick. It even works on wounds that are already infected."

Rav looked at Finn's feverish temperament. "Give it to Finn," he ordered.

"Are you sure?" Lyra continued to avoid his gaze.

"Aye."

Lyra smiled and set the pot aside, then reached for another vial, which she smeared onto the bandages. Her hands moved quickly, and Rav soon had been rebandaged. He examined the dressing, finding it tight but not inflexible. This new paste felt thick, tingling on his skin, and smelled bitter. Next, she brought out more cloth and coated it in Tibald's paste.

She looked to Robert. "His arm or his leg?"

"Leg," Robert answered. "You need two legs to run."

Lyra cut off Finn's old bandages and wrapped the new ones around his thigh.

"*Ah.*" Finn tensed.

Robert rushed to comfort him.

"He will be fine." Lyra went to wash her hands in a bowl. "By the end of the night, any infection will be gone. Set the leg up and put a bucket under it to catch any fluid that dribbles out." She returned to wipe Rav's and the mutant's blood off the examination table.

Rav stared at her, feeling a niggling suspicion. Where would Tibald have obtained such powerful medicine, and if it had come from the Sink, then how had Lyra recognised it?

Lyra laughed to herself and shook her head.

"What's so funny?" Rav asked.

"It is not something you would understand," she replied. "If Tibald realised how he had behaved in front of me, he might get quite the shock. He is a child."

"A child? Are you someone important to be calling a Champion who has travelled the Sink a child?"

"No, I am not important, I just found his rudeness amusing. Seeing a child act like a child is always funny."

Rav laughed.

"Why are you now laughing?" she spoke. "You are an infant."

"An infant? I thought you were only joking at Tibald's expense."

"As you said, Tibald is a Champion who has travelled the Sink. You can only be an infant compared to that."

"But *I* haven't behaved like a baby," Rav protested.

Lyra laughed harder than before. "To... to hear a baby claim it is not a baby..." She calmed herself. "You have misunderstood the joke."

Despite Lyra laughing at him, Rav felt no contempt or hostility coming from her. "Can you explain the joke to me?"

"I cannot. I can only tell you that 'infant' is not an insult. Infants are not judged on what they have done, but on what they have the potential to do."

"You're right; I have no idea what you're talking about."

"Hopefully, that will not always be the case." Lyra smiled, lighting up the room. "One day, you might grow up and understand the joke. If you meet someone else like me then, perhaps you can laugh with them."

Rav sighed. He was having a difficult enough time trying to process Tibald's words, never mind whatever Lyra was talking about. He gathered his equipment and headed for the door, where he paused, unable to ignore the niggling suspicion that had wormed its way into his head.

"Lyra, why have you come to Pitt?"

"I am looking for something, but you do not need to worry—it has nothing to do with you or your people."

"You're a lone traveller?"

"I am."

"I hope that's true."

"And I hope that you think about my joke, Rav Carvell. The day you can laugh is the day you will see the world for what it is."


Rav clutched his wounded arm to stop it moving so much as he jogged out of Ghoul Wood, his spear and shield strapped to his back, hurrying to the Carvell House. Barging through the door, he set down his equipment beside the entrance and clomped down the hallway, arm stinging.

"Cyrn?"

"In here," Cyrn called from his bedroom, stepping out just as Rav arrived. "Come, we'll speak in private."

Rav peeked in at Enna seated facing away from him at the end of their bed, twirling some fur from their bed's cover around her finger. Cyrn shut the door behind him before leading Rav to a small living room at the end of the hallway that had been furnished with a square table and two high-back leather chairs like the ones their parents used, both facing a stone fireplace built into the wall. As Cyrn took his seat, he pointed for Rav to close the door, sealing them inside the cool gloom, only a shaft of pale light shining in through a circular, warped glass window set into the far wall. Door shut, Rav took his seat beside Cyrn and told him exactly what had occurred during the hunt, going as far as to describe as many of Tibald's expressions and mannerisms as he could remember.

"Thank you, Rav." Cyrn leaned forward as if to hug him but settled for patting his back upon seeing his wounded arm. "It can't have been easy. I only realised Tibald was specifically targeting me when he decided to take you along with him. I didn't have time to explain everything to you then."

"Did you know what Tibald was planning?"

"I knew he wanted to prove he could be trusted by taking care of you during the hunt and to show his commitment to his duties by slaying the mutant." Cyrn tapped his foot against the table leg. "I suspected he might try to make a good impression on you because if you spoke about him positively, it might have influenced my decision, but I knew you'd never fall for something like that. Still, I didn't know he had such a thorough understanding of *that* event. I'm sorry he put you through that."

"It's good news overall, though, isn't it?" Rav grinned. "We know what Tibald wants. You can pretend to have some interest in joining Tibald but keep on putting off leaving Pitt until we're ready to escape, then we'll disappear. Better still, if you do show some interest in joining Baron Hewett's army, Tibald might even tell you more about it in an attempt to impress you, making it easier for us to find any gaps past Stone's Way to slip through."

"That does sound good, doesn't it?" Cyrn murmured, turning away to stare at the cold ash lying in the fireplace.

"Aye." Rav stood and paced beside his chair. "And if Tibald keeps trying to get to you through me, I'm confident I'll be able to hold him off. That will give you more time to figure out how Baron Hewett's soldiers are positioned, right? I won't be your weakness; I'll be your strength."

"You already are my strength, Rav." Cyrn pressed his knuckles into the hard-leather armrests of his chair until they went white, voice trembling. "You were strong when I was weak, so it's my duty to be strong for you now."

The grin fell from Rav's face as he stepped back around to see Cyrn's eyes glistening with tears, never leaving the fireplace. "What's wrong? This is good news. Don't cry, please don't cry. I... I..." He held Cyrn's shoulder. "You never cry. Cyrn, what's wrong?"

Cyrn rubbed his eyes and wiped away his tears as though suddenly realising they shouldn't have been there. "Nothing." He smiled up at Rav. "It's just been a hard couple of days."

Rav spotted the strain at the corner of Cyrn's mouth, the emptiness in his gaze. "You can tell me if something's wrong. It's not about *that* event, is it? That was all my fault. It was my decision, my mistake, not yours."

Cyrn hardened his expression, all traces of sorrow wiped away. "It was *my* mistake, Rav. I should've been the one to do it, not you. How could I have stood by? Contender Warrit barged into *our* house, into *our* kitchen, and snatched *our* Ma by the hair as she ate breakfast, dragging her down the hallway screaming. And I stood watching in the kitchen doorway with Pa, only thinking about how doing anything other than standing there would tarnish our Name for breaking the law."

He shook his head. "How could I have possibly thought our ancestors would have been ashamed at my intervening?"

"That's not true and you know it," Rav huffed. "You were willing to let Ma get taken to preserve the righteousness and honour of the Carvell Name. Any one of us would happily suffer as long as our Name remained unblemished. When all of us are dead, our Name and its reputation will live on, either with our Bloodline or with our memory." He squeezed his fist. "Because of me, the Carvells might be seen as treacherous, murderous thieves."

"That doesn't matter," Cyrn snapped. "*I* should've borne the dishonour of killing him, not you. You were a child, my little brother, and it was my duty to protect you. Instead, I watched on as you sneaked up behind him and stabbed that kitchen knife into his neck. I failed you. I should've carried that burden, but instead, I let you do it, and it's crushing you."

"And what about afterwards?" Rav retorted. "Who was the one who chased out Contender Warrit's men? Who freed Pitt from their pillaging and saved townsfolk too scared of dishonouring their Names to fight back? Who formed the Ghoulsmen?" Rav held his brother's gaze. "Who faced Pitt's citizens for me? Who buried the bodies? Who cleaned the house and made everything appear to return to how it had been before?"

Cyrn dropped his head as he grumbled. "Everyone did that, not just me. Everyone in Pitt accepted some dishonour in ignoring what had happened. That's how strong the Carvell Name is, Rav; they were all willing to share that burden for us."

Rav stared at him a while longer, stomach sinking. How strong it *was*. Before he spoke further, Rav caught his tongue, skin suddenly prickling as a strange shiver wriggled through him, Cyrn's words overlapping with past memories of this conversation. This felt... wrong. Cyrn had told him about how he felt bad for not murdering that garrison soldier himself many times before and Rav had explained that he'd never wish for Cyrn to ever feel the way he did. Cyrn's words felt more like a re-treading of their past conversations than it did a real concern he currently had. Was Cyrn trying to hide what he was really crying about?

"We've been over this before." Rav pulled a weak smile. "Whatever we did back then, we can make up for by what we do now. If you need more help, tell me."

"Thank you for being my brother." Cyrn took a breath and slapped his thigh before standing, smile bright. "I'll be fine. Whatever comes next, know that I love you, and I'll do anything to protect you and our family."

"I will too, Cyrn. You're not alone... you're *never* alone. Whatever you need me to do, I'll do."

"I know you will." Cyrn ruffled Rav's hair. "You're a Carvell. Don't let anyone tell you otherwise."

Rav couldn't stop his shaking. Why did it feel as though something had gone horribly wrong?

Out the back of the Carvell House, Rav stood in a small training ground built between the building and the town wall, staring at the wooden, scarecrow-like training dummy opposite him. He raised his spear high before striking down as hard as he could. *Thwack*. Rav winced at the recoil but nothing else changed, the choking knot of emotions stuck in his gut unbroken. *Not hard enough*. As the training dummy shook in place, he squeezed the spear tighter, his hands aching, and struck again. *Thwack! Ah!* The sting had him hissing through his teeth, but still the knot remained, sitting in him like he'd swallowed a stone. *Coward*. He smacked the dummy's torso, *thwack*, this time unable to hold his spear any longer. He dropped his weapon, hands raw, and gazed at the darkening sky, forehead scrunched and jaw clenched. Cyrn was hiding a problem; it was obvious. So why… Rav dropped his head. Why couldn't he bring himself to force his brother to tell him what it was?

Why was everything always going wrong? Why was it that no matter how hard he tried to fix things, he was never able to?

The sky darkened further as evening set in. Rav watched the lengthening shadows, waiting for them to warp into the 'Zet Ar. He was going to have to watch as the Ghoulsmen figures were brutalised all over again despite his best efforts.

Blood pounding in his skull with every beat of his thumping heart, everything seemed to fade and blur around him as if a veil of fog had covered it all, sights of buildings smeared into dull streaks. Rav wiped his face and rubbed his eyes, but it all stayed bleary, the Carvell House somehow looking fragile, as though it could be torn like paper at any moment.

Turning away, he left his spear behind and started running, his feet turning on their own down faded streets, dashing past cheery faces of Pitt's townsfolk congratulating him on the hunt until he arrived at a familiar door with Blaine carved above it. Rav raised his hand and knocked.

"Rav." Kayla's expression dropped from joy into concern as she opened the door. "Are you alright?"

"I'm fine, I'm fine." Rav scratched his bandaged arm as a fierce itch set in, wincing as he rubbed too hard. "Can I come in?"

"Of course."

Kayla ushered him into the short entrance corridor before glancing around the lively streets at people muttering to each other about young love. After giving them a sheepish smile, she shut the door and guided Rav through to a small room with cushioned wooden chairs surrounding a square table, all set up beside a lit cooking fire. Rav slumped down in the chair closest to the flames and leaned over the table while Kayla lit a candle for better light.

"There's something wrong with Cyrn, and I don't know what it is," Rav groaned, voice shaking. "I made some progress with our escape plan today, thinking that I'd found a way out of the mess we're in, but then he... he started crying, Kayla. He treated my good news like it was the end of the world."

"Oh, Rav." She sat beside him and stroked his back.

Rav raised his head to gaze into her eyes, face pale and hanging. "I know you said you wanted to help more, so please help me because I don't know what to do."

Kayla reached out to hold his cheek in her palm, stroking it with her thumb as she gave him a gentle smile. "What kind of help do you want?"

Rav held her hand against his cheek as he leaned into its warmth. "Can you tell me about what's been going on in town? Just for now. I... I need to know that what I'm doing matters."

"Aye, I can do that. The most recent news is that Ronin Luke has been going around town telling tales of Champion Sar's victory against the mutant badger and about how you were the one to draw it into the open." She leaned close to whisper in his ear. "You're a hero, Rav. You helped kill the monster that attacked poor Finn."

Rav released her hand as he shook his head. "Is there anything else? I don't want to have to think about Tibald."

"Hmm..." Kayla leaned back and touched her bottom lip, her dark eyes gleaming. "A maid from Franz's Tavern is being courted by a miner."

Rav broke into a cheeky smile as he watched her. "Oh?"

"He travels to see her at the end of his shift every day and always brings her a gift. Yesterday, he had a shiny stone, and the day before that, he brought flower petals..."

Rav pulled Kayla out her chair and onto his lap, leaning her back against him, his arms wrapped around her waist as he listened.

"Rumour is, she's starting to like him despite her cold behaviour. The other maids think he's sweet, though they do wish he'd wash before coming to the tavern; apparently, he has quite the smell after his shift."

Rav rested his chin on her shoulder. "I wish my life was like that."

"You want a reputation for smelling bad?" Kayla laughed.

Rav tutted. "No, not that part. I meant the part where he can solely focus on her. He probably thinks about her all day during work and then rushes to see her once his shift is over. I want that for us. I want to finish work in the pelt shops and come running to you.

"My Pa used to tell me and Cyrn about how he would carve small pieces of wood into flowers or birds as gifts for my Ma when he was courting her. He told us time and time again how honoured he was to court her and how much he wanted to join with her Carvell Bloodline to become part of its ancestry. The Carvell lineage was so special to him, and I want to share that with you."

"Rav…" Kayla turned to face him, noses touching, breath tickling.

"So many other Names have joined under the Name Carvell, all bound within the sacred ceremony of marriage. It's… humbling." Rav dropped his gaze. "It's my duty to carry their legacies onward, but I'm failing, Kayla. I don't have the time to carve you flowers or visit you every day. We might not even be able to get married in Pitt, and if we do, it won't be the grand celebration of Carvell traditions that it should be. We won't be free to enjoy ourselves or excited for our future together; we'll be preparing to flee Stone's Way and face the dangers of the outside world."

"I don't love you for your traditions, Rav; I love you because of who you are. Our lives are messy now, but one day they won't be, and we'll have everything we want. We just have to wait a bit." Kayla's eyes shone as though she could see that future. "We're going to get married and have children, then we'll watch them grow up and fall in love themselves. Nothing is more important than that. You bring me safety and hope, which are the greatest gifts you could ever give. You never have to worry that what you're doing doesn't matter. It will *always* matter to me." She leaned down, cupped his face, and kissed him deeply.

Rav held the moment for as long as he could before he broke into a burst of giggles, smiling so wide it started to ache.

"I take it you're feeling better," Kayla cooed.

"I couldn't not be after that." Rav gazed into her eyes. "Do you have any solutions to my Cyrn problem?"

"Enna's not been feeling well lately." Her voice went soft. "Cyrn might be worried about her, and with all the stress Tibald's causing, maybe he couldn't keep suppressing his concern."

Rav went wide-eyed as he grabbed Kayla's shoulders. "How sick is she?"

"It's not too bad." Kayla patted his hand. "She's just nauseous. I think that's why her appetite has been odd recently."

"I didn't know." Rav dropped his hands back to her waist and shook his head. "I've been..."

"Focusing on your own problems."

"Aye. I'll visit her tonight to check on her."

"And then you need to wash and sleep." Kayla leaned in once more but brushed past Rav's lips to his ear. "You know I think you're handsome, but with the dark circles under your eyes and the grime on your skin from Ghoul Wood, your good looks are getting hard to see."

Steps lighter, Rav exited Kayla's house with a goofy grin, his breath easy now that part of the tangled, crushing knot in his gut had loosened. Heading east, he stopped by Aunt Judy's to make sure she was alright and to thank her for her help in Ghoul Wood.

Perched on the side of her bed, she pinched his cheek with a satisfied smile. "That was all you, silly boy, but it's good to know you're taking on board some of my common sense."

Heading home in the setting sun, the long shadows pooling through Pitt started to twist, calling him to battle the 'Zet Ar with their phantom voice. Rav kept his eyes on the streets ahead as he fought to ignore them, hurrying home before the shadows completed their transformation into the great braying beast. Inside the candlelit hallway, Rav shut the door behind him and readied to dash upstairs when soft humming caught his ear. Enna's voice. After slapping his cheeks, he strode towards her room and knocked on the closed door, flinching back as the shadow his fist cast over the wood by flickering candlelight grew wicked horns.

The humming stopped. "Come in," Enna called.

Rav eased the door open to see Enna sitting up alone in bed with the fur covers over her legs, sewing square sections of hide together with thread. While larger than his room, the simplicity remained the same, two wardrobes set against the back wall along with a large chest at the foot of the large bed. Opposite the bed sat a wooden desk littered with paper slips and beside it was a small alcove containing a chamber pot and washbasin.

"Cyrn's at the Council Chambers," Enna said as she set the hide aside to face him, somewhat wistful yet melancholic.

"I came to see you." Rav wiped his sweaty hands on his legs. "How are you? I'm sorry I didn't notice your illness earlier; with Tibald and the hunt, I haven't been paying attention to much else."

Enna's face glowed with delight, its homely warmth revitalised in full as she smiled at him. "Aye, I know how hard you're working for us." The hand resting on her lap twitched.

"I'm alright, Rav; you don't have to worry about me. It's just a bit of nausea and dizziness from something off I ate. A few more days resting like this, and I'll be healthy again." She suddenly grimaced and clutched her gut, glancing at the chamber pot. "Now, I'll need some privacy. Goodnight, Rav. And thank you for checking on me."

As she stood, the shadows on her face warped, the face of the 'Zet Ar cast over it. Rav flinched back, nodded goodnight, then darted out and upstairs to seal himself in his room.

Lying in bed, Rav watched as the shadows came to life on the wall opposite him, the Ghoulsmen figments appearing standing in formation ready to fight the monster towering above them. After taking a moment to gather his focus, Rav began.

*Scatter*, he commanded, and all the Ghoulsmen except himself dispersed to flank the charging 'Zet Ar.

The beast committed itself to trampling Rav's shadow. Cyrn and Wakeman thrust their spears into its back leg, but as usual, it did nothing to slow it down. This was the important part, the part where his timing had to be perfect.

*Dive*, Rav screamed in his mind at his shadow. Would the mutant still clatter into it like it always did? His shadow obeyed, launching itself out the 'Zet Ar's way in a great leap. This time, the 'Zet Ar only made contact with his trailing legs.

*Crack*. Though they were just shadows, Rav heard his shadow's bones break. But it hadn't died. Rav pumped his fist. While his shadow's legs were mangled, it was still crawling. It was the first time any figment had survived the 'Zet Ar's charge.

Rav ordered the remaining Ghoulsmen to continue attacking the 'Zet Ar's back leg, and Cyrn managed to thrust into the same place he had before, this time breaking through the 'Zet Ar's hide. It bleated, and Rav stared with elation. Then the 'Zet Ar used its superior speed to retreat from Cyrn before turning around to charge once more. This time, Rav's timing was off, and Thorley's shadow dissipated into nothing. Then

Tido's, then Tobias'. Cyrn and Wakeman banded together, but nothing changed. The mutant carried out another massacre. Even wounded, it had still won. Rav panted in the dark.

# Chapter Twelve

Rav tried to sleep in, but his arm ached like a rotten tooth and kept waking him up. He peeked under his bandages and saw that the cuts had already scabbed over, determining that it was just sore rather than infected. He lay on his back, staring at the ceiling, thinking about what it would take to beat the 'Zet Ar. Those distracting the 'Zet Ar needed to survive at least one charge each. If he spread the Ghoulsmen out further, he could give Cyrn and Wakeman's figures more time to attack the mutant, and from there, they'd at least have a chance to kill it. All it would cost was everyone else's lives. Rav gritted his teeth and thumped his fist into his feather mattress, staring up into the dark but finding no new answers. How could he? He already knew the truth. If they fought the 'Zet Ar, people would die.

Seeing the dark lightening with dawn, Rav swung his legs off his bed and headed downstairs to the kitchen. The long central table was lined with benches on either side and had five bowls on it, Benji stirring a large pot of flour and oats with water into a thick gloop over a cooking fire at the back.

"Morning, Rav," Benji called, voice bright.

"Aye, morning," Rav grunted, taking his place and handing Benji his bowl. After filling it, Benji handed it back, Rav thanking him before picking up a spoonful, blowing on it until it no longer steamed, then eating, bland but hot porridge warming his stomach.

"Morning, Rav." Enna entered the kitchen with a yawn. "Did you not sleep again?"

He swallowed another spoonful of porridge. "Not really. Are my eyes bloodshot?"

"Aye." Enna sat at the table and handed Benji her bowl after greeting him. "You're starting to look like a ghoul."

Rav pulled a half-smile. "I've got yellow eyes and rotting skin, do I?"

"Nearly." Enna laughed as she received her filled bowl back and started eating.

Rav watched her for a moment, noting her clear eyes and easy demeanour. "You seem much better today."

"Oh, I'm not better yet, but I need to eat if I want to recover. You should eat too; your cheeks look a little thin."

"It's good to see you both eating well." Cyrn joined them at the table, kissing Enna as he sat next to her. "Thanks, Benji," he said as he received his bowl of oats.

Benji used a poker to disperse the coals in the fire, then lifted the pot off its hook and set it on a blackened patch of stone beside the fireplace. "If your parents arrive while I'm away, tell them I'm just lighting the fire in the office." He stepped out as Cyrn nodded.

Rav stifled a yawn with his hand before rubbing his face in an attempt to energise it. "I didn't know Enna was ill. You should've told me, Cyrn."

Cyrn dropped his spoon on the table with a clatter as he jolted in his seat. "Hmm?"

"My illness, dear." Enna stroked his arm, glancing at Rav, who'd snapped his head towards the noise. "You know, the reason why I'm taking time off work. I told Rav that the Healer said my nausea would pass."

"Ah, right." Cyrn settled back down and scratched his chin. "Who told you Enna was ill?"

Rav squinted at him uneasily. "Kayla."

"Did she say anything else?"

"No."

"Well, as Enna said, her nausea should pass soon; it's nothing to worry about."

"I was just telling Rav that he looks like a ghoul," Enna interjected before Rav could speak.

Cyrn focused on Rav and nodded. "He does. You're not taking being part of the Ghoulsmen too seriously, are you?" He faced Enna. "What was the story?"

"Out from the swamps of Ghoul Wood crawled the desiccated corpses of Pitt's dead to devour those who'd slain them." Enna shrugged. "Something like that anyway."

Cyrn eyed Rav. "The dead can't do anything, only the living can. Stories are just stories. Get some sleep. Keep well." Staring at his porridge, he smirked. "But maybe I should tell Tibald about it; it's a good warning of what happens to those who harm Pitt."

Enna changing the subject hadn't gone unnoticed by Rav. He watched Cyrn eat a mountain of food like normal, failing to find any trace of his earlier alarm.

Benji walked in holding a piece of card. "Tibald Sar has invited you all to a feast tonight to celebrate the hunt," he announced, handing Cyrn the card. "He's also invited your parents and Kayla."

Rav scowled. "I can't deal with more of his scheming. Does he ever rest?"

"It was nice of Tibald to invite Kayla for you, though," Enna commented.

"No, it wasn't. He probably wants to toy with her like he toyed with me. It's all plans within plans."

"What did I tell you?" Cyrn thumped the table with his palm. "I'll handle Tibald. You can enjoy your evening with Kayla."

Rav pulled a fake smile in thanks. After seeing Cyrn crying yesterday and his strange behaviour this morning, he wasn't so sure he could.

Rav met with Kayla in another dusty storehouse filled with grain to continue preparing food for their escape and told her about the feast.

"Do you think Tibald knows about our custom after successful hunts?" Kayla asked.

"I'm sure he does. This whole evening is going to be about him ingratiating himself with us. I can only hope that he gets some part of the ritual wrong, but I doubt that's going to happen." Rav pinched between his eyes. "He'll also have another purpose for hosting this event, which we'll have to figure out. Don't believe anything he says."

"I won't."

After they'd finished, Rav and Kayla headed to the Carvell House to get ready for the feast. Once Kayla had changed into her black silk dress that shimmered in the light, she helped dress Rav in his Carvell ceremonial robe, which was made from melted coins that looked like scales. Purple flowers and vines were stitched over its surface, running up either side of his sternum before leading down each sleeve, with wide cuffs hanging from his wrists.

"Seeing you like this makes me even more excited for our wedding," Kayla commented as she ensured all the stitching ran in line. "I can't wait for you to dress up in celebration of me."

"I'll look even better to celebrate our marriage; I'll polish the scales until I glimmer." Rav smiled. "And you'll be wearing one of these as well. We'll get to shine together."

Kayla traced his chin as they gazed at each other.

"Are you ready?" Healanor called.

"Aye," Rav shouted back.

They arrived downstairs to see Cyrn, Enna, Senior Carvell, and Healanor all dressed in their ceremonial robes.

"Let's go." Cyrn led them to the Council Chambers.

The Council Chambers consisted of large halls filled with various tapestries depicting Pitt and Stone's Way, some of which dated back to when their ancestors first settled here, all lit by chandeliers. At the end of the ground floor were stairs leading up towards the meeting room Tibald was using to host the celebration. As Rav watched his family climb the stairs, he noticed how much Kayla stood out in her black dress, the lone pool of darkness among the shimmering gold. Rav winced. It wasn't fair for her to stand out like this. The sooner she joined the Carvell Bloodline, the sooner she'd receive her own robe and then everyone would see her glimmer.

"Welcome," Tibald greeted them at the top of the stairs, dressed in a black formal robe. "Thank you all for coming."

"Thank you for inviting us," Senior Carvell said. "It smells delicious."

"I've prepared a special meal for us with some of the provisions I brought with me." Tibald directed them inside the room. "Once my trade caravan arrives, I'll be able to share food like this with all of Pitt."

A long table had been set up in the centre of the dining room, adorned with a tablecloth and candles. Servants rushed in and out of a side room from where the succulent scent was coming from.

"I can't wait to try it," Senior Carvell spoke.

Cyrn looked at the empty seats. "Where are Jingo and Ronin?"

"They're helping the cooks at the moment but will be joining us for the feast." Tibald puffed out his chest, chin slightly raised in an attempt to appear dashing as he guided them forward, voice dripping with forced charm. "I believe it's customary for *all* those who participated in the hunt to be celebrated."

"Oh? You know our customs?" Healanor asked.

"I hope so. It would be a shame to miss anything out." Tibald laughed, and Healanor laughed with him.

Rav's stomach churned as he watched Tibald's performance. How his parents managed to speak to Tibald without grimacing baffled him. Kayla tapped Rav's foot with hers, and he forced a smile, as though he'd found Tibald's remark amusing.

Tibald led them to the table, where he'd allocated seats for everyone. Tibald was seated at the head, with Cyrn and Enna to his right and Jingo and Ronin to his left. Rav sat opposite the Champion, Kayla to his right and his parents to his left. He tried not to glare as he faced Tibald.

"How's your arm, Rav?" Tibald asked. "Is it healing well?"

"Aye." Rav touched it. "Lyra's bandaged it well."

"Excellent. I was very impressed by what you did for young Finn. I didn't have enough medicinal paste to give him any at the time, but I returned to Lyra's hut this morning to offer him some, only to learn that you'd already given him your own."

Rav's parents looked at him with pride; however, he had to stop himself wriggling with revulsion. Tibald was only highlighting Rav's good deed so that he could tell everyone about what he'd done without seeming as if he were self-aggrandising. Kayla tapped Rav again under the table.

"I couldn't have given Finn my paste if you hadn't gifted it to me in the first place," he responded.

"It was a generous act. You've raised a fine young man," Tibald spoke to Rav's parents. "My medicinal paste is made from herbs that only grow in the Sink, so not only is it rare, it's also very effective. It can prevent infection as well as remove any infection that has already set into a wound."

Rav massaged his temples. If Tibald was going to keep selling the Sink to them, it was going to be a very long evening. Jingo and Ronin soon came out of the kitchen dressed in the same attire as Tibald and took their seats, finally bringing a halt to Tibald's tirade about how great the Sink had been for medical advancements.

"Let's begin the celebrations," he announced. "To a victorious hunt."

"To a victorious hunt," everyone followed, bowing to the table.

Four servants placed small plates with badger meat in front of Tibald, Rav, Ronin, and Jingo. They all tucked in barehanded, each racing to scoff down the food.

"Champion Sar is first," Senior Carvell announced as Tibald swallowed his last piece of meat.

Rav gulped down the last of his food, coming second, followed by Ronin, then Jingo.

"You know our custom very well," Healanor spoke to Tibald.

"I enjoy learning the practices of the places I travel to," he replied. "I believe this ritual is to remind us that we too are beasts and can be devoured just as quickly by the prey we hunt."

"Indeed." Healanor nodded. "Thank you for taking the time to learn our ways. It's been years since an outsider bothered."

Tibald smiled. "Thank you for having such a rich history for me to study."

Kayla leaned towards Rav. "You're making that face again," she whispered. "Hide your scowl. Tibald has been nothing but pleasant."

"No, he..." Rav took a breath. "I'll try to do better."

The first dish was a sweet carrot soup and the second was a blend of meats rolled in thin pastry with a sweet dipping sauce, served alongside an assortment of fried vegetables. Rav suffered through bouts of people telling Tibald that the food was amazing followed by the Champion explaining how he'd come across the recipe or a specific ingredient in a certain part of the Sink during his travels. The worst part was that the food *was* spectacular. No matter how much Tibald droned on, Rav found himself smiling as he discovered another delicious flavour. If Tibald planned to win over Pitt by using his coming caravan to feed them, he might just succeed.

The conversation waned as the last dish, a hot cheese that melted in the mouth, was served and eaten.

"I trust you've all enjoyed yourselves," Tibald said.

"Aye," everyone clamoured, banging the table.

"I'm glad." Tibald brought his hands together. "I hope Pitt can enjoy food like this every day in the future. But I haven't just invited you all here to celebrate a successful hunt, I also have something I wish to discuss with you. I know I've talked a lot about the wonders of the Sink, but as you already know, the Sink *is* a dangerous place. Your fears are based on some truth."

Everyone shuffled uncomfortably.

"Rest assured, I'm not going to conscript you or any other such nonsense—I am not those who came before me." Tibald paused. "Perhaps it's best to start by telling you why Baron Hewett is staying at Greenfield..." He pursed his lips. "Our recent expedition through the Sink ended because Baron Hewett was defeated; however, the reason we lost is not because we were lacking in strength or strategy, it's because we ran out of supplies. The Sink *is* filled with resources, but the abundance of mutants and other armies makes settling down in an area to mine stone and ore for constructing fortresses very difficult. Which is why Baron Hewett, in alliance with a dozen other Barons, has decided to set up an enormous supply line into the Sink.

"This supply line will require the people guarding it to remain *outside* the Sink and will also require miners, loggers, and stitchers to keep working so that we can transport their produce into the Sink. Once we establish a foothold to gather resources from the Sink, we can start sending things, such as food, back here. Those who wish to keep away from the Sink can, and those who want to compete for the Sink's resources can still benefit from their help."

"You want to turn Stone's Way into a garrison," Cyrn murmured.

"Yes, Stone's Way's unique terrain would make it an excellent garrison, but rest assured, the soldiers staying here would be managed by a Baron who would stay with them to keep them under control. There won't be a repeat of previous events."

Rav tensed, but everyone's attention went to Healanor, whose breathing turned shallow until Senior Carvell held her hand. While she remained pale, her breath steadied.

"Your lives would return to the way they were before the Sink," Tibald continued. "You'd have soldiers all around you to defend your home and wagons waiting to buy all your produce. Pitt would be safe and rich. Is that not what you want?"

Rav clenched his fist beneath the table, teeth grinding against each other. Wasn't Tibald basically asking them to become slaves in their own home, where they'd work while guarded to produce goods under the promise that one day they'd get paid in food? Having seen so many soldiers, and even Ronin, call them slaves, Rav didn't believe for a moment that they'd be treated fairly. Instead of marching into Pitt to arrest them all, Tibald wanted them to build their own prison around themselves. And what would happen when Barons lost their soldiers? What would this supply line be used for then? They'd conscript soldiers from Pitt, just as they'd planned to do before.

Tibald could never be trusted with their lives no matter how many mutants he hunted or how many feasts he held. Rav looked around himself and flinched upon seeing his family seeming to be seriously considering Tibald's proposal. Surely, they were just playing along, right? Rav hoped that was true, but there was something in their frowns that told him they weren't. Even Cyrn was deep in thought. He shivered.

"It's a lot to think on, I know," Tibald spoke. "I don't need your answer now. You're welcome to meet with others in Pitt to discuss my plan and I'll be available to answer questions during my stay here."

"Thank you," Cyrn said. "I think we'd best head home to talk about this."

"As you wish." Tibald grinned from ear to ear.

Rav pulled Cyrn into a side room as soon as they got back to the Carvell House.

"You can't be considering this." He grabbed Cyrn by his collar. "*Everything* Tibald's promised relies on us trusting him, and he's proven time and time again that he *can't* be trusted."

Cyrn's voice was calm. "Tibald's not asking us to trust him, Rav."

Rav frowned. What had he missed? "Then his plan doesn't make any sense. Who's going to make sure the garrison doesn't take over Pitt? Who's going to ensure we actually get paid? Who's going to watch out for us?"

Rav noticed the glisten in Cyrn's eyes as tears welled.

"You?" Rav's frown deepened. "But you'd have to have the same authority as Tibald, and the only way to get that would be..." Rav shook his head with a snarl. "No, that can't be. I won't let you do it."

Cyrn's temperament stayed even. No, Rav was wrong. It was suppression. Cyrn was straining to keep himself stoic. "Tibald had a similar plan for you when he told you to go into exile. I'm sure this is just the first part of his offer," Cyrn whispered, the tremble building within him unable to be hidden any longer.

"Tibald's going to tell me that if I join Baron Hewett in the Sink, I'll be able to protect Pitt."

Rav loosened his grip, face contorted in imploring pleading. "Then let's run away. The Sink's too dangerous for you to consider going there. You'll die, and when you do, we'll all be enslaved anyway. Fight with us on the road. Fight to help us all escape."

Cyrn's voice wobbled. "I might not be able to run, though, Rav."

"Why not?"

Cyrn took a breath as fat tears rolled down his cheeks. "Because Enna's not sick... she's pregnant."

# Chapter Thirteen

Rav froze as a thousand fears stormed his mind. Enna would have to stay in Pitt to give birth and recover, then the baby would have to grow strong enough to travel. Cyrn would never leave her behind—no Carvell or any of the Ghoulsmen would. None of them could escape until Enna was ready, and without them to lead, no one from Pitt would go. They were trapped here. The Sink, Baron Hewett, Tibald—they'd all ruined something supposed to be special.

Rav felt his own tears welling but stopped them before they fell. Cyrn wouldn't see them fall. No one would. Any coming child was something to be celebrated, but a child of the Carvell Bloodline, a child who'd be his niece or nephew, a child who'd further the Carvell legacy deserved so much more. None of this was that child's fault, and Rav refused to show any sorrow for its existence.

"It's already been a few months," Cyrn continued. "Enna can't run around avoiding enemy soldiers. It's too much of a risk for the baby. Even now, she should be being tended to by a Healer, but I can't have one around her, or Tibald will figure out what's going on. He can't know about this." Cyrn held Rav by the shoulders. "You know how insidious he is—he'll threaten my child and force me into obeying him. That cannot happen."

"It's not going to," Rav swore.

Cyrn squeezed Rav's shoulders harder. "How, though? How can we hide it? Enna's eating as much as she can to prepare for the birth and to hide future signs of her pregnancy, but that's not going to work forever."

"Easy, Cyrn." Rav struggled out of his grasp. "I don't have an answer now, but I will find one. *We* will find one."

"There's only one solution I can see," Cyrn stated. "If I agree to join Tibald now, I can leave Pitt with him, and he'll never find out about my child. He won't be able to threaten them, then. We've got a favourable deal with Tibald now because he doesn't think I have any exploitable weaknesses, so we must keep it that way. I can protect us all—"

"You're not going to the Sink," Rav snapped. "Do you want your child to grow up without you?"

"Better that than not having them grow up at all."

"What kind of thinking is that? You'd let your child get raised as a slave?"

"That's only if I die."

"Which you will."

"Then you find another way out of this mess," Cyrn huffed.

"First of all," Rav hissed through gritted teeth, jabbing Cyrn in the chest with a pointed finger, "Enna being pregnant is not a 'mess', it's a blessing. Don't you ever forget that. Secondly, what's the point of us fighting for a peaceful life if not for our families? Everything we do is for our Bloodline. Condemning the Carvell lineage to slavery is unacceptable. And lastly, if you're going to risk your life for us all, you'd better make it count. Becoming another corpse in the Sink changes nothing." Rav caught his breath. "You're going to be a father. Have some pride."

"*I am proud*," Cyrn yelled.

"Then act like it."

They stared at each other, faces taut with anger.

Cyrn was the first to look away, his snarl fading into solemnity. "There is another option," he muttered. "Only Enna and I need to stay in Pitt. Wakeman's good enough to—"

Rav snorted. "Don't even bother. What would you say if I was in your position? We're family; I'll never leave you behind. We're not going to put Enna or your child in danger by running, so we'll stay here until we can all travel together. That's the plan now. Somehow, we'll make it until after Enna's given birth and recovered, then we'll all head out with our new baby Carvell."

Cyrn locked eyes with Rav once more, but the fight had left him. "Thank you."

Rav dropped his head to stare at the floorboards, a twisted knot of joy and guilt writhing in his chest. "You don't need to thank me. You've already risked your life so many times for me, now it's my turn to do the same for you."

Rav stayed up deep into the night, staring at the shadow of the 'Zet Ar. Staying in Stone's Way increased the chances they'd encounter the mutant, so he desperately tried to think of a way to defeat it without having to sacrifice anyone, but he was unable to. When the battle finally commenced, he opted for the same strategy as last night, where the Ghoulsmen split up to give Cyrn and Wakeman's figures time to attack it; however, the scenario didn't play out as it had before. The 'Zet Ar targeted Cyrn's shadow from the start of the battle, and once it had killed him, it focused on Wakeman. It countered Rav's strategy as though it had expected it. Rav's mouth went dry. As though it had learned from Rav's previous attempts. The 'Zet Ar took no injuries as it massacred them all.

The mutant bleated in victory yet again, and when it did, Rav felt as if the shadow were looking straight at him, gloating. With no clues as to why these visions had started, he'd made no progress in understanding why they were happening to him, but tonight was the first time it occurred to him that he might not be fighting by himself. Was it possible that someone or... something was controlling the 'Zet Ar? Just as Rav was practising fighting it, was it practising fighting the Ghoulsmen?

These visions had begun the day he'd first found traces of the 'Zet Ar, so it *was* likely that they were connected. Had the beast formed some kind of bond with him, or was something else guiding them to fight each other? Was there a way for him to find out? Cyrn was too busy and didn't know much about the Sink, which left Tibald, who could never be trusted with knowing something like this. Who else was there?

...Lyra.

If Lyra really was from the Sink, then perhaps she would know what was happening to him. He didn't know anything about her, but she was his best option. Now, he just needed to find some time to talk to her.

Rav spent the second half of the night thinking about Enna's pregnancy. He tossed from side to side in his bed, unable to get comfortable. He was going to be an uncle and he was going to have to deal with Tibald Sar for much longer because of it. He'd assured Cyrn that everything would be alright, but would it? They were now stuck in limbo, having to delay leaving while hiding Enna's pregnancy from Tibald, which seemed impossible. Conflict was inevitable, but what choice did they have? Rav already loved his coming niece or nephew, and he was never going to let Cyrn sacrifice himself for Pitt, so this was the only way forward.

The part that made it all so horrible was that he was getting his wish. He'd wanted to stay in Stone's Way longer and now he was going to. Rav got up and punched a wall. *Thud*. Why were all his good intentions being warped? Why couldn't anything ever go well? He was trying so hard, but all his effort was wasted.

*"Silly boy,"* the memory of Aunt Judy chided him.

Rav rubbed his tender knuckles. What would she say right now? Probably something like, "Your effort hasn't been wasted, Rav. If things are falling apart *with* you trying, imagine how bad they'd be if you weren't."

Then there was Kayla. She'd also be in danger if they lingered here, but he knew she'd be just as willing to protect Cyrn's child, who would also become her niece or nephew. Safety and hope were the gifts he had to keep giving. As the outside dangers encroached, it was his duty to stand tall before them, and maybe if he managed to protect the Carvell Bloodline, his ancestors would forgive him for dishonouring them.

# Chapter Fourteen

Rav woke late, body aching, exhaustion catching up. Peeling himself from his bed, he hurried downstairs to eat cold porridge before heading into town, the sun already halfway towards its peak. Was seeing Lyra the right decision? He rubbed his eyes as he paced along the street to the western gate, Ghoul Wood laid out beyond it, when a commotion caught his ear from across town, seeming to come from the main, northern gate. Rav set off running over, raised voices becoming clearer as he arrived.

"Get out my way," a man with an oily accent snarled. "Someone as filthy as you standing in the way of someone like me should be a crime."

A man with bronze skin and braided black hair dressed in full-plate armour was sneering down at Pitt's gate guards from horseback. Behind him rode two men and a woman dressed in copper-green scale armour, the men's black hair like their leader's, while the woman was bald, with sharp features.

"Then answer me, who are you, and why have you come to Pitt?" the old guard demanded, standing firm.

"He is Contender Greeshe Pattik," the woman announced. "Here to Challenge Champion Tibald Sar and become Baron Hewett's new Champion."

"So, get out my way," Greeshe followed. "I'm going to kill Tibald and claim my place at Baron Hewett's side, which means I'll be *your* Champion. You don't want to annoy me, do you?"

"Get down from your horse and show our townsmen some respect," Rav yelled.

Greeshe faced him. "And who are you?"

Rav met his gaze. "Rav Carvell, brother of Elder Cyrn Carvell."

Greeshe snorted. "I've never heard of you, and seeing as neither you nor your brother have the Contender title, why don't you shut up and step aside?"

Rav laughed. "Do I need to remind you that since it seems you're not currently part of Baron Hewett's army, if you harm any of us, you'll have attacked his citizens and will be arrested by him? And besides, it's four of you against my entire town; you'll die long before you step into the arena with Tibald." Rav stepped up to him. "Why don't you get down from your horse, apologise for your rude behaviour, and then go politely request to kill Tibald."

"I'd listen to Rav if I were you, Greeshe."

Rav turned around to see Tibald sauntering over to them with Jingo and Ronin either side of him.

"He's one of Pitt's best fighters; I've personally witnessed his skills with a knife."

"Tibald." Greeshe grinned. "Do you know how far I've travelled to kill you?"

"You should've come from farther away. Now that your journey is at its end, so is your life," Tibald retorted. "Are you ready to duel today, Greeshe?"

"The sooner I become Champion, the better."

"Very well, let's fight when the sun is at its highest. The arena is over there, towards the mine." Tibald pointed. "Our duel will be overseen by Pitt's Elders."

Rav rushed to the Council Chamber, bursting into an office furnished like his Pa's, where Cyrn sat furrowed behind the desk, looking up from the papers he'd been reading.

"The man Tibald's going to duel is here," he panted. "He's going to Challenge Tibald today."

Cyrn rubbed his chin. "Already? Shouldn't he want to rest a day before the Challenge?"

"Maybe Greeshe is confident he'll win?" Rav paced in front of the desk. "What do we do if Tibald is killed? Greeshe doesn't seem as clever as Tibald, but he's much more arrogant. Also, how will Baron Hewett react? I've never seen a Challenge before; I don't know what to expect."

"I doubt Tibald will lose, especially after you told me how he fights." Cyrn leaned on his desk with his elbows. "I'm not sure what Tibald is planning here. Perhaps this is just a Challenge that he must face? But the timing is too coincidental with his proposal yesterday."

Rav shook his head. "He can't have planned the hunt, so he can't have planned the feast. I don't think Tibald could have coordinated all of this. Also, how would he have known when Greeshe was arriving?"

"That's true. We'll just have to see what happens, then."

Rav had to delay his visit to Lyra to spend his morning rushing around Pitt to help get everything ready for the Challenge. Tibald had spread news of the event through the town by having Jingo and Ronin go around telling everyone about it, and a huge crowd gathered near the mine in anticipation of the event, jostling and clamouring in excitement. It was rare for Pitt to host events like this, especially since the Sink had appeared, and its citizens were riled up for the upcoming Challenge. Reuben had constructed a makeshift arena by nailing posts into the ground in the shape of a large square, then wrapping several ropes around them to clearly mark its boundaries. A small podium had been built for the Challenge to be conducted from.

The Carvells dressed in their ceremonial robes and followed Cyrn to the arena in a procession, Kayla joining them from the crowd. Cyrn took his place standing at the podium, while his family stood beside him. The entirety of Pitt was bustling around them, discussing the upcoming event.

"They're talking about Greeshe," Kayla told Rav as she slid her hand into his. "He's treated everyone from Pitt like servants and is already hated. They all want to see him lose. Is his behaviour what you meant by outsiders looking at us with derision?"

"Aye, it is."

"Then let's hope he doesn't become Champion."

"Settle down," Cyrn's voice boomed, quelling the crowd. "Pitt is honoured to host the Challenge of Contender Greeshe Pattik for the position of Baron Hewett's Champion, currently held by Champion Tibald Sar. It's been more than thirty years since Pitt has held a Challenge, so let me remind you of its laws.

"Champion Sar and Contender Pattik will duel to the death within the confines of the arena. They are to fight with their own strength and *only* their own strength. Poison and other such methods of killing are banned. This is to be a contest of skill to decide who the superior fighter is. Anyone who interferes with the Challenge will be made Nameless, set to forever wander the world without a home or family. Is that clear?"

The crowd shuffled under the weight of Cyrn's words.

"Then let's begin the Challenge by welcoming contestants Champion Tibald Sar and Contender Greeshe Pattik."

Everyone turned to the town gates, where Champion Sar, in full-plate armour, led his retinue out towards them. Behind him came Contender Pattik with his guards. The crowd became riled up once more. Tibald and Greeshe entered the arena and stood before the podium, while their guards handed the weapons they would be fighting with to Cyrn for inspection.

"These are the weapons you intend to wield?" Cyrn asked the duellists as he sniffed, then wiped Tibald's spear and Greeshe's glaive, along with several daggers, on white cloth, checking for poison.

"They are," they replied.

"Do you swear on your Name that you will follow all laws of the Challenge?"

"I swear it by the Name Sar."

"I swear it by the Name Pattik."

"Take your weapons," Cyrn ordered, returning them to their owners. "This is a true Challenge for the position of Baron Hewett's Champion. Tibald Sar, do you acknowledge and accept?"

"I do."

Cyrn nodded. "Greeshe Pattik, do you give your life to make this Challenge?"

"I do."

"Then let your ancestors witness this Challenge and be made proud by your efforts."

They each took their places on either side of the arena, where Greeshe flourished his glaive.

"Are you nervous, Tibald? You should be." Greeshe stretched his neck. "Do you know how I learned that you were all the way out here in this little town? One of your own soldiers told me. That's right, you've been betrayed. One of your soldiers wants you gone, so he provided me with the opportunity to come here and Challenge you. Someone who isn't respected by the soldiers they lead is not worthy of being Champion to an Ah'ke, and I'll prove it by killing you."

"Your petty attempts to distract me will not work," Tibald responded. "I think everyone here can see who is unworthy."

"Who cares about the opinions of people no better than slaves?" Greeshe laughed. "When Baron Hewett takes me into the Sink, I'll become Ah'ke too. With such power, all but those like us will grovel at our feet."

The crowd gasped at his words.

Greeshe grinned, facing his audience. "*That* is your place, you just don't know it yet."

"*Enough*," Tibald barked. "You Challenged me, so accept the consequences."

Cyrn gazed at the two fighters. "Ready? *Fight*."

They dashed towards each other. Greeshe stabbed at Tibald's neck, the tip of his glaive aiming for the gap between Tibald's breastplate and helmet, but Tibald turned his body to the side, dodging the attack, then countered with a thrust to Greeshe's waist. Greeshe blocked Tibald's spear by pulling the glaive's butt back across his body before swiping the blade of his glaive in front of him to deter Tibald from advancing any further.

They stepped away from each other as the crowd roared. After taking a moment to size each other up, Tibald jabbed at Greeshe's knee before storming forward to push him back. Greeshe hurried to defend himself, retreating further to bait Tibald into overextending; however, Tibald had already retreated, using the ample space and time he now had to flourish his spear.

Rav shook his head in disbelief. "Is he...?"

"Aye," Cyrn answered.

Tibald swept out with his spear, smacking it against the shaft of Greeshe's glaive with a great *thwack*. Greeshe made to grab Tibald's weapon with his free hand yet was too slow, as Tibald was already following up the attack by swinging the spear butt into Greeshe's knee, forcing Greeshe to step back.

Tibald levelled his spear and thrust it directly into the centre of Greeshe's breastplate.

*Clank.*

From there, Tibald continued his assault, a relentless figure repeatedly slamming into Greeshe's armour.

*Clang. Clang. Clang.*

Greeshe attempted to break Tibald's momentum but proved too weak to divert Tibald's strikes and was forced to endure the barrage until, eventually, Tibald pulled back, and Greeshe could finally catch his breath.

"It's just a performance," Rav whispered. "Tibald's toying with Greeshe to show off his skills for the crowd; he's created a story where he's the hero defeating a villain for all of Pitt to see. Cyrn, I don't like where this is going."

"Neither do I."

The audience was frenzied, enraptured by Tibald's brutal domination. Tibald feigned going into another barrage, and once Greeshe retreated to avoid it, Tibald turned his back to him. The crowd laughed at Greeshe's humiliation. Greeshe hurried to cut Tibald behind his knee, but Tibald swatted the thrust aside without even looking. Greeshe tried moving faster, striking harder, his movements growing increasingly reckless. He snarled, throwing his full body weight behind each of his attacks, which Tibald simply dodged over and over again.

Rav shook his head.

Greeshe looked desperate. He struck a wide blow, opening himself up to a lethal attack, but Tibald hit Greeshe's leg instead. Greeshe slipped in the muck and collapsed in a heap. He rushed to his feet, only for Tibald to knock him down again, muddying his armour brown. The sequence repeated until Greeshe started wildly swinging his glaive at Tibald's legs. Tibald avoided every blow.

Panting in the muddy pit, Greeshe struggled to his knees, staring up at the man above him.

"Pathetic." Tibald's voice rang clear for all to hear as he watched Greeshe pull himself to his feet with his glaive.

"*Aahhh*," Greeshe roared as he flung himself forward.

Tibald used his incredible footwork to manoeuvre behind Greeshe and stabbed him through the back of the head. Pitt cheered as Greeshe's corpse flopped to the ground, but Rav shivered—the kill was no different than when Tibald had slayed the mutant.

Greeshe's guards rushed into the arena to kneel at his body, their wailing voices rolling through the air as they chanted in an unknown language.

Tibald removed his helmet, bowed to the corpse, then faced the townsfolk. "As long as I am your Champion, no one will dare to disrespect Pitt or its people. It is my duty and my honour to fight for you all. For as long as Baron Hewett rules Stone's Way, Pitt will be safe and Pitt will prosper."

The crowd cheered once again.

"We have to stop him," Rav hissed to Cyrn. "He's going to get Pitt's support. What if they believe in his proposal?"

"Quiet," Cyrn hissed back as Tibald approached the podium. He stood tall before Tibald and the crowd. "I hereby announce the victor of the Challenge to be Champion Tibald Sar."

The crowd bowed towards Tibald, completing the Challenge.

"Thank you for overseeing the Challenge," Tibald spoke to Cyrn. "I hope it has given you some idea of what I am capable of. Perhaps you can better see the validity of my proposal now?"

"Aye, I can better envision it."

"Excellent. By the way, I can teach you the manoeuvre I used for my last strike. Of course, I can only share the hard-won secret techniques I learned in the Sink with those who are part of Baron Hewett's army, but that does mean that *everyone* who joins us will get the opportunity to learn it." Tibald tilted his head to indicate the audience, voice going soft. "Every citizen of Pitt could use it to better defend themselves... if they agreed to become part of the garrison."

Cyrn nodded. "I see."

Tibald winked at Cyrn. "Think about it. I could benefit from your skills and you could benefit from mine. If the two of us fought together, we'd be unstoppable. I'll be resting in my quarters." He began walking back to Pitt. "Come talk with me sometime."

The crowd parted as he walked through them. Rav paled as he saw the amount of respect Tibald was being shown.

"Cyrn, what do we do?" he whispered.

"Nothing," he whispered back, still maintaining his decorum as the crowd bustled back to Pitt and they followed. "Although Tibald's managed to build a good reputation with our citizens, it's not to the point where they'll agree to join Baron Hewett's army, and they certainly won't accept a garrison being set up in Stone's Way."

Looking at the crowd's awed expressions and hearing their vibrant discussions about Tibald's charm and skill, Rav wasn't so sure anymore.

"Though," Cyrn grumbled, "the amount of progress Tibald's made in such a short time *is* unsettling. He likely wants to use others to influence my decision, hoping I'll be swayed by a large enough crowd, but that won't work. No matter how much food or entertainment he brings to Pitt, I trust our people to listen to me, not Tibald."

Was that the same trust Rav had to have when watching his family listen to Tibald's stories? Perhaps trusting each other was all they could do.

Cyrn patted Rav on the back, then joined the crowd heading back to Pitt, adding his own remarks about Tibald's devious fighting techniques to the conversation. Rav watched Cyrn subtly imprint the idea of Tibald being deceitful among those around him with nothing but a few choice words. His brother was doing his work, and he had his own to attend to. Rav set off to Ghoul Wood to find Lyra.

# Chapter Fifteen

It was mid-afternoon when Rav reached the edge of Ghoul Wood. He paused to scratch his itching arm. Was Lyra really from the Sink? Maybe she'd recognised Tibald's medicine from somewhere else. And what if she *was* from the Sink? What if she was another one of those blind fanatics who was only hiding her greed? He hadn't sensed any hostility from her, but that didn't mean she had none. Though, she had been working as a Healer and he'd witnessed the care she'd taken when helping him and Finn. Rav took a breath as he thought out a plan. He'd pretend to be visiting because of his wounded arm, then mention the 'Zet Ar to test how she would respond to him. If she knew something and didn't turn crazed, then he could ask her about the visions he was experiencing.

He hurried into the trees, stopping once he reached Lyra's hut.

"Come in," Lyra called after he knocked on the door.

Rav entered the hut and hurried to shut the door behind himself. Robert and Finn had returned to their home in Pitt after Finn had begun recovering, leaving Lyra alone. Lyra's face and Healer robes were freckled with flecks of mud, her hair matted with sweat, yet Rav couldn't help but gawp at her beauty as his every thought scattered.

"Is your wound healing well?" Lyra asked. "You should not need another dressing."

"Aye, m-my arm is fine," he stammered. "Thank you for helping me."

*Ah*. How was he going to lead the conversation now? He looked at her dirty clothing. "Ha... Have you been somewhere? Is it part of your search?"

"Have you come to interrogate me?" Lyra smiled. "I do not mind answering your questions as long as you are polite."

"I wasn't..." Rav could see in her eyes that she knew. He collected himself. "It's not an interrogation; I just have some questions for you."

"Then come sit down. I will make us tea." Lyra put a pot of water over the fire to boil before sitting opposite Rav at the table. She stared at him with her haunting blue eyes.

"I... um..." Rav's mouth went dry. Why did he find it so hard to talk to her?

"This morning, I explored more of Ghoul Wood to try and find what I am looking for, but that is of no concern to you," Lyra said.

"I'm not here to ask about that anyway." Rav finally found his focus. "First, I would like to confirm that you have travelled to the Sink."

"I have."

"But you don't behave like the others I've met who have been to or are going to the Sink."

"That is because I am not like them." She traced the table edge with the tip of her finger, following it to an indent, which she then tapped, everything so fluid it seemed almost fated. "Have you heard of the World?"

Rav stared at her finger, enthralled by the thought that it was where it was always meant to end up. "The place where we live?"

Lyra shook her head and drew back her hand, breaking Rav's stupor. "It is more than that. It is the air we breathe, the water we drink, our creator, and our purpose. The World is the silence and the noise. I am a follower of the World's will, going wherever I am guided to enact its plans."

"Right..." Of course, she was crazy. Everyone from the Sink would be. "Does the World care about Pitt, or are we allowed to exist in our own way?"

"If the World requires your help, it will let you know. As I told you before, you are an infant, not judged on what you have done, but on what you have the potential to do. Everyone in Pitt has a part to play in the World's plan, you just have not been informed of the role you must perform yet."

"So... killing us is bad?"

Lyra nodded, expression stern, her entire body taut, as though she'd suddenly borne the weight of the world. "Killing you would be the gravest crime I could commit because it would prevent you from performing your role in the World's plan."

Rav watched her with squinted eyes while she spoke, leaning closer, not seeing even a slight quiver in her stance. Jaw tense, lips pursed, eyes clear, she wore the same face he did when speaking of his Name or his parents or of defending Pitt. Was it really true? Just as a sliver of hope fluttered in his stomach, Lyra continued.

"However, that does not mean I will help protect you. For you to be killed by each other or by mutants is also the will of the World. Only a very rare and special few are granted our protection."

Rav sucked his teeth as he leaned back in his chair. "Ha, wouldn't it have been nice if you'd only said that first part? You might not be the same as those like Tibald, but you're not too different either, are you?"

Lyra covered her mouth as she giggled. "There is no need for someone like me to lie to a babe like you. I have told you the whole truth, not teasing snippets. Besides, were I to have only mentioned the first part, you might have believed me now, but would you not always be waiting for a trick, like with Tibald?"

He rubbed his jaw, feeling a creeping smile start to rise at her oddness. "I suppose so. Well, even if you won't help us, at least you're not going to attack us. Since you've been to the Sink, I was wondering if you could tell me about 'Zet Ar. I already know that 'Zet Ar are powerful mutants from the first section of the Sink, the... Ar'za, I think it's called. What I want to know is how intelligent they are and if they have any strange abilities."

"Your pronunciation of Ca'ah e Ggome is very bad." Lyra tutted. "You must use your throat more to better mimic the sounds of the concepts you are trying to convey."

"Ca E Gome? What's that?"

Lyra sighed. "Just call it the language of Earth and Thunder. The words 'Zet and Ar are Earth and Thunder, where 'Zet means changing flesh and Ar means monstrous. These mutants are rather intelligent, capable of organising those of its kind weaker than itself into formations and other such feats. As for their abilities, besides possessing great strength and size, they have nothing else. Children like Tibald would struggle to face them, while babes like you would be slain outright."

Rav scratched his cheek with a sweaty hand. Did that mean his visions weren't being caused by the 'Zet Ar? *Wait.* What had Lyra said just before...?

"You said that this 'World' has a plan and that it can communicate with us. How does it do that?"

Lyra's eyes gleamed. "You are asking about being Called, a phenomenon that began when Ga'thew', the Sink, first appeared. When someone is Called, they see a possible future that the World wants them to achieve within Ga'thew'. It then becomes their purpose to bring about this future and for people like me to help them do it."

Rav sat forward. "How do you know if someone has been Called?"

"There will be a connection between us as the World links our lives together. It is unmistakable. If you had been Called, I would know it just by looking at you."

Rav sucked his teeth. So, his visions hadn't been caused by that either.

"Are you seeking answers for something specific?" Lyra asked. "I have travelled far and seen many wonders, so I may have encountered what you seek."

"I..." He had to find a way to defeat the 'Zet Ar. What choice did he have but to trust her? "I've been having these waking nightmares where I can't tell if I'm awake or asleep, and I see things that aren't really there."

"That sounds exactly like the effects of sleeping within Ghoul Wood."

"Aye, but these visions happen even if I sleep in Pitt, and I see a 'Zet Ar rather than ghouls. Every night, I watch my friends get killed by the mutant."

Something about Lyra changed at his words, as though her delicate features suddenly became predatory. "How curious. Is that all you see during these nightmares?" She leaned closer to him.

Rav leaned back, his skin feeling itchy under her gaze. Telling her was a mistake. Sweat ran down his back. "Aye, that's all I see." He wasn't going to tell her he could control the visions or anything else about them now.

"Perhaps it is a warning of things to come," Lyra said. "Perhaps *something* is trying to save you. You should do whatever you feel like doing after seeing these visions; maybe then, they will go away."

The way Lyra had said "something" was the same way she said "World", and her eyes were currently glistening with fanaticism. How could he have been so foolish? He should've run back to Pitt the moment she'd confirmed she'd been to the Sink.

"I don't think that's true, but thank you for your help anyway." Rav hurried to the door.

"*What do I look like to you?*"

Rav jumped and turned, not understanding how Lyra had suddenly gotten right behind him. She inspected him so closely that he could smell the sweat and bitter herbs lingering on her skin.

"You're, um, very beautiful... obviously."

"You think I am pretty?"

"Sure." Rav hurried to nod.

Lyra beamed and stepped away, but she never stopped staring at him. Rav flung open the door and dashed back to Pitt. He kept checking over his shoulder, terrified that she'd be right next to him once again, but fortunately, the path behind him was clear. Rav reached his home and raced inside.

"Is that you, Rav?" Cyrn called from a side room as Rav slammed the door behind himself and leaned against it, panting. "Listen, I've spoken to Tibald, and he's expecting his trade caravan to arrive tomorrow, so we need to be prepared to receive it." Cyrn stepped into the corridor. "Also, I might have a new plan for our escape. It's a bit dangerous, but if it goes well, we'll all be able to..." He stopped talking and studied Rav's face. "You really do need to get some sleep."

Rav struggled to respond. The longer he remained tongue-tied, the harder it became to say anything. Besides, didn't Cyrn already have enough to worry about with Tibald and his child? And Lyra *had* said she wouldn't kill anyone.

"Aye, I'll go to sleep early tonight."

"Good." Cyrn ruffled his hair. "We'll get through this, I promise."

Rav nodded. "Cyrn, do you think Lyra's pretty?"

"Lyra?" Cyrn tilted his head in thought. "She's a little plain-looking, but I'm sure she'll find some suitors in Pitt if she wants to. Why?"

Rav's heart was thundering. No wonder no one else had commented on how beautiful she was... they couldn't see it.

# Chapter Sixteen

Rav spent the next day fretting over Lyra as he waited for Tibald's trade caravan. He stood by the main gates all day, but the caravan didn't arrive, and as it grew dark, he returned home to inform Cyrn. Cyrn told him to wait again tomorrow, explaining that it was important for him to take charge of unloading its goods so that Tibald's men wouldn't be able to survey Pitt's storerooms.

Cyrn then went over his new escape plan, where he would pretend to agree to join Tibald and travel to Greenfield with him, keeping him out of Pitt so that Enna could give birth in safety. During Cyrn's stay there, he would use his new status to delay the garrison setting up in Stone's Way until everyone was ready to leave, then he'd run away from Greenfield and join them on the road. It was an enormous risk for him to bear, but it *was* possible to pull off. The biggest problem would be getting Tibald to believe that he really had accepted becoming part of Baron Hewett's army; otherwise, Tibald might leave a few soldiers to monitor Pitt in his absence or come up with some other contingency plan to ensure Cyrn's loyalty.

After another loss to the 'Zet Ar—which now always targeted Cyrn and Wakeman's figures first, making it impossible for Rav to fight back—Rav headed out to the main gate and waited in the drizzle until midday. Tibald came and stood beside him, also staring off into the distance.

"Where's my caravan, Rav?"

"It clearly hasn't arrived yet."

"I paid the Ghoulsmen to ensure it would have safe passage through Stone's Way."

"Maybe it broke down somewhere and needs repairs."

"Then why hasn't the caravan sent a rider ahead of it to inform us that it's going to be delayed? We've spent so much time working to become friends; I'd hate for all of that to be undone because of something silly like this." Tibald put his arm around Rav's shoulders, who tensed at his touch, having to brace himself as Tibald pressed down on him.

"If you've harmed my caravan either deliberately or by incompetence, I'm afraid I would have to hold you accountable, which means bringing more soldiers to Pitt for a rather invasive investigation." Tibald squeezed his arm tighter, coiling it around Rav's neck. "I'm sure you don't want that, so why don't you find out why it hasn't arrived?"

Rav grabbed Tibald's arm and struggled to pry it off him. "I'll speak to Cyrn."

"Yes, do that." Tibald relented his constriction and released Rav, who hurried to step away from him. "This caravan is supposed to play a very important part in bringing Pitt and Baron Hewett together. I really do hope nothing bad has happened to it."

Cyrn's forehead wrinkled as he listened to Rav's relay of his conversation with Tibald in the side sitting room.

"Get ready to leave; we're heading out into Stone's Way to find out what's happened," Cyrn said, stomping towards the door. "We need to check on Wakeman and the others to make sure they're alright."

Rav paled as he hurried to follow him out. "Do you think they're in danger?"

"If Tibald's caravan has been attacked, then it's possible the Ghoulsmen have been too. If they've encountered enemy soldiers or mutants, they could need our help."

Rav gulped, glancing at the dark shadows in the corner of the room. "You don't think this has anything to do with the 'Zet Ar, do you?"

"That's what we're going to find out. Come on, hurry; I want to get to the Alley Camp before sunset."

Rav rushed off to get changed into his armour in his room, mind racing. If they really did meet the 'Zet Ar, they would have to run. There was no way they could beat it. If the other Ghoulsmen had already faced it… He shook his head, scattering that line of thought.

Once ready, he collected his shield, spear, and crossbow, along with a few knives, before joining Cyrn in jogging towards Pitt's main gate, seeing his family and Kayla waiting there with stern expressions, Kayla playing with the sleeve of her furs as she gazed at him.

Rav slowed, stepping behind Cyrn as he wrestled to still the tremble that had suddenly taken over his lip. How many times had he left Pitt like this to go fight invading soldiers? He dropped his head, guts clenched tight in an ineffective attempt to calm the squirming jitters coursing through him. Out there was a beast unlike anything they'd ever faced before and in here was a man just as terrifying. It had never been like this. How could he assure Kayla that everything would be alright this time? How could he tell his parents that he'd succeed again?

Cyrn slowed too. "Take a breath," he whispered, never turning. "I'm here. The Ghoulsmen need us."

Rav gazed up at his brother's wide back and did as ordered, the tremble in his lip finally controlled. Wakeman, Thorley, Tido, and Tobias were waiting. He gritted his teeth and ran level with Cyrn once more as they reached the gate, Cyrn winking at him as he did.

Senior Carvell stood closest to the gate, Healanor to his left, then Enna and Kayla.

He stepped forward, stoic and upright, carrying the dignified weight of the Carvell Name. "We've come to say goodbye," he said loudly and clearly, looking them both in the eye. "Be strong, be brave, be loyal. Be Carvells."

Cyrn wrapped him up in a strong hug, while Healanor stepped before Rav with the same stoicism and stroked his cheek.

"The blood of our ancestors flows through you, blood that built Pitt and sired its future." She pulled him into a hug. "It *will* bring you home."

Rav squeezed her back, then hugged his Pa while Cyrn hugged his Ma. As his parents stepped back again, Kayla walked to him and Enna to Cyrn.

Kayla broke her stone face with a soft smile, Rav clenching his jaw as he fought off the tremble in his lip once more. She tidied the front of his furs so everything ran in line, as though he were about to attend another banquet, then leaned in towards his ear on her tiptoes, breath tickling his ear.

"Don't die," she whispered, her hand grabbing his furs starting to shake. "Everything else can be fixed, just don't die."

Rav forced a chuckle to hide his own shaking, raising his chin as he gently pushed her back. "I won't."

Cyrn also finished his goodbye with Enna, the hand he had on her waist sliding onto her belly.

"Before you go," Tibald called as he walked over to join them with an unashamed grin, "I must say something."

Rav and Cyrn turned to face him, Rav's fist clenching.

"While it is the Ghoulsmen's responsibility to make sure my caravan arrives safely, I am here to offer my help if you need it. Should you find things to be beyond what you can handle, please return to Pitt, where I'll gather my soldiers so we can head out to deal with the threat together."

"Thank you," Cyrn said, although his expression remained flat rather than grateful.

"Rav, might I speak with you alone?" Tibald requested.

Rav followed him a short distance away from his family.

"Have you thought much about our conversation in Ghoul Wood? I know Ronin's cruel words ruined things then, and for that I'm sorry, but your path to salvation is still very important."

Rav nodded slowly, watching Tibald's every movement.

"I know this might seem like an odd time for me to bring this back up, but when you're out in Stone's Way, why don't you consider what you're doing and if it's really helping you make up for your crime? I know my suggestion for you to go into self-exile must have been daunting, but I truly believe exile is the only way for you to be rid of your guilt. I've thought about it some more, and maybe I can offer you some help by inviting you to follow me into the Sink when I return there.

"Don't decide now; take your time to think about what you're doing and if it's really changing anything. Sometimes, when you're powerless, you must rely on others to help you, and I'm here to offer you that help."

Rav pulled a bitter smile, feigning acknowledgement of Tibald's words. "Thank you for your advice," he forced out before hurriedly walking back to Cyrn, worried that his smile would slip into a scowl.

The pair soon set off into Stone's Way.

"What did Tibald want?" Cyrn asked.

"He was trying to prey upon my insecurities by bringing up *that* event and how I can make up for it. He invited me to join him in the Sink, just like we thought he would. His behaviour was strange, though. Did you notice how he didn't appear to be that bothered by his missing caravan? I know he said that he cares about it, but he seemed more focused on saying that we were responsible and offering us his help, especially after he repeated himself to me."

"Aye, I noticed that too."

"I've got a feeling that this missing caravan is a much bigger part of his plan to get you to join Baron Hewett than we think."

"I do too."

They soon lost sight of Pitt. Rav surveyed the hills around him. For some reason, Stone's Way didn't look so beautiful to him today. Everything appeared to be the same as it had when they'd left just over a week ago, yet he had an inkling that told him it wasn't.

They made it to the Alley Camp without any issues, but Rav couldn't shake off the tension that had seized him. He tried having the Ghoulsmen figures flee from the 'Zet Ar that night, yet even then, it caught them all. No hope. Rav shuddered. Was that what had changed? Was that why Stone's Way felt different? Somewhere out there, the beast was waiting to massacre them for real.

# Chapter Seventeen

Rav and Cyrn were up at dawn to continue to Bear Camp, following a longer route over the hills that allowed them to watch the road for any signs of the caravan, of which there had been none so far. As they walked, the misty raindrops swelled, blurring the distant hills.

Cyrn sniffed the air. "Can you smell that?"

Rav wrinkled his nose as he caught the scent of iron and earth, spitting on the ground as the stench of metallic rot crawled down his throat. "Has another group of soldiers been killed?"

"Let's find out."

They followed the scent to a battlefield a short distance away from the road. It was another massacred group of soldiers wearing Baron Kiln's blue and white armour, with a few rotting ordinary goats as well as a Spine among the bodies. Rav held his breath as he looked over them, swatting at the flies swarming the area. The soldiers' bodies had also been gnawed on. Cyrn signalled for them to carry on moving towards Bear Camp; however, it wasn't long until they caught another rotten stench, leading them to more bodies.

"Cyrn, what's been happening out here?"

"I don't know. No more detours; we need to get to Bear Camp as soon as we can."

Rav jogged after Cyrn, having to watch his footing over the uneven ground that had been pocked by dozens of goats' hoofprints. It was like they'd taken over the entire area. The poor weather made it difficult for Rav to see ahead of them, which was made worse when the sun started to dip as the day ended. He could only hope that there weren't any Spines between them and Bear Camp.

As they got close, Rav heard the clamour from dozens of voices ahead of them, not recognising any of the accents.

"Get down," Cyrn hissed. "It sounds like there are soldiers staying at Bear Camp. We'll sneak up to them to see who they are."

Rav crouched and followed Cyrn around a few rock formations leading towards the camp. Cyrn stopped and pointed above them at a blurry figure. It was a scout dressed in Baron Kiln's colours, standing on top of a tor. Cyrn signalled for Rav to wait where he was, then he moved around the tor, where Rav lost sight of him. Rav stayed as still as he could, hoping that if the scout did look at where he was standing, the sheet of rain between them would make Rav look like just another rock.

Cyrn burst up from behind the scout and held the scout's mouth shut as the two struggled. It didn't last long, Cyrn breaking his neck before dropping the scout's body headfirst off the edge of the tor, then climbing back down to Rav. Rav inspected the body, which, after the impact, looked as if they had simply fallen.

"Have all of Baron Kiln's surviving soldiers come to Stone's Way?" Rav asked.

"That's what it looks like." Cyrn sighed. "I spotted more of them at Bear Camp when I climbed up."

"What are they doing here? I thought Baron Hewett had taken over Greenfield with an overwhelming victory."

"Maybe Baron Hewett's victory wasn't as grand as Tibald had us believe... or maybe there's something else going on. We can learn what's going on later, but we need to find the other Ghoulsmen first."

Cyrn led them to lie down at the top of a craggy tor just a few hundred feet from Bear Camp. Rav crept to the edge and looked down at Bear Camp's flat hilltop, where years of caravans camping on it had left the ground barren—just a thin layer of mud glazed onto hard rock. A large fire burned in the centre of several makeshift shelters, under which a few dozen soldiers milled around. To the side stood a wooden cage with four figures locked inside. Wakeman's enormous frame was unmistakable despite the constant pattering rain blurring everything.

"*They've been captured,*" Rav hissed.

"Aye. Keep note of how the soldiers are positioned so we can come up with a plan to free them."

Rav pulled out his notebook and sketched everything he could see with shaking hands. As they watched the camp, a unit of four soldiers walked up to the cage, the leader walking ahead of the others. Rav snarled at their loud brashness, sauntering around Bear Camp as though they owned it, the pencil in his hand almost snapping as he squeezed it. Straining his ear, he caught the rain-muffled conversation.

"Wow, look at you, big fella. You're everything I was told you are." He laughed. "You'll make an excellent labourer... after you heal, of course." The leader's laugh turned sickly. "I've been told you killed three of our own before you were caught today, so I'll carve three scars into your back. Don't worry, you won't die. The trick is to cauterise each wound with a separate blade after every cut. I'll make sure you make up for the lives you took by working for us until death."

# GHOULSMEN

"Come closer," Wakeman growled, voice rumbling as he grabbed the wooden bars and shook the cage. "Maybe I can manage a fourth."

"Still got some fight left in you, eh? You won't for much longer, heh heh heh. Contender Olden, you like breaking in slaves like this one, right? Why don't I give him to you once I'm done disciplining him?"

A large man came over to the cage from the makeshift shelters. "I can definitely get him to grovel. And you, Contender Ive? Have any caught your eye?"

Contender Ive leered at them with slick malice, gaze shifting from Ghoulsman to Ghoulsman before he settled on Thorley. "The ginger one might provide some entertainment. As for the rest... at best, they can act as bait for mutants." He laughed.

"*You're going to die,*" Wakeman shouted. "All of you are going to die. The other Ghoulsmen will come and hack you to pieces. There won't even be corpses left."

"The other Ghoulsmen? That's only two people, isn't it?" Ive laughed louder. "You think that two people are going to kill all of us? I've... I've never heard something so funny."

"They'll find a way."

"What a wonderful threat." Olden chortled. "If two people wish to attack us, then I say let them, eh, lads?"

The other soldiers laughed.

"You *Ghoulsmen* are no better than rats," Olden said. "When you hide in your holes, you're a nuisance, but once you come out, all it takes is a good stomp to crush you. Soon, we'll have enough soldiers to invade Pitt and kill Tibald Sar along with his men, then we'll put your families in cages with you. There is no hope for your rescue. It was admirable of you to try running to Pitt so you could warn them about us, but it was also just too predictable. You should've stayed in your hole like the pathetic rats you are."

Wakeman pressed his face between the cage bars and unleashed a guttural roar at him, spittle flying, forcing Olden and Ive to step back.

Ive sneered, waiting for Wakeman to run out of breath before licking his lips and tutting. "Oh, I'd save your voice for the screaming you'll be doing later, heh heh heh." He turned to his partner. "Why don't we start in the morning, Contender Olden, so we don't disturb the mutants tonight?"

Olden glanced east, his posture stiffening a moment as though he'd seen something terrible through the hills. "That's a good idea." Turning to face Wakeman again, he tilted his head in taunting. "It'll also give our captives some time to anticipate the pain they'll soon be experiencing. No matter how excruciating you think torture is going to be, it's always so much worse when you experience it for real." He kicked the mud-slick ground to spatter muck over Wakeman. "You have one night to decide if you're going to accept your new status as our dogs or if you'll cling to your pride, only to be broken down after suffering."

"I'm going to kill them," Rav hissed. "*They're* the ones who are going to suffer."

"Aye, but we need to be smart about it. I can see a path we can use to reach the cage undetected when it's dark, but once we're there, we'll be spotted before we can get them free. You'll have to go alone while I cause a distraction."

"Whatever I have to do, I'll get it done."

"Then listen closely."

Rav waited until the sun had completely set before moving, allowing the 'Zet Ar to kill the Ghoulsmen shadows as quickly as possible to get his vision over with. The camp's central fire was blazing fiercely to provide enough light for the soldiers to see across the hilltop and acted as a beacon for Rav to follow, guiding him towards his path. He had to loop around Bear Camp and then approach it from the boulder field on the north side of the hill, where he would have enough cover to get close to the cage without being spotted. Cyrn was somewhere nearby, watching for when he was in position to draw the soldiers' attention.

Rav reached the boulder field and gazed up from the shadows. Even though it was night, the soldiers still had many people keeping watch over the area, along with the occasional patrol, forcing Rav to pick his moment to approach the cage carefully. At least the patrolling soldiers were all carrying torches, making them easy to spot. He could count three soldiers standing at the front of the cage, keeping watch over the Ghoulsmen, as well as two others keeping lookout over Stone's Way close by, all armed with spears.

Rav set his spear and shield down to wipe his sweaty hands on his furs, then checked on the four knives he'd tied into a bundle to ensure they would stay together if thrown. He waited until one of the cage guards made a joke, causing the others to laugh, to don his mask, collect his weapons, and start advancing.

Due to the lip of the hill blocking the firelight from reaching this side of Bear Camp, Rav could move safely up the hillside in the darkness until he was just below the cage. The soldiers were still chatting among themselves. Rav grabbed the bundle of knives and slid them over the hill's lip to the edge of the cage before dashing back into the black. He peeked up and saw that the knives were gone from where he'd slid them. The Ghoulsmen were alert and armed.

Rav waited on the hillside, struggling to control his rapid breathing. The next part of the plan was the most important. He peeked his head up and wished with all his heart that Cyrn would see him before the soldiers did.

"*Waaah,*" Cyrn roared from the other side of the camp, catching the guards' attention.

The campsite surged into life as soldiers swarmed over to Cyrn's position. The cage guards stayed where they were, but now, they all had their backs turned to Rav, who leaped up and stabbed one of them through the neck. As the man collapsed, the others turned to face Rav, who whipped his spear across to the soldier on his right, smacking him over the head to send him tumbling to the ground.

"*Enemy over here,*" the remaining soldier shouted while he thrust his spear at Rav, forcing Rav to block the attack with his shield.

Rav stabbed at the soldier's leg, and the soldier dodged to the side, setting himself between Rav and the cage, then braced behind his shield. Several soldiers were already rushing over to support their comrade. Rav charged forward with his shield and crashed into the soldier, slamming him against the cage, where Wakeman grabbed him before slicing his throat with a knife.

"Two enemies coming from your right, Rav. You've got a moment before they get here," Tido said.

Rav raised his shield high, then smashed it down on the cage's bolt lock, splintering the wood but not breaking it.

"*Block right,*" Tido shouted.

Rav reacted in an instant, managing to stop a spear from skewering him. Wakeman kicked the cage door, further damaging the lock as Rav faced his new opponent, taking a defensive stance in the hope he could protect Wakeman long enough for the Ghoulsmen to break out. The soldier facing Rav approached at a steady pace, and another soon joined him. Rav kept his spear pointed at them, but when they split up to flank him, he had to keep shifting between the two.

"*Three more soldiers coming from your left, Rav,*" Tido called.

"You'll soon be surrounded," one of the approaching soldiers said. "Give up now and maybe we won't torture you."

Rav sneered. "Soon isn't quick enough."

Tobias and Thorley kicked the cage door with Wakeman. *Crack.* Wakeman burst out and grabbed a dead soldier's spear while Rav dropped back to his side.

"Is there anything else you need to do?" Wakeman asked.

"Cyrn said he'd take care of himself."

"Then let's get out of here."

The soldiers backed away as Tido and Thorley also picked up spears, giving the Ghoulsmen time to race down the hillside and into the night.

"Cyrn said... we should hide in the boulder field... while they pursue us," Rav panted.

"They won't risk chasing us in the dark," Wakeman grunted. "Where are we meeting up with Cyrn?"

"Follow me."

Rav led them back around Bear Camp, to where he and Cyrn had scouted from. There were cries of "*Attack*" followed by screams and dozens of soldiers holding torches lined up around where Cyrn had ambushed the campsite from, but Cyrn was hidden somewhere in the dark just outside of the light's reach. Two soldiers charged out of the formation, and in flashes of orange firelight, Rav watched Cyrn stab one of them so hard that he lifted the soldier off the ground. He then crushed the head of the other with a punch from his shield.

"Stay in formation," Contender Ive screeched. "We have to surround him."

"That's six dead, Contender Ive," Cyrn bellowed. "Are you going to carve into my back too? Two Ghoulsmen is too many to deal with you; I alone will be enough."

"*Forward march*," Contender Ive yelled, but when his soldiers lit up the area with their torches, Cyrn was nowhere to be seen.

"Cyrn needs to get here as soon as he can, then we need to find somewhere safe for the night," Wakeman whispered. "We can't be out here."

"Why not?" Cyrn asked as he emerged from the shadows.

"You were right about the 'Zet Ar being nocturnal; every night, it prowls Stone's Way hunting anyone vulnerable," Wakeman explained. "I'll tell you more later, but right now, we need to leave."

The Ghoulsmen set off for one of their emergency shelters—a short dug-out tunnel between two leaning boulders in a nearby rock formation just long enough for them all to cram inside—Cyrn guiding them by experience in the darkness.

"Please tell me there's flint and firewood in here," Rav whispered as he followed after Cyrn, crawling past him in the tight space to reach its end, where a small fireplace had been dug into the dirt wall.

*Tch*. Sparks flew, lighting up Cyrn's blood-soaked face, then landed on a pile of shavings within the alcove. A small fire bloomed to life as the rest of the Ghoulsmen huddled inside the hole, everyone silent and wide-eyed as the new light exposed Cyrn's matted furs, blood dripping onto the ground as though he'd been doused in it.

"Are you hurt?" Rav asked.

Cyrn shook his head. "Wakeman, what's been happening out here?"

Wakeman wiped his own bloody hands on his furs before speaking. "The most important thing for you to know is that the soldiers aren't our biggest problem. The reason why none of them pursued us is because they're scared of the 'Zet Ar."

"Terrified," Thorley corrected, voice trembling. "They're *terrified* of the 'Zet Ar."

"Aye, terrified." Wakeman nodded. "I haven't seen it, but I've felt it. It's like a storm made flesh, Cyrn. Your skin prickles when it's around and you can hear thunder rumble when it's fighting.

When Baron Kiln's soldiers first started moving into Stone's Way, they were in small units that could easily hide, but those groups kept getting annihilated by the 'Zet Ar, so they've had to gather together at Bear Camp and use their numbers to deter the monster."

"Do you know where the 'Zet Ar stays when it's not hunting?" Cyrn asked.

"Somewhere to the east of Bear Camp," Wakeman answered. "But we don't know its exact location. We haven't gone looking for it and we shouldn't. The 'Zet Ar must have also had an impact on the other goat herds because all of them, Spines included, have been migrating eastwards."

Cyrn took a breath. "I don't know much about these 'Zet Ar, so I'm not sure how to fight one. Thorley, is there anything else you can tell us?"

Thorley gave a helpless shrug as he shook his head. "No, I only knew what they were called."

Cyrn pressed his knuckles into the dirt wall beside him as he glowered. "We'll deal with the soldiers first, then. What was your plan before we arrived?"

"Originally, we wanted to come to Pitt and warn you straight away, but then we found some of the massacres the 'Zet Ar had carried out and decided to hide while we learned where it was hunting so we could avoid it," Wakeman said. "While we were waiting, the soldiers gathered at Bear Camp, so when we finally headed out, we ended up getting captured."

"I see... Well, we can't defeat the soldiers or the 'Zet Ar alone." Cyrn sighed. "Which leaves only one option. We'll return to Pitt and ask Tibald for help."

"Will he help us?" Tobias asked.

Cyrn told them about what Tibald had done in Pitt.

"If you think Tibald can be trusted, then we'll join you."

"It's not that I think he can be trusted, I just can't see another way out of this situation," Cyrn muttered.

Rav thought back to the last thing Tibald had said to him before he'd ventured into Stone's Way. *"Take your time to think about what you're doing and if it's really changing anything. Sometimes, when you're powerless, you must rely on others to help you, and I'm here to offer you that help."*

Didn't it now sound as if Tibald had known he would encounter a situation he couldn't solve? A situation that would make him feel useless, exacerbating his guilt for not being able to make up for his crime and driving him to further consider Tibald's idea for him to enter the Sink to achieve salvation.

Tibald's offer of help was too convenient for their current circumstances, especially when Rav considered *how* these supposedly vanquished soldiers had arrived in Stone's Way. This whole scenario felt as though it had been orchestrated, but he couldn't understand how it all pieced together.

"Before we do that," Rav spoke up, "did Baron Kiln's soldiers attack a caravan coming through here?"

"I haven't seen or heard a caravan come through Stone's Way." Wakeman looked to Thorley, Tobias, and Tido, who also shook their heads. "We might not have noticed it, though."

"With how important this caravan is supposed to be, there's no way you wouldn't have noticed it. It should have been heavily guarded, leading to a battle, and Baron Kiln's soldiers would have had to store its goods somewhere, but I didn't see anything at their camp." Rav faced Cyrn. "What if there was no caravan? What if the caravan was just an excuse Tibald made up to get us to come out here and discover the invading soldiers?"

Cyrn sucked his teeth. "That's possible; Tibald's definitely crafty enough to do that. If that is what he's done, then his wider plan is to..." He frowned. "During the Challenge, Pattik said that one of Tibald's soldiers sent him a message containing Tibald's location. Tibald didn't seem fazed by that, though, playing it off as a distraction, but what if it was true?"

"Tibald doesn't seem like the type of person to allow any dissent among his soldiers," Rav commented.

"Aye, he doesn't. How likely is it that the person who came to Challenge Tibald was both incredibly vile and not very good at fighting? It's almost like he was selected to play the part of Tibald's 'villain' so that Tibald could get Pitt's support for killing Pattik. I think Tibald deliberately sent one of his soldiers to tell Pattik his location."

"Tibald wanted to make himself look like a hero." Rav gasped. "Is he doing the same thing here?"

"Aye, he could be. Tibald was excited by the prospect of us fighting together, so maybe he's created an enemy for us to fight against. What was his plan? To let a portion of Baron Kiln's army escape, then herd them towards Stone's Way, where he knew that we would come into conflict with them? Then, because there are too many soldiers for us to fight alone, we'd have to ask him for help. Tibald will get to protect Pitt, bolstering his reputation with everyone while also further proving his dedication to his duties, like he did by hunting the mutant badger. He'd also have an easier time convincing people to let him turn Stone's Way into a garrison with the promise of preventing an attack like this in the future."

"He can't get away with it," Tido spat.

"He'd organise for our home to be attacked, putting our families' lives in danger just to further his own selfish goals. We can't ally with him, Cyrn. I'll never fight by his side." Rav faced Cyrn, whose eyes were hard, his face twisted into a ferocious snarl.

"The only other question I have," Cyrn growled, "is where does the 'Zet Ar fit into all of this? I don't know if it's possible for Tibald to have brought it with him from the Sink."

"If he could control monsters like that, what need would he have with you?" Wakeman asked.

"I also don't think Tibald would be capable of controlling something that powerful," Rav added, thinking over his shadow skirmishes with the beast.

Cyrn went quiet before he punched the ground. "Even if this is all Tibald's plan, what else can we do but follow along with it? We're up against enemy soldiers *and* the 'Zet Ar. We'll need his help to protect Pitt."

"We can't fight the 'Zet Ar even with Tibald and his eight men," Rav muttered. "I..." He gulped, trying to steady the quiver in his voice.

"We can't be sure of that." Cyrn patted Rav's back. "With traps and a good formation, killing it *will* be possible."

"Possible, maybe, but it's not worth it, Cyrn. Most of us *will* die. I've seen it." Rav slumped against the cave wall. "Every night, I watch us fight that beast, and every night, it kills us all, barely taking a wound in return. And it's not just strong, it's clever, capable of learning from its mistakes and avoiding positions where it becomes vulnerable. Traps won't work as well as you think. Maybe with Tibald we'd last longer, but most of us would still die."

Cyrn grabbed Rav by the shoulders and faced him, deep lines of concern etched into his forehead. "Rav, what are you talking about?"

Rav gazed at his brother with hopeless eyes. "The only way to hurt it is by having someone bait its charge while the others attack, but at best, its target will be crippled for life, likely to die from infection or blood loss after. Do you think Tibald or any of his men will make that sacrifice? It'll be us, Cyrn." He dropped his head. "There'll be no victory even if we slay the mutant."

Cyrn puffed out his chest and hardened his expression with determination. "I know you're scared, we all are, but you can't let nightmares about the beast sway you. What happens if it comes to Pitt? What happens when we leave Pitt and travel

Stone's Way with our families? There's no choice but to fight, so have faith that we'll succeed."

Rav pushed him away while shaking his head. "They *aren't* nightmares, but if you won't believe me, then maybe you'll believe Lyra." He faced the other Ghoulsmen, seeing them all shifting uncomfortably as they listened. "She's a Healer from the Sink and knows about 'Zet Ar like this one. She knows how dangerous they are. One of the Sink's horrors is here, massacring people across our home—"

"Then what would you have us do?" Cyrn snapped. "We can't do nothing, Rav."

"*I don't know*," he huffed. "I've been thinking and thinking, but I still don't know."

Itchy silence settled in the tunnel.

"This Lyra," Tobias murmured. "Would she help us?"

"No." Rav kicked the ground with his heel. "She said if we were to die, then that would be the will of the World she follows."

Thorley gasped before covering his mouth. "If this Lyra is who I think she is, she won't help us, unless... What else did she say to you, Rav? Does she know about your nightmares? Did she say anything about you being Called?"

Rav shook his head. "I haven't been."

Thorley dropped his head with a tut.

"Listen," Cyrn sighed. "We need to rest tonight, then head to the Alley Camp tomorrow before returning to Pitt. Now that Baron Kiln's soldiers are aware that we know about them, they might launch a hasty attack on Pitt, so we need to get back quickly and help prepare everyone to defend the town. I don't know about 'Zet Ar, but we've been killing soldiers for ten years—we know how to do that. We'll discuss what to do about the monster later. Maybe Tibald can get reinforcements from Baron Hewett."

Everyone nodded in agreement before settling down for the night, Cyrn adding another bundle of wood to the fire, dazzling sparks flying as it crackled.

Rav slumped to the ground, his eyelids so heavy he couldn't lift them, but his wounded arm was aching after the fight, keeping him from falling asleep. Breath stifled, he wriggled to find a comfortable position but was unable to, too aware of how Tibald's scheme was coiling around him, constricting him until the only path left to follow led exactly where Tibald wanted it to. He was the badger trapped in smoke, Greeshe stuck in mud, but as Cyrn had said, what choice did they have? Wakeman mentioning the goat herds moving towards the 'Zet Ar had also reminded him that 'Zet Ar could control their kind and lead formations. There were two armies next to Pitt. Three if you counted Baron Hewett.

Allying with Baron Hewett and his army would work, but what price would the Baron ask them to pay for his help? Rav snorted, the answer obvious. What was the point of paying for their lives *with* their lives? How else could they kill the 'Zet Ar without most, if not all, of them dying, though? Rav shivered, his eyes stinging with tears.

It wasn't just their plan to escape that was in tatters... everything was. He'd worked so hard to stop the Sink's malice from reaching Pitt, but Pitt was going to face bloodshed anyway. Kayla was going to see the encroaching horrors ruining their beautiful home. Why was he so powerless? Had he been cursed? Was this the price you had to pay for dishonouring your lineage? It was all hopeless. Rav curled up on the freezing ground as the tears he'd been holding back broke free and streamed down his face.

# Chapter Eighteen

"*Silly boy.*"

Rav rubbed his eyes as he woke, seeing sunlight seeping through the cracks in the rock above him. He listened to everyone breathing deeply around him.

*Three armies, three armies, three armies.*

He massaged his temples. It would take sacrifices to wound the 'Zet Ar, and it would take an army to defeat it.

...Or would the 'Zet Ar defeat an army?

Rav sat up, mind alight, his fatigue gone. What if Baron Kiln's soldiers and the 'Zet Ar fought each other?

Cyrn stirred beside him, scratching his chin as he sat up. "We should get moving," he grumbled, waking everyone else up.

"Wait," Rav spoke as everyone else sat up. "I have an idea. It requires sacrifices to hurt the 'Zet Ar, but those sacrifices don't have to come from us. Why should we put our lives at risk when others far more deserving of death are close by?"

Wakeman pinched between his eyes while he listened. "Are you talking about Baron Kiln's soldiers? How would you get them and the 'Zet Ar to fight, though? They'll never go anywhere near its territory."

Rav's eyes gleamed as he grinned. "I think I can lure the beast to them. If the 'Zet Ar really is fighting me during my visions, maybe it would leap at the opportunity to kill me for real. I'll act as bait and draw it to Bear Camp. If I wear blue and white, it might mistake Baron Kiln's men as my allies."

"That's insane," Tido gasped. "How are you going to get close enough to the 'Zet Ar for it to attack you but manage to outrun it until you reach Bear Camp? What about all the goats and Spines that migrated eastwards with it?"

"You'll also be attacked at Bear Camp," Tobias added. "What if you get trapped between the two forces?"

"Aye, I know it's dangerous, but if we do it this way, all the danger would be directed at me, not at Pitt." Rav faced each of them in turn with a pleading look. "Let me keep Kayla's life peaceful for a little longer. Help me avoid following Tibald Sar's scheme and keep Cyrn from being forced to join him. I can protect everyone."

Cyrn laced his fingers through his hair. "I still don't understand these visions you've had. How do you know that the 'Zet Ar will chase you?"

Rav locked eyes with him. "Even if I fail, it's worth the risk. The Ghoulsmen exist to protect Pitt, so let me try this. I'll tell you everything later. If you really think Baron Kiln's soldiers will start marching to Pitt, then we must act quickly."

"It's so risky, though, Rav." Cyrn gazed at the Ghoulsmen, expression shifting between a hopeful smile and a despairing grimace. "*If* you can get past the Spines, *if* the 'Zet Ar chases you, *if* you can outrun it, *if* it attacks Baron Kiln's soldiers, *if* you can then hide from both armies. If, if, if. *If* they'll even mutually destroy each other. What if the 'Zet Ar and the Spines kill all the soldiers, then kill you?"

"Aye, it's all ifs, but I'd rather take those ifs than the guarantee that Pitt will come under attack. Could you at least help me solve some of the problems?"

Cyrn picked at the dried blood on his sleeve. "Well, we could reduce the chances of Baron Kiln's soldiers killing you before you reach Bear Camp if you arrive at night when they won't see you until it's too late."

"You said this 'Zet Ar is quite intelligent, right?" Wakeman leaned forward. "Why does it have to see you at first? Can't you shout at it to catch its attention? Then, if it attacks, you'll have a good head start, and if the plan doesn't work, you won't have taken too big a risk."

"The boulder field next to Bear Camp would provide good cover for your escape once the two armies start fighting," Tobias added.

"We could alert the soldiers about the 'Zet Ar's arrival so they have time to prepare a defence. That way, they'll have a chance of hurting it, and if they're preparing for an attack on their camp, they can't start marching towards Pitt." Thorley grabbed Tido and Tobias' shoulders as he grinned.

"And if one of us returns to Pitt to warn Tibald, we can carry out both plans. Five of us to stay out here and one person to get reinforcements in case it goes wrong," Tido finished.

Rav gazed around the cave with a gleam in his eye. "It doesn't seem so hopeless now, does it? You wouldn't even have to come with me; I could get the 'Zet Ar alone. I can do it. I can—"

"Rav," Cyrn interrupted. "This plan is still extremely dangerous, even if all those things go right."

"But there's a chance."

"Rav's right, Cyrn," Wakeman spoke. "It *could* succeed."

"Well... you certainly can't do it alone, so I'm coming with you. I can help protect you from the mutants and the soldiers."

"I can lead Tido and Thorley to the boulder field next to Bear Camp. We'll hide there until you've brought the 'Zet Ar to the soldiers, then help you during the battle," Wakeman said. "Tobias, as the fastest of us, you should be the one to head to Pitt and get Tibald. We need to be careful when we're moving around Stone's Way because Baron Kiln's soldiers will likely be looking for us now that it's light. If they spot us, they'll pursue us this time."

"There are two main objectives we have to achieve before we do anything else," Cyrn said. "First, we must know what Baron Kiln's soldiers are doing. All of us will travel together to Bear Camp for safety to spy on them, then if they're still there, we'll split up. I can cause another distraction with Rav so that Wakeman, Tido, and Thorley can enter the boulder field while Tobias starts running back to Pitt.

"Second, we'll need to find out where the 'Zet Ar is. Rav and I will go looking for it during the afternoon, which should also help us lose our pursuers after our distraction. From there, Rav will need to attract the 'Zet Ar just before evening so that it can see us once we have its attention. When that's done, we'll lead it to Bear Camp during sunset, arriving in the dark, where we will hide in the boulder field." He clenched his fist with a snarl. "Wakeman, Thorley, and Tido, you need to be ready to kill anyone following us. After that, we just have to hope everything works out while we retreat to the Alley Camp. Tobias, run as fast as you can to Pitt and tell Tibald to meet us there. Is that clear?"

"Aye."

"Then let's crush our enemies and save our home."

The Ghoulsmen sneaked out to find a group of dead soldiers, and soon everyone was disguised in their armour. Wakeman, Thorley, and Tido also pillaged spare spears and shields to arm themselves. Once everyone was armed and ready, they started winding their way over to Bear Camp. Fortunately, it was still overcast and raining, providing the Ghoulsmen with some cover as they moved; however, they still took their time approaching Bear Camp, constantly on the lookout for enemy scouts. They scampered up rock faces and dived into valleys, using the complex terrain to stay out of sight as they crept closer. Soon, they heard soldiers talking—Baron Kiln's men were still at Bear Camp.

Rav peeked around a boulder, seeing the camp full of movement as soldiers packed away their makeshift shelters. "They're getting ready to leave," he whispered.

Cyrn turned to face Tobias with grim seriousness. "Start running to Pitt now, but be careful. Wakeman, lead your group west until you're out of sight before looping back to enter the boulder field. Rav, start moving east and get ready to sprint. I'm going to make sure the soldiers stay here."

Everyone nodded, then set off.

Rav skulked away, thinking about the task ahead of him. He thought through every battle he'd fought against the 'Zet Ar during his nightmares, analysing its strength and speed so he could know how far away from it he'd have to be to reach Bear Camp before it killed him. By his estimation, it was about ten times as fast as him at a full sprint; however, if he used the complex terrain of Stone's Way well, he could force it to slow down enough to get away from it. By running through narrow passages and getting out of its line of sight, the 'Zet Ar would have to take longer routes than he did to reach the same destination while also stopping to search for him when he hid.

"Contender Ive," Rav heard Cyrn bellow. "I killed six of your soldiers yesterday. I wonder how many more I'll kill today."

"Where are you hiding, Ghoulsmen rat? Come out and face me," Contender Ive shouted back.

"I see that you've decided to run away," Cyrn's voice came from a different location. "That's a wise decision; I wouldn't want to stay here either with someone like me lurking around. I've already killed two more of your scouts today. Who knows how many of you will die during the night?"

"*Find him,*" Ive screeched.

"You seem busy, so I'll come back once it's dark again. Against me and the beast, let's see how long you'll last in Stone's Way." Cyrn laughed.

"I'll kill you and enslave your family. There'll be nothing left of Pitt but ashes after we attack."

Rav flinched as he heard shuffling to his left and pointed his spear towards the noise, grip tight, ready to thrust. Cyrn scurried out from around a boulder and crawled back up to his position. Rav lowered his weapon.

"We'll have to watch them for a while to see if my words worked," Cyrn whispered. "I hope Ive and Olden aren't clever enough to see through my provocation. Calling them cowards for leaving might have been too obvious, but hopefully the threat of me attacking them while they're travelling and reminding them of the 'Zet Ar will make them think staying at Bear Camp, where they're fortified, will be the safest option tonight."

They sipped from their waterskins and chewed dried meat while they kept watch over Bear Camp. It looked as if Cyrn's plan had worked, as soldiers began rebuilding their shelters while others hammered wooden posts into the ground around the hill to act as a barricade. A patrol unit had been formed to search the area around the hill, led by Contender Olden. They were scouring the area where Cyrn had shouted from.

"We can't have them searching around the boulder field, or they might spot Wakeman's group moving towards it, so we'd better show them that we're not there," Cyrn said as he got up. "Are you ready to start running? We'll be heading into mutant territory; make sure you're prepared to face them."

Rav checked over his equipment one last time, ensuring that his knives were all strapped tight to his belt. "I'm ready."

"Then the rest of the plan is up to you."

They ran to the top of a hill where they could easily be spotted from Bear Camp, then dropped into a valley, heading east.

"That's them. Hunt them down."

Rav heard the patrol give chase. As he ran, he scanned his surroundings, envisioning which paths through the terrain would be useful when they were returning with the 'Zet Ar right behind them. He stumbled, and Cyrn caught him.

"Watch where you step," Cyrn warned.

The ground beneath them was pocked with hoofprints, and Rav had to keep an eye on where he placed his feet in case he twisted his ankle. There were no goats in sight for now, so the brothers continued following their tracks while maintaining their distance from the pursuing patrol unit. The distance between them and their pursuers increased until the patrol stopped and spread out in a line.

"What are they doing?" Rav panted.

"They're herding us into the mutant territory by making sure we can't come back out the way we came in. Ignore them; focus on what's in front of us. Judging by the number of hoofprints, about a hundred goats have moved this way, and look at this." Cyrn pointed to several larger cloven hoofprints. "There must be at least twenty Spines."

They continued deeper into mutant territory, losing sight of the patrol behind them.

*Tak, tak, tak.* The sound was coming from around the boulder in front of them.

Cyrn signalled for Rav to climb on top of the boulder, so Rav jumped up with Cyrn's aid, then lay flat on the rock, watching as an ordinary goat walked around it towards Cyrn. As soon as it saw Cyrn, it charged, and Cyrn raised his shield to block its horns. Now that it was distracted, Rav readied his spear and stabbed it through the back of its neck from above. It dropped dead.

"Can you see any others?" Cyrn whispered.

Rav looked around them. He shook his head before climbing back down to the ground. They encountered a few other goats along the way, but none of them were Spines and were dispatched with little commotion.

"Judging by these tracks, we should see the main herd once we reach the top of the next hill."

Cyrn was right. Gathered around a river in the distance were so many goats huddled together that it looked as though a black, brown, and white cloud had blanketed the land. A dozen sets of spiked black horns stood out from the herd. *Meh. Meh. Meh.* The bleats were endless.

"I can't see the 'Zet Ar, can you?" Cyrn asked.

"No, but it must be here. Look, what Wakeman said is true." Rav lifted his sleeve to show his prickled skin. "It really does feel like a storm is coming."

It wasn't just the tension in the air, Rav could also feel a pull coming from his mind, like an invisible tether had connected him to the 'Zet Ar, drawing them towards each other. He suddenly felt as if he was destined to fight the beast, destined to slay it or be slayed by it, as though all his life had been leading to this moment. And there was a strange growing excitement about their coming battle.

"We'll watch them from here, but if we don't see the 'Zet Ar by the afternoon, we might have to sneak closer," Cyrn said.

The time for battle was nearing, the sun starting its descent. Rav kept thinking, kept planning, looking over his sketch of Bear

Camp to find where the best path for them to safely reach the boulder field would be.

"We can move this way to reach the boulder field," Cyrn pointed out. "This rock formation will provide cover, then we can change direction and squeeze through this narrow section, where Spines and the 'Zet Ar won't be able to fit."

Rav nodded, then he discussed the route back to Bear Camp that they would follow while they were being chased by the 'Zet Ar. "That should bring us to the top of the last hill before Bear Camp," he finished. "From there, it's a sprint to the bottom."

Cyrn gritted his teeth. "Let's hope we're quick enough."

"We will be."

Cyrn scanned the herd once again. "I still haven't seen the 'Zet Ar. What if it's staying further away from the rest of the goats?"

"If we can hear the goats bleating, I'm sure they will hear us shouting. We'll get the 'Zet Ar's attention either directly or by riling up the other goats."

"You seem quite calm for someone about to face a stampede of mutants."

Rav chuckled, a sudden wave of terror seizing his mind before memories of Pitt; Enna, the future of the Carvell Bloodline within her; his parents; and Kayla rose above it to break him free. He stilled his trembling hands. "I am scared, but that doesn't matter. I have to do this, Cyrn. Nothing's going to harm Pitt, not if I can stop it." He smiled. "Besides, I've got you with me."

Cyrn smiled back at him.

"Shall we begin?" Cyrn held out his hand.

Rav grabbed it. "Aye."

Cyrn pulled Rav to his feet, where they stood at the top of the hill, side by side.

*"I guard my home with all I am,"* Cyrn sang.

*"To honour those who gave me life,"* Rav sang with him.

*"We march far to conquer our foes,*

*"A Bloodline to keep out all strife,*
*"Go forth and fight 'til your last light,*
*"Gifting land and lineage to our flesh made young,*
*"We'll love and marry for our blood to carry,*
*"Into the future bright."*
Silence.
And then it roared.
*MUUUUUUH!*

# Chapter Nineteen

It was like thunder rumbling.

The goats all turned in their direction and started charging. The ground was shaking. There was a cacophony of bleating. Rav could feel the beast coming for him. What had he done?

"Come on." Cyrn pulled him down the hillside.

Rav didn't dare look behind him as he raced after Cyrn; even that slight action might slow him down enough to be trampled. He spotted the path they were going to follow back to Bear Camp and dashed towards it, grazing his arms and legs on rocks he scraped past in his frantic rush to reach safety. Along the tether connecting Rav's mind to the 'Zet Ar came an immense feeling of malice and desire for destruction.

"It's coming, Cyrn. The 'Zet Ar is after us."

"Even without it, these goats are enough to raze Bear Camp." Cyrn scrambled to the top of a rock face and reached down to lift Rav up after him. "Hurry."

Rav grabbed his hand and was pulled to the top in one motion before they continued fleeing, the path they'd travelled to reach the herd blurring by. Night was fast approaching, the setting sun stretching the shadows around them. Goats swarmed through the twisted rock formations and over each steep hill as they chased after the brothers, the stone cracking under their hooves. Rav squinted as he faced the bright horizon, hoping the goats would be more bothered by it than he was, but the rumble behind him was only getting louder as the goats got ever closer. He slipped in a divot, and searing pain shot up from his ankle.

"It's just a bit further. Don't slow down now," Cyrn shouted.

"I'm trying," Rav roared, gritting his teeth as he continued sprinting.

The fleeing figures of the patrol could be seen ahead of them, each also in a mad scramble to escape.

"*Faster, men.* We have to warn the camp, or we're all going to die," Contender Olden yelled. "What have those madmen done?"

The stampede rushed ever closer, Rav now able to hear their braying breaths at his back. He surged after Cyrn, climbing up the steep hillside in front of him, legs burning. All he had to do was make it to the top and then down into the valley on the other side, then he'd reach the hill Bear Camp was built atop.

The sun had left only a fading pink glow in the sky. Rav watched it with gritted teeth, wishing it would just disappear and bring the darkness they desperately needed to hide in.

*TAK.*

A Spine was right behind him. He pushed himself harder to clamber over the lip of the hill, his gaze locked on the last few boulders they'd have for cover before they began their exposed final dash towards Bear Camp.

Cyrn suddenly slowed to become level with him while brandishing his spear. "*WAAAH.*"

*MEH.*

The Spine lunged at Cyrn with its wicked horns. Cyrn dodged the strike before speeding up again and squeezing between two boulders to prevent it from following him. Rav could hear another Spine breathing at his back and threw his spear blindly over his shoulder.

*MEH.*

A hit. He'd gained more time.

He crossed the hilltop and started dropping into the deep valley at the same time as Cyrn, but the Spine pursuing his brother had also caught up with them and went for another headbutt. Rav punched at its head with his shield.

CRACK

His shield splintered as a sharp pain shot through his hand, his efforts diverting the attack just enough to miss Cyrn.

Cyrn grabbed Rav's shoulder and pulled him down the valley. "It's the last sprint, Rav."

The ground rumbled as though it were about to crack as the main body of the herd caught up to them. The brothers raced down the hill in the open towards the last twisted rock formation before the boulder field. Cyrn flung his spear into the eye of the front-running Spine, knocking it down to disrupt the others behind it while Rav looked across the valley. Bear Camp had four massive bonfires burning to light up the area along with dozens of lit torches hanging off the wooden barricade that had been constructed. Baron Kiln's soldiers were standing in formation behind it, armed and ready to face the coming threat. Rav glanced at the stampede heading towards them. It was an endless stream of fur and horns. The soldiers would—

"*Dive,*" Cyrn screamed.

Rav dived, a Spine's horns tearing his furs but failing to gore him. He tumbled down the hill and just about managed to find his balance before he lost all control. A goat went rolling past him. So many goats came pouring over the hilltop that many ended up falling down the hillside in bleating balls of hooves and horns. Rav and Cyrn zigzagged down the hill.

Rav threw away his broken shield and pumped his arms as he dashed towards the rock formation. He slammed into the stone to stop his momentum, then darted in between two rock faces, following the narrow route to the boulder field. He checked behind him, relieved to see Cyrn also shuffling along the narrow gap with him.

*MEH.*

A Spine butted and snarled at the entrance, mouth frothing, doing its best to claw its way after them as night arrived. All Rav could see was black ahead of him. He scraped along, fighting off the rising panic that threatened to suffocate him. In between his and Cyrn's ragged breathing, he could hear the battle raging around them.

"*Hold together,*" Ive cried. "*Push them back,*"

*MEH. MEH. MEH.*

Rav felt in front of him, finding nothing—they were out of the rock formation and in the boulder field.

*Tak, tak, tak.*

It was coming from the right.

Rav drew a knife as he squinted. A crescent moon, an array of stars, and Bear Camp's bonfires provided just enough light to make out the largest boulders around them.

"Cyrn," he hissed.

"I'm here." Cyrn put a hand on Rav's shoulder.

*Tak, tak, tak.*

It sounded closer.

"Where is it?"

"Quiet."

*Tak, tak, tak.*

Rav could smell unwashed hide and rotten breath. Cyrn pulled him further into the boulder field. Everything went quiet, Rav and Cyrn holding their breaths as they wove between the rocks. Aside from the screams of battle, there was—

*MEH!*

Rav spun around to see a horned shadow charging straight at him and leaped out of its way.

"*Waaah,*" Cyrn roared, drawing the Spine's attention.

"*Cyrn.*" Rav recovered from his fall and jumped up to stab the Spine in the back.

*Meh.* The Spine bucked. Rav felt weightless... *Crack.* He struck a boulder, then collapsed on the ground. He lay there wheezing, his back in agony.

"*WAAAH,*" Cyrn continued to roar.

*MEH.*

Rav's body refused to get up and go help. "Cyrn." He slumped forward. "*Cyrn.*"

*MEH.*

"Fight me. Come and fight me," Rav cried out. If he could just get the Spine to attack him instead, then Cyrn would have a chance to run, but the Spine wasn't listening to him. He drew a knife and flung it at the Spine's bucking figure.

*MEH.*

It bleated in pain. He'd hurt it? How? Did that matter? Rav got another knife, ready to do it again, when—

"*Waah,*" Wakeman bellowed as he stabbed the Spine with his spear again.

Tido and Thorley thrust out after him, crippling its hind leg. Rav could now see their figures in the dark, working together to finish off the beast. It gave a final bleat as it dropped dead.

"Rav?" Cyrn called out. "Where are you?"

"Here, I'm here."

Cyrn stumbled forward with his arms outstretched until he touched Rav, grabbing him to lift him to his feet. "Can you walk?"

"I'll be able to in a moment... I just need to catch my breath first," Rav panted. "My legs are fine... I hurt my back. What about you?"

"I'm fine. Let's get out of here." Cyrn knelt to lay Rav across his shoulders, then picked him up. "Wakeman, what's happening at Bear Camp?"

"Last I saw, the soldiers were doing well," Wakeman said. "There are dozens of goats, but with the barricade and a strong formation, the soldiers are holding them back."

"What about the 'Zet Ar?"

"I haven't seen it. Did it chase you here?"

"It did," Rav said. "I'm sure of it."

"Well, it hasn't joined the battle."

Cyrn led them a short distance west, towards a nearby hilltop from where they could watch the fight, bleats echoing off stone while soldiers barked orders. Baron Kiln's soldiers stood with their spears raised in one large formation behind their barricade, facing the herd of two hundred goats charging up the hill to Bear Camp, two dozen Spines among their ranks. Soldiers at the rear kept feeding the bonfires, building them into beacons that burned away more and more of the darkness.

"They're just goats," Contender Ive bellowed above the bleating cacophony, his voice carrying far into the clear night. "We have the fire to blind them and the hill to tire their charge. Stand strong, stand firm, and we'll slaughter them."

The goats charged without care into the barricade, clattering against it before being driven back by soldiers wielding spears. The goats didn't even flinch from the blows, and with more of their kind driving them forward from the back, those wounded were forced into the melee once more.

"I've never seen goats like this," Wakeman whispered. "It's like they can't feel any pain. Is this the effect of the 'Zet Ar controlling them? Where is it?"

Rav was still tethered to the 'Zet Ar; however, while he could feel its viciousness, he didn't know which direction it was coming from. Was it watching the battle, like they were? Perhaps it was trying to spot Cyrn and Wakeman among the soldiers, knowing they were its greatest threat.

*CRACK.*

Part of the barricade collapsed under the relentless blows of the goats, leaving the left side of the soldiers' formation exposed.

"*Shields,*" Ive cried, organising a frontline of shield-bearers to block off the gap while spearmen formed behind them to stab at the coming herd, but even with their quick reaction speed, the soldiers started to get pushed back under the weight of the pressing beasts.

"The left flank will buckle if nothing changes," Cyrn muttered. "They're getting injured."

With the sheer number of horns wildly flailing around, it was inevitable for the shield-bearers to take blows no matter how good their teamwork was. Another wave of goats crashed into them, and several soldiers were knocked back. Contender Olden rushed forward to plug the gap before the fault spread through the whole formation, bolstering the defence as the wounded soldiers were pulled back for treatment.

"Around me," Olden called loudly and clearly above the braying, rallying those nearby to attack with greater ferocity.

While the goats didn't flinch under their strikes, many were still peppered with wounds and soon lost their strength.

"Ready," Contender Olden bellowed. "*Heave.*"

The shield-bearers stepped forward, regaining some of their lost ground.

"*Heave.*"

The frontline advanced again and again, driving the goats back until they reached the original barricade line at the edge of the hill. They shoved the frenzied goats back down the hillside to crash into the others running up.

Thorley gasped. "They've turned the battle in their favour."

While the frontline held off further attacks, the backline repaired the barricade as best they could.

"But the 'Zet Ar hasn't joined in yet." Rav pinched between his eyes. How could he force it to reveal itself? *Ah.* If he could sense what it was feeling through their tether, could he also send the 'Zet Ar a feeling to goad it into fighting?

Rav concentrated on the tether and thought about how happy he was that the goats had been driven back. The battle raged on without change. Rav was sure he'd managed to send his emotions across to the 'Zet Ar, so if it hadn't responded, then it didn't care about that enough to come out.

So, what did the 'Zet Ar want? It wasn't to destroy the soldiers, or it would have attacked them long ago.

And then it hit Rav. It wanted him.

Was it waiting to find out where he was?

Rav stared at the battle, picking a location at the back of the formation to observe. If he were there, how would he feel? Scared for sure. Maybe a little hopeful after the barricade had been repaired. If he saw a wounded comrade, he'd feel sad and angry.

Rav concentrated on the tether again and began feeding the 'Zet Ar a stream of emotions related to what was occurring within that small space. Then waited. And waited. Until. Back along the tether came a string of emotions that told Rav one message.

I found you.

*MUUUUUH!*

Rav swore the air shook.

*DOH DOH DOH.*

Something enormous lumbered up the hillside across from Bear Camp where the goats were charging from.

Rav's hair stood on end, his body shaking. It felt as if the air around him had turned heavy, weighing him down as a thunderstorm approached. It was the beast from his nightmares, the monster that had massacred the Ghoulsmen shadows, the mutant that had come from the Sink to take his life. With fur as dark as night and horns like curled spears, the 'Zet Ar stood as tall as two grown men at the peak of the hill and roared again.

*MUUUUUH!*

Everything trembled.

The behemoth barrelled towards Bear Camp, aiming straight for the spot Rav had been focusing on.

"*Crossbows,*" Contender Ive screamed across the chaos. "We have to slow it down before it reaches the barricade."

Several crossbowmen shot at the 'Zet Ar, but the bolts shattered against its hide, not slowing it in the slightest. Panic spread among the soldiers, and the frontline stumbled backwards. The pressure on the barricade grew as more goats crashed into it.

"Now is the time to give everything you have if you want to live," Contender Ive cried out. "This is our greatest trial before we reach the Sink. Survive tonight and we'll all become as rich as Barons. Olden, take charge of the formation. I'll deal with this beast."

The soldiers rallied at his words, entering a killing frenzy, their ferocious attacks slaying goat after goat to drive them away from the barricade. Contender Ive gathered several soldiers and marched towards the arriving 'Zet Ar before bracing behind the barricade. It looked as if the 'Zet Ar was going to run straight into them, but just before it did, it jumped. Rav watched it sail over the barricade and land next to where it thought he was, looming over the five soldiers there. A swipe of the 'Zet Ar's hoof sent two of them flying off the hilltop, then it headbutted another, turning his body to paste. The last two fled, but the 'Zet Ar gave chase and gored them in the back. It shook its head and flung the bodies off its horns.

*MUH.*

It was the same victorious bleat Rav had heard every night since its arrival. He seized up. That would've been the end of the Ghoulsmen—butchered in a few simple moves. He couldn't ever let the 'Zet Ar find them.

Cyrn shivered. "How can something like that exist?"

The 'Zet Ar stood still for a moment, as though it was waiting for something, but Contender Ive didn't wait with it, leading his unit to stab the 'Zet Ar in the back while it was distracted. The beast jolted as though pricked and darted around to face them. Two members of the unit threw themselves at the 'Zet Ar with their spears, but the 'Zet Ar jumped over them, this time aiming to land on top of Contender Ive. The Contender dashed underneath it and thrust his spear into its belly. The 'Zet Ar crushed Contender Ive beneath itself but landed straight on top of his spear, which was driven deeper into its abdomen before the shaft snapped under its weight.

*MUH.*

It went into a rage, wantonly running around while swinging its head from side to side to smash swathes of soldiers in its rampage.

Rav wanted to cheer—it had been hurt. The 'Zet Ar was injured and none of the Ghoulsmen had to die for it to happen.

The 'Zet Ar suddenly stopped its rampage and glared around itself.

*Oh no.* Rav desperately tried to calm himself, but his emotions had already travelled along the tether to the 'Zet Ar. It knew he was alive. It knew it had been tricked.

"Forget about the goats and get the monster," Contender Olden ordered, rushing at the 'Zet Ar once more. "Aim for its eyes."

The soldiers responsible for guarding the barricade had already scattered due to the beast's fury and now put their effort into attacking the 'Zet Ar, hacking at it from all sides. Blow after blow struck its hide, leaving little more than scratches. But the power in the strikes held it in place for a moment.

"Keep going," Olden roared.

"*Ahhhh,*" a soldier leaped at the 'Zet Ar's face with a dagger.

The beast ducked its head, blocking the dagger with its forehead, but the soldier used both hands to drag the dagger down towards the mutant's muzzle.

*MUUUUH.*

The beast whipped its head around, throwing the soldier into a crumpled heap on the ground, then charged straight ahead, trampling over everything in its way as it escaped the encirclement and galloped to the edge of Bear Camp.

"Reform," Contender Olden commanded. "Get to the barricade."

It was too late. While they'd been focused on the 'Zet Ar, the Spines had battered down the wooden posts and came charging into the camp. Rav looked away from them and stared at the 'Zet Ar. When the soldier had attacked it with a dagger, an immense feeling of pain had been transmitted to him through the tether. He squinted, hoping the 'Zet Ar would step into the light so he could better observe it. Was that...? The 'Zet Ar turned its head, and Rav confirmed that there was, indeed, a dagger handle sticking out of its right eye.

The beast was half-blind. It snarled, then charged back into the fray, carving a line in soldiers' blood that ran straight through the camp.

"This battle's nearly over," Cyrn said. "There's no way the soldiers are going to be able to kill the 'Zet Ar; it's just too powerful. We should get a head start to the Alley Camp while the goats finish off the rest of the soldiers."

Rav had recovered enough strength to stand on his own, and after thinking about being so terrified that he was going to abandon Stone's Way so that he could mislead the 'Zet Ar into heading away from Pitt, he started the run back to the Alley Camp with the Ghoulsmen.

"Cyrn," Wakeman panted, "even with Tibald and his soldiers, we won't be able to kill that thing. We can set traps for the 'Zet Ar, but from what I've seen, I'm not sure if it will be tricked by them, never mind if our traps would manage to hurt it. It took a spear to its underbelly and carried on fighting without issue."

"The spear *did* hurt it, though," Cyrn said, "which means we *can* pierce through its hide, in the right places. Its right eye was also destroyed by that dagger, so that's two vulnerabilities we can exploit. If we can get it to fall onto something sharp or attack its face, then we'll defeat it. It's not hopeless. I'll also ask Tibald to send for Baron Hewett and his army to help fight it."

"Is that..." Wakeman bared his teeth and shuddered before massaging his temples. "You know what asking for their help means, right?"

"I do," Cyrn answered. "The 'Zet Ar's just too strong for us to defeat alone; we'll have to work with Tibald and Baron Hewett to stop it. We need to do whatever we can to stop that monster from ever getting to Pitt, or it'll destroy everything we've fought to protect."

Rav kicked the ground with a snarl, scattering loose topsoil into the dark, pain flaring up his leg from his ankle. He spat with a hissing wince, limping on as fast as he could manage, but with his ankle burning in pain, he slowed, watching the other Ghoulsmen stride ahead of him until they started to vanish into the darkness.

Stinging wounds flared up all over his arms and legs from the grazes he'd picked up during the chase as he pushed himself on, the worst being where the badger had scratched him. Just as he stumbled, leg on the cusp of buckling, a large figure dropped out of the darkness ahead and grabbed his collar to steady him.

Wakeman draped Rav's arm over his shoulder, then lifted him so Rav only had to run on his good leg and carried him forward.

"Come on, Rav," Wakeman grunted. "This night's nearly over. It's just a little bit further."

Still too slow, Cyrn also dropped back and propped up Rav's other side, he and Wakeman sprinting to catch up with Thorley and Tido while carrying Rav between them.

"Are we really going to ally with the man who brought soldiers into Stone's Way to attack us?" Rav wheezed. "I can't stomach it. Isn't there some way to get the 'Zet Ar to kill Tibald and lay waste to Baron Hewett's army too?"

"Tibald is in Pitt, Rav," Cyrn panted. "We can't lure the beast there, and we won't survive luring it all the way to Greenfield. We've done what we can."

"Cyrn," Rav pressed. "Maybe Baron Hewett being this Ah' ke means he can handle things like the 'Zet Ar. But you can't. Tibald can't. If the Sink has turned something like a goat into a monster like this, imagine what it's done to actual predators, like wolves. If asking for Tibald and Baron Hewett's help means you must go to the Sink with them, then it's better for us to make our stand here where we can at least die in our home."

"I know. I've thought about that already, but I told you my plan before, didn't I? I'll just be pretending to ally with Tibald. When we're all safe, I'll run away with everyone."

Rav hung his head. "That's..." *Extremely dangerous for you to do.* After taking a breath, he raised it again and gave his brother a firm nod. "I believe in you."

The further away from the 'Zet Ar Rav ran, the weaker his connection to it through the tether became until he was only vaguely aware of its existence.

Supported on both sides, Rav found his body slumping unbidden as exhaustion sapped his remaining strength, the ache in his back throbbing so much it left him breathless. Head lolling, he fought to remain thinking. How could he get Tibald and his soldiers to be the ones sacrificed to wound the 'Zet Ar in the coming battle? A trap within a trap, perhaps? But how could Tibald be fooled by something like that and wasn't the 'Zet Ar too dangerous a foe to use in such a plan—

A spot of something wet and warm soaked through his furs above his waist to touch his skin. Rav unhooked his arm from Cyrn's shoulders and hopped on as he hurried to touch his left side, finding the substance viscous and sticky—blood. But after running his hand under his clothes, he didn't find any cuts. Rav stuttered in his hobble, Wakeman groaning while Cyrn lifted him back up. Did that mean the blood was coming from...?

Rav looked at his brother.

# Chapter Twenty

"You're bleeding," Rav whispered.

Cyrn kept facing ahead. "Aye, I am."

"It's from when you fought the Spine, isn't it? You said you were fine."

"I *am* fine, that Spine caught me with its horn is all. I can still move and fight and do everything I need to."

Rav tried to wriggle off Cyrn's shoulder, but Cyrn grabbed his arm and held it in place. "Put me down; I should be the one helping you if you're hurt."

"You're too slow and, as I said, I'm alright. Trust me."

Rav slipped his arm out of Cyrn's grip and raised his hand in another attempt to slide himself off Cyrn's shoulder, but instead brought it around so Cyrn was only under his armpit and pressed it down over Cyrn's side to slow the bleeding. Warm and slick, Rav breathed a sigh of relief, his brother's blood already thick as it continued clotting. The bleeding had stopped; the wound couldn't have been too deep—most of the blood that had soaked into Rav's furs like thin jelly formed from old blood that had already been absorbed by Cyrn's furs.

Cyrn winced under his breath as he stepped over a rock but continued moving as normal. Rav pressed his hand firmer onto

Cyrn's side, the signs of pain Cyrn had been hiding becoming more and more apparent. How was he even still moving?

Wakeman looked across to Cyrn and shifted further under Rav, taking more of his weight, Cyrn breathing easier as they continued. Rav also leaned more on Wakeman while doing his best to run on his own as sweat streamed down Cyrn's face. Guided by starlight, the Ghoulsmen hurried to the Alley Camp, and soon, the sun began to rise again, lighting the eastern sky pink.

"We're being followed by a unit of four soldiers," Cyrn muttered as he looked over his shoulder. "Hide behind the next hill, then we'll ambush them."

"Can you fight?" Rav asked Cyrn.

"Aye."

"*Should* you fight?"

"There's no time for this, Rav."

Rav held his tongue. They followed Cyrn's instructions and waited out of sight for the pursuing soldiers to get closer.

"Can *you* fight, Rav?" Wakeman asked. "I noticed you flinching whenever I touched your back."

"Aye, I can," Rav stated. If Cyrn was going to keep fighting, then so was he.

"We've only got three spears anyway," Tido said. "Two of us will have to stay back."

"I'll use a knife," Cyrn said.

"I can throw some knives as well," Rav added.

"Rav and I will fight one of them together while you three handle one soldier each," Cyrn commanded. "Once we've killed them, we'll continue moving."

As Rav waited, he began to shiver as though his body were racked with fever. In the quiet, all he could hear was his rattling heart as it worked hard to keep him awake.

"What did you mean by you 'pretending to ally with Tibald'?" Wakeman whispered to Cyrn.

"Our plan to leave has changed," Cyrn responded. "We're still going, it's just gotten more complicated. I'll explain everything later." He nudged Rav's shoulder. "And I'll also be waiting to hear your explanation about what's going on with this 'Zet Ar."

"It's..." Rav sighed. "It's hard to explain."

"Start working on it, then. If you have any information that can help us defeat it, we need to know."

Rav rubbed his eyes as he tried to focus. "The 'Zet Ar's objective is to kill me—that's the most important thing."

Cyrn nodded. "We can use that. Quiet now, the soldiers are close."

"Where are they?" Rav heard a soldier ask. "Hurry. Since they're the ones who brought that monster to attack us, they must have a safe place to retreat to. We must find it, or we'll be stuck out here with the beast."

"I can't see them; it's like they've disappeared," another soldier replied.

Cyrn signalled for the Ghoulsmen to get ready, and as the sound of the soldiers' footsteps got closer, he ordered the attack. Rav dashed out of hiding and threw a knife at the first soldier he saw. The blade clanged off the soldier's helmet, knocking him backwards. Wakeman dispatched his target with a clean thrust of his spear while Tido and Thorley did the same to their opponents. Cyrn pounced on the soldier Rav had knocked down, but the soldier was already retreating.

"*It's you,*" he screeched. "You killed my comrades. They were mothers and fathers, brothers and sisters—good people working to bring honour to their Names, and you had a beast butcher them all."

"You attacked us first," Rav spat. "None of them would have died if they hadn't invaded Stone's Way."

"Attacked you?" The man's face contorted with twisted hatred. "We offered you a place at our side; we offered you a part of the glory we were going to claim, and you rejected our goodwill. Even then, we were still going to add you to our ranks so you'd have a chance of obtaining a part of the Sink's spoils. That beast is evil by nature, but you... you're so much worse. You had the path towards honour right before you and yet you *chose* to walk a life of shame. You're the real monsters."

"I must commend you for your courage," Cyrn said as he closed in on the soldier, wary of the man's spear. "You've seen one of the true mutants that inhabit the Sink slaughter an entire group of soldiers and yet you still want to go there and face hundreds of them. I'm impressed by the depth of bravery fanaticism inspires. Do you really not fear for your life?"

The soldier hesitated, giving Cyrn a moment to dash close to him and tear the spear out of his hands. The soldier punched at Cyrn with his shield, but Cyrn dodged to the side before stabbing him under the armpit with his knife. The soldier screamed.

"What a waste of life," Cyrn muttered as he grabbed the man, spun him around, then lifted his chin to expose his neck, his knife pressed against it.

"You're... wrong," the soldier managed to speak through bloodied teeth. "Soon, only those families who've benefitted from the Sink will matter anyway. I did the only thing I could do to bring honour to my Name. The only future awaiting families like yours is one where you grovel at the feet of those better than you. Your Name will be worth less than mud."

"At least we'll be alive to experience the future, whatever it may be." Cyrn cut the man's throat, a spurt of crimson spraying across the mud before it all ran slick down his chest. He threw the body down and raised his hand to gather the Ghoulsmen. "Let's keep moving."

He collected a spear and shield, as did Rav, then the Ghoulsmen set off once more.

"They're mad, utterly mad," Rav spoke. "How could any of them still think they could survive the Sink after facing the 'Zet Ar? They're all so deluded, it's almost... sad. I can only think that they're all suffering from some kind of mental affliction."

"They don't deserve our pity," Cyrn said. "Don't forget that. Those people made their choices with rational minds."

"I know. It's just that when he talked about their families, I thought about how they see us and how we see them. We *have to* kill them to protect ourselves, and I wondered if they think the same way. If they have Names and families and speak of honour, then they can't be that different to us, but somehow, they've twisted everything those words mean to justify the atrocities they commit."

Cyrn sucked his teeth. "There's no point trying to rationalise the minds of madmen; it's best to simply put them down so they can't cause further destruction."

Tibald wasn't at the Alley Camp when they arrived. Cyrn ordered them all inside to rest, and Rav collapsed into a heap on his bedding. Cyrn's words had been branded into his mind and Rav couldn't fall asleep with them staring at him. 'Put them down' was too callous... or was it? What had he just done? He'd sent a mutant to slaughter dozens of people to save his home without a single thought about what it meant to orchestrate their deaths. Maybe that soldier was right; maybe he was a monster. But maybe Cyrn and Aunt Judy and Kayla and everyone who supported him were right too. Maybe being a monster wasn't so bad. Maybe it was necessary.

Then why were Cyrn's words glaring at him like that? Why did they refuse to fade away and let him sleep? Perhaps there was something acceptable about acknowledging that he was a monster, but he couldn't accept the same of his brother. Rav didn't want Cyrn to be a monster like him, and yet, it appeared that he was. He could only hope that once they left this place, the cold malice building inside them all would fade away so they could become their normal selves again.

"Rav..."

Rav startled awake, not knowing when he'd fallen asleep. The other Ghoulsmen were milling around the camp, tending to their weapons in beams of bright sunlight that shone through cracks in the cave roof, the largest coming through the chimney hole. Suddenly, Rav felt his connection to the 'Zet Ar become slightly stronger before fading. Then it happened again and again and again. He sat up.

"What is it, Rav?" Wakeman asked.

The connection grew stronger for longer this time before it faded.

Rav shivered, going pale as his heart started to pound in his chest. "I think the 'Zet Ar's trying to find me."

"How?" Cyrn grabbed his spear and raised it towards the cave entrance, as though the beast would burst through at any moment.

"I'm connected to it and I can sense what it's feeling, but when we ran away from it, the sensation grew faint. The 'Zet Ar's now moving around to find out which direction the connection is strongest in so it can hunt me down." He flinched at the connection strengthening once more, a tremble starting in his hands, then racing up his arms to his lip, his entire body soon shaking as the 'Zet Ar moved ever closer. "It won't be long before it finds the exact direction it needs to run in to find me."

Cyrn stamped his spear butt into the ground as he closed his eyes in thought. "How far away is it?"

Rav tensed to steady his erratic breathing. "It's still very far away, probably on the other side of Stone's Way after I tricked it into running there, but thinking about how fast it is, once it starts running in a straight line, it won't be long before it gets here. Maybe half a day?"

Cyrn opened his eyes and looked up through the chimney hole. "It's already afternoon. By the time the 'Zet Ar arrives, it will be night, when it will have the advantage in the dark... You said it's chasing you, Rav?"

"Aye."

"Are you willing to act as bait again?"

Rav forced a nod.

Cyrn took a breath. "We'll prepare traps at the Alley, where we can drop boulders on top of the 'Zet Ar, using you to lure it into the narrow space. The high walls can keep the 'Zet Ar contained and allow us to stay out of its reach while we attack it. Hopefully, Tibald will arrive in time to help us, and with his assistance, we might have a chance of killing it."

Rav shook his head. "That's not going to work. If we fight the 'Zet Ar, it *will* kill us. I've seen it happen. It learns from its mistakes; tricking it won't be as effective again."

"Well, what else can we do?"

"I don't know."

Cyrn put his hand on Rav's shoulder. "Then, this is the best plan we've got. We'll make it work. Everyone, get ready. We need to gather as many boulders at the top of the Alley as possible."

Rav wanted to put his head in his hands, but he stopped himself, mindful of those around him. He couldn't show the despair he felt; he had to keep morale as high as possible for the coming fight. He slumped back down. Even with that, there was no hope. The 'Zet Ar was going to kill them all to get to him.

"Come on, Rav." Wakeman handed him a spear and shield as the others headed to the Alley. "We all need to work together if we want to overcome this."

Rav looked up at him, tears in his eyes. "All I ever seem to do is bring harm to those around me. Do you think this is all happening because of what I did? Are my ancestors making me suffer? None of you deserve this."

Wakeman ruffled Rav's hair. "No, Rav, you're not being punished. It's not your fault that the Sink exists. Everything you've done has helped protect your home and your family, not destroy it. Just two days ago, you saved me from becoming a slave. What you're doing is making things better, not worse."

"This is different, though... The 'Zet Ar is coming for us simply because I exist, and I don't know why. There's nothing I can do about it."

"Aye, there is—you can fight with us."

"Of course, you know I will. It's fine if I fight an unwinnable battle, but I can't let anyone else do that, not for me. Cyrn certainly can't, not with his duty to his Bloodline. He *has to* live."

Wakeman flicked Rav's head. "Have we fought the battle yet?"

"No..."

"Then how do you know we won't win? Rav, we can only make good choices, not control good outcomes. None of us know what will happen. We can only decide what to do in the moment, and I believe that making the right decisions now *will* lead to a better future. I disobeyed my Pa and he made me Nameless, exiling me from my home, but it was only because I left my home that I found you and Cyrn and Stone's Way. I made the right choice and suffered for it, but that suffering was temporary. Fighting the 'Zet Ar *is* the right decision to make now. Have faith in us."

"But everyone's already tired and Cyrn's wounded. We couldn't defeat the 'Zet Ar at our best, never mind now."

Wakeman huffed. "We don't know that, and remember, the 'Zet Ar is injured too. Blind in one eye, and having been running around Stone's Way all day, this is the best time for us to face it." He grinned in excitement, eyes alight as his breath quickened.

"Can you not see the opportunity you've given us? The opportunity that you've given me? You're not alone in your anger, Rav, you never are. Now is my chance to act, to defend *my* home. To prove my courage and valour and show everyone that my being Nameless has done nothing to diminish my character. You've done your part; now it's time for me to do mine." He gave Rav a playful nudge. "Let me fight unburdened. Let me guard your brother's back. Let me have my moment."

Rav couldn't help but smile back, chest burning with renewed vigour. "You won't be guarding his back; you'll be standing shoulder to shoulder, Wakeman. You're already as good as Cyrn. I just wish you could see it yourself." He stood taller, shaking his head with a laugh. "Where did you learn to talk like this? I can *feel* my blood pulsing through my body."

Wakeman smirked with a wink. "I've read a lot of books."

Rav raised an eyebrow. "But I never see you read."

Wakeman's smirk softened, his gaze becoming unreadable. "I haven't in a while. Reading reminds me of home."

They went quiet as Rav thought over what Wakeman had said.

"Thank you, Wakeman. I know what to do now."

"Come on, then." Wakeman headed for the cave exit, beckoning Rav to follow him. "We've not got long."

Rav made to get up, then pulled a pained expression before sitting back down again.

"Can you move, Rav?" Wakeman rushed to his side.

"Aye, I just need a moment to stretch. I'll be able to get to the Alley for my part in the plan, though, don't worry."

"Do you need me to carry you?"

"No, get to the Alley as fast as you can to help the others." Rav stretched his back into a painful position, causing genuine sweat to form on his brow. "I'll join you soon."

"As long as you're sure you'll be alright."

"Aye, I will be." He used his spear as a walking stick to stand up. "See, better already."

"I'll come back to check on you."

Rav nodded as Wakeman left... then picked up his spear and marched to gather his equipment. The answer had been so obvious that he felt stupid for not realising it sooner. The beast was coming for him and him alone; the only reason Pitt and the other Ghoulsmen were in danger was because he was with them. If he ran far away from Pitt, the 'Zet Ar would follow him away from everyone else. From there, he could find a way to survive long enough for Cyrn to find another way to kill it, or if he died, maybe the mutant would be satisfied with that, having achieved its goal, and leave Stone's Way.

There was no way the other Ghoulsmen would let him sacrifice himself like that. *This* was the right decision. He tore a blank page out of his notebook and wrote:

*Cyrn,*

*I won't let you die for me. I have a way to protect Pitt on my own. When you have an army, come find what's left of me and kill the 'Zet Ar. Until then, I'll be hiding in a place where the beast might just fall.*

*Always thinking of you and our family,*

*Rav*

Rav stuffed his pouches with as much food as he could carry and started running.

# Chapter Twenty-One

Rav gritted his teeth as he raced east towards the Stone Steps, following familiar hills towards Crevice Camp. If he used its eroded and brittle landscape as cover to hide in, he might just survive long enough for Cyrn to gather an army and come save him. He also thought about what Cyrn had said about the 'Zet Ar having two vulnerabilities that they could exploit—it was half-blind and could be hurt if it fell onto something sharp. The Stone Steps was the perfect place to take advantage of those weaknesses.

His back and ankle were already screaming, slowing Rav down as his breaths became hisses. He had time, though. With the 'Zet Ar tracking him by trying to feel which direction their connection was strongest, as long as he kept moving, it would be far harder for the 'Zet Ar to find the right direction to run in.

As he ran, he kept checking over his shoulder, hoping he wouldn't see Cyrn or Wakeman chasing after him. Cyrn would figure out where he was going from his message, but Rav hoped his brother would prioritise gathering reinforcements. Rav shook his head and focused on the path ahead. Cyrn was smart enough to not waste the opportunity he'd created for them. Cyrn had asked Rav to trust him and now Cyrn needed to trust him in return.

Rav limped on, the pain in his back flaring until it was all he could think about. He pushed thoughts of his family and Kayla to the front of his mind to keep moving; the pain was worth it if it kept them safe.

*Just. Keep. Going.*

Rav pressed on until his throat went dry and sweat weighed his furs. He sat on a rock and guzzled from his waterskin, trying to conserve the little water he had, but his thirst was insatiable, and it was only after the first quarter of the water was gone that he could swallow without his throat grating against itself.

There would be streams to refill his waterskin from on the way, but every time he stopped, the 'Zet Ar would get closer. Rav sat there for a moment, trying to calculate if he'd move faster drinking lots of water with more breaks or if he were dehydrated and ran without stopping.

The tether grew stronger. Rav jolted up. He was wasting time. No more breaks. He tied some cloth as tight as he could around his ankle and carried on running.

The afternoon passed and soon the sun was setting, but Rav still couldn't see the Stone Steps in the distance. Where was he? He rested on another hill and flicked through his notebook in the fading light to find the route across Stone's Way and into the Stone Steps towards Crevice Camp, matching a lone tree to his left to a sketched one to see that he was close to his destination even if he couldn't see it yet. It would be night by the time he arrived, though; he'd have to finish the last part of the journey in the dark. Then what would he do? Rav grimaced as he looked over his sketched map of the Stone Steps, reading through every warning he'd written about dangerous places to travel within it. It was too risky to traverse in the dark. He'd recover during the remainder of the night when he got there and continue in the morning.

The sun started sinking below the horizon, its orange disk glowing over the hills behind him to look like a crown. Rav concentrated on the tether. It had been some time since he'd last felt any significant flare from it. He tried to sense something from it to find out how much closer the 'Zet Ar was when a wave of panic rushed through him. What if the 'Zet Ar had carried on heading towards Pitt? If the 'Zet Ar had realised what he was doing, then it might have done just that, aiming to kill Cyrn and Tibald before they could gather reinforcements. What if it were going to attack his home? What if he'd left the Ghoulsmen down a man for the coming fight? Rav shook his head. The 'Zet Ar couldn't be that clever. *Right?* He waited where he was with a white-knuckled grip on his spear and shield.

*Rage. Destruction. Domination.*

Rav flinched as the tether flared to life. The emotions were much stronger than before; the 'Zet Ar was nearer now. It *was* chasing him. Rav sighed with relief. *Wait.* Wasn't the beast much closer than he'd expected it to be? It must've started heading straight towards him, which meant it had locked onto his position. Did that mean... it had been suppressing its emotions so that Rav couldn't sense its rapid progress? The 'Zet Ar had been duped by the tether once and was now using it as a weapon itself. Rav set off sprinting.

The last of the daylight faded before he arrived at the Stone Steps, leaving him with only dim crescent moonlight to navigate with. The hillside seemed to stretch on into infinity before him. Surely, he should be there by now? The ground squelched beneath his feet as though he were walking along the tongue of a great beast, heading straight down its throat. All it had to do was swallow and all his hardships would disappear...

Rav slapped his cheeks, waking himself back up. He had to give everything to stay alive no matter how doomed everything felt.

He fell into rhythm with his aching—*Step, breath, ow. Step, breath, ow*—until finally, his feet slapped against flat, hard stone. Rav walked in a circle just to be sure, confirming that the area around him was all flat rock before dropping to his knees. He'd made it. Now, he had to find a crevice and sleep. He crawled across the surface of the Stone Steps, finding a cove next to a boulder and huddling into it.

*Drip, drip, drip.*

Rav woke to the sound of raindrops. *Water.* Vision bleary, he stumbled over to a puddle on the rockface and pressed his lips to the stone to drink it dry. By the faint light, he could tell it was almost dawn; he hadn't slept long. His connection to the 'Zet Ar was now strong enough for them to send faint feelings to each other constantly. Rav got up and pressed ahead.

Before him lay the Stone Steps—an enormous plain of flat stone whose surface had been eroded by hundreds of years of heat, ice, and rainfall, causing it to be brittle and riddled with craters, like flaking skin. It wasn't just the stone's surface that had been worn away by water, though. Beneath the flat top layer, thin but powerful underground rivers had also carved out the stone, leaving much of the terrain hollow. Multiple narrow ravines now lacerated the land where the top layer of stone had succumbed to its own weight and collapsed into the rapids below, leaving great gouges in the landscape. The sheer drops all around Rav reminded him to be extra careful about where he stepped, lest his weight caused the thin section of stone he was standing on to finally also collapse, sending him plunging into the torrent of water flowing under him.

He peered down one of the circular well-like holes beside him, seeing bare rock at the bottom. A fall like that would kill him, but it was a welcome sight. If there was no water at the bottom of a hole, the underground rivers that had carved it in the first place had likely changed direction, meaning that further erosion hadn't occurred and the path was probably still safe to travel. He pulled out his notebook and checked the clear path across this section of the Stone Steps that had been trod, following it as closely as he could. Still, he tested the stone in front of him by tapping it with his spear just in case.

One of the native lizards scuttled out of a crack.

*Cheep.* A flock of tiny birds flittered overhead as they scavenged for easy pickings.

The lizard rushed to hide again.

Rav faced the sky to let the icy-cold rain splash over him. Where was he going? A small campsite had been built inside a canyon towards the centre of the Stone Steps. That's what he needed to reach. Then, he was going to hide away. There was no way the 'Zet Ar would be able to find him quickly in this landscape, and even if it did, it wouldn't be able to fit into the narrow canyon. Rav wiped his face. Although the 'Zet Ar was a goat and probably good at climbing, due to its increased weight, it would hopefully have a treacherous time searching in here, where one wrong step would send it into freefall.

Step by step, Rav walked until he reached the edge of the thin canyon he was aiming for, which was about as wide as his shoulders. He looked down at the rock shelves leading into it. Rainfall had worn away the soft stone of this canyon, leaving only the harder stone layers behind after everything else had been washed downstream. It looked like a set of giant steps led to the canyon floor, each about his height.

*Muuuuh.*

Rav turned around to see a small figure bounding towards the Stone Steps in the distance. The tether came to life, sending a constant stream of malice towards him. The 'Zet Ar was here. Rav jumped down onto the first rock shelf, hoping the 'Zet Ar hadn't seen him. *Ah!* His ankle buckled under him as he landed. Rav clutched the limb, pain burning, breath hissing through his teeth. Something had torn. He bit into his furs to quiet his whimpers and lowered himself to the next layer, then the next until he reached the canyon floor.

It was dank down in between the stone walls and there were great patches of moss growing all around him. Rav shuffled forward, having to turn sideways to fit through an extremely narrow section of the canyon. His back scraped against the wall as he moved, causing him to tear up. At the other end, his arm brushed against a bulging moss patch. A swarm of insects buzzed out in a cloud to choke the air, biting his face and neck.

*Tok, tok, tok.* The sound of hooves much heavier than even Spines' thumping on rock echoed down to Rav. He kept wishing to hear a startled '*Muuuh*' or feel a sensation of fear come along the tether as the 'Zet Ar fell through the surface layer, but the constant stream of fury directed at him didn't stop. He hobbled over to a grimy stone slab that marked Crevice Camp and slid it aside before crawling into the small space behind it. After covering the entrance again, he searched the cave to find a candle with flint, and soon the cave glowed pale yellow.

It was cramped and dark but also clean and dry. He measured out the dried meat he'd brought with him, rationing out a week of food for himself. If he didn't move much, he might be able to stretch that out further. There were also lizards and bugs to eat if he was starving. Water was a larger issue; however, if it kept raining like it had been today, he would have enough to drink. The candles would have to be used sparingly, but that didn't matter. He'd made it. There was no way the 'Zet Ar would be able to fit down here, much less find him.

*Muuuh.*

Rav brought his elation back under control, doing his best to not let any more information about his situation leak out to the 'Zet Ar. He blew out the candle and curled up into a ball to keep warm. Now he just had to wait—*tok, tok, tok*—listening as the 'Zet Ar hunted for him.

*Ee. Eeeeee. Eee. EEEEEEEE.*

Rav slapped at his ear.

*...Eeee.*

It was hard to tell how much time had passed. The light shining through a crack by the camp entrance told him it was day, but he wasn't sure if it was still that first day or the second. Once the 'Zet Ar had reached the Stone Steps, its speed had drastically slowed, presumably because it had to progress so carefully, and then the tether had returned to the way it had been when Rav had watched the beast at Bear Camp. It had been some time since Rav had heard it moving. Was it resting? Maybe it was—

*Doh.* The stone shook, dust falling onto Rav's face.

*MUUUH.*

Rav sat up. It was here, right above him. He wished it were just passing through the area, but after waiting a while, it had yet to move. Had it spotted him jumping into the canyon, then sneaked over to him? He took a deep breath, stilling his trembling hands. He was safe down here. The 'Zet Ar couldn't reach him.

*Doh. MUUH.*

Rav checked his cuts to see how healed they were, confirming it was the second day, as he'd eaten and drunk in candlelight. Everything ached; his ankle was badly swollen, he couldn't lie on his back, and he needed to pee. He doused the candle and emerged from the camp, straight into a swarm of insects.

"Pah." Rav spat and hurried to close the cave entrance behind him before heading out of the cloud.

*Doh.* The canyon walls rattled again, driving the bugs into further frenzy. Dust shifted onto Rav's shoulders and shards of stone clattered against each other as they fell into the canyon. He looked up as he relieved himself, squinting at the bright sky. What was the 'Zet Ar doing?

*Doh. Clatter.* At the top of the canyon wall where he'd first climbed down, he saw the giant shadow of the beast rear back on two legs and then slam its hooves down with thundering strength.

*Doh. CRACK.* The top edge of the canyon broke off and then shattered as it hit the floor far below it, releasing a cloud of dust into the air.

Was it...? Rav watched as the end of the canyon he'd climbed down from disappeared in rubble. It was. It was trying to collapse the canyon; it was going to bury him alive.

Rav scrambled back into his cave and grabbed his equipment before hurrying back out, insects and lizards scurrying around him. With the 'Zet Ar destroying the entrance he'd climbed down from, he had to run to the other end of the canyon to climb back out, and he had to do it as fast as he could. If the 'Zet Ar broke the other exit before he climbed out, he'd be trapped down here and crushed.

*Doh.* The 'Zet Ar had shifted along the top of the canyon and started breaking another section rather than heading straight to the other end. Rav exhaled in relief. He had a chance to escape. He ducked under the dust cloud as he moved to hide his figure, grit coating his skin. First, he had to get out of here, then... Rav stumbled. What would he do then? He'd been planning on hiding, but now he couldn't do that and his backup plan to enter places the 'Zet Ar couldn't fit was crumbling around him. Once he climbed back up, he'd be back on the flat stone surface with nowhere to hide from the 'Zet Ar.

But what other choice did he have? He'd just have to run for his life and hope the 'Zet Ar fell before him.

*Wait.*

He thought over the trodden paths through the Stone Steps, realising there was one nearby. If he fled there, he could move safely across the surface and gain some distance from the 'Zet Ar while it had to slow down in case it fell. It wasn't much, but it would have to do.

Rav shuffled along, flinching at the lizards rushing past him. One jumped on his back, and he wriggled to throw it off while insects buzzed in his ears, managing to squirm under his fur hood and into his armour.

*Doh. CRACK. Crash.* Another section collapsed. Rav could see the end of the canyon floor.

*Doh. CRACK. MUUH.* An enormous shattering shook the entire canyon. Wind rushed behind Rav, bringing a great rolling dust cloud with it to engulf him. He couldn't breathe, coughing and spluttering as his eyes stung, blind to anything but grey, fighting to escape the suffocation. He charged forward, desperate to find fresh air, and at last, he did, emerging from the cloud coated in dust and spewing grey saliva. He hunched over, chest heaving, feeling as if his mouth were filled with sand.

*Doh. Crack.*

He trudged on, reaching the set of giant steps leading back up to the top of the canyon. Now, he had to climb them. After tying his spear and shield to his back, Rav jumped up. *Ah.* His ankle couldn't take the violent motion. He was going to have to pull himself up with his arms.

*Doh. CRACK.*

Sweat mixed with dust to scratch and scrape him as he heaved himself up each step, getting closer to the surface with every wince. His ankle was a problem. Rav tried to think of a solution, but other than just gritting his teeth and ignoring the pain, he couldn't find one. How was he going to move fast enough when he was level with the 'Zet Ar? He wasn't.

Rav started to shake. He was going to die. The idea hadn't seemed so bad before, but now he found himself trembling. *No.* He forced his hands to go still. Maybe he would die, but he wouldn't die like this. Not as a coward. He'd do his duty to his Name and give everything he had to live. That's what Carvells did, and he *was* a Carvell.

Rav waited just below the lip of the surface level, peeking out at the 'Zet Ar, which was busy burying the camp he'd been hiding in. He readied his spear and shield, tying the support around his ankle even tighter. Memories of how useless spears were against the 'Zet Ar's hide flitted through his mind, but he discarded them. If he had to stab the beast, he'd make sure it felt it. The time to make a run for it was approaching. Rav took a breath and whispered,

*"I guard my home with all I am,*
*"To honour those who gave me life."*
*"Don't die."* Kayla's words echoed in his mind.
*"We march far to conquer our foes,*
*"A Bloodline to keep out all strife.*
*"Go forth and fight 'til your last light."*
*"I couldn't wish for a better brother,"* Cyrn's words followed.
*"Gifting land and lineage to our flesh made young,*
*"We'll love and marry for our blood to carry,*
*"Into the future bright."*
He burst up and ran without looking back.
*MUUUUH!*

# CHAPTER TWENTY-TWO

Rav sprinted along the trodden path, crying in pain. The 'Zet Ar bounded towards him but kept stopping before moving again. Rav listened to its movements, hoping to hear it fall. He wasn't so lucky. He glanced over his shoulder to see the 'Zet Ar dancing nimbly over the rock surface. Despite its size and weight, it still had the climbing ability of a normal goat, allowing it to chase after Rav at a decent pace. Rav stared ahead, envisioning the path he had to take, when he spotted an anomaly—he couldn't see a section of stone in front of him. It had fallen away, leaving a gap as long as he was in the stone platform. He'd have to jump it. Worse than that, it meant the path he was following might not be safe anymore.

The 'Zet Ar was hopping across the stone behind him, catching up. Once it reached the area Rav had climbed up from, it started tapping the stone it was about to step on before moving. It knew the ground was unstable and was treading its own way across. Rav gritted his teeth. Why was it so clever? The sound of rushing water got louder as Rav neared the gap. He sped up and leaped over the ravine, crashing to the ground on the other side. He hurried to get up and keep moving but found that he couldn't—his ankle could no longer bear any weight.

He looked back at the hulking black beast hunting him down. The 'Zet Ar was making steady progress towards him; it wouldn't be long before he was gored. The 'Zet Ar looked at him with what seemed like a grin. It revealed its delight at Rav's agony through the tether. It was going to trample him, just as it had trampled his shadow every night since its arrival. It bleated as though laughing, as though it had just realised something obvious. Rav watched in horror as, instead of continuing its process of testing the ground it was stepping on, it stepped exactly where Rav had, following the safe path he'd travelled. It bleated again in triumph, sneering at Rav with a single oily eye. Rav's hope of it falling buckled. Tears blurred his vision and his lip wobbled.

*MUH.*

The beast had misplaced its hoof, and its leg had broken through the stone surface to dangle into an empty gap. It pulled its hoof back up and tested the way ahead like it had before. Rav rubbed his eyes, clearing the despair that had blinded him. He still had to survive; that *thing* wasn't unbeatable. The more his vision cleared, the better he saw the monster. Its right eye still had a dagger hilt sticking out of it, while its remaining good eye was haggard from lack of sleep. It was also limping from where it had landed on Contender Ive's spear, and its front hooves were cracked from slamming against the stone. Its black fur didn't seem so menacing in the daylight. It was exhausted.

Rav crawled to his left, where the mutant couldn't see well, and searched the ground around him. It was just as flaky as the rest of the stone, leaving many loose sections of rock. He pried up a chunk and threw it at the monster, watching the rock arc through the air before landing far short. But when it shattered against the stone surface, it broke a hole through it, opening a small gap into the empty darkness below. The 'Zet Ar turned its head in Rav's direction, and Rav finally felt the sensation he'd been desperate for: fear. Rav laughed as he dug up another piece of stone with deranged energy.

Piece by piece, hole by hole, Rav wore away at the stone surface the 'Zet Ar was crossing. The 'Zet Ar moved faster to get off the fragile stone and broke more of the ground around it, slipping into holes and jumping over others. Rav doubled his efforts, slinging rocks as fast as he could to chip away at the path. The 'Zet Ar just needed to fall and then it would all be over. The path Rav had followed had started out as a wide area of stable ground but was soon ground down to a thin route with steep sloping sides with an abyss either side.

The 'Zet Ar was forced to slow once again as its weight crumbled some of the stone it was standing on. Still, it was getting closer. Rav ran out of rocks to throw and rolled to a new patch where the rocks were smaller, the 'Zet Ar ever closer. Rav targeted the mutant, trying to knock it off balance. Flinging the stones from the mutant's right meant that it couldn't see them coming and had to stabilise itself to take the blows; however, it was heavy, with hooves built for narrow gaps and horns protecting its head. The rocks did little to deter it.

Rav paused his pointless barrage and wound up his throwing arm as he took better aim, focusing on its tender blind eye. One powerful, stinging blow it could not see coming was all it would take for it to slip. He took a breath, then threw, *crack*, missing, the stone bouncing off the beast's forehead without a mark. Scratching up more flaky rock, he found another stone and tried again. The beast slowed further, rearing up to use a hoof to protect its eye, then shuffled closer. All it would take was timing. Rav took a breath as he weighed a stone in his hand, feeling its shape to envision how it would fly. He cocked his arm back and threw.

*Thewsh.*

The stone arced through the air in a perfect curve and landed under the mutant's weak leg as it was stepping forward. The beast slipped.

*MUH.*

It slid down the side of the path, scrambling at the rock to find purchase but breaking the holds it tried to cling to.

Rav watched it get closer to the edge little by little. *Please just fall.*

Its bad leg fell off the side of the wall, hanging into the chasm, and was soon followed by its right. Rav held his breath. But the 'Zet Ar worked with all its strength to dig its front hooves into the stone and managed to bring itself to a stop.

*No.*

Rav grabbed more stones and flung them at its hooves and head, hoping to stun it into losing the last of its grip, but the mutant shook its head, using its horns to deflect the stones. It kicked at the steep slope and found purchase.

*MUUH.*

It dragged itself back up bit by bit, muscle and sinew bulging beneath its hide, until it arrived back on the path. It glared at Rav with terrified fury, blood leaking from its wounded eye and nose from where a few stones had bypassed its horns. Crimson dripped onto stone.

*MUUUH.*

It lumbered up to the gap and leaped. There were no more stones near Rav. He threw his spear with all his strength. The weapon struck the beast straight in the chest... and bounced off its hide without having any impact. Rav watched it tumble into the rapids as the mutant landed on the stable rock. It loomed above him. Rav crawled away from it, heading off the trodden path, wishing for the stone to hold for him but not for the monster. The 'Zet Ar stood there, panting, watching Rav wriggle.

Rav dug his nails into the stone and kicked with his good leg, hauling himself away.

*Tok, tok, tok.*

He continued to struggle. Where could he go? There was a deep well-like hole in front of him as wide as two spears lying end to end. Could he climb down there? If it was filled with water, he could fall into it and survive another moment. What else could he do?

*Crack.*

A section of stone broke under the 'Zet Ar's weight but didn't fall away.

Rav crawled faster. "*AHHHH.*"

*DOH.*

The beast's giant cloven hoof slammed into the ground next to him. Rav rolled onto his back, staring up at the monster leering over him. Rancid spit and blood dripped from its maw, splattering on Rav's face as it raised a hoof above him. This was it. Should he think of Cyrn, or Kayla, or his parents? They wouldn't want that. They wouldn't want him to resign himself to death. *At least die fighting.*

Rav fumbled at his belt for a weapon and clasped the cold handle of a knife. His adrenaline surged, and suddenly, everything became clear, as though he could calculate everything around him.

He knew how fast the 'Zet Ar's hoof was falling and how it would break every rib in his chest as it crushed his heart. But he also saw a perfect blind spot on the 'Zet Ar's right. If he could shift himself up enough to whip his arm around...

As the 'Zet Ar stamped down, Rav twisted to the side and threw his knife.

"*AAAH.*"

*MUUH!*

The knife flew like a bolt to pierce the 'Zet Ar's remaining eye, and as the beast reeled back, its hoof shifted just enough to the side to only scrape across Rav's chest. Rav used his momentum to wriggle out from under the beast as it flew into a stomping rage, cracking the ground around it. Rav squirmed away, taking choking breaths, his shield left behind. The beast roared, both eyes bleeding. Rav crawled towards the well. The mutant huffed and snorted, flicking its head from side to side to clear away the blood, then continued stamping the ground around it.

Rav reached the well-like hole and pulled himself forward to look over the drop. His heart seized. At the end of a drop several times his height was rock, not water. He couldn't jump down. The muscles in his chest spasmed where the 'Zet Ar's stomp had torn them, stopping him from breathing. Rav writhed there, mouth frothing, trying to take a breath. The 'Zet Ar recovered from its frenzy and cocked its head, listening for him. Rav hit his chest with a fist and gasped, shocking his lungs into working again.

*Tok, tok, tok.*

The 'Zet Ar walked in his direction. It also refused to stop. It also refused to die. Was that why they'd been pitted to fight each other? To see whose will would break first? Rav would have laughed if it didn't hurt so much.

Rav rolled out of the 'Zet Ar's way, careful not to make any more noise, hoping the beast would carry on walking into the well-like hole.

It started sweeping the area in front of itself with its hooves.

*Scrape, scrape.*

Rav winced mid-roll.

The 'Zet Ar snapped to look straight at him.

Rav froze.

*Scrape, scrape.* It started heading in his direction.

*Faster*, Rav urged himself on. He no longer had something to aim for, he was just crawling in the opposite direction to the 'Zet Ar.

*Scrape, scrape.*

The mutant cleared another area and moved on to the next.

Rav rolled onto his chest and grunted. The mutant caught the sound, skipping forward straight to the next patch of ground. Rav threw a stone into the well hole, but after listening for a moment, the mutant ignored it, not falling for the trick.

Rav's chest almost seized up again, but he managed to hit it in time to prevent that from happening. Every noise he made brought the 'Zet Ar closer and he was breaking apart. He searched around him, wishing to find something he could use to survive. *Nothing, nothing, nothing.* He trembled. The beast would soon loom above him again. *No escape.* The beast was going to win and run free again. Cyrn, Kayla, the Ghoulsmen, Pitt, everyone was still going to have to fight it after everything he'd done. If he was going to die anyway, then...

Rav looked at the well-like hole again as an idea emerged. Maybe it could help him after all. *Doesn't the beast commit itself entirely to its attacks?* His eyes went wide. Now that was a dumb idea, but he had no good ones, so why not try it? Maybe he'd survive, and if not... Rav gritted his teeth. You had to make sacrifices to hurt the 'Zet Ar, and maybe his sacrifice would take the beast down with him.

Rav threw himself towards the edge of the hole, forced himself to stand, and bellowed, "*WAAAAH.*"

*MUUH.*

The 'Zet Ar charged. Its horns were right before Rav. He turned and jumped over the hole.

*MUH.*

The 'Zet Ar struck air but couldn't stop its momentum, the ground breaking underneath it as it slid towards the hole. It kicked out, jumping after Rav. Rav reached out as far as he could as he hurtled through the air, the other side getting closer and closer. The 'Zet Ar flailed behind him, but it was too heavy and its jump was too weak. It swiped its hoof at Rav in a last attack, snagging the back of his furs.

He just about managed to grab the edge of the well hole with one hand, but his grip didn't hold. Rav slid down the side, scrabbling at the rock to find any purchase until he drove his fingers into a crack, stopping an arm's length below the surface. He clung there, toes slipping on a protruding piece of stone, fighting with all his might to avoid falling after the beast.

*MUUUUUH!*

Rav glanced down to see a dust cloud at the bottom of the hole. His grip was failing. Succeed and live or fail and die. Rav faced the sky once more as he braced himself. Blood ran down his hands from his broken nails as he built his power, his toes managing to find grip on the slippery stone. *Go.* He lurched up, his entire body hanging in the air for an instant before he grabbed the lip of the hole with one hand. This time, his grip held. He flung his other arm up after it and, with an exhausting heave, just about managed to pull himself out of the well and onto the rock platform.

He lay there panting, ragged breaths shaking him. His thoughts sloshed around his head as if he were drunk. It took a moment before he gathered enough energy to think again. He was Rav Carvell. He was in agony. It had fallen. Rav sat up. The 'Zet Ar had finally fallen.

He peered into the well hole, seeing nothing but dust. It couldn't have survived that fall... right?

*MUH.*

Rav stared in shock, expecting to see the 'Zet Ar climbing out of the dust cloud. It couldn't be killed. It was still coming for him. He was powerless to stop it. He listened to the mutant's cries, waiting for the inevitable. Then its cries quietened. Rav blinked. He focused on the tether, feeling... dread. The 'Zet Ar was panicking. It wanted to live but knew that it wasn't going to. The 'Zet Ar's thoughts became weaker and weaker until they stopped.

It was dead? Somehow, that didn't make sense. How? Why? Did that mean he'd defeated it? Had he... won? Rav went still, then his joy erupted.

*I WON.*

Rav struggled to his knees and overlooked the hole. The dust had cleared, leaving the still body of the 'Zet Ar clear to see. He was safe. The Ghoulsmen were safe. Rav watched his tears fall into the well hole. Finally, he'd succeeded at something. Finally, he'd done his duty. He wiped his eyes, but when he opened them, he didn't see the Stone Steps.

# Chapter Twenty-Three

"Rav..."

Rav found himself in Ghoul Wood, and as he looked around, the scene distorted as if he were underwater. It was another vision, but this one was far more powerful than the others; he could see the gnarled bark of the trees and the fetid green surface of the swamp in front of him. He didn't recognise where he was, only knowing that it must have been somewhere deeper in the woods than he'd ever been by the fog of rotten air surrounding him.

The swamp began to simmer, bubbles shaking the stagnant surface, causing steam to drift into the air. Rav stepped back as the simmering grew violent, the swamp now boiling, when something under the water caught his attention. Something small and black. Black like nothing, black like emptiness, black like the end. It seemed to suck in everything around it, drawing in all the light. It was a cube. A broken cube. One of its corners was missing. Rav couldn't comprehend what he was seeing. It wasn't a 'thing'; it was the absence of anything that gave shape to a 'thing'. It was something that didn't belong in the world.

A desiccated hand burst out of the swamp water, breaking his fixation. A creature hauled its rotting body out of the swamp, heading straight for him. Its eyes were set in a skull that was missing most of its skin, leaving dead veins lying across the bone. It had no nose or ears or tongue, only teeth. A ghoul. Hundreds more hands broke the surface of the boiling swamp as an army of ghouls heaved towards Rav. Rav stumbled backwards, but the ghouls didn't attack him, instead lining up before him, waiting for him to command them.

"Rav..." the voice called. "Find me..." It giggled and the vision faded.

Rav returned to seeing the 'Zet Ar's corpse. His blood froze, and his skin prickled as a new understanding dawned on him. Fighting the 'Zet Ar had been a trial for him and now he was being presented with a reward. He vomited down his chin and chest, too weak to spit it further, acidic bile burning his throat as horror coiled around his heart. Had some entity been puppeteering him all this time? Had *it* caused all this death and destruction? Why? Rav leaned forward and spat out the foul taste in his mouth, watching it dribble into the hole.

Turning away, he rubbed his face, escaping that dread for a moment.

What would happen now?

He gazed at endless barren stone and the cracked wounds leading into plummeting darkness pocketing it.

How far away was Pitt?

He teetered on his feet as a swirl of dizziness struck.

How bad were his wounds?

He hugged himself tighter as his teeth started chattering.

Why was it suddenly so cold?

Looking up, he squinted into the bright light, the sun high in the sky, but he still felt ice set in his bones. At least the cold seemed to numb the ache racking his entire body.

Rav pried open the front of his furs to check on his chest, grimacing at the sight of his red and grey ribs, equal parts blood and dust. There was a large laceration going from his right shoulder down to the left side of his waist where the 'Zet Ar's hoof had scraped across him, and he was sure several of his ribs were broken. Rav pulled his furs back in place, holding them tight. If the cut split open, he'd be disembowelled.

"Drink," his rational mind ordered.

Rav fiddled at his pouch and found his waterskin intact. He brought it to his lips and sipped from it between shivers, the water freezing as it went down his throat and into his empty stomach. He had to keep drinking. He had to fight through this. He wasn't going to die now that it was over.

Over... what was over?

The 'Zet Ar was dead, but Cyrn was still going to gather an army using his promise to join them as payment. He had to tell Cyrn the 'Zet Ar wasn't a problem anymore.

Rav looked up. The stone plane seemed to stretch to the horizon in front of him, distances growing strange as colours melded together as if the world were a roiling mass of vibrant paste. All he could focus on was the well hole, so he set about crawling around it. If he could find the path he'd taken to get here, he could find his way back.

Rav eased on, finding himself looking down into the ravine splitting the stone surface, nausea swirling the water in his stomach. He had to turn away and close his eyes to stop everything from spinning. He needed to jump again. He needed to land on a section that hadn't been broken by the battle. Once he was across, it would be much easier to travel.

He flung himself across the gap, crumpling on the other side with a shriek as searing pain burst up his leg from his ankle, what was broken within it now grinding and mangled. Breathless, throat raw, voice hoarse, his screaming faded quickly, and a dry, wheezing chuckle emerged. He'd made it. All he had to do now was crawl.

Rav heaved his eyelids back open, not knowing how long he'd been unconscious for. After gathering his bearings, he realised he was past the camp that had been collapsed by the 'Zet Ar and was now about halfway out of the Stone Steps. The sun was low in the sky. It would soon be dark. He'd have to stop moving in case he lost track of the path he was following and fell. Where would he sleep? Rav shivered with cold, skin feeling as if it were frostbitten. He wouldn't survive the night without a fire. A fire with what, though? He had no flint, no wood, and this land was barren. A bird circled overhead.

"Rav... find me..."

Rav shook his head. He couldn't start seeing things now, not when he had to concentrate. *Keep moving.* He had to get out of the Stone Steps before dark—that was his best hope of survival.

A hole suddenly appeared right in front of him, startling him backwards. Was the ground falling? Was it... Rav recognised its shape. It was the broken cube he'd hallucinated in Ghoul Wood. He touched the supposed hole, confirming that there was, in fact, still rock there—it was just a vision. As Rav moved past it, he saw another cube-shaped spot ahead of him. It was as if a hole had been cut into his mind; there was always a cube-shaped gap everywhere he looked.

Rav ignored it and lumbered on. The sun was setting, stretching the shadows and dyeing the stone gold. The lone bird circling above him had become a flock. He was *so* close now; he could see the end of the Stone Steps. If only he had the energy to get there. The temptation to sleep creeped up his limps, paralysing them before moving up to his head. All he had to do was shut his eyes and he'd sink into blissful slumber, but if he did, would he wake again? He forced his eyes open as he tried to regain control over his body.

Exhaustion was winning, fending off his attempts to stay awake by sapping away any feeling he had. There would be no pain if he gave in to it, no anguish, just peaceful nothing, as though he were floating in a void. Or falling. Rav shocked back to reality, his heart in his throat. The sensation of plummeting passed. He hadn't fallen after all. It was hard to tell what was going on. The sun had set. It was dark.

Maybe he was going to die after all. No. He couldn't. Not until Pitt was safe.

Rav looked ahead into the black, with no idea where he was. How far had he crawled? The stone underneath him was all flat, so he must still be in the Stone Steps. He rolled onto his aching back and gazed at the glittering stars. He'd done his best, he really had, but now he needed to sleep. Maybe he'd wake up feeling better? Rav laughed at the thought, well aware that it was just an excuse for him to give up. Was giving up so bad, though? He'd done the part that mattered, the 'Zet Ar wouldn't harm anyone he loved, so shouldn't he get to rest?

As he mulled over the dilemma, one of the stars started shining brighter than the others, catching his attention. He focused on its warm, orange glow. It flickered, birthing a dozen tiny new stars around it. Beautiful.

As Rav stared, the star became hard to keep track of and he had to strain his neck to follow it. Why did it keep shifting from side to side? *Stay still, little star. Not so little.* It grew bigger and bigger until he could feel its heat on his skin.

"*Rav,*" Wakeman shouted, rushing over to him with a torch. "He's here," he called behind him before kneeling at Rav's side. "Where's the mutant?"

"Are you real?" Rav reached up to touch him but couldn't feel Wakeman's face.

"Aye, I am. I need to know where the 'Zet Ar is, or we're all going to die."

Rav frowned at him. Was this just another vision? Did it matter? "You don't need to worry about that; it's dead," he murmured, trying to remember if this really was what Wakeman looked like.

"Dead?" Wakeman gasped. "How? When we told Tibald there's a 'Zet Ar in Stone's Way, he nearly fell over in fright."

Rav wheezed at the thought. "The great Tibald Sar was so scared of something I tricked into jumping in a hole? I wish I'd seen his face." He let out a gravelly chuckle. "I wonder how he'll look at me now—"

Wait, was this really Wakeman? Rav grabbed Wakeman's bristled furs, still unfeeling even as he saw them pricking his palm. "You have to tell Cyrn that we don't need to bring an army into Stone's Way to fight it. We don't need Tibald's help."

"You can tell him yourself."

"Rav?" That was Cyrn's voice.

Another star blazed up to him, and with it came Cyrn. Rav stopped caring whether he was hallucinating or not; if the last thing he saw was his brother, he could die smiling.

"Where's the 'Zet Ar?" Cyrn knelt by his side, next to Wakeman.

"It's dead; we don't have to ally with Tibald anymore." Rav pawed at Cyrn's beard, unable to tell if he was touching it. As he looked up at his brother, the centre of Cyrn's face disappeared as a gaping black hole in the shape of a cube appeared.

"*No,*" Rav screamed. "Go away. Don't ruin this. *Get out.*"

"What's wrong? Rav, what's going on?"

"Get out of my head. Why?" Rav cried. "Why are you ruining everything? Let me die in peace."

"You're not going to die." Cyrn held Rav's face. "Listen to me. You're not going to die."

Rav watched droplets of water fall out of the empty void that was Cyrn's face and splash on him.

"He's delirious," Wakeman said. "We need to get him to a Healer."

Rav looked at him, and Wakeman's face also vanished, replaced by the cube.

"Find me..."

"No." Rav kept shaking his head.

"Help me lift him," Cyrn said. He and Wakeman picked Rav up. "We need to get him to Lyra before he gets worse."

They started running. Rav kept staring at the sky, trying not to look at the empty faces either side of him. When would this nightmare end? One by one, the stars died out until everything he could see became sickening nothing. The entire sky became that giant cube. Rav had no choice but to face it and its suffocating blackness.

"He's not breathing," Cyrn shouted.

*Lungs seizing*. Rav hit his chest, gasping again. The cube remained looming above him. He went deaf and blind as he was consumed by the void—

—Piercing blue eyes cut through the darkness, gazing down at him.

"Can you help him?" Cyrn's voice was shaking.

"I cannot," Lyra answered as she examined Rav. "He has an infection, likely from the 'Zet Ar. None of my medicines are strong enough to treat it."

He was lying on the medicine table in Lyra's hut. When had he gotten here? Rav shifted his head to see Cyrn, only to jolt his head back in place after seeing Cyrn's empty face once more. It was better to see Lyra's haunting eyes than that.

"People can survive infections, though, right?" Cyrn said. "He just needs water and time to rest while we keep the wound across his chest clean. Then his body will heal itself, won't it?"

"The infection is not from the wound, it is within him." Lyra touched the side of Rav's mouth. "This is the 'Zet Ar's saliva. It has entered his body and is killing him from the inside."

"What can I do, then?" Cyrn growled, his words seeming to fall out the void as he clenched his fists. "There must be something that can save him."

"There are herbs capable of treating infections like this, but they are all within the Sink and you do not have time to go there and gather them."

"Medicine from the Sink can heal him?"

"Yes. That is the only way to save his life."

Cyrn jolted, the terror weighing on him lifting as the cube covering him curved like a half-smile. "Keep him alive for a little longer. I know where I can get some. If Wakeman arrives with my family while I'm away, tell him I'll be back soon."

Rav heard the door close, finding it hard to think. His once-freezing body was burning as if his bones were hot coals, and some of his feeling returned with the heat. Pain. His chest was in agony. All he could hear was screaming. He stared up at the knotted wooden beams of the ceiling above him, struggling to breathe.

# Chapter Twenty-Four

Rav heard the door swing open.

"Heal him," Cyrn ordered.

"I don't know how." It was Tibald. "I also don't have much medicine left."

"You did this to him," Cyrn shouted, "*so, fix it.*"

"I already told you that I had no idea there was a 'Zet Ar in Stone's Way. Do you think I'd be mad enough to try and control something like that? They're the entire reason we have armies in the Sink. Only Ah' ke like Baron Hewett can face them alone; the rest of us have to stick together in large groups to deter them."

Rav wanted to jeer at Tibald, telling him how he'd faced a 'Zet Ar on his own and lived, but he remained paralysed, only able to listen to the conversation.

"You're the one who brought the soldiers," Cyrn pressed. "We wouldn't have been out there if it wasn't for your scheming; we know there was no trade caravan. Make up for what you've done and help my brother."

"First, I need to know if I can even do anything." Tibald's voice was cold. "Lyra, are you certain that Rav's got an infection and that it's not venom? And would the medicine I possess even be effective at curing him?"

"The 'Zet Ar Rav fought ate meat, so its saliva is filled with rot. It *is* an infection, and your medicine *would* heal him."

"So, what are you waiting for?" Cyrn said. "Give it to him."

"Why?" Tibald asked. "I don't care about Rav's life, and seeing as you've figured out my plan, I doubt you're going to ally with me now."

"I'll swear on my Name to join you if you save my brother's life."

"I don't believe you; I think you'll run away at the first opportunity you get."

"Then, I'll kill you and take the medicine off your corpse," Cyrn growled.

"Maybe that threat would have worked another time, but right now, you're injured and exhausted from running all night. Try again." Rav could hear Tibald's grin. "You know what I want, Cyrn; the only thing of value in Pitt is you. Since you won't become my friend, I'll have to find another way to guarantee your loyalty."

Cyrn went quiet. "So, this is what's beneath your charm. For you to think I'm the only thing of value in Pitt... makes me *really* want to crush your head. You spent so much time in Pitt listening to us all as we talked about our beliefs, yet you learned nothing. You thought you were so clever scheming against us, thinking that I was your only opponent, but it was Rav who unravelled your plans. It was Rav who defeated the 'Zet Ar. My brother has been the greatest hindrance to your plans and you've been too blind chasing after me to realise it."

Everything went still... until Tibald started laughing.

"Brilliant, utterly brilliant. This is why I want you, Cyrn... this is why we *need* you in the Sink. Please know that you almost convinced me to do it. If Rav really was as incredible as you said, I would heal him this moment and do everything I could to recruit him, but once again, I don't believe you." He chuckled at himself, his empty head shaking from side to side. "You expect me to believe that someone like Rav, someone so burdened by his own self-loathing from an event nearly *ten* years ago that he leaped at my false offer of salvation, was able to understand my plans?" Tibald snorted with contempt. "No, I refuse to believe it. And I know from experience that defeating a 'Zet Ar simply isn't possible for people like me and you, much less for someone like Rav.

"I don't know what happened out in Stone's Way or the Stone Steps, perhaps Rav really did get lucky, but that is not skill or cunning or power. So, if you want me to save your brother, try again."

Rav writhed on the table, doing his best to form his words, setting his mouth frothing. *Kill him, Cyrn.* Tibald had put everyone in danger, and he needed to die, not be bargained with. He twitched and twisted, fighting to force his body to attack Tibald.

"What's happening to him?" Cyrn moved to Rav's side. "Why're his eyes so bloodshot? Lyra, help him."

Cyrn's face was still missing. Rav started to cry. *Ignore me and kill him*, he tried to mouth. As long as Tibald was alive, they'd never be safe.

"There is nothing more I can do," Lyra said. "Rav is on his own."

"*Tibald,*" Cyrn roared, "*give him the medicine now.* If my brother dies, I'll spend the rest of my life hunting you down."

"If Rav dies, I'll treat my mission to recruit you as a failure and invade Pitt with Baron Hewett's army. I will kill everyone who resists and enslave the rest of you. There is no win for you here, Cyrn. Submit, and maybe you can salvage something from this mess. What are you willing to give up to save your brother's life?"

*Give him nothing.* Rav writhed harder.

"I... I..." Cyrn looked down at Rav. "There is something I can tell you about. My true weakness..." he whispered. "Once you know, you'll be able to guarantee my loyalty, but in return, I want two things. First, save my brother, and second, I want to Challenge you."

"Only Contenders can Challenge Champions."

"Then you'd better talk to Baron Hewett and get him to make me a Contender. Tibald Sar, you put our lives in danger and have proven yourself to be a person of despicable character. I do not trust you. Pitt will never be under your control. It is better for the Sar Name to die here than for you to continue bringing shame to your ancestors by committing further atrocities."

"Hmm... I agree to the first condition. As for the second, what would be the point in getting you to work for me only to kill you just after? I cannot agree to your Challenge; it makes no sense to me."

"We can discuss the second condition later, just heal Rav now," Cyrn yelled.

*Don't do it, Cyrn. Don't you dare.*

"Deal," Tibald stated.

*No.* The strain became too much for Rav and everything went black.

Rav clenched his jaw, neck squirming. He was burning, boiling, suffering. He ground his teeth until he tasted blood. Every breath hurt so much he thought he was going to pass back out.

"Get more water; we have to cool him down, or the fever will kill him," Lyra barked.

"I thought you said this medicine would heal him," Cyrn shouted back. "You said it was the only way for him to survive."

"It will heal him *if* he manages to endure through this. It is like pouring alcohol on an open wound—the pain is a sign of cleansing. Kayla, come here. Your presence by his side might help soothe him."

*Kayla?* Rav would have smiled if it were possible.

He felt Kayla clasp his hand. "Don't die," she whispered in his ear.

*I won't*, Rav promised just before he lost his grasp of reality and fell into a slew of vivid nightmares.

"Rav... find me..."

"My dear boy, get better," a woman cooed, voice strained and shaken. "Please."

"Fight through this," a man growled. "I know you can overcome the pain. You are a Carvell."

"Come back to me, Rav. You said we're going to get married and live the life we've always wanted, so you need to wake up and make that happen."

"Silly boy." Someone stroked his cheek. "You'd best get up soon."

"Rav... find me..."

Rav covered his ears.

"Are you awake?" It was Cyrn's voice.

Rav forced his eyes open, desperate to see his brother, but Cyrn's face was still missing.

"What did you do, Cyrn?" Rav rasped. "What did you offer Tibald in exchange for the medicine?"

"Don't worry about that, Rav, I'm taking care of it. At the moment, you're my greatest concern. It's been difficult watching over you while you healed. I..." He choked up. "I never want to see you like that again. I can't tell you how happy I am to see you awake."

Rav was sure he was crying, but Cyrn's expression remained hidden beneath the black void.

"Cyrn, please tell me our family is safe."

He nodded. "With you getting better, all of us are."

"You didn't give Tibald your weakness?"

"It's more complicated than that."

"*How could you?*" Rav seethed. "The Carvell Bloodline deserves to be free, not held hostage."

"The Carvell Bloodline deserves to be *alive*, and we all are."

"You told Tibald that Enna is pregnant, didn't you?" Rav spat. "You gave up your child for me."

"I did, but I have a plan. I'm going to Challenge Tibald and kill him. Once I'm Baron Hewett's Champion, I'll have the authority to protect Pitt. Then, our plan continues where we left off, with us all running away from here after I escape from Greenfield. We *will* leave this all behind, I promise."

Rav's rage sputtered as the wind left him and exhaustion set in anew. "Tibald will never accept your Challenge," Rav wailed. "He said it himself. And you should never have put my life before your child's. The Carvell Bloodline is all that matters."

"Aye, *our* Bloodline must be protected, which is what I've done. Also, Tibald knows the only way for me to stay loyal to him is if he keeps my child alive, even if they're a prisoner. As long as we're all living, we have hope to change our circumstances. As for the Challenge, I'm working on it. If I can get Baron Hewett to accept my request, Tibald's wants won't matter."

"I hate this, Cyrn. I can't stomach it."

"Well, I couldn't stomach watching you scream and writhe," Cyrn snapped, thumping the table with his fist, the entire thing rattling. "You were dying and I found a way to save you, so you could at least be grateful for that."

Rav went quiet as he listened to Cyrn's laboured breathing. "I am grateful to be alive, Cyrn. But I'd rather be dead and have our Bloodline be free."

The cube covering Cyrn's face grew larger until it consumed Rav once again.

"Rav... find me..."

"Where are you?" Rav cried out.

"We're all here, Rav."

Rav peeked up, seeing a dozen faceless people. He had to focus on their hair, clothes, and voices to determine who they were. Wakeman, Thorley, Tido, and Tobias were here, reuniting the Ghoulsmen. Along with them were Rav's parents, Enna, Benji, and Kayla.

"Aunt Judy said she wanted to visit you again but was unable to," Cyrn added.

His family were all unharmed. Rav wiped away his tears. "I'm so happy to see you all."

"It's not just us who wanted to see you," Kayla said. "If Lyra's hut was bigger, everyone in Pitt would be gathered here."

Rav found it hard to think, his memories fluttering around his head. He tried snatching at a few, but they drifted out of reach. Finally, he grasped one. "What happened at the Stone Steps? How did you find me in time?"

"When Wakeman arrived at the Alley without you, I guessed what you'd done, and after reading your note, I knew where you were going," Cyrn spoke. "Tobias brought Tibald and his soldiers to the Alley that evening, where, after I told Tibald about the 'Zet Ar, he sent Ronin and a few soldiers riding to Greenfield to gather an army while we discussed what to do. Tibald chose to return to Pitt and fortify it, but none of the Ghoulsmen wanted to let you hide from the 'Zet Ar alone, so we decided to head to the Stone Steps to help you." Cyrn's voice wobbled, and he coughed into his fist to clear and steady it before continuing.

"We were delayed by a few Spines that were chasing after the 'Zet Ar, and after killing them, we reached the Stone Steps, where Wakeman spotted a flock of birds hovering over you. We picked you up, then came back to Pitt." He paused, breath unsteady as though struggling to find his words. "How did you manage to kill the 'Zet Ar?"

Rav started the story of what he'd done.

"When it was about to stamp on me and I felt the knife on my belt, it was like everything became clear in my mind. I knew exactly how to move to dodge its hoof and where to throw the knife, all in an instant."

"That's incredible," Kayla gasped, a bright smile audible in her voice. She stepped forward to hold Rav's hand.

Rav's face fell, his hand going limp within Kayla's grasp. "But it still wasn't good enough; I could have done better." He sucked his teeth. "If I'd thrown the knife earlier, I could have avoided this." He pointed to the wound on his chest. "And I could have stopped the 'Zet Ar from dribbling on my face. If I wasn't so sick or injured—"

"Enough of that," Wakeman interrupted. "You're doing alright now. We had a group of soldiers *and* a monster from the Sink to face, but we all came out alive. Asking for anything more is being greedy."

"Aye, we're all safe," Healanor said. "It was a shock for us too. When Tobias came running into Pitt, I thought something far more terrible had occurred. If Tobias hadn't persuaded us to guard Pitt, we all would have marched out to fight."

Rav gulped at the thought of his parents trying to fight a Spine.

They continued talking about their experiences, and Rav learned that Pitt was growing tense with more of Tibald's soldiers lurking around after Ronin had brought part of Baron Hewett's army over. Fortunately, Baron Hewett was away from Greenfield, meeting with other Barons to discuss his plan to build a supply line into the Sink and wouldn't be coming to Pitt. Yet.

Rav blinked, and everyone disappeared. Everyone except Lyra. She was reading a book by the fire, looking picturesque with her porcelain features glowing in the light. It was hard to believe that there had ever been anyone else here. What was happening to him? Between the fever and his visions, his sense of reality was unravelling.

"Have I been Called?" he whispered.

"No, you have not been Called." Lyra shook her head, still reading. "You are still a baby."

"Then, what's happening to me? I know you know something; I saw how crazed you became when I told you about my visions."

She lowered her book with a click of her tongue and faced him. "I do not know what is happening to you, but I can tell you a secret." She placed her book on a side table and strolled over to kneel at his side, leaning over to whisper in his ear. "The Ghoul Wood dreams are not ordinary dreams."

Rav tutted. "Everyone knows that."

Lyra leaned back, her expression stone. "No, they do not." She broke into a soft smile and shrugged. "However, there is no need for you to worry about this; if the World wants you to know something, it will lead you to the answer. When that time comes, Sisters like me will aid you in your journey."

Rav twisted as he threw his arms upwards, face scrunched in irritation. "What are Sisters? Who are you? Why do you never speak clearly?"

Lyra flicked his forehead and poked his nose. "I am Called Ha'th Bey Riene. When you understand this, you will know me and those like me. Just like when you threw your knife, everything will become clear."

"Hath Bay Reen?" The words scratched his larynx. "Should I call you Hath?"

"Ha'th Bey Riene is not a Name like yours," Lyra said, chuckling, "it is a sound the World made at my creation. It *is* me. Calling me Ha'th is like calling me torso; it does not make sense."

Rav's head spun. "How could you not have a Name? How can you have no reputation? Whose lineage do you come from?"

"I come from the World. There is no point in questioning me further about this; as I said before, you will not understand me until you understand my Name."

Lyra's non-answers were infuriating. Rav took a moment to gather his breath.

"You said that I should do whatever I wanted to do after seeing those visions, and I did, but they haven't gone away. If the World isn't causing them, what is?"

"I do not know." Lyra shrugged. "I did think that the World was guiding you to defeat the 'Zet Ar; however, that might not be true. Perhaps there is more to your visions."

Rav clenched his fist. "*More?* More than killing that monster? More than forcing me to risk my life and the lives of those I love? If this 'World' exists, then it's evil for doing this to me."

"*Quiet,*" Lyra snapped, her calm façade replaced by fanatical fury. "You do not know what you are speaking of. Part of the reason I am unsure if your visions have come from the World is precisely because they appear destructive. I do not know the World's plans, and this may very well be part of them, but you have not been Called and you have not been led to the Sink, leading me to believe that there is some other power guiding you." She turned around and washed her hands in a bowl before checking over her medicinal vials, the vein on her forehead bulging.

Rav decided that it was better to not pursue the matter, as it wasn't wise to anger the person taking care of you. If Lyra wouldn't help, searching for the cube might be the only way to get rid of his visions, but the idea of obeying that voice made his skin crawl. Would he become a puppet of whatever this entity was, forced to obey it lest he be tortured like this? Would it keep sending him trials like the 'Zet Ar? Would it keep putting those he loved in danger? If that was the case, it was better for him to tolerate the visions himself and spare those around him.

"Rav... find me..."

# Chapter Twenty-Five

"It's good to see you sleeping so peacefully." It was Cyrn's voice. "Lyra said you're healing well and that you might be able to hear me, so I thought I'd speak to you. Maybe it will help you wake up. I... I've... I'm handling things in Pitt. I know you don't approve of what I've done, but I had to do it anyway. I couldn't let you die, I just couldn't. Please also know that Tibald won't get away with what he's done. We've succeeded in getting him to accept a Challenge. In three days, Tibald Sar will be just another corpse."

Emptiness swirled, nothing all-consuming as it descended to devour him. "Rav... find me..."

"Lyra said I could spend the morning preparing for the Challenge by your side. I thought seeing you would help focus my mind. I told everyone that I'm confident in being able to kill Tibald, but truthfully, I'm a bit nervous. I'm stronger than him, bigger than him, and I've got a few tricks prepared, so I know I've got a good chance to win, but you never know how a fight will go until you're in one. If only there was a book about how to kill Tibald that I could follow.

"We've come up with a plan for me to handle his speed, though it does require me to be at my best the entire fight. Tibald's just so quick that if I can't contain him early, I'll never land a blow and end up dead in the mud. It's going to be difficult.

"I know Pitt's citizens will be cheering for me. That'll give me some extra strength, but it might not be enough. That's why I wanted to stay with you. If the time comes when I need to push myself beyond my limits, I'll think of you and remember what I'm fighting for.

"I know this Challenge is meant to be for the future of Stone's Way, but for me, it's all about you, Rav. When I saw how grievous your injuries were at the Stone Steps, how you'd faced that beast alone to protect us all and suffered for it, I felt this rage fill my stomach, and it hasn't left since.

"I couldn't do anything about the 'Zet Ar, but I *can* do something about Tibald. This Challenge is the perfect opportunity for me to unleash my fury. When I'm feeling scared, I'll dig into that fire and become angry instead. I'll give everything I have to butcher Tibald Sar and finally have my moment. I hope you can wake up in time to see it."

"Rav... find me..."

"*Cyrn.*" Rav gasped awake. He was back in reality now, he was sure of it. He looked around the room but only saw Lyra sitting in her chair, reading.

"Calm yourself, Rav," she said, coming over to his side. "Your body is still healing."

"I don't care. Where's Cyrn?" He pulled himself out of bed and slumped onto the floor, snarling as he worked to gain complete control over his weakened limbs once more, forcing them to get him standing. "Cyrn's going to tell Tibald something he shouldn't." He snatched up his robe and furs from a chair at the end of his bed. "I need to tell him he can't"—Rav paused as he realised the burning pain that had been racking his body was gone—"save me."

"You have been drifting in and out of consciousness for a week while the infection cleared out," Lyra said. "Cyrn is currently preparing for the Challenge in Pitt, so you will have to wait to see him. Whatever he was going to tell Tibald in exchange for the medicine has already been told."

"No... How could he be so stupid?" Rav wheezed, flinching as he finally noticed that he'd already been changed into a loose robe with a loin cloth wrapped around his waist. He also sucked in a sharp breath as he saw that he was standing next to a small bed that had been moved into the hut, not the medicinal table he thought he'd been lying on. A week... Had it really been that long? Easing open the top of his robe, he examined the now scabbed-over cut across his chest.

"I had to use a needle and thread to close that wound," Lyra commented. "Some sections are still being held together, so do not twist too much, or it will split open again."

"And my ribs?"

"They will take a month to heal. Regaining your consciousness is a good sign and will save me from having to feed and clean you, but your back and ankle are still damaged. It will be at least two months before you are able to move as you did before."

"I can't be stuck here for two months; there's too much for me to do." Sweat dotted Rav's brow as he struggled to piece together what had happened from his fragmented memories. Was Cyrn Challenging Tibald today? Wasn't Cyrn injured? Surely, he couldn't have healed in a week after being gored by a Spine, so was he fighting while wounded?

"I need to leave." Rav found his robes folded beside his bed and stuffed on his boots, wincing as he moved.

"That is not a good idea."

"I don't care." He grabbed a knife and marched out of the door.

He was shivering and shaking, wheezing as he trudged back to Pitt, but though his body was tired, his mind felt wide awake. Unable to see the cube anymore, he wondered if his visions had finally ended. Maybe they'd return in the evening. But that didn't matter right now.

He emerged out of Ghoul Wood to see that it was midday, the sunlight bright, giving him a clear view of the Carvell logging grounds. No one was here. He heard a commotion coming from near the mine and ran towards it as quickly as he could on his bad ankle, heading around Pitt's wall. What he was doing was reckless, but all he could think about was his brother fighting for his home.

As he neared the mine, he saw an enormous crowd packed around the arena Tibald had fought Greeshe in, and among Pitt's citizens, Rav spotted two dozen soldiers wearing armour that had a large mountain insignia imprinted on their backs. Since when were so many of Baron Hewett's soldiers in Pitt?

Ronin was standing at the podium, saying something that Rav couldn't hear. Was the Challenge about to start? Rav moved faster.

"*Fight,*" Ronin shouted.

*Clang.* The sound of metal clashing against metal rang out from the arena. Rav was now close enough to see two figures wielding spears—one enormous, one lithe—fighting in the arena. Cyrn and Tibald were already in battle. The crowd was fully focused on the arena as the two fought, wincing at close cuts and flinching at heavy swings as though they were the ones duelling.

Rav wormed his way through the crowd until he was near the front. Tibald was wearing his full-plate armour, polished to gleam in the sunlight so his Blood Palm sparkled. He held a spear and a buckler, his face hidden behind his visor. Cyrn stood opposite him in his thick fur armour, wielding a spear and shield. His helmet had his menacing-looking Ghoulsmen animal skin mask pasted onto the front of it.

Tibald shot off with his movement technique, spear blurring. Cyrn strode forward to meet him, shield raised, his own spear pointed forward. Rav clenched his fists, digging his nails into his palms. Could Cyrn deal with Tibald's speed? It was Tibald's greatest strength, and if Cyrn was too slow, he'd never even hit Tibald.

Tibald's spear flashed. Cyrn *was* too slow. But as Tibald's spear drove towards Cyrn's throat, Cyrn attacked Tibald without regard to his defence, sweeping his spear in an arc around himself. Tibald shifted back to block with his buckler while aiming to continue his initial strike, but when Cyrn struck his buckler, Tibald was sent stumbling backwards by the sheer power in the hit. Cyrn followed up by punching at Tibald with his shield, forcing Tibald to use his movement technique to retreat in a spray of mud.

Rav caught his breath. Cyrn had survived. No, not only had he survived, he'd also counter-attacked. The crowd's cheers were so loud the ground seemed to shake. Once he was a safe distance from Cyrn, Tibald flexed his arm, clearly stung from the blow.

Cyrn was unrelenting and dashed at him, closing the distance between them. Tibald appeared caught off guard by the fast action and found himself cornered. Despite moving faster than Cyrn, he was stuck within a small enough area for Cyrn to still pin him down with his greater size and reach. Cyrn jabbed, then whipped the butt of his spear around in an overhead slam. Tibald dodged it, manoeuvring around to Cyrn's flank, but Cyrn punched his shield at the space Tibald was moving into, and Tibald had to retreat again to avoid the blow. Rav watched as Tibald was herded deeper into the corner of the arena, move by move.

A surge of pride coursed through him like never before, beckoning him to sing and shout and proclaim to all the world that Cyrn Carvell was his brother, that he shared the same blood as such a great man. But it was far too soon; the battle wasn't over yet.

Cyrn moved with his shield outstretched to cover as much space as he could before attacking Tibald with another quick set of spear jabs to contain him. As Rav watched Cyrn's actions, he realised it was a planned strategy. Cyrn had watched Tibald duel Pattik and was now using that knowledge to deal with Tibald's abilities.

Tibald dodged again and again, looking increasingly desperate to escape the chain of attacks, but Cyrn kept him trapped by predicting Tibald's every move. Cyrn would stab into an empty space, only for Tibald to somehow appear there, as if Cyrn had seen the future. Tibald was seen through. His speed was being controlled. And if he made one mistake, Cyrn was strong enough to end the fight in a single blow.

As Tibald got pressed closer and closer to the corner, the crowd grew louder and louder. Victory was within sight. Cyrn stabbed again, then cut the spear tip down and swung his shield in an uppercut. Tibald glided to the side, then ducked, then stepped back. He jabbed with his own spear, but Cyrn's shield was already in place to block it, the uppercut having been a feint. Tibald lost ground again. Rav leaned closer, tense and breathless. Just a little further and Tibald would have no more room to dodge in.

Cyrn strode forward. Tibald had no choice but to move back. He was stuck right in the corner near Rav. The butt of Cyrn's spear swept up, and with nowhere to run, Tibald dodged straight into the path of the subsequent shield drive. Rav gasped. This was it; Tibald was finished. Once Cyrn smacked him with his shield, Tibald would crumple.

Tibald didn't try to dodge, instead bracing himself for the coming attack. The shield connected and Tibald was shoved away. Away from the corner. He'd managed to bounce off the outside of the shield. Cyrn had helped him get away. But he was still hit. It was a harder blow than the first; he had to be injured.

Tibald glided away from Cyrn and into the full space of the arena once again. The strike hadn't slowed him. Cyrn hesitated, seemingly unsure whether he should continue pursuing Tibald. Tibald seemed to laugh as he watched Cyrn, and Rav realised Tibald wasn't as weak as he'd pretended to be. The first blow had knocked him back, but not as severely as Tibald had displayed. He'd baited Cyrn into using a strike he'd thought would cripple Tibald, only for him to escape.

Tibald set his stance again and waited. It looked as if he were hoping for Cyrn to unleash another barrage of attacks so that he would tire. Or was *this* an act so that Tibald could rest after the previous exchange? Rav didn't know. It looked as though Cyrn didn't know either.

There was a flicker of movement while Tibald waited—his arm twitched where he'd been struck. The strike *had* injured him. Even if it wasn't as bad as they'd thought, it had still done some damage. Rav exhaled in relief.

Cyrn moved in to confront Tibald. This time, Tibald attacked with much more aggression, using the space around him to manoeuvre around Cyrn to jab at his sides. Cyrn tried using his size to press Tibald back again. *Whoosh, whoosh, whoosh*. Cyrn's spear and shield kept hitting air. Tibald dodged yet another strike, sailing into empty space at Cyrn's flank, and drove a clean thrust into Cyrn's side. Rav flinched.

*Clang*. Tibald's arm shook. Cyrn was heavy. Sunlight glinted from the hole in Cyrn's furs, indicating that he too was in full-plate armour. Cyrn didn't shift under the strength of Tibald's attack and went straight into another barrage. *Clang. Clang. Clang*. On and on, around the arena. But Tibald was getting better at reading Cyrn's moves and his counterattacks began to rain down. Rav trembled at the sight. Cyrn couldn't be losing, could he? But it was plain to see that if Cyrn weren't so much bigger and stronger than Tibald, he wouldn't have been able to compete at all.

Cyrn stabbed with his spear, then whipped the butt into Tibald's side. Tibald moved towards Cyrn's shield, baiting out a shield bash that he then shifted around to get to Cyrn's exposed flank. Tibald locked onto a gap that would lead straight to Cyrn's guts. Cyrn desperately whipped his spear across his shield to prevent Tibald from getting closer and repeating his earlier thrust. It worked. Tibald was forced backwards but still managed to deliver a clean thrust into Cyrn's exposed shoulder.

Cyrn turned into the thrust with a roar, and at the same time, he dropped his own spear to free his hand so he could catch Tibald's spear. He'd stopped the thrust from sliding down between his ribs to kill him, but the spearhead had still bitten deep into his shoulder. Cyrn held Tibald's spear, pulled the point out of his shoulder, and swung his shield into the wooden shaft. *Crack.* The spearpoint broke off, reducing the spear to a staff. Tibald dropped his spear and dashed to pick up Cyrn's.

Rav went pale. If Cyrn lost his spear, he was dead. Tibald grasped the shaft and heaved the spear up, where it bent before he lost his grip, and the weapon slapped into the ground, splintering from the impact. Cyrn was standing on the butt of the weapon. Tibald drew a dagger as Cyrn swiped at him with the bloodied broken spear point, chasing him away from the spear. Tibald retreated.

Cyrn picked up the broken spear. The point had fallen off and the shaft had snapped, only hanging together with splinters. He threw it out of the arena and drew his own dagger. It was to be a close-quarter fight. Rav regained some hope. Cyrn could better use his greater size and strength like this. No, it was better than that. As soon as Tibald came close, Cyrn wouldn't even need his dagger—he could crush Tibald with just a hand.

Cyrn attacked first again. *Swipe, swipe, swipe.* Tibald kept dodging. Blood kept leaking from Cyrn's shoulder. Tibald moved inside Cyrn's shield to strike at his neck, but Cyrn barged into Tibald, then drove his dagger at Tibald's waist. Tibald twisted enough for the stab to hit his armour. *Thump.* Tibald stumbled back, then glided away.

"*WAAAAAH,*" the crowd roared.

It was the first time Cyrn had been so dominant in an exchange. He kept moving, striking Tibald again to almost fell him before moving into a shoulder charge. *Clank.* Their armour smacked into each other. Tibald was stunned and staggered back, guard open. Cyrn lashed out with his shield and landed another clean blow on Tibald's torso; however, Tibald's armour absorbed most of the damage, giving him time to recover and use his footwork to retreat out of reach again.

"*Agh,*" Rav groaned. Why was Tibald so fast? How long was he going to keep running away like this? Surely, he couldn't keep this speed up forever.

Cyrn took a moment to rest, tightening the straps around his wounded shoulder to slow the bleeding.

Tibald saw him and dashed in.

Cyrn released the straps and prepared to defend against the coming attack, but Tibald dashed back to his initial position as fast as he'd left it. Cyrn held his stance a while longer before seeing Tibald relax. He went to tighten his straps again. Tibald shot off once more... then retreated once Cyrn readied himself. Rav's face swelled red with rage, knowing exactly what was going on. So many times, the Ghoulsmen had done this same thing to their opponents, using their greater manoeuvrability over Stone's Way to harass their enemies until they weakened.

Cyrn reached for his straps. Tibald shot off. Cyrn kept working at them, calling Tibald's bluff. Tibald moved in for a killing strike, dagger slicing at Cyrn's open right side. Cyrn still didn't move. Rav gritted his teeth. Cyrn would take a blow here; he couldn't defend in time. Cyrn finally moved once Tibald was right in front of him and threw a fistful of blood into Tibald's face, spattering the front of his visor red to blind him.

Tibald immediately backed off, wiping off as much of the blood as he could while Cyrn sprinted towards the spot between Tibald and the far corner he was retreating into. Cyrn arrived just as Tibald did and punched with his shield, knocking Tibald out of his footwork to stop him from escaping. Now, it was Tibald's turn to flounder. He swiped out with his dagger to deter Cyrn, but Cyrn didn't care for the weak slashes, marching right into them to let his armour block the strikes.

Cyrn stabbed straight at the gap between Tibald's breastplate and helmet, right where his neck was. Tibald found his footing again just in time to twist away, causing Cyrn to miss his strike, his dagger slicing shallow across the back of Tibald's neck rather than through it. Blood spurted through the air in a short burst, falling to the muddy ground while Tibald scampered off.

Once Tibald was safe, he tore off his helmet to clear his vision. Cyrn charged at him and kicked his foot across the ground to spatter mud at Tibald, who hid his face behind his arm. Cyrn followed up by discarding his shield, throwing his dagger at Tibald, and then diving forward to tackle him.

Rav gasped at the drastic action. The dagger bounced off Tibald's armour but caught him by surprise, allowing Cyrn to complete his tackle. Cyrn brought Tibald to the ground, pinning the Champion underneath him.

"*WAAAAH,*" Rav roared with Pitt.

Tibald tried to wriggle free, but Cyrn didn't budge, using his weight to keep Tibald down while he wrapped his fingers around Tibald's throat, strangling him. Blue eyes bloodshot and blond hair messy, Tibald writhed with everything he had as the arena thundered. Rav grinned from ear to ear, tears streaming, singing with all his heart.

*"I GUARD MY HOME WITH ALL I AM,*
*"TO HONOUR THOSE WHO GAVE ME LIFE,*
*"WE MARCH FAR TO CONQUER OUR FOES,*
*"A BLOODLINE TO KEEP OUT ALL STRIFE,*
*"GO FORTH AND FIGHT 'TIL YOUR LAST LIGHT,*
*"GIFTING LAND AND LINEAGE TO OUR FLESH MADE YOUNG,*
*"WE'LL LOVE AND MARRY FOR OUR BLOOD TO CARRY,*
*"INTO THE FUTURE BRIGHT."*

Even when Cyrn's arms began to shake. Even when his movements grew sluggish. Even when Tibald took a breath. Blood pooled around them, pouring out of Cyrn's gut.

"*AHHH.*" Cyrn used the last of his strength, squeezing with all his might.

It wasn't enough. Tibald drove his knee up into Cyrn's wounded side and finally shifted Cyrn off him. Cyrn collapsed in the mud, Tibald's dagger buried into a gap at his waist. Tibald struggled to his feet, soaked in blood, and stood over Cyrn.

Cyrn was beaten. Cyrn was bleeding. Cyrn was dying.

Rav trembled, powerless to stop it. It was happening again. His family was under attack, and no one was doing anything to save them. Memories from the past of his Ma cowering as that garrison soldier towered over her overlapped with the sight before him. Cyrn was going to die and everyone else was just watching. Someone had to *do* something. *He* had to do something.

Rav hesitated. It was that moment that had led to all of this. But everyone said it was worth it. Everyone said he'd done the right thing. Everyone wanted to save their family. If he had to suffer it all over again...

For his brother, he would.

Just as Tibald was about to deliver the final blow, Rav threw his knife with everything he had. "*AAAHH.*"

Tibald turned his head. The knife sliced into his ear before the handle smacked him in the temple, knocking him to the ground.

"*Cyrn,*" Rav cried out as he rushed to his brother's side, ignoring the pain flaring across his chest.

He kicked Tibald in the face to make sure he stayed down as he arrived before kneeling to check on Cyrn. So much blood. It was everywhere, staining Rav's hands as he tried to staunch the bleeding. Cyrn's chest heaved as he tried to say something. Rav pulled off his brother's helmet… to see Wakeman's pale face staring up at him.

# Chapter Twenty-Six

"Rav..." he rasped.

What was happening? Everything started to spin.

"You made it." He coughed. "Sorry you had to see me lose."

Rav shook his head, wishing the sight before him was just another nightmare. "Y-you haven't lost," he stammered. "A-as long as you're alive, you haven't lost."

Blood kept pouring. Wakeman kept paling. Everything kept spinning.

"I think... the dagger's buried too deep... for me to be saved..." Wakeman held Rav's cheek. "I had to do it. Do you understand? You did so much for us, I had to do this for you. You're... family. My family... Better than my family... I wish I was a Carvell." He sighed. "Too fast, Tibald was just too fast..."

Rav blinked again and again as hot tears welled in his eyes, Wakeman's paling face going blurry. "You *are* family." He clenched Wakeman's furs in his fists as he held him. "Family isn't just in a Name. You are my brother, just like Cyrn. You hear me?"

A small smile played across Wakeman's lips as he gently nodded. "My brother," he whispered.

"*Where is Lyra?*" Rav screamed, looking around. "We need to get him to Lyra."

The crowd stared silently back at him, some with open mouths.

"Why is no one doing anything?" He grasped Wakeman's hand in his, but Wakeman didn't grasp his back. He looked down and choked on a sharp exhale as he saw Wakeman's unblinking eyes staring at the sky, with a permanent smile etched on his paled face.

"*Rav,*" Healanor Carvell bellowed from the crowd. "For the crime of intervening in a Challenge, I strip you of the Name Carvell and declare you Nameless."

A terrible tremble seized him, Rav's hand shaking in Wakeman's as the words smacked into him worse than any Spine's charge. Dazed, he continued his gormless stare, his Ma's decree echoing in his head. Ronin jumped down from the podium and sprinted to Tibald's side, hurriedly wrapping a cloth around his head as Tibald lay unconscious. The crowd surged into the arena, circling the three of them. *This is all just a nightmare. Please let it be another nightmare.* Rav kept wishing to wake up, but nothing changed. His hands remained red. Wakeman was still dead.

"I'll have you executed for attacking a Champion," Ronin hissed at him.

Rav looked up to see Baron Hewett's soldiers all marching straight towards him. This was all real. What had he done? Nameless. Pitt's citizens looked between Rav and the arriving soldiers, hesitant for a moment before they stood steadfast together as a barrier between them, fists clenched. Ronin paled as he looked up at them, a shaking hand on his sword pommel.

Robert's voice cut through the growing clamour. "You should leave now, Rav. No one will harm you as you do."

"Rav... find me..."

Rav ran through the crowd as soldiers tried to chase after him, townsfolk banding together to slow them. Where could he go? Where could he hide? Empty black dots grew around him as visions of the broken cube appeared once more. There was only one place that remained clear. Only one place that promised safety. Rav headed for Ghoul Wood.

"Is this Pitt's justice?" Ronin roared behind him. "To let an attempted murderer go free after interfering with an honourable and fair Challenge? To protect a man who'd shame the vows taken by both combatants to fight with valour to the death? To tarnish the sacrifice of the man who fought so bravely for your home? Control your townsmen, Cyrn, or Baron Hewett will."

"*Halt,*" Cyrn bellowed.

Rav froze and turned to look at his faceless brother, recognising his Carvell ceremonial robes. He was standing at the podium with the other members of the Ghoulsmen at his side.

"Protect Champion Sar," Cyrn ordered.

The soldiers chasing Rav looked between themselves before returning to the arena and forming a defensive circle around Tibald and Ronin. Rav waited, hoping Cyrn had a solution to his current situation. Cyrn seemed to stare straight at him, then motioned with a slight tilt of his head for Rav to keep running. Rav continued moving to Ghoul Wood, only slowing once he was within the treeline. What now? Nameless. He wasn't welcome in Pitt anymore. Even Cyrn wanted him to stay away. There was nowhere for him to go. Nowhere but the path in front of him. He kept walking, heading deeper into the woods.

The stench and cold didn't bother him, rather, Rav embraced them. They were what he deserved. How could he have been so stupid? How could he have interfered with the Challenge without fully understanding what was being fought for first? ...Or was it the other way around? How could everyone else have been so stupid? How could they have watched on as Wakeman was killed? Why hadn't Cyrn intervened? Why had he left *him* to do what should've been done all over again? If it had been Cyrn who had acted, maybe he'd have succeeded. Maybe Wakeman would still be alive. Rav slapped his cheeks. Maybe they'd all be at war with Baron Hewett, rushing to flee from everything they'd protected before the Baron arrived with his army and butchered whoever he caught.

Rav paused his step as his eyes welled up, sorrow saturating his very bones as a shiver took hold of him. Wakeman was dead. He looked at his hands, the blood coating them having formed into a dry crust, thinking about what happened to corpses, how they went stiff, then bloated, then rotted. Wakeman would be cold. Pale to the point where he'd look bruised. And he'd reek. There was no dignity in death.

Rav shook his head, scattering his tears like crystal droplets. For Wakeman, there would be. All of Pitt would decorate and praise him. Everyone would honour the man who'd given his life trying to protect a place he wasn't even from. Rav sucked in deep, choking breaths, and with every exhale came a guttural wail unlike any noise he'd ever made before. It was rough and broken, dense and hoarse, something far more unnerving than the 'Zet Ar's roars.

Wakeman would never offer any more advice or share any more of his experiences again. Never ruffle his hair or pat his shoulder. Without Wakeman here, everything felt so... hollow. What had even been the point of the Ghoulsmen? What was the point of anything when they weren't all alive to appreciate it? There was a gaping, endless wound in Stone's Way that could never be filled. Rav broke his sobbing as he laughed at himself. How could he have ever wanted to stay here? If only he'd worked harder to leave, then maybe they'd all be alive and well. What was the point of a home without your family?

"There you are."

Rav flinched, spinning to see the figure who had sneaked up behind him. Jingo stood between the trees with a lit torch and sword.

"There's no escaping punishment this time, Rav," Jingo growled. "Come back to Pitt without a fight."

Rav stood frozen.

"Cyrn said he wants to see you," Jingo said, growing more confident as each word came out. "Yes, your brother has called for you to come back to Pitt and then travel to Greenfield. You listen to your brother, don't you?"

"No," Rav croaked. "Cyrn would never want me to go to Greenfield. You're lying. Why didn't you kill me? You could have. You didn't need to announce your presence. Why do you want me alive?"

"I told you," Jingo snapped, "Cyrn has ordered you back to Pitt."

"A hostage. That's all I'd be. Another Carvell under threat to keep Cyrn obedient." Rav shook his head. "I've already brought my brother enough trouble."

"*Not* another Carvell. You're Nameless now, remember?" Jingo's sneer deepened. "Why do you always cause everyone so much trouble? If you'd just do as you're told, you could make all this so much easier. You could've made *everything* so much easier." He spat in the mud. "To think we were willing to have you march beside us just to recruit your brother. Tibald's assessment was right: smart enough to notice some of what's going on, but too stupid to think of any clever counters. All you can do is all you have done—recklessly thrash around to ruin everything for everyone."

Rav stepped back from him.

"Don't bother, Rav." He smirked. "Or is it Nameless Rav now? I know you're injured."

Rav raised his guard. "You are too."

Jingo stepped closer and brandished his sword. "Maybe a small cut is needed, something painful but harmless to teach you your place. Tibald could forgive me for that, right? Now that we know about Enna, Cyrn will have no choice but to forgive small incidents like this. I warned Tibald not to treat you people with too much respect, I told him that it would make you too prideful. That's something we'll have to tear out of you all so that when people like me give you orders, you'll grovel on your knees and obey them."

He lunged towards Rav, blade slicing at Rav's thigh. Rav hobbled to the side just enough to avoid it. His left ankle burned with agony, the stitches in his chest on the verge of tearing. But Jingo stumbled, the knee the badger had scratched buckling, and he had to stab his sword into the ground to stop himself falling over. Rav shuffled away from him, scanning his surroundings for anything that could help him.

"Get"—Jingo found his balance and tore his sword from the mud—"back here." He whipped his torch back and forth in fury as he gave pursuit.

Rav couldn't run far, and Jingo had already halved the distance between them. He spotted a short tree with dense foliage and headed for it, pressing his back to its bark as he raised his fists. Jingo stopped before it, face bloated in gloating.

"What was the point in that? All you've done is make me angrier. Cutting you won't be enough of a lesson." He grinned. "If you don't come with me and do everything I say, I'll find that girl, the one with the shiny black dress, and I'll cut her too."

Rav stayed put. *Just a bit closer...*

"How about this?" Jingo tilted his head. "I'm going to hold a torch next to that sweet black-haired girl's face for all the time you're wasting now. Better come quickly, or you might not fancy her all that much when I'm done."

Rav scoffed at him, lowering his fists to open his defensive stance, providing Jingo an even easier opportunity to attack.

"Why would I fear your threats? You're nothing but an ugly idiot barking at the wind without your master's orders. I killed a 'Zet Ar and you couldn't even hit a cripple with your sword. You're pathetic. It's a wonder Tibald even keeps you around. What would your ancestors think having seen you fail at fighting the badger, then fail at hitting me? Surely, they must be ashamed. And what will Baron Hewett think when he hears the same? You want power and glory in the Sink? No, I think you'll be stuck cleaning chamber pots and washing clothes while everyone else claims everything they ever—"

"*AAARGH.*" Jingo charged forward with a great swing.

Rav dropped to the ground, watching as Jingo's torch touched the distorted air.

*BANG.*

For an instant, everything burned red.

"*AAAHHH.*" Jingo collapsed backwards, sword and torch forgotten as he held his smouldering face.

Rav pounced, picking up the sword and driving it through Jingo's waist. The screams grew louder. Rav kept pushing the sword down, Jingo pinned in place. Only once the hilt touched Jingo's body did Rav clamber to his feet and stand over him. Bits of Jingo's hair still burned, the acrid stench filling the air, and scorch marks covered his ears. Jingo tried to say something, but his lips were too blistered to form anything but horrid screeching.

"You could've made everything so much easier if you'd just left us alone," Rav spat, mimicking Jingo's tone. "While you must've forgotten about the fumes, I hope you still remember the ghouls. I don't know what you see while dying in here, but I hope it's far worse than the nightmares."

He hobbled away, Jingo's screams getting quieter and quieter as he headed deeper into the trees.

# Chapter Twenty-Seven

Night came, but Rav felt neither hunger nor thirst. He kept walking in the dark, uncaring, and soon, the day passed. Followed by a second day and then a third. Ghoul Wood swallowed him whole. This deep, the rot pervading the air was so thick it felt as though it were keeping him upright. Keeping him going. The lack of sleep plagued his brain until he began to see Wakeman's face in all the trees, always with his final smile.

On the fourth morning, filthy and starved, Rav arrived at an area where the air was choked with fog. Still, he walked on even when the ground softened to mud, then bog, then swamp. Rav peered into the murky water. His eyes had sunken into his face, black from lack of sleep, and his cheeks were thin, mere skin on bone, showing the veins beneath. He'd truly become a ghoul now. A truly monstrous appearance for a truly monstrous person.

He waded into the swamp, the putrid water rising to his knees, waist, chest, neck, then climbed out the other side of the swamp and kept going. On and on he marched until he finally arrived at a place he recognised. It was the swamp from his vision, the place he'd seen after killing the 'Zet Ar.

"I'm here," Rav croaked. "This is where you've been leading me, isn't it? Do what you want with me. I don't care anymore."

"Rav..." the voice called him further.

A shadow of the cube hovered above the water, inviting him to approach it. Rav walked into the water, and this time, he was submerged. Dark, silent, and without constant threats or Wakeman's dead face, it was peaceful beneath the surface. How long had it been since he'd felt like this? There was nothing but numbing coldness that lulled him to sleep. Rav smiled. Wouldn't it be nice to stay here forever? He lowered his head, releasing himself to float freely, and as he drifted towards the centre of the swamp, a semblance of clarity returned to him.

Cyrn must be worried. He'd abandoned Pitt when it needed him. Would everyone be punished for his crime? He had to return to face the consequences. Kayla—

The thoughts stopped as the current carried him past the centre of the swamp. Ants crawled under his skin, burning, itching, biting. He needed that feeling again, that clarity. He'd murder to have it. Rav seized control of his body and swam back to the centre of the swamp for the missing part of his mind.

*There.*

Kayla would miss him. He had to marry her. He had to explain himself to his parents. He had to scatter Wakeman's ashes over Stone's Way.

Rav reached out to the swamp bed and felt a smooth cube the size of his palm.

*Breathe.*

He grabbed the cube and rushed to the surface to fill his lungs, bursting up with a great gasp. He needed to get out. He needed to get back. Rav crawled out of the water and lay on the bank, panting. The broken cube sat in his hand, just as black as his visions had shown him, and by some strange instinct, Rav pressed it to his head.

"*AHHH.*"

The cube fused with him, melting into his skin before dissolving in his blood. His vision warped, and when it cleared, Rav saw himself as a real ghoul, tearing at some unknown soldier's body, then devouring them whole. Salty blood and fetid flesh. He wasn't alone, either; he was just one of a thousand ghouls, all feasting on the corpses of what used to be an army. He felt a rush of power he'd never thought possible as he sensed a connection between himself and the other ghouls, as though they were part of him, like extra arms and legs. Rav stood to survey them all, flexing his fist. Every ghoul here was his to command. It was *his* army destroying another. He could clench his hand and have a thousand monsters savage anyone in his way.

The vision faded just as Rav was about to try to command them. He coughed as he returned to reality. *More...* he needed to see more. The details of where he was and who he'd killed were already lost; only that overwhelming sense of power remained. Rav tried to fall back into the vision but flinched upon seeing Lyra kneeling at his side, inspecting his neck with fanatical eyes. What was she doing this deep in Ghoul Wood? Why had she followed him all this way? All the way to whatever had sunk into his forehead. Whatever it was, it couldn't be good. He punched at her, but Lyra caught his hand with ease and held him still. Rav bit and clawed, giving everything to break free from her grasp, yet he remained immobile, Lyra's strength far beyond what she should've been capable of.

"Calm down, I am here to help you, Rav. I have been following you since you entered Ghoul Wood, waiting to see if you would find what I am searching for. And you have." She touched the back of his neck with a loving tenderness. "It is here. Pa'cr. Wait... it is not complete, but I suppose that does not matter. Rav Carvell, you have been Called, and"—she gazed down at him with a wild madness—"you are also Ah' ke."

Rav gasped, shaking as a searing headache throbbed behind his eyes, his vision starting to sparkle and blur. "What? How?"

"That cube is a Pa'cr, a Heaven's Tear. It contains a part of the World's laws, and now that it has fused with you, you are able to use that part of the World's power. Baron Hewett has obtained a Heaven's Tear that contains the power of 'weight', allowing him to become as heavy as a mountain. Your Heaven's Tear will enable you to do something just as magnificent or perhaps something even more special. Come, we must go to the Sink so that you can enact the World's will." Lyra picked Rav up by his collar and slung him across her shoulders as though he were a fur stole before setting off marching back towards Pitt.

Rav flailed, trying to wriggle from her grasp again while dread sat like cold sweat across his skin as he realised he was being carried like a light sack of grain. "*Put me down.*"

"We do not have time to waste with you walking," Lyra said, squeezing harder. "We must get to the Sink as soon as possible for you to start training."

Rav winced, suddenly all too aware of how easy it would be for her to break his bones. "I'm not going to the Sink," he spat. "I need to stay here. I need to find out what's happening in Pitt." He kicked at her, but Lyra was unfazed.

"We will have to walk past Pitt on our way to the Sink. You can say goodbye then."

"Say goodbye? What makes you think I'd ever follow you to the Sink? I almost died fighting *one* 'Zet Ar."

"If you do not go to the Sink, how will you complete your Heaven's Tear and carry out the World's will?"

"Why would I want to do any of that?"

"Because it is your destiny."

"My destiny is to protect my family." Rav slapped at Lyra's face; however, she blocked all his strikes with one arm. "How are you so strong?"

"I have been Called Ha'th Bey Riene and am in Heaven. I will teach you about it during our journey. For now, think about it like that moment when you threw your knife at the 'Zet Ar.

Sisters like me exist in that state of clarity all the time due to our connection to the World. And the destiny the World has given you is far greater than protecting your family."

Rav gave up fighting her, his weariness catching up to him. "The World's plan? All I saw was—"

Lyra slapped him with the back of her hand. "Do not tell anyone what you saw; it must be kept secret from everyone, including those like me. Telling anyone diminishes the chance of you being able to succeed in bringing about the future you must make real. If what you must do means you have to kill others, it is better for you to take them by surprise. That includes Sisters. While I am certain that I would sacrifice myself for the World, we are all taught that to ensure we complete our duties, it is better for us not to know our fates to prevent us from betraying the World."

"That's madness. What if I saw myself massacring you and all your family?"

"If that is the World's plan, then I must help you achieve it. Though, I do not have a family like yours, so I do not need to worry about that."

Rav wanted to continue arguing, but he knew it was futile; judging by the zeal stirring in Lyra's eyes, she would drag him to the Sink if she needed to. He would have to find another way to placate her.

The insatiable drive that had brought him to the centre of Ghoul Wood was gone, leaving him hanging like a limp doll across Lyra's shoulders. As his eyes closed, he recalled the sense of power he'd felt during his Calling and had to admit that it was tempting. Ah' ke. With power like that, he could protect his home by himself, killing anyone who tried to invade Stone's Way... if that even was his home anymore. Nameless.

Rav yawned, and when he opened his eyes again, Lyra was still carrying him. Holding his head up, he spotted a tree thicker than the other black-barked, gnarled ones ahead of them, its leaves thin like needles and rust orange, recognising it to place them much closer to Lyra's hut.

"You carried me all the way here? How long has it been?" he managed.

"Two days have passed. You are malnourished. I have fed you and restitched your wound, but you will need to recover for at least a month, or even with my help, you will die in the Sink."

Rav was too tired to bother telling her he still wasn't going there. Pitt needed his attention. What would he say to his parents? His Ma's declaration making him Nameless rumbled in his ears. Would they even want to see him? The ground beneath him shook along with Rav's heart. He'd never thought that before.

"Stop breathing so much." Lyra shrugged her shoulders to stop his gasping.

It was late morning by the time they reached Lyra's hut. Rav applied a multitude of medicinal pastes on cuts he'd accumulated during his vacant march to the Heaven's Tear and ate until his stomach heaved while Lyra packed all her possessions from the hut into two enormous bags, each the same size as her. She also broke the floor under her bed to retrieve a suit of exquisite full-plate armour and a sword a foot longer than any he'd seen before, all of which she carried without issue. Rav watched her pour a vial of liquid on the hut floor before she ushered him out the door.

Lyra threw another vial into the hut, shut the door behind them, then set off marching to Pitt. Rav looked over his shoulder to see smoke starting to seep through the gaps in the hut roof, and soon, the entire structure was engulfed in blue flames along with the willow tree hanging over it.

"Why burn it?"

"Sisters like me seek Heaven's Tears and others know this. They often follow us in hopes of stealing what we have found. Nearly everyone in the Sink would kill you to get the power you now have; it is safer for you if no one knows that you are Ah' ke while you are so weak. No traces of you can be left until you are strong enough to protect yourself."

More trouble.

Rav pursed his lips. "Do *you* want my Heaven's Tear? If I give it to you, can you go to the Sink while I stay here?"

Lyra shook her head. "Sisters cannot fuse with Heaven's Tears; we are already connected to the World. Your Calling is for you to complete." She glanced up at him. "I do not understand why you are not excited for this. It is rare for someone to be able to fuse with a Heaven's Tear and rarer to be able to find one. This is the greatest gift you could ever receive. Most of those Called to the Sink must perform their duty to the World with nothing but their own strength."

"And I don't understand how you can't see that the Sink is ruining my life. It's ruining all our lives."

Lyra laughed as though he were a child speaking on things he had no knowledge of. "The Sink will *give* you life. You have been connected to the Sink since it appeared, from you being able to see my true face, to your Heaven's Tear guiding you towards itself. No matter where you go, the Sink will follow because the World needs you."

He really had been cursed. No wonder everything kept going wrong. Maybe if he hadn't been here, Wakeman would still be alive.

As they left Ghoul Wood, Lyra stopped and faced him. "I am going around the town. I will meet you at the place you call the Alley. If you are not there by morning, I will come get you."

"Aye." Rav looked at her, uncertain if she was offering to protect him or threatening to drag him away.

She grinned.

Both.

Rav changed his clothes and donned a cloak, using its hood to cover his face, then waited for the sun to set before sneaking into Pitt. There was no one around the Carvell logging grounds and no guards keeping watch at the gate. Rav stepped lightly into Pitt, heart pattering, but all remained still. No fight awaited him, the path to his house clear. Had Cyrn arranged this? Had his brother believed in and been waiting for his return?

Rav stuttered in his stride, chest stifled. How could he face him? He pinched his arm and pressed on, braced for whatever lay ahead. All was quiet as he walked down streets of shut windows and hushed conversations. So much had changed in just a few days. Gone was his warm and inviting home, free from the horrors of the outside world. The wound opened by Wakeman's death was already festering.

It was as if he were walking through an endless creaking mineshaft that grew more unstable the closer he got to the Carvell home. Would he be chased away again? Would his family call him Nameless and chastise him for bringing shame to the Carvell Name? He arrived at the door and froze. As long as he never knocked, he'd never have to face his family and therefore never have to know if they'd truly cast him out. Perhaps that was better. He took a deep breath, clearing away his cowardice. He hadn't given up against the 'Zet Ar, and he wasn't going to give up here. Whatever his family thought of him, he would accept it.

Just as he was about to knock, the door cracked open a sliver.

"Rav?" Benji whispered.

"Aye," he croaked, mouth dry.

"Come in." Benji pulled him inside, shut the door, and hugged him.

"We didn't know what had happened," Benji choked up. "Cyrn was worried that you'd never come back."

Rav's lip wobbled, his breathing quick and shallow, his eyes glistening with fat tears that rolled down his cheeks. "Of course I came back, I was just in Ghoul Wood for a few days."

"Rav?" Cyrn rushed into the corridor with Enna beside him. "*Rav.*" He wrapped his brother in a tight squeeze. "I was so scared I'd never see you again."

"It's alright." Rav squeezed him back. "I'm alright."

"Everything happened so fast. I never expected to see you at the Challenge, and when I saw those soldiers looking to kill you, I just thought about getting you away from them. Then Jingo set off on his own and—" Cyrn choked on his words as he sobbed.

"I know. I killed him."

Relief crossed Cyrn's face.

Rav heard footsteps coming down the stairs and looked up to see his parents, hand in hand, watching him as they descended. One moment his Ma was smiling, the next wincing, the next seething, then it all melded together into some grotesque, stretched flatness as she seemed to force herself back to being stoic and upholding her decorum. But her eyes couldn't change, ringed red, slightly squinted, and sunken deep with terror that should never have existed, as though her soul had been pricked by the tip of a knife.

The wrinkles etched into his Pa's face had deepened as though his entire being had cracked, the puffy, dark bags under his eyes seeming tender. With great effort to overcome the weight of his exhaustion, he managed a soft smile, breaking custom as relief restored a little pallor to his grey cheeks. Rav stumbled forward to the stairs as they reached the bottom and kneeled before them in a deep bow, his head touching the floor at their feet, unable to control his shivers.

"I..." He steadied his lip. "I know I am no longer a Carvell and have no right to present myself before you, but—"

"Come here, you stupid boy." Healanor grabbed his arm and pulled him up into a hug. Senior Carvell wrapped his arms around Rav too, enclosing him in a loving embrace between them.

"I had no choice, Rav," his Ma whispered. "With Cyrn's new position and those soldiers and Tibald Sar and the town watching, I..."

"You're still alive." His Pa stroked his hair. "At least you're still alive."

Rav cried in choking sobs.

"What's this?" His Ma gasped. "It looks like there's a hole in your neck." She traced the back of his neck in the same place Lyra had.

Rav touched the spot, his skin feeling normal. "I'm fine, see?"

"There's a square-shaped mark on your skin that's blacker than night. It really does look like there's a hole." She licked her thumb and rubbed at the mark. "It doesn't come off."

Rav brushed her hand away. "Leave it; it's probably nothing."

"What about the rest of your injuries? The last time I saw you, you could barely mumble. And you're so thin." His Pa guided him into the kitchen. "Come eat."

"Lyra helped me heal. I'm okay," Rav protested as he was seated at the table, everyone looking at him with concern.

Senior Carvell set a wedge of cheese and some bread before Rav. Rav nibbled at it until his Pa nodded in satisfaction.

*Lyra*. Lyra was waiting for him. Rav wanted to tell them about her but couldn't find the words to do it. He'd just returned, yet now he was going to bring them another problem. He ate in silence. Lyra was his problem, so he'd deal with it. His curse couldn't cause further destruction to those closest to him.

"Benji," Cyrn said, "could you inform Kayla that Rav's back?"

Benji nodded and left as everyone took their seats around Rav.

Enna held his arm and smiled at him. "Thank you for everything, Rav. I know how hard you fought to protect me and my baby."

"It wasn't good enough, though, was it? Does everyone know now?"

"Aye, everyone that matters."

No one could sit still at the table, the Carvells fidgeting or picking at their clothes. Their smiles were pure but fleeting, happy in the distracting moment, yet knowing that it wouldn't last. Rav looked around, recognising the sight from his childhood, the same smiles present a year after Baron Kiln had marched off into the Sink with half the town. Seasons had changed and yet there was no word from them, only ever more soldiers following and stories about the horrors that lay within the Sink. When family was gone forever, it left a raw wound in everything that could never be looked over.

"Have Wakeman's ashes been scattered?" Rav asked.

Cyrn nodded. "When Tibald recovered, he insisted that we dealt with his body, fearing that it could cause dissent among Pitt's citizens if people saw it for too long. Most of Wakeman's ashes were scattered in Stone's Way, near the Alley Camp where he liked to watch the sunrise, but some were kept so we can deliver them to his home... if we can find it."

Rav teared up again. "We've lost, haven't we, Cyrn? Tibald's going to take over Stone's Way, you're going to join Baron Hewett's army, and Wakeman's dead. The Sink's going to ruin our home even after all we've done to protect it. What was the point?"

Cyrn hit the table, *bang*, everyone flinching back as Rav's plate rattled. "We haven't lost and we're not *going* to lose. The Carvell Bloodline is still alive, which means we can keep fighting. This is just a setback. Do you remember what

Wakeman said about how we were only retreating now so we could have the possibility to take back Stone's Way in the future? That's all this is.

"I've already joined Baron Hewett's army, and as you saw at the Challenge, his soldiers now obey me. I can ensure that Pitt is treated fairly while a garrison is built in Stone's Way. Baron Hewett is only leaving for the Sink after he's established his supply line, which is going to take three years to build. Three years, Rav. That's three years for me to find an opportunity for us to still escape."

"How many more of us are going to die between now and then due to Tibald's schemes? He'll never let you go, Cyrn. Now that he knows about your child, you're trapped. We're all trapped. Even I'd rather become a slave than see a single drop of your child's blood spilt."

"I'll keep fighting until we're all free."

"And look how that's turned out. It's not enough. We're not good enough to beat him."

Silence settled in the room as everyone looked between the two brothers.

Rav stared at Cyrn as he mulled over his brother's words, unable to find any new answers beyond blind hope. How could they win? It wasn't that Tibald was too clever, it was because Baron Hewett was supporting him that the Ghoulsmen couldn't just kill him. The only way they could rid themselves of Tibald Sar and Baron Hewett was if they had an army of their own...

*Wait*. Rav flinched, dropping his head in thought. What about his Calling? Surely, an army of ghouls could sweep away Baron Hewett and anyone else in his way. If he became Ah' ke, couldn't he free Cyrn and the rest of his family? Couldn't he just visit the edge of the Sink, learn to use his Heaven's Tear, and then come back to free his family? He even had Lyra to protect him.

Besides, if he did nothing, then everything he loved would be razed anyway.

"Sorry," Rav whispered. "It's not hopeless. I'll keep fighting for us, just like you, Cyrn."

Cyrn pulled a small smile and nodded.

Healanor sighed. "I... I can't take back my declaration, Rav. The punishment for intervening in a Challenge is clear, and with Tibald taking over Pitt, I'll have to enforce it. You are still a Carvell by blood but not by Name. Accordingly, Pitt is no longer your home. If Tibald catches you, he has the right to execute you."

"It'll be worse than that," Cyrn said. "Tibald will torture you if he finds you. He's too vindictive to accept you attacking him."

Nameless. Homeless. Rav trembled.

"Until we can find a way to rectify the situation, you'll have to hide," Senior Carvell added.

Rav took a deep breath. Staying away while he sorted out his connection to the Sink was better anyway; that way, his curse would only affect himself. Also, hadn't Lyra warned him to keep his possession of a Heaven's Tear a secret? If he let it slip, more greedy people could come to Pitt looking for it. Aye, no one else could know, not even his family. Keeping away was for the best.

"I understand." He stood. "I have brought shame to the Carvell family and must accept the consequences of my actions. But this is not the end. Three years... I will return to Stone's Way within three years, wielding enough power to free us all."

"Aye," Cyrn cheered, rousing everyone.

Rav saw their faces, brimming with support but not belief. And why would they believe him? He hardened his expression. It didn't matter. He would claim the powers of the Sink or die trying. What was his life worth without his family anyway?

Benji arrived not only with Kayla, but with Tobias, Tido, and Thorley too.

The Ghoulsmen trudged into the kitchen with heavy steps, heads hanging, cheeks pale, eyes bloodshot. Tido and Tobias sniffled as they saw Rav, fresh tears beading. Rav rose from his seat to hug them at the table head, both feeling thin and feeble, as though they could crumble.

"How can he be dead?" Tido whispered, squeezing Rav tighter. "Why did we let it happen? Everything was always fixable as long as we were all alive..."

"I was so certain he'd win," Tobias mumbled in his other ear, face buried in the furs at Rav's shoulder. "The way he spoke before the Challenge, the way he carried himself for us, for Stone's Way... Maybe if I'd attacked before you did, we could have saved him." He lowered his voice further, becoming barely a breath. "Why was I such a coward? What's the point in Names and laws and legacies when they stop you from helping family? I've no need for honour; I just want my friend."

Rav held them close as they bawled into him, knees on the verge of buckling under their weight, but, somehow, he managed to stay standing, holding himself firm despite the shards of sorrow piercing his heart.

Across from them, he saw Thorley white with shock, no sign of the boyish playfulness that always seemed to glint around him. This man was hollow, gormless, limping through events without recognition, the wrenched wound in his mind so big it blotted out almost everything around him.

"It's good to see you, Rav," he said listlessly. "At least you're alive."

Behind Thorley, Kayla floated, gaunt and sharp in the corridor leading into the kitchen, fretting and fidgeting, looking to catch his Rav's eye over Thorley's shoulder, finally smiling when she did.

"There was nothing more for you to have done," Rav murmured to Tido and Tobias. "Had you acted, you'd be Nameless like me. You'd have undermined Wakeman's sacrifice and further worsened Pitt's relationship with Baron Hewett. Right now, we could be fleeing across Stone's Way with what little we could carry, looking behind us as everyone too slow was cut down by Baron Hewett's army. Perhaps we'd all risk everyone's lives for Wakeman, but he wouldn't want that. He *didn't* want that. That's why he's a Ghoulsmen."

Releasing them, he stepped forward to hug Thorley. "I'm sorry."

"Oh, it's not you," he muttered, arms limp at his sides. "It's the Sink. What can I do about that?"

Rav held his shoulders and faced him, but Thorley ducked his gaze, glancing behind at Kayla. "You've someone who's missed you more than me waiting." Thorley pushed Rav passed himself towards her.

Kayla smoothed her dress and stood tall, looking behind Rav as she forced herself stoic. Rav turned back to see his family all watching them, all pained. Holding Kayla's hand, he led her away and upstairs, taking her into his room before shutting the door. Holding her by his bedside in candlelight, he stared at her, chest crushed by the weight of his broken promises. Kayla dropped from decorum and wilted like an autumn leaf.

"How have you been?" Rav pulled her closer, feeling her bony frame. "Your cheeks look thin."

"Have you seen yourself?" Kayla snapped, holding Rav's chest with scrunched fists. "You look like a walking corpse, Rav. How can you worry about me when you're like this?"

Rav wrapped his arms around her waist and swayed, resting his chin on her collarbone. "Because I love you."

Kayla softened in his arms, falling into his swaying rhythm as she stroked the back of his head.

Rav closed his eyes, nose filled with the scent of woodsmoke that lingered on her skin and dress. "I'm sorry I couldn't keep you safe. I'm sorry we can't get married. I... I'm sorry I can't make you a Carvell."

Kayla looked at him, lifted his chin, and gave a soft snort as though facing a fool, almost seeming hurt by his words. "Do you think I care about your Name? All I care about is you, Rav. I'll stay by your side no matter what you're called."

Rav looked into her eyes, seeing such tenderness and love. He blinked, breaking the connection at a prickling thought. Was she seeing the same in him, or could she see his shame and embarrassment? "Really?"

Kayla touched his nose with hers. "Aye, really. I told you, didn't I? You don't have to bear dishonour alone. Even if you hate it, even if you fight to change it, I'm willing to share your life with you, whatever life that may be. Shows for Baron Hewett and Tibald Sar don't matter to me." She leaned back and wiped the tear rolling down his cheek with the tip of her finger.

"And there is a way for us to still get married. You can convince a Baron to give you a Common Name. I know all the Barons we've seen have gone mad, but there might be some far away from the Sink that are still sane. After we escape, if we settle on their land and you serve them well, they'll gift you a Common Name."

Rav kissed her forehead. "You know the likelihood of that happening is so low it's practically non-existent, right?"

"I do."

He chuckled. "Aye, alright, then. If that opportunity exists, I'll find it; if it doesn't, I'll make it. What kind of storybook hero would I be if I can't keep your hopes alive?"

They held each other a while in silence, melded together as they shifted in place, unified as they bobbed in an imaginary storm until Kayla broke from his arms and led him by the hand back downstairs.

"It's unfair for me to keep you to myself, as much as I'd like to," she cooed. "This goodbye should be proper, not the easy send-offs we have when you venture out into Stone's Way."

Returning to the kitchen, Rav glanced in surprise at Kayla as he heard laughter from within.

"Aye, that was a good jape, Thorley," Tido guffawed. "Rotten entrails buried in shallow dirt under bedding. I remember watching Wakeman turn his mattress over again and again in frenzy as he tried to find where the stink was coming from."

"Oh, the moment when he noticed the disturbed topsoil was glorious," Tobias followed. "The shock on his face, then the grin he gave when he saw us all laughing at him. It almost made me sympathise with the poor goats that must've had to see such a terrifying sight whenever he went out to hunt them."

Rav walked in to see his family animated as they talked around the table with mugs of ale, even his parents sitting forward as they listened to the Ghoulsmen's stories.

Cyrn wheezed as he slapped his thigh. "He dug the entrails out barehanded and chased after us with them, everyone scattering out the Alley Camp and into the hills. I was so sure I was safe, I stood taunting him from the adjacent hilltop, but he squeezed something black and oozing into a ball and threw it at me, hitting me just below the chin." He shook his head with revulsion. "I've never smelled anything so rancid. I hunched over and vomited all over my new boots."

Thorley scoffed. "At least you got away. He caught me and rubbed some old blood in my hair. I almost had to shave it off."

Everyone rumbled with laughter, Rav joining them as he thought back.

"That was the summer Wakeman taught me how to swim in the Herd River," he spoke up, sitting with Kayla beside Thorley, close to the warm hearth. "We'd spend mornings and afternoons splashing in shallow water to cool us from the hot sun."

"So he told you," Tobias mused, winking at the other Ghoulsmen. "That was the year you decided to grow your hair long, and it became so matted we almost pinned you down and sheared you. Thank Wakeman for coming up with the genius plan to have you swim long enough for it to come loose again."

"I thought you looked rather handsome," Healanor said. "At first."

Everyone snorted, and Rav sat back with his mouth wide open in a feigned gasp.

"If not for your Pa telling me you were already a man and needed to make a man's mistakes, I'd have done something myself. It was lucky we had Wakeman to sort you out."

More laughter followed.

"Ah, do you remember when we lost that gold ring?" Tido asked. "It wasn't even that valuable, yet Wakeman dragged everything out of Bear Camp looking for it, ranting about how he wouldn't let anything we'd fought for go to waste. I nearly cracked a rib laughing when he found it in his pocket."

"The better part was when he put it on and couldn't take it off." Cyrn chortled. "We had to cut it free."

"What about that winter storm the year I arrived?" Thorley grinned at Cyrn. "So much water poured through the Alley Camp chimney, I thought we'd drown. Only you and Wakeman were tall enough to reach the gap, standing on chairs with that stretch of hide to try and guide the rain into the buckets we carried. Do you remember how Wakeman laughed? Soaked and freezing, he roared back into the storm, hair matted to his face as the wind howled." He lowered his head. "That was the moment

I decided to stay with you. Someone Nameless braced against a storm and you braced with him. I've never forgotten it."

Rav tapped the table with his nail, his other hand laced between Kayla's fingers. "Aye, I remember what little of that I could see. Blinded by the spray and gasping for breath, I'd always thought we'd looked so pitiful he'd been laughing at us, having found a sliver of joy within the torrent. He was always good like that."

"Oh, for sure it was both," Cyrn rumbled. "At one point, we were laughing so hard we dropped the hide and dumped all the water over Tido. That just made us laugh more."

Story after story passed until Rav noticed pale pre-dawn light starting to seep through the window shutters. Everyone else caught it too, the conversation fading to a tense silence as they looked between it and Rav.

Rav stood. "I should leave now before Pitt wakes up. Tibald can't know that I've been here."

"Wait a moment." Cyrn also stood from the table. "I've prepared some supplies for you." He left the kitchen before soon returning with a large bag in one hand and a cloth-wrapped bundle in the other. Opening the bag, he showed Rav food, waterskins, and camping gear stored inside. "There are also these." Cyrn unwrapped the bundle and took out the top item. "First, your notebook and pencil. With its maps, I know you'll find your way home."

Rav traced the leather cover, face grim. After a gulp, he tucked it safely in his bag.

"The second is this," Cyrn murmured as he held out a small clay urn. "These are the last of Wakeman's ashes. If you find his home while you're away, you can scatter them there."

Rav froze. Could something so small really contain even a piece of his friend? His brother? He blinked again and again; however, the sight didn't change the urn no matter how many times he saw it anew. Sure, maybe Wakeman's cremated arm could fit, but what of his honour? What of his loyalty? His bravery? Humour? Joy? Love? Comradery? Wakeman's character was far too large for something like this to hold.

Rav's hand trembled as he received it from Cyrn. He cupped it close to his chest.

"And lastly, there's this." Cyrn lifted out a newly polished chainmail shirt, yet chain links by the waist still had a faint gleam of red from the blood that had poured through them, a few at the bottom still broken where Tibald's dagger had clipped them as it was driven by. "You should have it. He'd be glad to know part of him is still protecting you."

Rav released a hand from the urn clutched to his chest and took it, stumbling forward as its heavy weight unbalanced him before standing firm. "I'll wear it all the time," he promised, staring at the shirt as though he could see Wakeman still wearing it. Could he ever hope to fill it like Wakeman had? In size and character. How much honour, love, and loyalty did he need to do something like that? He gulped, Wakeman's legacy towering before him just as daunting as the Carvells' had been.

His Pa clicked his tongue. "Go on, son; put it on. I want to know how it fits." Senior Carvell coughed. "I need to see that you'll be safe. As safe as you can be."

Rav nodded and headed upstairs, followed by Kayla, who brought up his bag along with clean fur armour given to her by Cyrn. With Wakeman's ashes set on his bed beside his chainmail, Rav undressed, then pulled his under-furs over him as normal, but Kayla stopped him from doing anything more. Picking up a needle and thread from his bedside table, she sewed his under-furs tight as he wore them, ensuring they'd be held in place however he moved, never parting to expose any easy gaps he could be cut through. Finished, she let him step into his leg armour and stitched sections of its hide tightly together before he shoved on his boots, thick leather creaking as he wiggled his toes. They both turned to the chainmail shirt laid out on his bed. Breath gathered, Rav lifted it above his head and draped it over his shoulders, Kayla helping stop it from scrunching, where it sat like an everlasting hug.

Kayla cracked a smile, pointing at the mail hanging to Rav's mid-thigh. "I never realised just how muscled Wakeman was; his shirt looks almost like a dress on you."

"Aye." Rav twirled before her. "But I'll manage. It's like his hands are always on my shoulders now."

Kayla rolled up the bottom and tucked it into Rav's waistband, then adjusted his belt to keep it in place. Last came his top layer, the thickest furs tied over his torso, so Wakeman's mail could only be seen at his collar, wrists, and waist.

Kayla brushed it all down, her final touches bringing everything to run in line.

"Do I look like a Ghoulsman?" Rav asked, gazing down at a sight so familiar yet somehow so different to how it had ever been before.

Kayla shook her head as she bit her lip, tears welling in her eyes. "No, Rav. You look like something more than just Pitt's protector. A soldier, maybe." She stroked his cheek. "Will this be enough? I know how dangerous it is out there."

Rav leaned in and kissed her, savouring the softness of her lips for as long as his breath could hold. Pulling back, he winked at her with a dashing smile. "I'd survive with less than this to see you again. As I am, I *will* be back. I promise."

She gave him a fierce nod and kissed him again. More light spilled through the window. Rav broke away, tucked Wakeman's urn at the centre of his bag, slung it over his shoulder, then headed downstairs, where he found his family waiting for him in the corridor.

His Pa strode forward to inspect him with a big grin. "Ha, look at you. Aye, you'll be alright. How could you not be? You're my son."

His Ma followed him and stroked Rav's hair with a gentle hand. "Our dear boy of our great Bloodline. Hide when you can and fight with all your might when you must. Once all this mess is sorted out, we'll meet again and make our ancestors proud."

Rav twitched, ready to hug them, but a slight tremor in their eyes stopped him. They were doing everything they could to stand tall before him and not crumple into weeping heaps. They were working hard for everything to appear well, manageable, possible, all for his confidence, for his courage. Rav simply nodded, stern, unafraid, assuring them of his survival in the same manner.

Cyrn and Enna approached him next as his parents stepped back, Cyrn poking at his armour in various places. "How does the chainmail feel? Is it not too loose?"

Rav shrugged, feeling the weight on his shoulders. "I'll have to eat some more to get it to fit."

"Aye," Cyrn said, laughing. "You do that."

Enna clasped his hand. "Be smart, Rav." She held his palm to her warm stomach. "As you always are. For all of us."

Rav's stomach jittered, his conviction wobbling as the masquerade of assuredness he and everyone else hid behind teetered on the verge of destruction. He turned away from his brother, sister-in-law, and the future of the Carvell Bloodline, facing the Ghoulsmen, all of whom were beginning to crack, smiles falling lopsided, hands shaking, tears welling.

"Be brave for me," Tobias said, clipped.

"S-stay s-strong," Tido followed.

Thorley kept blinking, but still, tears trickled down his cheeks. "Keep us in mind," he added.

Last was Benji. "There will always be a home for you here," he stammered. "Remember that."

"I will," Rav choked out, heart rattling.

*Tap, tap, tap*, Kayla moved lightly down the stairs to his side and pressed her forehead against his. "Promise me you won't die," she whispered.

Rav steadied his rapid breathing. "I won't die."

He looked down the corridor once more, head held high, shoulders broad, and strode down it, boots thumping against the wooden floor. Yet as he reached for his spear and shield leaning beside the door, he froze. What was the point in this? Sure, they were all giving him support, and sure it would help, but what if he did die?

Turning around, he dashed to gather his parents in a great hug, squeezing them hard as they hugged him back. Waving his hand, he beckoned everyone else to join, embracing them all, and there, cheeks ruddy, no one cried, all shuddering on the cusp of breaking yet held together by each other.

Birds started tweeting, golden light peeking under the doorway as the tip of the sun broke the horizon. The hug crumbled, but the warmth in Rav's chest remained.

Cyrn guided him to the door as everyone else watched on, arm wrapped around his shoulder. Leaning closer, he whispered. "I know where you're going. I'll trust that if you're going there, you have a plan."

"I do," Rav stated, eyes locked forward. "Three years. I'll be back within three years. Believe in me." He took a last deep breath, his chest rising with vigour as he felt the chainmail supporting him. Wakeman had faced the Challenge without flinching. To honour Wakeman, to continue his legacy, Rav had to face the Sink just the same. He opened the door and stepped out into the dawn light.

# ABOUT THE AUTHOR

Alex Hughes lived in Zambia until the age of six, before moving to England and the historic cathedral city of Canterbury. At 17 he was diagnosed with severe depression and left school to recover.

While recovering, Alex started reading novels from East Asia such as The Godsfall Chronicles, City of Sin and Divine Throne of Primordial Blood, which inspired him with fresh ideas from a different philosophical and cultural perspective. He put his imagination to the page and had written five novels by the age of 23, when he was accepted onto (and completed) the Faber Academy Submissions and Editing Course.

You can follow Alex on X (formerly Twitter) @ghoulsmen

# Thank you

Thank you to my mother for all the help you've provided. From reading to feedback to advice, all of it has helped shape me into the writer I am today.

Thank you to my father for all the support you've given over the years as I pursued my dream of being an author.

Thank you to my sister for your constant encouragement and enthusiasm for my work.

Thank you to Cassandra Davis for believing in Ghoulsmen and for your work in bringing Ghoulsmen to the world.

Thank you to Lauren Counsell for your work editing Ghoulsmen into its best self.

Thank you to George Green for the immense kindness you showed me and the guidance you provided when I was just starting to write.

Thank you to those who helped me shape Ghoulsmen into a position to be noticed, Rose Tomaszewska, Catherine Cho, and Brendan Durkin.

And thank you to everyone who has given feedback for Ghoulsmen over the years, especially my aunt, Maria Martin, and everyone from Faber Academy.

Printed in Great Britain
by Amazon